About the Author

Rachael Johns is an English teacher by trade, a mum 24/7, a chronic arachnophobic and a writer the rest of the time. She rarely sleeps and never irons. A lover of romance and women's fiction, Rachael loves nothing more than sitting in bed with her laptop and electric blanket and imagining her own stories.

In 2016 *The Patterson Girls* was named General Fiction Book of the Year at the Australian Book Industry Awards. Rachael has finaled in a number of other competitions, including the Australian Romance Readers Awards. *Jilted* won Favourite Australian Contemporary Romance for 2012, *The Patterson Girls* won the same award for 2015 and she was voted in the Top Ten of Booktopia's Favourite Australian Author poll in 2013.

Rachael lives in the Perth hills with her hyperactive husband, three mostly gorgeous heroes-in-training, two fat cats, a cantankerous bird and a very badly behaved dog.

Rachael loves to hear from readers and can be contacted via her website www.rachaeljohns.com. She is also on Facebook and Twitter.

Also by Rachael Johns:

Man Drought

The Hope Junction novels
Jilted
The Road to Hope

The Kissing Season (e-novella)
The Next Season (e-novella)

The Bunyip Bay novels
Outback Dreams
Outback Blaze
Outback Ghost
Outback Sisters

Secret Confessions Down and Dusty: Casey (e-novella)

The Patterson Girls
The Art of Keeping Secrets
The Greatest Gift

RACHAEL JOHNS

TALK
OF THE
Town

mira

First Published 2017
Second Australian Paperback Edition 2018
ISBN 978 1 489 24691 2

TALK OF THE TOWN
© 2017 by Rachael Johns
Australian Copyright 2017
New Zealand Copyright 2017

This is a work of fiction. Names, characters, places, and incidents are either the product of the author's imagination or are used fictitiously, and any resemblance to actual persons, living or dead, business establishments, events, or locales is entirely coincidental.

Published by
Harlequin Mira
An imprint of Harlequin Enterprises (Australia) Pty Ltd.
Level 19, 201 Elizabeth St
SYDNEY NSW 2000
AUSTRALIA

Cataloguing-in-Publication details are available from the National Library of Australia www.librariesaustralia.nla.gov.au

Printed and bound in Australia by McPherson's Printing Group

MIX
Paper | Supporting
responsible forestry
FSC® C001695

A note from Rachael Johns

Can you believe it? *Talk of the Town* is my tenth print book for Harlequin Australia and my twentieth published story, but who's counting?

One of the questions I most get asked by readers is what inspires my stories and where my ideas come from. As most writers would probably agree, this is not an easy question because every book is different. Some ideas come fully formed in your head (my book *Man Drought* was a little like that); some start with one tiny seed (*The Patterson Girls* began when I drove past a paddock of purple weeds); others grow from a real-life experience (*Outback Blaze* was inspired by a tragic fire at my husband's workplace), but most ideas are like jigsaw puzzles—with a little bit of all the above working together to create inspiration magic.

Talk of the Town was definitely like this. It grew out of my love for old buildings and my fascination for ghost towns. I always wanted to write about a ghost town, but I wasn't sure how until one day three or four years ago, I had a brief dalliance with jogging. Every day I used to run around our town (or rather try to run) and I distinctly remember going past an old house that someone had mentioned was haunted and having a visual of a young woman who'd moved there to live alone. I imagined how such a woman might feel should someone tell her the house was haunted and this one line landed in my head: 'She had enough skeletons in her closet, she could deal with a few ghosts.'

And it was from this line the story grew. As with many ideas, I started asking questions—Who was this woman? What were her skeletons? What on earth had happened to her to make her move to a new rural town all alone? What if the house she'd bought wasn't only haunted and run down but was located in an actual deserted (ghost) town?

I had other stories to pen and this woman was put on the backburner for a number of years, until last summer I visited an ice-creamery with my husband and our sons while we were holidaying in the south-west of WA. Suddenly I decided that I wanted my next rural romance to be set in dairy farming country and I had a clear image of a dairy farmer who was a single dad and still grieving the tragic loss of his wife. I can't explain why, but I knew this hero was the guy I'd been waiting for for my ghost town heroine and that it was time to write this story.

But although I thought cows were kinda cute, I knew absolutely nothing about life on a dairy farm, so before I could start I had to do some research. Researching for *Talk of the Town* took me to a real working dairy farm in Waroona, Western Australia, where I had to get up before the crack of dawn to watch the early milking get done. Although I'm not a morning person, the process fascinated me and I decided getting to watch the sunrise every single day would be pretty special. I couldn't wait to get started on my story.

The dairy industry across Australia has been through some hard times of late and I've touched on some of them briefly in this book. So as you read, I hope you'll remember how important dairy farmers (heck, all farmers) are to all of us and, if you can, shop local!

Happy reading

Rachael Johns

Talk of the Town is dedicated to all my wonderful and faithful readers who have been with me on my journey to this, my tenth print book! Your support and enthusiasm for my stories means the world. Here's to ten more good reads together!

Chapter One

Megan McCormick froze at the sound of a car door slamming outside. She'd been there five days already and hadn't seen or heard anyone, which was exactly how she wanted it.

Thankful she always kept her door locked, she cocked her head to one side and listened to the distant mumble of conversation. The part of her that wanted to know who was out there pushed to her feet, but she'd not even taken one step before she fell back onto the seen-better-days sofa. She clutched her needle and the half-made black and white tea-cosy against her chest as if she were some kind of granny, not merely twenty-five years old. Her heart racing, she looked down into her lap to see her hands trembling.

You're being ridiculous!

Did she really think whoever was out there had come because of her? The media might have been interested in her in Melbourne, but it was highly unlikely they'd track her down all the way out in rural Western Australia. She laughed nervously at her paranoia and forced herself to stand again. This time she dumped her crocheting on the sofa and strode across to the front window. Her fingers still shaking, she peeled back the curtain only enough to peek outside.

On the normally deserted road right out the front of the run-down, early 1900s shop she'd just moved into, she saw a once-white ute. Not far from the ute stood a tall, tanned man scratching his head and a little boy tearing around madly with a football. There'd been the occasional vehicle pass through the deserted town site since she'd arrived, but only two or three a day, and every time they did, she held her breath, praying they wouldn't stop.

None ever had, until now.

The man and boy looked out of place on the main street of Rose Hill, a tiny town, stuck somewhere in the late 1970s when most of its residents had abandoned ship for one reason or another, or so said the estate agent.

'Dad!'

Meg startled, the curtain jolting in her hands, when the little boy shrieked and then she watched as he kicked the ball. He'd been aiming for his father but the oval-shaped ball veered in the other direction and landed in one of her tiny, weed-ridden garden beds. She let go of the curtain as if it were on fire, her heart stammering as the voices came closer to her hiding spot.

'Not bad, mate,' said the man.

She heard the patter of small feet and then the few thuds of bigger-sized shoes scrambling in the undergrowth right outside her house.

'There it is,' shouted the boy. And Megan started breathing again. Maybe now they'd get back in their car and stop intruding on her solitude.

'Awesome,' said the dad. 'Let me change the tyre and then we'll have a few more kicks.'

What? No! Her heart jumped back up into her throat; at the same time the little boy shouted, 'Yes!'

She could almost hear him punch the air in excitement but the prospect made her palms sweat. What if the kid fell and scraped his knee? The thought of having to go outside and offer first aid made her feel physically ill. Silently, she prayed the summer sun would mean they didn't hang around too long. As she forced breath in and out of her lungs, she told herself to be thankful it looked like a farmer who'd got a flat rather than someone from the city, who might have needed her assistance.

As she stood there, still clutching the curtain, she thought of the whole array of things she'd learned these past few years—some useful, some most-definitely not, and one of them ... how to change a tyre. She'd surprised herself by how much she'd enjoyed the car maintenance course but perhaps it had been because it reminded her of her father and brother. They'd both been car mad and when she'd been reading the textbooks or tinkering with the test cars she'd felt close to them. Then again, if she were honest, eventually she'd enjoyed almost all her courses—anything and everything that had kept her busy and stopped her *thinking* had been a blessing.

Shaking her head clear of those thoughts, Megan cocked an ear towards the window and listened. Although she hadn't heard the ute drive away yet, the chatter outside her window had ceased. Thinking the man had gone off to attend to the tyre and the boy to get up to who knew what kind of mischief, she risked peeling back the curtain again.

And when she did, her heart leaped up into her throat. Standing on the half-rotten windowsill outside, clinging to the glass like some kind of spider-man, was the boy. He took one look at her and he started screaming.

She screamed too as he jumped down onto the verandah.

'Ned?' the man shouted from his ute, startling her into action.

She yanked the curtain closed and stood, frozen, her heart pounding as she listened to the conversation unravel outside the window. The boy was crying now.

'What is it? Did something bite you?' The man sounded both frustrated and concerned. '*Ned*, you need to talk to me! Are you hurt?'

'I … saw … a … ghost.'

Oh! Megan stifled an amused gasp. Not that she found the boy's terror funny, but she'd never imagined he'd mistake her for a poltergeist.

'Don't be silly, son, there's nothing there.' Although she couldn't see through the curtains, the warmth in the man's voice made her imagine him ruffling the boy's hair. 'Maybe we should stop reading those Goosebumps books at night, hey?'

Goosebumps? She'd loved those books as a kid.

'No, Dad.' Ned's voice was vehement. 'I *definitely* saw something. The curtain moved and then a woman's face was there. She looked white and a little sick. *Exactly* like a ghost.'

Megan frowned, her hands rushing to her face to palm her cheeks as she made a mental note to get outside in the sun a bit more.

'And then,' the boy continued, his tone becoming more and more agitated 'when I screamed, she screamed too. What if she's angry with me? What if she comes after us? What if she …'

Megan had heard enough. Putting her crocheting down on the tarnished coffee table, she pinched her cheeks in the hope of adding obviously necessary colour and then marched across to the front door. After slipping her feet into a pair of boots, she took a deep breath and opened it.

The bright light of the midday sun almost blinded her but she stepped outside and shut the door behind her. Shielding the glare with her hand, she cleared her throat. 'Um, excuse me?'

The boy stopped rambling as he and the man turned to look at her.

Wow. Her gaze skipped from the kid to his father. Wearing dusty boots, khaki shorts and a blue chambray shirt pushed up to the elbows, he looked even better close up than he had from a distance. Her insides flickered a little, catching her by surprise. *No.* She'd moved here to get away from people—and, even if her situation were different, this man, with his cute little sidekick, was obviously off the shelf.

'I *told* you I saw someone.' The boy stepped closer to his dad as if he still believed she was a ghost. He had blond hair almost as light as his dad's was dark, and it was curly—so much that he looked like an honest-to-God cherub.

The man put his hand on his son's shoulder and drew him back against his body. Quite rude considering he didn't know anything about her and technically, they were the ones trespassing. *Unless …*

He recognised her!

Her heart hitched a beat and she braced herself but his expression relaxed a little.

'Hi,' he said, sounding *just* as good as he looked.

'Hi,' she managed, swallowing.

'Are you a ghost?' asked the boy; Ned, she remembered. Now he could see her in the flesh, he sounded more intrigued than terrified.

She looked down and forced a smile. 'Not last time I checked,' she said, pretending to pinch her hand.

Ned laughed. 'Well, what are you doing here then?'

'Um …' That question was far too complicated to answer, but she hadn't expected visitors so she hadn't come up with a plausible story. Rookie mistake.

'Sorry,' the man apologised, letting go of Ned and stepping forwards. He held out his hand but he didn't quite smile. 'I'm Lawson, Lawson Cooper-Jones, and this is my son, Ned. He doesn't mean to be rude—it's just we've been driving through Rose Hill for years and rarely seen any sign of life. You surprised us.'

'I'm … I'm Meg … Meg Donald.' Her new name almost caught in her throat, and her hand trembled as she reached out to accept his greeting. She couldn't recall the last time she'd voluntarily touched anyone. A pleasant spark shot up her arm at the connection and she hoped he didn't notice her cheeks flare.

'Pleased to meet you, Meg. Have you been here long?'

'Five days.'

He raised an eyebrow. 'Wow, I didn't even know it was for sale. Or are you renting?'

When she didn't immediately reply, he added, 'Sorry. None of my business.'

'I bought it.' She almost told him that the whole tiny town was pretty much on the market, and you could buy any one of the dilapidated properties on the once-main-street for not much more than you'd spend on a new car. But she bit her tongue, because although she had no reason to believe this man might be interested in such property when no one else had been for years, she didn't want to risk him telling someone who might be. One could never be too careful.

'Anyway,' she said quickly, 'I just wanted to check your son was okay. Nice meeting you.'

Megan turned to head back into the house, but before she closed the door behind her, Ned asked, 'Have you got anything to drink? It's *real* hot and I'm *real* thirsty.'

She froze, torn between pretending she hadn't heard him and offering him a glass of the orange juice she'd squeezed that morning. The garden might be overrun with weeds, but the old fruit trees out the back were strong and healthy. She had so many oranges and lemons she'd already used every baking, bottling and squeezing trick she had.

'Ned!' Lawson admonished. 'You've got water in your bottle in the car.'

The child groaned. 'But it's hot and yuck and tastes dirty.'

Even when he whined, he was somehow still adorable. Megan remembered how long and hot summer car journeys had felt when she was young.

She took a deep breath and turned around. 'Do you like orange juice?'

The little boy's eyes lit up and he nodded eagerly. 'Do I ever! Although I'm not allowed to drink it much.' He shot an accusing look at his father.

Lawson raised an eyebrow. 'If Meg's offering, you can have a treat. It *is* hot.' Then, he lifted his arm and wiped his brow with the back of his hand.

Ned started towards her as if about to come inside but she held her hand up to halt him. She'd spent the first three days cleaning so the place wasn't a total bomb, but that didn't mean she was about to invite strangers inside. No matter how hot the day, how endearing the boy or how good-looking the man. 'I'll bring your drinks out,' she promised, retreating inside and closing the door before man or boy could protest.

'Okay. Thanks,' Ned called as Megan leaned against the back of the door and sucked in quick gasps of air to catch her breath.

When she'd woken that morning, she'd lazed in bed, listening to the kookaburras laughing in the trees outside her bedroom window, relishing the freedom to do as she pleased and the sounds of nature that had been absent from her life for so long. The novelty of living alone in her own place hadn't worn off, but she knew that being alone and idle would drive her to insanity, or worse. She needed to keep busy, and so, determined to make the most of her time, she made a mental list of things to do to while away the long hours ahead. The house needed renovations and, although she had enough left over from her grandparents' inheritance to survive on for a while, she also needed to come up with a way to earn in the future.

Both these things had been on her to-do list. Entertaining a cute little kid and his even cuter father had not.

Again her heart shuddered at the thought of the two guys waiting outside and her stomach twisted as if someone were giving it a Chinese burn. She couldn't leave them waiting forever but what the hell had she been thinking, offering the kid a drink?

Ungluing herself from the back of the door, Megan forced her feet to move her across the house to the kitchen, where her shaking hands took a few attempts to open the damn fridge. The blast of cool air from inside helped clear her head. Why was she so jumpy? They didn't know who she was, so if she acted normal, they'd go on their way without another thought.

She took the jug of juice out of the fridge, grabbed three glasses— then put one back—and filled them to the brim. Leaving the jug on the bench, she carried two full glasses outside, kicking the door shut behind her as she handed Ned and Lawson their drinks.

The little boy gulped his down immediately, but his father thanked her first and then lifted the drink to his mouth and took a sip. Megan watched his Adam's apple move slowly in and out as he drank. Heat washed through her that had zilch to do with the outside temperature and everything to do with how pleasing he was on the eye.

At that thought her eyes snapped to his left hand in search of a ring and her heart sank. Of course there was a gold band glinting in the sunlight that streaked onto the verandah. What had she been expecting? That he got the child on eBay? And even if there hadn't been a Mrs Cooper-Jones, it wasn't like she'd want to interview for the position. Her last boyfriend had soured her on men.

'What brought you to Rose Hill?' Lawson asked eventually.

She swallowed. 'Oh, this and that.'

'I see.' He nodded once. 'You live here alone?'

'Yep.' Perhaps she should have made up a partner. Two people living out there might have seemed less peculiar.

'Well, thanks for the drink.' A slight frown creased his brow. 'Guess I'd better go change this tyre.'

He held the glass out and she took it, careful not to let her hand brush his in the exchange. She nodded and again tried to smile, her face aching from the sudden and frequent use of muscles that had barely moved in years.

'Wanna kick the football with me while Dad fixes the car?' Ned asked.

Megan blinked. She couldn't recall the last time she'd kicked a football, although her brother had been footy-mad and made her play with him lots as a kid. If Ned were entertained, Lawson might finish faster, right?

'Sure. That sounds like fun.' Her chirpy, enthusiastic tone sounded alien to her ears, but she took Ned's now empty glass and placed both glasses down by the front door. 'Lead the way.'

Ned looked up at her and frowned. 'It's hot out there. Maybe you should get a hat or something? And sun-cream. You don't wanna get burned.'

She looked to Lawson with amusement. 'That's one smart kid you have there.'

Lawson's smile stretched to bursting across his face as he reached over and tweaked Ned's cap. 'Yeah, he's not too bad.'

'Ned,' Megan said as she looked back to him, 'you're absolutely right, it is hot and I do need a hat and sun-cream, but I've only just moved in and I haven't unpacked them yet.'

Part of her welcomed the excuse not to go kick a ball, but the other half sagged in surprising disappointment. She might not have wanted company, but it felt surprisingly good to talk to someone besides her own reflection in the mirror. Maybe she should consider getting a pet.

'That's okay,' Ned said brightly. 'We've got a spare hat and sun-cream in the ute, don't we, Dad?'

Lawson nodded and that was that. She found herself voluntarily stepping off her front verandah and walking alongside them to the vehicle, where Lawson reached in to retrieve the hat and Ned conjured up a bottle of sun-cream. Lawson plopped the Akubra hat onto her head and then grinned down at her. She wondered if it was his wife's, although it didn't seem very feminine.

'It suits you,' he said, once again looking at her in a way that sparked goose bumps on the back of her neck. She couldn't quite tell if they were good or *bad* goose bumps.

Thankfully, Ned thrust the sun-cream at her, giving her an excuse to look away.

'You need any help with that?' Lawson asked as her fingers wrapped around the bottle.

'No!' She almost shrieked her reply, then quickly squeezed a dollop out onto her palm and rubbed it up and down her exposed arms.

'All right. Sorry.' Lawson shrugged one shoulder and backed away, sounding half-amused, half-offended.

As he went back to the tyre, Megan tried to regulate her breathing.

Beside her, Ned bounced the football in his hands. 'Ready yet?'

'Sure.' She followed him along the road to a spot out of the way of the ute.

'You stay there,' Ned ordered. 'I'll kick first.' He sprinted about twenty metres and then, with an intense look on his face, positioned himself to kick.

As the football sailed through the air towards her, Megan tried not to worry about the fact they were playing in the middle of a road. Where she grew up in the inner suburbs of Melbourne, playing on the street was a dangerous pastime. But Rose Hill was hardly a metropolis and she reminded herself that she'd seen more native animals on her daily runs in the forest that surrounded the town than she had cars on the road. With this thought, she threw herself into the game and tried to ignore the impulse to glance back towards the ute.

'Won't your mum be wondering where you are?' she asked when Ned ran close to her.

'Nope. She's dead,' he said matter-of-factly.

Her heart turned over at the thought that this cool little kid didn't have a mum. She'd lost hers in her teens—bad enough. 'Oh. I'm sorry.'

He shrugged one shoulder in exactly the manner as his dad. 'She died when I was little. I don't remember her.'

That piqued Megan's curiosity big time. *How'd she die? Do you have a step-mum? Or does your dad wear a wedding ring because he's still mourning the loss of the love of his life?*

Without meaning to, Megan found her head twisting to look back at the ute. Or rather to look back at *him*. The tanned skin of Lawson's lovely forearms glistened as he lifted the spare tyre onto the axle, and the back of his shirt was soaked in sweat.

'Come *on*, Meg,' Ned called again, forcing her to look away.

'Sorry.' She turned around to see the football hurling through the air towards her and reached out to catch it just in time.

'Nice one,' he cried and Megan smiled—*really* smiled—for the first time in a long while. They kicked the ball back and forth a few more times, all while more and more questions formed in her head about Ned and his dad. But with Lawson only a few feet away, she couldn't risk asking them.

When he finally swaggered over to join them, Megan couldn't help but wish he'd taken a little longer. Ned was such a cool kid and it had been fun to do something so normal for a change.

'Thanks for entertaining him,' Lawson said. 'We'll get out of your hair now.'

Megan resisted the urge to ask them in for afternoon tea good and proper. She'd succumbed to the desire to bake that morning and made far more scones than she could ever eat; the act of baking made her feel good though. 'No worries,' she said as she handed the borrowed hat back to Lawson.

Ned handballed the footy to his dad. 'Yeah, thanks Meg, see ya round.'

'It was fun.' She lifted her hand to wave.

Lawson hesitated a moment as if he wanted to say something, but then he shook his head slightly and turned to follow his son to the ute. Megan watched as Ned climbed into the vehicle. Lawson threw the football in after him and then got in the driver's side. A strange feeling washed over her as he started the ute. She hadn't wanted visitors, but now that they were leaving, her chest tightened at the prospect of being all alone again.

'Hey,' Ned leaned out of the window and called to her. 'Did you know your house is haunted?'

'What?' She stifled a chuckle.

'Your house,' he shouted, jabbing his finger towards it, 'is haunted. The whole town is.'

'Ned, there's no need to shout,' Lawson warned.

'Is that right?' Megan rubbed her lips together in amused contemplation as she lifted her hand to wave goodbye. She had enough skeletons in her closet: she could deal with a few ghosts!

Chapter Two

'Isn't Meg cool?' Ned said, half hanging out the window waving to her as Lawson pressed his foot down on the accelerator. 'She can kick a footy almost as good as you. Can we ask her over for dinner or something?'

Lawson swallowed—he wasn't in the habit of asking strangers round for dinner. Hell, he wasn't in the habit of asking *friends* round to dinner. His lack of a social life was something his sister berated him about constantly, but this was the first time Ned had said anything of the sort. While he had no intention of asking Meg out to the farm for dinner or any other reason, something made him put his foot on the brake pedal. Once stopped, he yanked the ute into reverse and then drove backwards up the road to the old general store where Meg had set up home. She was almost inside again but looked up at the sound of the ute and ... God, she was gorgeous.

The thought hit him like a physical blow—he hadn't noticed any woman in such a way since Leah.

But Meg's wavy, mahogany-coloured hair hanging down to her bum, and the fringe across her face hiding her eyes, drew his

13

attention. She was thin but ripped, and something—something he couldn't quite identify as clearly as he could her great body and amazing hair—intrigued him. Although he'd caught her looking once or twice when he'd glanced up from changing the tyre, she came across as shy and he found her quiet reserve compelling. Also, she'd been good with Ned.

'Was there something else?' Meg called, her brow creased.

Realising he was sitting in the ute gawping at her, he opened his mouth to speak but Ned got in first.

'Do you want to come over for dinner?' he shouted.

What? That had not been what Lawson was going to say. It didn't matter if he felt some weird, physical pull to this woman; he wasn't about to invite anyone into his and Ned's life without getting to know them on neutral ground first.

'Um …' Meg rubbed her lips one over the other, clearly as uncomfortable with the invitation as he was. 'Thanks for the offer, but I'm pretty busy unpacking and …'

Her voice drifted off but Lawson could fill in the gaps. *And she didn't know them from a bar of soap*—why on earth would she want to have dinner with them?

'We could help you unpack,' Ned suggested, his voice brimming with enthusiasm.

Meg's lips curved upwards and she met Lawson's gaze. 'Does he always have an answer for everything?'

He chuckled. 'Pretty much. Look, you're welcome to dinner any time,' he found himself saying, 'but how about I give you my number in case you ever need anything and—'

'That's very kind of you,' she called, stepping down off the verandah and coming back towards the ute, 'but I don't actually have a phone, so I couldn't call you anyway.'

'You don't have a phone?' asked Ned and Lawson at the same time.

She shook her head. 'I haven't got round to getting the landline connected yet.'

But what about a mobile? he wanted to ask. Network coverage might be dodgy out there in Rose Hill, but surely she *had* a mobile. He didn't know any woman who went anywhere without hers: not even his grandma, and she lived in a nursing home. And who in this day and age could live without wifi?

His surprise and concern must have shown on his face for she said, 'It's okay, I'll get it connected soon—and I've got a car so I can drive for help if there are any real problems.'

He guessed the car must be parked around the back because he couldn't see it.

'Don't you have an iPhone?' Ned sounded incredulous. For once Lawson was grateful for his son's tendency to say whatever came into his head.

'Nope,' Meg said with a shake of her head. 'Don't have one of them either.'

When she didn't offer any further comment or explanation, Lawson said, 'Have you met Cr— Archie yet?'

'Who?'

'Crazy Archie,' Ned said.

Lawson gave him a look, then, 'Archie,' he emphasised. 'He's an old guy who lives in the abandoned service station and keeps an eye on the town. Been here forever, or so it seems.'

'I filled my car up there the other day.'

He nodded. 'There's only a pre-paid machine now. I can't imagine Archie makes much from it, considering hardly anyone drives through Rose Hill any more, but I guess he gets what he needs.'

Meg shook her head. 'I haven't met him. I must admit, it's been so hot, I've pretty much barricaded myself indoors.'

'Well, rumour has it he's not very sociable but he might have a phone if you ever needed to borrow one.'

'Okay. Thanks. I'll go over and introduce myself some time.' She half laughed. 'And here I was thinking I was the only resident of Rose Hill.'

She sounded a little put out that she wasn't and that only piqued Lawson's interest more. What on earth was she doing living out here all alone? He wanted to ask but he also didn't want to be rude. Besides, he should be getting back to the farm to get ready for the evening milking.

'Well, we better be going, but here,' he leaned over and scrounged around in the glovebox for a pen and something to write on, 'have my phone number just in case you ever need anything. It's hard moving into a new town.' *Especially one as deserted as Rose Hill.*

He scribbled down his mobile and home number alongside his name on an old receipt and then he held it out the window to her. She hesitated a moment, before reaching out and taking it quickly. He didn't think himself *that* repulsive.

'Thank you.' She folded the receipt in half and tucked it into the pocket of her shorts.

'No worries and thanks again for the OJ. Have a great day.' Lawson took his foot off the brake and put the car back into drive.

'Yep. You too. Bye, Ned.' Her smile looked forced as she lifted her hand to wave them off again and this time, when he glanced backwards after driving a few metres up the road, she'd already vanished inside the house.

Ned spoke all the way back to the farm about how wicked-cool Meg was and how brave she must be to be living in a haunted house. As with many of his conversations when he got overly excited about something, he was happy to talk with only the occasional mumble of agreement from Lawson and that suited Lawson just fine. He should probably try and put Ned straight about the whole haunted thing, but he didn't have the energy, not when his head was filled with thoughts of Meg. He'd probably pay for it later when Ned couldn't sleep because *his* head was full of ghosts.

Ned was still talking when Lawson parked the ute in front of their old farm house. He leaped out the passenger side and ran towards the house, calling, 'Aunty Tab, Aunty Tab,' as he went. Lawson chuckled and felt a rush of love for his son as he went around to the back of the ute to grab their bags. It was good to have Ned home after a week away in Albany visiting his grandparents. He didn't want to begrudge Leah's parents their only grandson, but he didn't like spending even a night away from his kid. Tab sometimes jokingly called him a helicopter dad but he didn't care. He'd lost his mum and then Leah, he didn't want to even *think* about losing his son.

The door to the house flung open as Ned approached and Tabitha stood there waiting, one arm wide ready to grab him into a hug.

'God, boy, I've missed you!' She scooped him up and clung to him.

'I missed you too, Aunty Tab.'

'What are his grandparents feeding him?' she asked as Lawson approached carrying Ned's suitcase and his own overnight bag. 'Won't be long and I won't be able to lift him any more.'

Ned laughed and struggled free. 'Soon, I'll be able to lift you. Guess what? We just met this woman. She's living in the haunted shop at Rose Hill. She has no phones but can kick a football way better than you can.'

As Ned harped on about the virtues of their stranger, Tab raised her eyebrows and looked to Lawson. 'There's someone living at Rose Hill besides Crazy Archie?'

He shrugged. 'Seems so. I got a flat tyre driving through and she gave us a drink.'

'Intriguing,' Tab said. 'How about you two come inside, have some ice-cream and you can tell me all about it?'

'He won't eat dinner if he has ice-cream,' Lawson said as he toed off his boots and discarded them on the verandah.

'Yes, I will,' Ned whined as he did the same.

Tab grabbed Ned's hand and started inside. 'Don't be a spoil-sport,' she called over her shoulder. 'I haven't seen the kid in a whole week; besides, I need his opinion on my latest flavour. He's my chief taste-tester. We're like business partners, aren't we, Ned?'

Dinner was still a few hours away, but Lawson and Tabitha's mum had always been such a stickler for snacking. Her rule had been only fruit between meals and then if you ate all your dinner, you got dessert, which was the treat of the day. Being a young, sole parent, Lawson generally tried to do what he thought his mum would have done, but Tabitha sometimes reckoned he was a little too stringent. Knowing he was fighting a losing battle, he followed his sister and son into the house, dumped the bags in the hallway and then went into the kitchen.

'Was everything okay last night and this morning?' he asked as Tab took a container out of the freezer using her good arm. Lawson had gone down to Albany yesterday and stayed the night with his in-laws before bringing Ned home, ready for when the school year started next week.

'Fine, fine. The girls all behaved, although I think they much prefer it when you're around for milking. If only you had the same way with human ladies as you do with the Bovinae variety.'

He shot her a don't-start look and grabbed himself a beer from the fridge. He didn't usually drink pre-milking, but he decided to make an exception after his eventful afternoon. 'Want one?' he asked his sister.

'Maybe later with dinner—I've made some salads to go with the barbie. Besides, beer doesn't really go with ice-cream.'

Ned hauled himself up on the edge of the bench and watched as Tab wedged the ice-cream container between the bench and her hip and then scooped out a generous serving of her latest creation into a bowl. Lawson dragged out one of the counter stools, plonked himself down and took a sip of his beer.

'What flavour is it?' Ned asked.

Tab pushed the bowl towards him. 'Guess!'

Ned dug his spoon into the homemade ice-cream, lifted it to his nose and inhaled deeply—he took his job as Tab's chief taste-tester very seriously. 'It looks like chocolate and it smells like chocolate, but there's something else.' He paused a moment, his brow furrowed like some kind of devout wine connoisseur. 'Oranges!'

Tab nodded at Ned's victorious tone and then grinned at Lawson. 'The kid's got a gift. It's a milk chocolate ice-cream but I melted some Terry's chocolate oranges and made them into a fudge-like sauce, which I swirled through. What's the verdict?'

Ned licked his lips after the first mouthful. 'Totally rad! Are you gunna sell this one at the farmer's markets too?'

'That's the plan.' While Ned got stuck into the rest of his ice-cream, Tab leaned against the bench. 'So, tell me more about this mystery woman?'

Lawson shrugged and caressed the cool bottle in his hands. 'Not much to tell. She wasn't very talkative.'

'How old is she?'

'Maybe twenty-four or twenty-five? I'm not great at guessing ages.'

'So about my age. And what did she look like?'

He felt heat rush to his cheeks as he recalled all too clearly how long and luscious her legs had looked in those tight denim shorts.

'Oh my God. You're blushing.' Tab's lips split into a massive grin. 'I don't think I've ever seen you blush before. She must be really something.'

'*Tabitha*, please.' Lawson rolled his eyes. 'You need to get yourself a man and put all your romantic energies into him, because you're delusional. If my cheeks are red, it's because it's damn hot outside and I've just been changing a bloody flat tyre in full sun.'

'Okay. Whatever.' Tab shrugged but didn't stop smiling. 'Speaking of hot women, you just missed Adeline.'

'What was she doing here?' He tried not to sound irritated but ever since he'd relented and gone to the CWA Belles Christmas Ball with her she'd been like one of her dogs with a bone. He'd told her they were just friends, but she seemed to think he was simply playing hard to get.

'She wanted to talk about the P-U-P-P-I-E-S.'

Ned giggled. 'I can spell, Aunty Tab.'

'Really?' Tabitha placed her hand against her chest, feigning shock. 'What *are* they teaching them at school these days? Next you'll tell me you know your times tables or something?'

In reply, Ned began reciting the seven times tables through a mouthful of ice-cream.

Tab winked. 'Impressive.' Then she looked back to Lawson. 'You do realise if you succumb and buy a puppy from her—however cute they are—you'll never see the back of dear, sweet Adeline. She'll use checking up on the mutt as an excuse to come over and visit whenever she pleases. As much as I want you to … you know …' She pretended to ride a horse. 'I'm not sure Adeline is the right one for …'

'For what?' Ned asked, looking from Tab to Lawson when her voice drifted off.

'That's why I'm not buying a puppy from her.' He took another swig of his beer. Adeline was a nice chick and they'd been friends for a long time but he didn't feel that way about her. He'd tried not to be downright rude but he couldn't risk encouraging her either.

'Besides, we've already got two dogs,' piped up Ned. He glanced affectionately at their ancient Border Collie, Bonnie, as she slept—her legs in the air—on the kitchen floor. She'd been solely a working dog till a couple of years ago, but these days she spent more time indoors than out. Her son, Clyde, though, he was the best worker they'd ever had.

'Damn straight we do.' Lawson winked at Tab. 'He's wise beyond his years, this kid.'

'He sure is.' She beamed with pride at her nephew. 'And I reckon you and I can take a little of the credit for that.'

Tab was right. She'd hardly left their side since Leah's death and had barely dated anyone in that time herself, although sometimes he thought this had as much to do with having lost her arm as it did he and Ned. It was all well and good her worrying about *his* love life, but what about hers? Since her illness it had been non-existent, but she didn't want to talk about it any more than he did.

Absentmindedly, Lawson reached out to ruffle his son's hair and looked over at the clock on the microwave. 'Bloody hell, is that the time?' He took one last slug of his beer and then put the still half-full bottle down on the bench. 'I better head out and start helping Ethan bring in the cows. Ned? You gunna do the calves with Aunty Tab or come down to the dairy with me?'

Ned looked from Lawson to Tab and back again. 'I'll help Aunty Tab. You have Ethan after all.'

'That I do. See you both later.'

He stomped down the hallway and outside. Clyde, who'd been napping on the verandah, sprang to life the moment the screen door opened and was halfway to the shed before Lawson had even pulled on his boots. He headed after the hyperactive but hard-working Collie and on his way met Ethan coming over from their worker's cottage.

'Hey, mate. Thanks for your extra work today. I appreciate it.'

Ethan, an Irish guy who was the same age Lawson had been when he'd become a dad, waved his gratitude away. 'No worries. Tab and I had it all under control.'

Lawson stifled a smile. Ethan had a little crush on Tabitha, but at twenty-five, she thought a twenty-one-year-old far too immature. Without further conversation they prepped the rotary milking platform for the girls and then jumped on the quad bikes to encourage them all towards the dairy, with Clyde on the ground being his usual bossy self. Creatures of habit, the cows always headed towards the sheds at this time of the day, so it was really a matter of giving them a heave-ho, as they were, by nature, ladies of leisure.

As soon as Lawson and Ethan had gathered the first lot in the pens, Ethan turned on the rotary. Most days he put the girls on and, after they'd been milked, Lawson got them off at the other end. They worked well together and Lawson hoped Ethan would stick around longer then their last worker had. He pushed the rest of the mob into the back of the pen and was in position to let the first cow off the rotary by the time they came around.

He'd been working like this since he was younger than Ned. This was his life and he genuinely loved what he did, but it could also be monotonous, giving his mind a chance to drift off on the job. As he sprayed the udders with water before each cow disembarked the rotary, his thoughts wandered to meeting Meg that afternoon.

When she'd stepped out of the old general store, he'd been almost as surprised as Ned to see a real live person standing there. If she weren't wearing denim shorts, maybe he'd have thought she *was* a vision from a bygone era, one of the ghosts he'd been hearing about since he was a little kid. A few folks had still lived in the buildings on the main street back then; although apparently most of the shops had closed in the late seventies when a new highway was built that bypassed the town, so travellers and truckies heading south from Perth ceased stopping there. The pub had gone downhill thanks to dodgy owners, so people got out of the habit of going there. At one stage it *had* actually been the pub with no beer. These days it was nothing but the dangerous skeleton of a building, since a fire had almost burned it to the ground one night in 1989.

The general store had by then been losing business to the Food-land in Walsh, which was only a fifteen-minute drive away. But the town had well and truly breathed its last breath when the old store closed in the early nineties.

It didn't take much for a small rural community to die, especially when they were so close to bigger towns. Although there were farms in the region, the owners of those properties did their business in Walsh, Harvey or Bunbury, which was the nearest city. Rose Hill was known to locals as 'the old ghost town' and that's why it had been so surprising to see Meg there, looking like she was settling in for the long haul. Again, he wondered about her story. About why a young, gorgeous woman like her would choose to live in such a lonely place. It was a mystery. On the one hand it shouldn't be any concern of his why she'd chosen to live where she had, but he couldn't help feeling a little anxious about the idea of a young, single woman living in such isolation.

What if something happened? Not even something or *someone* sinister, but what if she broke her leg or got bitten by a snake? The fact that Crazy Archie was a few doors away did little to ease his worries. Not that he thought the old man dangerous, but rumour had it he was a bit of a drunk, so he might not be much help if disaster struck.

The sound of Ethan shouting something at one of the cows in his thick Irish brogue snapped Lawson out of his reverie just in time. On autopilot, he'd been about to unhook the chain that was in place to indicate when a cow had a lot of milk and needed to go round the rotary another time. Dammit, he needed to stop his mind wandering off—if he'd let this girl out, she could have got mastitis. He sprayed water off the next few sets of udders and then had to climb up to encourage a cow who'd decided to sit down and was thus interrupting the flow of traffic through the pens.

Clyde dashed in from the entry side of the pens and barked his disapproval at lazy Daisy, but it wasn't easy for the old girl to haul herself up in such a tight space, with dozens of her 'colleagues' standing around her.

'Halt the rotary. Cow down,' Lawson called to Ethan as he prodded at the heifer. He and Clyde eventually got her up and the evening milking continued as usual, with Lawson reprimanding himself every time he started thinking about Meg again. He didn't usually get hung up on things like this but he just hated the thought of something bad happening to her out there.

'Coming for dinner?' Lawson asked Ethan when they'd sent the last of the cows on her way and washed down the dairy.

'That depends on who's cooking,' Ethan said as they yanked off their gum boots and replaced them with their normal farm boots. 'You or Tab?'

Lawson chuckled—it was a well-known fact that he wasn't as gifted in the kitchen as his sister. 'Well, Tab made some salads this arvo but I'll probably wield the tongs over the barbie.'

Ethan screwed up his nose. 'No offence, boss, but you Aussie blokes literally burn meat. I'll come if you'll let me do the honours.'

'No complaints here,' Lawson said as he reached up and switched off the lights. The way his mind was right now, he *could* very well ruin the meat.

Ethan's ever-present grin grew wider. 'Goodo!' he said as they started towards the house, Clyde bounding ahead of them as usual.

Ned and Tab had finished feeding the calves and were sitting out on the front verandah. The Tupperware bowls with the salads had been laid out onto the table and it looked like she'd also started the barbecue. Ned jumped the few steps off the verandah to greet Ethan.

'Hey little dude.' Ethan held up his hand for a high five. 'I missed your face these last few days. And have you grown or have I shrunk?'

Tab laughed. 'That's what I said too.'

Ned followed Lawson and Ethan inside to wash up, talking the whole time about the mystery woman at Rose Hill. Lawson realised that even if he worked out how to get Meg out of his head, Ned probably wouldn't let him forget until something else out of the ordinary happened.

'Sounds like I might need to take a drive out to Rose Hill and welcome the new girl myself,' Ethan said as he laid out the sausages and steak on the grill top.

'Can I come with you?' Ned shouted from the other end of the verandah where he was lying alongside Bonnie.

Before Ethan could reply, Lawson said in a low voice so only he and Tab could hear, 'I get the feeling she's not too keen on visitors.'

'Even more intriguing,' Ethan mused.

For some reason the thought of Ethan going out there and introducing himself to Meg irked Lawson. But what right did he have to feel such a thing? Maybe he'd been wrong about her? Maybe she did want to meet people. And wasn't it the country way to make newcomers feel welcome?

'Shall I get us some drinks?' he asked, hoping to steer the conversation in a different direction.

'You sure can, big bro.' Tab smiled as she flopped down onto a seat at the outdoor table and propped her chin up with her good arm. 'My work here is done.'

Lawson retreated inside and returned a few moments later with three bottles of beer and a glass of milk for Ned. He handed round the drinks, pretended to supervise the cooking of the meat and then, once the steak and sausages were done to Ethan's standard, the four of them sat down to enjoy dinner.

Sitting back in his chair, Ethan lifted his beer in a toast to the view in front of them. 'How's the serenity?'

They all laughed at the Irishman, who since coming to Australia to work had made it his mission to watch every classic Aussie film he could lay his hands on. Not only did he watch the movies, he quoted them whenever he could, never failing to make those around him smile. But right now, with the sun setting over their pond, which, although dry at this time of year, still looked gorgeous with the backdrop of orange and purple sky, Lawson had to agree with his worker's sentiment.

His life might not have been a walk in the park but he wouldn't want to live anywhere else. While they ate, they talked about the new calves—Ned had already named the newborns. So far they'd been lucky this season and all births had been smooth sailing, but the springers were in the paddock closest to the house so they could keep an eye on them, know when they went into labour and intervene if necessary. Doctors and emergency services weren't the only professions on call—a dairy farmer never clocked off either.

Following dinner, Ethan and Tab offered to clean up while Lawson ushered a grumbling, I'm-not-tired Ned into the shower.

'You might not be tired, mate,' he said, 'but I'm stuffed and I can't go to bed until you do.'

With a roll of his eyes, Ned showered, got into his summer PJs, brushed his teeth and then climbed into bed. Sure enough, two seconds after Lawson kissed him good night and stepped out of his bedroom, Ned called out. 'Dad?'

Here it comes … The request for a drink, another bedtime story, perhaps a song—sometimes the list was endless. 'Yes?'

'I'm scared.' Ned was all bravado about being a big kid during the day, but his antics at night time reminded Lawson he was still just eight years old. The ghost talk *had* come back to haunt them.

He inhaled deeply and walked back to his son's bed. 'What are you scared of?'

'I thought I heard a noise. Maybe it was a ghost?'

Lawson clenched his jaw and resisted the urge to roll his eyes. 'There's no such thing as ghosts.'

'How do you know?'

'I've never seen one.'

Ned contemplated this for a few moments. 'Just because you can't see something doesn't mean it's not real. You can't see air but it's there or we'd all be dead. And we can't see Mum any more but you still say she's up there looking down on us.'

'True.' Lawson's eyes followed Ned's finger as it directed him to the ceiling scattered with glow-in-the-dark stars. Sadly, he didn't really believe in anything like an afterlife and he definitely didn't believe Leah or his own mum were watching them. It was a nice idea—something he'd told Ned when he'd come home from his first day at school sobbing about being the only kid in kindy without a mum. But it was in the same realm as fairy tales.

Ned shuffled over and patted the tiny strip of mattress beside him. 'Can you stay with me while I go to sleep? *Please?*'

Lawson lay down next to him—both their heads could barely fit on Ned's pillow and Lawson's feet hung over the end of the single bed, but if he didn't do as requested, Ned would take much longer to settle. And they did both need their sleep. It was early to bed and early to rise on a dairy and, for some reason, Lawson was more buggered tonight than usual.

'Love you, Dad,' Ned whispered as he snuggled into Lawson's side.

A lump rose in his throat. 'I love you too, little man.'

'I'm not so little any more. Ethan and Aunty Tab both said. And I'll be ten next year.' Considering it was January and Ned wasn't nine until June, that was stretching things a little.

Lawson smiled to himself. 'So they did and so you will; now get some rest.'

He put his arm over his son and tried to get comfortable. Comfortable or not, he'd likely end up falling asleep before Ned did, but he didn't mind that much. And if Leah had still been alive, she'd have happily cuddled Ned to sleep. Lord knew she'd comforted Lawson on many an occasion. His eyes watered a little. Leah had been the most kind, caring and loving person on the planet. Her family had moved to town when he was in Year Ten. When she'd first sat down next to him in English, he'd been immediately attracted to her—what red-blooded adolescent male wouldn't have been—but he hadn't known how much he'd come to rely on her in the terrible months ahead. She'd helped him through the loss of his mother, and she'd been there for Tab too, when their dad was too lost in his own grief to know how to handle his children's.

Ironically, much of what Leah had taught Lawson about grief and how to handle tragic loss had also helped him carry on when she was killed and the pain of losing her seemed insurmountable. It was true—the good died young.

'Dad?'

Ned's high-pitched voice broke his thoughts.

'Yep. What is it?'

'Do you think Meg might get scared out there all alone tonight?'

Lawson swallowed at the way his son talked about the stranger as if she were an old friend. 'I dunno, mate, I dunno.'

But, like Ned, he couldn't get her out of his head.

Chapter Three

Megan woke with a jerk at the sound of movement outside her bedroom door. Her heart stilling, she listened carefully for anything more as she read the time on her alarm clock. Six-thirty. Way too early. Without the enforced routines of the past four and a half years, the days stretched ahead; she'd been enjoying the luxury of sleeping in because it meant fewer hours to fill, less time to pass, before she could climb back into bed and put another day to rest. If there were an intruder, they'd have to deal with her wrath.

After a few seconds, she heard a slight creaking noise and her heart started up again like some heavy metal rock band inside of her. She glanced around frantically for something to use as a weapon and her eyes landed on a can of spray deodorant on her dresser. A golf club or cricket bat would have been preferable but, in the absence of either, the deodorant would have to do.

Careful not to make a sound, she crept out of bed and across the room to retrieve the can and then stilled again, listening. After a few minutes of silence, she let out a long huff of breath but kept a firm grip on the 'weapon' as she walked over to the door and carefully peeled it open.

Hesitating in the open doorway, she peered out onto the landing and down the stairs. Everything was still and as she'd left it when she went to bed. Finally she allowed herself a small chuckle that the day after Ned Cooper-Jones had said her house was haunted, she started hearing noises, which must have been the sounds of an old house shifting. Either that or her imagination playing tricks with her.

Whatever the reason, she was awake now and it would be good to get out for her daily run before it got too hot. With that thought, she went back into her bedroom, dressed in her running gear and then hurried down stairs. She grabbed a banana from the kitchen and wolfed it down, before heading outside, locking the front door and tucking the key inside her sports bra.

It was a beautiful morning—the sun was shining brightly across the deserted town, glinting off the rusty tin roofs of the decrepit buildings. She glanced left and right and sighed with relief when there was not a soul in sight. As she started running down the road in the opposite direction of the service station, the only sound for miles was the chatter of pink-and-grey galahs flying overhead.

Farmland and forest surrounded the little town, but Megan stuck to the main road as she didn't want to trespass and risk running into anyone; nor did she want to risk meeting a snake. *Eek*— just the thought gave her the heebie jeebies. She ran and ran—the road undulating with the landscape of gentle hills—until she guessed she'd gone about four kilometres, and then she turned around and headed back. Her calves burned a little and she was in dire need of a drink but she pushed herself a little further every day. Keeping her body in shape was more to do with her mental health than anything else but as the other thing that helped with this was baking, it was lucky she enjoyed exercising.

Once back inside, she filled the kettle, flicked it on and then immediately switched on the radio that sat on the windowsill.

Never much of a radio listener in the past, she now found the endless music and the chatter between the hosts comforting. Over the last few days, occasionally she felt like she was the only survivor of the apocalypse; mostly she didn't mind the feeling but the voices on the radio would hopefully stop her going insane from too much quiet.

While she waited for the water to boil, Megan popped two slices of bread in the toaster and grabbed a jar of her homemade marmalade out of the fridge. As she unscrewed the lid and lifted the jar to inhale the familiar aroma, she thought about Granny Rose. Her beloved gran was the only reason she had any idea how to make marmalade. Her heart ached thinking about Gran and all the pain she'd put her through. Megan wished she were still alive and she had the chance to make it up to her, but if such enormous wishes could come true, then wouldn't she just rewrite the past altogether?

She took the coffee and toast out onto the front verandah to eat. A rooster crowed from the direction of the old service station and wind gently moved the leaves of the jacaranda trees that lined the wide street. She sipped her coffee, munched her toast and enjoyed the peace as she wrote her to-do list for the day.

More cleaning—when she'd arrived her place had been caked in dust, not to mention such a number of eight-legged beasts she'd had to make a trip to Bunbury to stock up on insect killer. Although originally the general store, the building hadn't operated as a shop in over thirty years. The last owners had continued to live on in it for fifteen years after it closed—until they'd died of old age within two months of each other. Megan had bought the place from their daughter, who now lived in Sydney, so all interactions were through the real estate agent. The daughter had offered to have the building cleared and fumigated, but Megan had been happy to take the furniture and contents and slowly clean the joint herself, reasoning it would give her something to do besides sitting around and contemplating her navel. She'd promised to box up any personal, family-type items and send them on to Sydney, but the daughter had told her not to bother. Megan got the feeling she hadn't been close to her parents.

This was something she couldn't understand—she'd give anything, *do* anything, to see her folks again.

She swallowed the lump in her throat that arrived with that thought and turned her attentions back to the list. Perhaps she'd do a little gardening before it got too hot. So far she'd harvested two of the fruit trees out the back but there were others that needed the same treatment. All this physical work supplemented her running; a bonus considering there wasn't anything like a gym in Rose Hill for her to join. She chuckled at the thought and the sound felt alien to her.

When was the last time she'd laughed? *Truly* laughed?

Yesterday, when she'd found herself entertaining unexpected guests, she'd smiled again, and the buzz that came with that felt better than she could have imagined. Who would ever have thought that a smile and laughter would be something to celebrate?

Grinning from ear to ear, she inhaled the fresh country air and then picked up her mug and took another sip. As the caffeine took affect she started to feel halfway normal again. Sorting, cleaning, gardening, continuing with her list of what parts of the building needed more urgent repairs ... If she worked hard at this stuff until lunchtime, she would reward herself with a little baking, crocheting or maybe even some reading.

This had become a bit of a routine over the last few days—but it was *her* routine, so she told herself that this was okay.

The day planned, Megan stood, took her empty plate and mug inside and dumped them in the sink for later. Then, she went upstairs and got dressed in suitable gardening attire of light cargo pants, an old singlet and boots. This time of year she wanted her feet and legs covered in case she stumbled on a snake. Before going outside, she brushed her teeth, washed her face and pulled her hair back into a ponytail. The truth was she'd been a little lax about such things the last few days, but the previous day's unexpected visitors had reminded her of one of Granny Rose's nuggets of wisdom: 'Always wear good underwear in case you get in a car accident!' Or have an unexpected visitor, Megan thought.

She spent three hours in the garden, weeding the flower beds, picking more fruit from the trees and piling all the discarded foliage in a corner at the back of the big yard—something else to deal with later. Her arm and leg muscles ached by the time the sun grew too hot and she headed back inside for lunch. After food and another few hours sorting and carrying clutter from one of the bedrooms out into another pile at one end of the verandah, she finally decided it was time for a break.

She took her crocheting, a copy of *Harp in the South* and a plate of cookies she'd made yesterday out onto the back verandah and all but collapsed into the old rocking chair she'd put there. The temperature in the sun had to be mid-to-high thirties, but under the verandah it was just about bearable, and she wanted to sit in the fresh air. With the best intentions to read a few more chapters of her book, she dozed off within a matter of minutes, only to be woken who knew how long later by the clucking of a chicken.

Her eyes boggled at the sight of a plump, red hen only a few feet away from her. She sat up straighter, picked her crochet off her lap and put it on the milk crate beside her.

'Well, hello there,' she said to the animal. 'Where did you come from?'

In reply it clucked again and she smiled—it was as if the chicken understood her question. Pity she had no idea how to decipher *bok-bok-bok*. She glanced left to right and out over the backyard as if she might find a clue to the mystery, but to no avail.

'What am I going to do with you?'

While she kinda liked the idea of getting a few chickens and having fresh eggs daily, her yard didn't have an enclosure. And besides, she wasn't about to steal someone else's. Unless someone had driven through Rose Hill and dumped the bird, it had to belong to the only other resident of the town—Crazy Archie. Telling Lawson she'd go over and introduce herself had been a little white lie. But she couldn't just ignore the chicken. If it didn't get home safely by nightfall, it would be in danger of being eaten by the local foxes.

She felt a prickling sensation at the back of her neck as she realised what she needed to do. Whether she wanted to or not, it was time to meet her lone neighbour. Megan heaved herself out of the rocking chair, muscles screaming from the morning's exertion and her vertical nap. Then she stared down at the chicken as she tried to work out the logistics. If she got some grain or something from inside, could she lure it to follow her to the roadhouse Hansel and Gretel style?

Short of another plan, she barked 'Stay there' to the hen, then went inside and grabbed some sunflower seeds from her pantry. Whether chickens ate sunflower seeds or not, she had no clue, but it was the best she had until she got back to Bunbury for more groceries. Walsh was closer, of course, but no way was she shopping in such a small town, where the locals would know she was a newcomer.

'All right, chicken-licken,' she said as she dropped a sunflower down in front of the bird. 'Time for walkies.'

The chicken glanced down at the seed and then back up at her as if she were cray-cray. Undeterred, Megan took a step back and dropped another seed on the ground. She repeated this two more times, hoping the bird would get the idea, but it didn't.

Dammit. She shoved the sunflower seeds in her pocket and frowned. 'Are you friendly?' she asked, and received another *bok-bok-bok* in reply.

Perhaps she could leave it there and go over to find Archie, then tell him to come and get it. What if it wandered off and got lost while she was gone? Nope, that would not do.

Holding her breath, she took a slow step towards the chicken, stooped slightly and held out her hand as if it were a dog or cat she was trying to make friends with. When it didn't retreat or attack, she swallowed, put her hands out and tried to pick it up the way her granddad had shown her years earlier.

Success. It turned out chicken-licken was tame and quite happy to be held. Talking soothingly to the bird, she slowly stepped off the verandah and walked around the side of her building to the front. From there she turned left and headed along the cracked, weed-ridden footpath in the direction of the service station, which was a few hundred metres up the road on the way out of town towards Walsh.

Walking slowly Megan admired the abandoned redbrick post office and the double-storey pub with its gabled verandahs and faded red-tin roof. Across the other side of the wide street was a brown, wooden building, sign-posted as the town hall, and next door a gold plaque on a big rock indicated that long, *long* ago a school had resided in that spot. The historical buildings were far more beautiful than some of the modern monstrosities built in cities today, but, like the general store, they were all in dire need of a new lick of paint and a fair bit of handyman TLC.

It made her heart sick to think that once upon a time this little town would have been a vibrant hub, but at the same time she was glad she'd found a place of solitude at such a reasonable price.

A little further along the road she came to the petrol station, which was all boarded up. A big golden ram was perched on the end of a tall post out the front. In years gone by it would obviously have been lit up at night, but these days it was all faded and chipped. There were two bowsers still in use and a self-serve pre-pay machine in front of the main entrance, making it clear there was nothing to purchase but petrol there.

She heard the sounds of more chickens out the back and the bark of a dog, alerting its owner to her presence. For the first time since they'd started out chicken-licken began squirming in her arms, so she didn't have time to dither or deliberate about whether or not to dump her and run. As the side gate, she peered through the tiny square hole where the latch was.

'Hello, anybody home? I think I've found your chicken.' She held her breath as she waited for a reply.

'Hello?' came a gravelly voice a few moments later. Footsteps followed and then a grey-haired head appeared. The lips attached to the head cracked into a smile as their eyes met. 'I thought I must be hearing things,' he said.

There was warmth and friendliness in his voice and in the lines etched into his face that she hadn't been expecting.

'Did you say you've found my chicken?'

She nodded as he unlatched and opened the gate. A scruffy black and white dog stood at his feet. The chicken took one look at the canine and sprang from her arms, although, as it hurried into the yard, the dog didn't look the slightest bit interested in chasing it.

'He's not the best guard dog.' The man chuckled and Megan realised she hadn't said anything since he'd appeared.

'But he's adorable,' she said with a smile as she ruffled the dog's soft fur. 'I'm sorry to bother you, but your chicken appeared on my back verandah and I wanted to bring it back so it didn't get lost or hurt.'

'Thanks. That little witch is always making a run for it.' His grin grew wider and she noticed he was missing a fair few teeth, but aside from that and the fact he didn't look like he'd had a good meal in decades, he wasn't scary in the slightest. He didn't seem crazy as his nickname suggested either. At a guess she'd put him in his late sixties or early seventies.

'Well, I'm glad she's safe again,' she said. 'I'm … Meg by the way. I've just moved into the old general store.'

'I'm Archibald, but if you call me that I'll have to kill ya. Archie will be fine.' The man's bushy white eyebrows lifted as he offered her his rough-skinned hand. She forced herself to put hers in it and shake, trying not to flinch at the direct contact with another human.

'Anyway, what's a nice girl like you doing in a shit hole like this all on your own? I assume you are on your own?' he asked.

She actually laughed, not feeling at all threatened. 'You assume correctly, and I could ask a similar question. What's a lovely gentleman like yourself living here in a place like this?' Although she disagreed that it was a shit hole.

'Touché.' He dipped his head, his grey eyes sparkling. 'Can I offer you a cool drink as thanks for bringing back my runaway?'

While Megan's throat felt parched, she didn't want Archie to get the impression she wanted to become too neighbourly. Bringing back the chicken was her good deed for the day, but if she hung around any longer he might start asking her questions.

'Thanks,' she said, 'but I forgot to lock my house so I'd best be getting back.'

Archie snorted. 'Haven't locked my place ever, but maybe you've got more to steal than I do.'

He couldn't be more wrong. The only things she really cared about in her house were the photo albums and the crochet stuff she'd got from Granny Rose's estate, but she couldn't imagine going out without locking up. 'Maybe another time.'

'Maybe.' Archie nodded and she was glad he didn't make an issue of it. He seemed harmless enough but she'd chosen Rose Hill so she could lie low, so it wouldn't pay to start making friends with the neighbours. 'You know where to find me if you ever need anything, and thanks again.'

'You're welcome.' Megan smiled warmly, ruffled the dog's furry head one more time and then started home.

Once there, she went round the back, retrieved her crocheting and her book and took them inside, where the radio still twittered away. Despite the upbeat music, the stillness and emptiness of the house struck her. *This* was what she'd needed, what she'd wanted in order to heal and to start afresh. Still, she had to admit, talking to Lawson and Ned, and then Archie today, had been rather nice.

But they didn't know about her past and if they did, they wouldn't want anything to do with her.

Chapter Four

'Smile for Aunty Tab!'

As Tabitha snapped away on her iPhone, Ned looked to Lawson and rolled his eyes, but he smiled nonetheless as he stood there in the hallway, proud as punch, dressed in his school uniform ready to face the new school year.

'And now the two of you,' Tab instructed. 'Outside on the verandah.'

'That's my boy.' Lawson ruffled Ned's hair and grabbed his hand as they followed his sister outside. Although he didn't love being photographed any more than his son did, he was grateful that she insisted on keeping a record of these special moments. Leah would have been doing exactly the same. She'd recorded Ned's first three years in beautiful handcrafted scrapbooks and had been halfway through the fourth when she died. Lawson kept them under his bed and got them out to look at more than he would ever admit to anyone, even Tab. Sure, he loved looking back on photos of Ned as a baby, but even more than that, he liked reading Leah's comments and running his fingers over her handwriting.

As Tab positioned them on the bottom step outside, she shook her head at Lawson.

'What?' he asked, lifting his hand to his chin. 'Have I got Vegemite on my face or something?'

'You took Ned to get a hair cut on the weekend. Did you not consider getting your own chopped while you were there?'

'Nothing wrong with my hair.' He ran his hand up and through it. 'I can almost tie it up and haven't you heard? Man–buns are *all* the rage.'

The expression on her face told him exactly what she thought of that.

He laughed.

'Can we go now?' Ned leaped up, eager to get to school. He was always like this to start with—the excitement of seeing his friends again spurring him on—but as the year dragged on, his enthusiasm waned a little. Farm mad, exactly like Lawson himself had been as a boy, Ned often asked if he could stay home and help.

'Okay, okay. I get the message.' Tab shoved her phone in her pocket, then offered her hand to help Ned up and pulled him into a hug. 'You have a fun first day. I might have a new ice-cream flavour for you to test after school.'

'Thanks, Aunty Tab,' Ned said as he broke free and ran towards the ute, his Minecraft backpack bopping up and down behind him.

'See ya later, sis.' Lawson lifted a hand as he followed after his son.

Normally Ned took the bus, but the first day of the year most people drove their offspring, which meant Lawson had left Ethan to finish up the milking and get the cows back out to pasture. The farm was only a ten-minute drive out of Walsh, but the way Ned went on you'd think it was ten hours.

'Can't you drive faster, Dad? When are we gonna get there? I can't wait to tell all the kids that someone's living in the haunted house. Can we go out and see her again soon?'

'Maybe,' Lawson said, not about to admit to Ned that he too had been unable to get the mysterious redhead out of his mind over the weekend. Something about her had captured his interest, and he wasn't sure how he felt about that.

The small car park at school was already filled with dusty four-wheel drives when they arrived. Lawson's vehicle was the sole ute, just as he was pretty much the token male in the sea of mums yakking to each other as they ushered their children towards the school gate.

'Hi, Lawson,' called Tennille Wellington, the older sister of his best mate, Funky (christened Sam), from where she was locking her youngest into a pram.

'Hey there.' He waved and crossed over to join Tennille as Ned ran ahead of him and joined the other kids all dressed in blue and yellow school uniforms. They looked like a tribe of Eagles fans, which annoyed the local Dockers supporters no end. These days Lawson didn't have time to get too hung up on football.

'Can I help you with anything or anyone?' he asked as Tennille hooked a big nappy bag on the back of the pram. She and her husband, Boots (christened Toby), had five kids under seven—just the thought made Lawson's head spin but nothing seemed to faze Tennille.

'I'm all good.' She started pushing the pram towards the gate, her younger children shuffling along beside her. 'Is Ned excited about being back?'

'Crazily so.'

'That's great,' Tennille said and then lowered her voice. 'So, I hear the new junior room teacher is young and gorgeous.'

Lawson raised an eyebrow and shoved his hands in his pockets as he walked. 'And the reason you're telling me this is …?'

She made a tsking noise with her tongue. 'You know young female teachers come to the country for one reason and one reason only.'

He played dumb. 'What? To gain good teaching experience?'

Tennille whacked him on the arm. 'They're man-hunting.'

Lawson scoffed as he helped her manoeuvre the pram and her kids through the gate. 'Maybe you should tell Funky about her then.'

'Oh come on, *please*. That brother of mine doesn't have a settling-down bone in his body, but you …' Her voice drifted off but Lawson knew what she was thinking. He had a kid and the kid needed a mother. Besides, he'd married once already so why wouldn't he do it again?

'If you're set on playing matchmaker, I suggest you aim your Cupid's bow in another direction. You know I'm not interested.'

Honestly, he got sick of the whole damn town trying to set him up with people. For two years they'd allowed him his grief over Leah and then suddenly almost everyone he knew had turned into an obsessed matchmaker, as if two years was long enough to mend his heart. He'd contemplated making up an online girl-friend, but he'd confided the idea to Tab and she'd pointed out that eventually he'd have to manifest a real live female for public scrutiny, so he'd scrapped that idea. Even *if* he was contemplating dating again, which he was not, he doubted many women would be interested in hooking up with a single dad. And between run-ning the farm and looking after Ned, where was he supposed to find the time to date?

Tennille sighed. 'Pity.'

'Hey gorgeous,' called a high-pitched female voice from across the yard.

Lawson didn't need to look up to know who the voice belonged to and to know that the 'gorgeous' was supposed to be him. For once, he was glad to see Adeline hurrying towards them as it meant an end to this ridiculous conversation with Tennille.

'Ooh, is that because the rumours are true and you have a thing with Adeline?' Tennille said under her breath.

He ignored her. It didn't matter what he said anyway, the local gossips would never let the truth get in the way of a good story.

'What are you doing here?' he asked, trying not to sound rude as Adeline stopped in front of them, wiggled her fingers in greeting at Tennille and then leaned forwards and pulled him into a hug.

'I'm taking first-day-back photos for the *Walsh Whisperer*,' she said, pulling back and lifting the camera that hung around her neck to show him. Editor for the local paper was just one of her many volunteer roles.

'What's *that*?' piped up Tennille's five-year-old daughter, Natalia, pointing to the camera as if it were a live insect necklace.

They all laughed.

'This is a camera,' Adeline spoke slowly. 'People used them to take photos before smart phones.'

'Oh,' was all Natalia said in reply, but her eyes were wide as if she wasn't sure whether Adeline was pulling her leg.

She placed a hand against Lawson's arm. 'Can I get a photo of you and Ned?'

'Shouldn't you be taking photos of the kids who are starting school this year?'

'I'll get the kindy crew later,' she said, and then all but dragged him away from Tennille and over to where Ned was already playing handball with his friends. 'Neddy,' she called, 'come over here a moment.'

Lawson cringed and smiled apologetically at his little man, who was too polite to ignore the request of an adult.

'Hi, Adeline,' he said, looking longingly back at his mates.

'Hello, Neddy.' She stooped a little and reached out to straighten the collar of Ned's polo shirt. 'Are you super excited to be back at school?'

She elongated each word, speaking as if Ned were two years old, not eight. It grated on Lawson's nerves and he couldn't help comparing her to Meg on Friday afternoon. She'd spoken to him like an equal. Then again, she'd also kicked the footy with him and he couldn't imagine Adeline doing such a thing. She may be wearing a classic RB Sellars pink chambray shirt, work shorts and RM Williams boots, but she looked more like a catalogue model or Farmer Barbie than someone who actually worked hard enough to get dirty.

'Yeah,' was Ned's monosyllabic reply.

'O-kay, excellent. I just need to get a quick photo of you and Daddy for the *Whisperer* and then you can go back to your little friends.'

Ned grimaced in much the same way Lawson wanted to, but they both understood Adeline wasn't the type to take no for an answer. They posed as she instructed and were happy when the bell rang, giving them an excuse to get away.

'I was wondering, now school's back,' she said, before Lawson could escape after Ned towards his classroom, 'whether you'd like to go out for lunch sometime?'

He shuffled from foot to foot, trying to work out how to let Adeline down gently. Adeline was a friend, a die-hard supporter of keeping the town alive and undoubtedly one of the best-looking women in the district, but he just didn't *feel* anything like that for her. He didn't feel anything like that for anyone and it wasn't fair to get her hopes up.

'I'm pretty busy on the farm right now,' he said, his cheeks heating even though this was the truth. 'We've got heaps of new calves and we need to service the machinery leading into seeding. There's also a lot of fencing needing repair.'

He felt like a schoolkid clutching at excuses for why he hadn't done his homework.

She offered a sympathetic nod. 'I understand. So how about I bring a picnic out to you one day? I'll even bake my famous cream puffs for dessert.'

Lawson swallowed, his traitorous taste buds standing to attention. Adeline was president of the local branch of the CWA Belles—a group of young farming women determined to keep the institution alive—and there was no doubt she could cook.

He summoned a smile. 'That sounds great, and I'm sure Ethan and Tab will appreciate it as well.' Then, before she could set him straight, he added, 'I've gotta go meet Ned's new teacher. See ya round.'

Ned had already unpacked his bag and was laying out water bottle and stationery items on his desk by the time Lawson got to the classroom. Tab had spent two nights the week before labelling all Ned's new things. He'd tried to help, but she'd insisted he didn't do it properly and she was probably right. She might only have one arm, but she did most things better than most people who had two.

Ned's teacher this year was Mrs Warburton, a woman who'd also taught Lawson and Tabitha when they were at school and yet didn't look like she'd aged at all in that time. Teaching would give a lot of folks grey hairs but it seemed to keep her young.

'Hello, Lawson dear,' she said, noticing him lingering on the edge of the classroom like a spare part.

'Hi, Mrs Warburton. I'm stoked Ned has you this year. You're still one of my favourite teachers.'

She smiled warmly. 'And you're still one of my favourite students, but don't you think it's time you called me Joanne?'

He wasn't sure he could do that but he promised her he'd try.

Mrs Warburton patted him on the arm and then went around the room to the other parents. Lawson went to say goodbye to Ned.

He squeezed his shoulder. 'I guess I'll be making tracks. You have a good day and I'll see you when you get off the bus this arvo.'

'Bye, Dad.' Ned grinned and threw his arms around Lawson's middle. 'You have a good day too.'

When Mrs Warburton called the class to attention, Lawson slipped out the door and headed for the car park. As he turned his key in the ignition, he felt a little lost without his sidekick in the passenger seat beside him. He'd got used to having Ned around over the summer holidays and knew from experience it would take him a few days to readjust to being alone again. He decided to go visit his grandmother—her cheery personality always made him feel better—but when he drove out of school, he turned right instead of left onto the main road that would lead him to the local nursing home. A few hundred metres up the road, he realised his error but he didn't do anything to correct it.

He drove on towards Rose Hill—yes, it was a detour, a very long detour—but he couldn't bring himself to turn around. Meg had been slipping in and out of his mind all weekend, leaving a tight feeling in his chest every time he thought about her being so isolated. He didn't know what he planned on doing when he got there and truth be told he felt a little stalkerish as he slowed his ute in front of the old general store.

If he hadn't seen and spoken to her on Friday, he wouldn't believe that someone actually resided here. Quite aside from the peeling paint on the verandah, the drawn curtains and glass door so dirty you couldn't see through it, the sparse dry garden beds with nothing but weeds growing made the place look sad and lonely. It needed a little colour.

Maybe he could buy her some pot plants to put on the front verandah as a housewarming gift? Or would that give her the wrong idea? Dammit, what exactly *was* he doing there?

He looked down at the plain gold wedding band on his finger and then twisted it round. Just thinking about another woman didn't feel right when the love of his life was buried in the local cemetery. He missed Leah more than he could ever explain to anyone but, despite having Ned and Tab, he was starting to feel a little lonely. The blokes he'd grown up with had thought him crazy settling down so young, but now they were all pushing thirty and starting to get into serious relationships themselves. Aside from Funky—who reckoned there was plenty of time for that kind of stuff—a few of his friends had recently got engaged and another one was having his first baby.

Once again, Lawson felt on the outer and had experienced the odd twinge of something he could only identify as jealousy when he saw how content his friends were. He didn't begrudge their happiness but he couldn't help wishing life hadn't dealt him such shitty cards. He and Leah should almost be celebrating ten years of marriage together, instead he was living with his sister and hadn't so much as kissed a girl since a one-night stand he'd had six months after his wife died. A one-night stand fuelled by grief and drunken stupidity and which he'd regretted mere moments after the act. The poor girl had been horrified when he'd sprung from her bed and been physically sick, feeling as if he'd cheated on his wife.

Luckily she had been a backpacker waitressing at the pub and had left Walsh not long after, so he hadn't had to relive his mistake every time he went for a beer.

But he'd made the decision then not to use another woman like that and he hadn't felt tempted to renege on it once. He kept himself busy with Ned and the farm and told himself that was enough, so he didn't know what to do with the fact that Meg was suddenly taking up real estate in his head.

The engine idling, Lawson stared at her building, contemplating getting out and saying hi. He could play things by ear, suss out his feelings and see if he felt anything more than the urge to look out for her.

Remember me, Meg? Well, I was just passing through again and I thought I'd see how you were settling in.

Would she buy that excuse? And if she did, then what? Would she ask him in for a drink? Did he want her to? Would there be awkward silence as they tried to make small talk? His gut twisted as questions whirled through his head.

No! He wasn't ready for whatever this was, so he pushed his foot down hard on the accelerator and zoomed back out of town.

Having wasted precious time on a stupid whim, he probably should be getting back to the farm, but unsettled, he felt the need to see his grandmother more than ever. He called Tab and told her he was popping in to see Gran and that he'd pick some pies up from the bakery for lunch. Then, he turned his stereo up loud to drown his thoughts and drove back into Walsh, arriving fifteen minutes later at the hospital.

Jenny, a girl who'd been a few years above him at school, sat behind the reception desk when he entered the building. He chatted briefly to her, then turned right towards the residential wing. The old people were all sitting outside on the verandah, enjoying fresh air and cups of tea in plastic beakers. He hadn't been to any nursing homes in the city, but he understood they weren't like this at all. Here the nurses looked after the six residents as if they were family.

At eighty-four his gran was the youngest resident—she had Parkinson's too far gone for her to look after herself. Despite this she had to be the most positive person he'd ever known; Tab had inherited the same disposition and he reckoned one of the reasons he'd been so attracted to Leah was that she'd been the same. They were glass-half-full women who always looked on the bright side and saw the best in people.

'Hello, my love.' Gran's eternal smile grew wider and her eyes lit up as she saw him. He leaned down and kissed her on the cheek, already feeling a little better just for seeing her. 'Where's that gorgeous great-grandie of mine?'

Lawson kneeled beside her portable recliner. 'Sorry, Gran, you're stuck with only me today. I've just dropped Ned off for his first day back at school.'

She reached out a shaky, papery hand and patted his check. 'You are just perfect, my darling. Now, tell me what's been happening on the farm? How are the cows? You know I miss that fresh milk more than anything in here.'

'Why'd you never tell me that before?' Lawson frowned, feeling a stab of guilt that she'd been there a few years and he'd never thought to ask her if she wanted him to bring some. His father's mother, she'd lived in a cottage on the farm till Lawson had married Leah and she'd insisted the young couple needed their own space. Then she'd moved into Walsh to one of the seniors' units owned by the shire, but she'd come out to the farm almost daily. When Dad had his heart attack three years back, his then new wife had insisted they move to Bunbury to be nearer medical help should he need it, so Lawson had moved back into the main house with Tab. Now Ethan lived in the cottage and on the rare weekends Dad and Sandra made the trek to see how things were ticking along, they stayed at the pub in town.

'Oh, you know I don't like to cause a fuss,' Gran said.

'I'll bring you some in tomorrow,' he promised, glad of something he could do for her.

'What other news have you got for me?'

Before Lawson could think of anything, the door from inside opened and he automatically looked up. He bit down on a groan as his eyes met with Adeline's.

She winked at him as the door clunked shut behind her. 'Fancy running into you twice in one day. How lucky.'

Wasn't the word he'd use. But Adeline's great-grandmother Penelope was also a resident, so she had as much right to be there as he did.

'Fancy that,' he said, forcing a smile.

She flitted across the courtyard and perched herself on the arm-rest of old Pen's chair. 'Hello, grandmother darling. I've brought you some photos of my puppies.'

Adeline conjured an iPad with a sparkly pink cover out of her handbag and angled it so her grandmother could see as she swiped her fingers across the screen. Penelope stared at the photos, her eyes agog, but she didn't say anything. Poor thing had suffered a stroke on the farm about a year earlier, two days after her hundredth birthday. Lawson wondered what she must make of today's technology.

One of the nurses arrived and stood on the other side of Penelope's chair, oohing and aahing over the photos.

'Oh my Lord, Adeline, they're too cute for words.'

'I know, right.' She grinned as if the compliment were on *her* appearance, but maybe that wasn't fair. He was in a shit of a mood this morning.

Len, the only man among the residents, piped up from over in his corner. 'Lemme see the puppies,' he demanded gruffly.

'Of course.' Adeline leaped up and took the iPad over to Len. All the old dears wanted a looksee and Adeline patiently took the iPad around to each of them, commentating on the temperaments of the pups as she swiped through the photos. Lawson looked over his gran's shoulder and had to admit Adeline's baby Maremma sheepdogs were adorable.

'I've been trying to get Lawson to take one for Ned,' Adeline said, smiling in a conspiring manner at Gran.

He shook his head. 'I don't deny they're cute but even if I were in the market for another work dog, Maremmas are watch dogs, not herders.'

'Perhaps, but you could always train them to keep an eye on the cows.'

He folded his arms across his chest, wishing she'd go back to Penelope and leave him alone with his gran. 'Strangely we don't have much of a problem with predators where the cows are concerned.'

'They make great family pets as well,' she countered. 'Ned would love it and I could come over and help him train it so it would be no hassle for you. I have dogs and bitches available, he can take his pick. What do you say?'

'I'll think about it,' he finally conceded, having no intention whatsoever of doing so.

'Adeline,' called the nurse, 'do you mind holding the door open for me while I take Penelope back inside? I think she'd like to watch a little TV.'

'She's a firecracker, that one,' muttered Gran with a shake of her head as Adeline and the nurse pushed her great-grandmother back inside. 'Penelope was a good few years older than me but from what I've heard she was exactly the same. Now, where were we? Any local gossip I should know about?'

'My guess is that you're more likely to be privy to that kind of thing in here than I am.' But once again, his mind drifted to Meg. 'Although when Ned and I were driving home from Albany the other day we got a flat tyre in Rose Hill and met someone.'

'You met someone in *Rose Hill*?'

He nodded. 'A young woman has moved into the old general store.'

'Well, I never. What on earth would she want to do that for? I haven't been out that way in years but unless it's undergone some miraculous revival I thought only ghosts lived there these days.'

'And the caretaker,' Lawson reminded her.

'Oh yes,' Gran mused. 'Apparently a bit of a recluse, but I guess you'd have to be to live in a place like that. I wonder what your girl's story is and I do hope she's okay out there all alone. Maybe *she* should get herself one of Adeline's puppies.'

His mind hung up on the way Gran had called Meg *his girl,* it took a second for Lawson to register what she'd said but when he did it felt like she'd given him a Nobel Prize—winning idea.

'Gran, you are a genius.' He leaned forwards and kissed her on the forehead. 'Pure genius.' A puppy would give him a reason to go out to Rose Hill and check on Meg. And afterwards, knowing she had the company of a dog with the protective nature of a Maremma, he could stop worrying about a woman he'd only met once.

Gran laughed half-heartedly as if she had no idea what he was talking about.

'I'd better be off now,' he said. 'If I don't get home soon, Tab and Ethan will be whingeing that I'm not pulling my weight.'

Gran smiled. 'We couldn't have that. You give that girl a hug for me. I love you both.'

'And we love you too. I'm sure Tab will be in some time this week. See ya soon.'

After a quick kiss on her cheek, he went inside to the lounge area where the residents spent much of their time watching day-time television. To his relief, Adeline was still there, brushing her grandmother's long grey hair.

He cleared his throat. 'Adeline, can I talk to you a moment?'

She sprang up from the seat she'd been perched on, dropped the brush in Penelope's lap and beamed at him. 'Have you recon-sidered that offer to take me out to lunch?'

'Uh, no. But I have reconsidered your offer to take one of the puppies,' he said, before she could harp on about the lunch thing.

'Ooh, seriously?' Adeline clapped her hands together.

'Yes. When will they be ready to leave their mum?'

'They're ready right now. You can come out and choose one whenever you want. Today even.'

He shook his head. 'I need time to get a few things organised. How about Wednesday?'

'Wednesday is perfect. And if you need any help working out what you need before then, just give me a call. Ned is going to be beside himself!'

Lawson smiled and then dipped his head to say 'goodbye', but he didn't bother to set her straight.

Chapter Five

Another day, another delivery of eggs on her doorstep. Megan chuckled as she stooped to collect them. She hadn't seen Archie since the chicken episode but everyday following she'd woken up to anything from five to ten eggs on her doorstep. There were only so many eggs a girl could eat, so every evening she'd walked along to the old servo and deposited a box full of home-baked goodies for him—everything from cakes, biscuits and slices to a quiche that he could eat hot or cold for lunch or dinner.

They hadn't exchanged words or even seen each other during these transactions, but it was strangely comforting knowing he wasn't far away. She had faith that the barking of his dog would alert Archie to her delivery and usually when she was halfway back to her place she heard the unlatching of the gate and smiled, safe in the knowledge that her endless baking was going to a good home.

Her fridge, freezer and pantry were full to bursting as the joy of being able to cook whenever and whatever the hell she wanted hadn't yet lost its gloss. As much as she could, she made use of the eggs Archie delivered and fresh fruit from the trees out the back, but her supplies of flour, sugar, butter, milk and the like were dwindling fast. The time had almost come when she'd have to venture further afield to restock and her blood pressure rose just thinking about it.

Rose Hill and this house were her safe haven. Every trip to civilisation carried a risk. Although she was about as far from Melbourne as you could get without leaving the country or travelling to the remote north, and she'd dyed her hair darker and cut herself a thick fringe, there was still the fear that someone might recognise her, that she'd never be able to escape her past. A shiver snaked down her spine as she carried the eggs back inside and went to the fridge to see if she could find a spot to put them in. She might need milk and fresh veggies, but perhaps she could go another couple of days surviving on cake and cookies. *We might not be able live on bread alone, but cake, on the other hand …*

Chuckling to herself at this thought, Megan flicked the kettle on for her morning coffee and poached herself a couple of eggs for breakfast. After eating, she looked down at her list of tasks that needed to be done and decided to tackle the polishing of the old staircase. It had been beautifully crafted in an era where nothing was rushed, but years of wear and tear had tarnished its original charm.

She took cloths and wood polish and got to work. Despite the temperature already heating up, the area surrounding the stairs was strangely cool, and this wasn't the first time she'd noticed. She suspected a draft sneaking in through a gap in the floorboards but hadn't been able to determine exactly where it was coming from.

She put this from her mind and before long began to work up a sweat. Each step took longer than she'd anticipated but the results gave her a sense of accomplishment she hadn't felt in a long while. Time passed quickly. Her imagination ran away with her as she fantasised about what it would have been like to grow up in this house—to have the forest practically in her backyard and not have the worry of traffic when she and her brother played out on the street. Somehow, she believed, if this had been her family's home, they would all still be living happily.

Lost in her thoughts, with the radio in the background, she almost leaped out of her skin at the sound of a heavy knock on the front door. She peered slowly over the stair railing towards the two glass doors at the front. They were so dirty you couldn't see through them, but she hadn't cleaned them because she didn't *want* anyone looking in. At the sight of a tall silhouette on the other side, she bit her lip so hard it almost bled.

Maybe dirt wasn't enough. Maybe she needed to hang curtains on the door like the old ragged ones on the windows.

Another knock sounded and then a bark. Her shoulders slumped at the realisation her visitor must be Archie, but she still deliberated about opening the door. Exchanging food was one thing but getting to know each other was quite something else. Then again, what if he were in trouble? She pushed herself off the steps, leaving the polish and cloth where they were, and wiped her hands on her shorts as she went to open the door.

She gasped at the sight of Lawson Cooper-Jones, her visitor from the previous week, standing on her front porch. And, as if he hadn't been appealing enough on his own, in his arms he carried the cutest bundle of puppy she'd ever laid eyes on.

She couldn't help herself. 'Oh my,' she said, reaching out and stroking the top of said puppy's head. 'She's adorable.'

He grinned back at her and something inside her twisted and made her blush. 'She's a he and he's all yours, if you want him.'

Her brain, which had frozen when hit with such cuteness, clicked back into gear. Had she heard right? He'd brought her a puppy? *Why?*

Her chest squeezing, she stepped back a little, her defences shooting up around her. 'What? But he looks like a purebred. He must have cost a fortune. I can't accept such a gift.'

Lawson cocked his head to one side as the puppy wriggled in his arms. 'Do you like dogs?'

She swallowed. 'Of course.' He'd see right through her if she tried to lie. Who wouldn't melt and fall in love at first sight with such a thing?

'Is there any reason you can't have one?' he asked. 'Are you allergic?'

She bit her lip and shook her head. Hadn't she thought about getting a pet these last few days? The brief company of Archie's chicken had brought her more joy than she'd thought possible. Talking to an animal seemed more acceptable than talking to oneself and she hadn't had a pet since the fire. Her eyeballs prickled at the thought and she pushed it aside to focus on the puppy. This dog would be good company and a fabulous running companion, but what was Lawson's ulterior motive?

'Good. Then he's all yours.' His smile widened and it felt so genuine she couldn't help but relax a little. She might not have the best record as being a good judge of character, but something told her Lawson didn't have a duplicitous bone in his body. 'I got mates rates for her. A friend of mine breeds them and has been after me to take one forever, so you'd really be doing me a favour. Not that you owe me a favour or anything, but …'

His eyes when he grinned were almost as adorable as the puppy's big, brown soulful ones. How could she resist either of them?

'What breed is he?' she asked, reaching out and touching the pup's head.

'A Maremma.' As he replied, Lawson thrust the dog towards her and she was helpless but to open her arms and accept this very precious gift. 'They're Italian sheepdogs, but have become better known recently in Australia since the movie *Oddball*. Have you seen it?'

She shook her head as the puppy lifted its head and licked her face.

Lawson laughed and she didn't think she'd ever heard such a beautiful sound. 'You should watch it. It's supposed to be a kid's movie but it's a cracker. I saw it with Ned at the cinema and then we had to get it on DVD. I've lost count of the number of times he's watched it. It's based on a true story about a dog who saved the penguins on an island from foxes.'

'It sounds cute,' she said, unable to help laughing as *this* little Maremma slobbered all over her.

'So you'll take him?' Before she could give Lawson an answer, he continued, 'Look, it may sound crazy, but I can't rest at night knowing you're out here, so isolated and all alone. Knowing you have this little guy around will help me get my beauty sleep.'

She let out a most unladylike sounding noise—a half snort, half laugh. As if Lawson Cooper-Jones needed beauty sleep! But it was the way he voiced his concern that both squeezed and melted her insides. It had been so long since anyone gave a damn about her that she had to swallow the emotion in her throat and blink back tears.

'How old is he?' she managed, holding the dog close and knowing she couldn't give him back even if she wanted to. She was a lost cause.

'Ten weeks. And fully toilet trained, according to my friend, Adeline. What are you going to call him?'

'I have no idea. Also, I haven't got anything for him. I'll need to get a bed, food, a leash, some toys … What else do puppies need?'

'I've got all that in the back of my ute. I'll be back in a sec.' And with that he turned and jogged back to the dirty utility parked on the road directly in front of her house.

Megan caught herself staring and averted her gaze from his arse. 'What do you want to be called?' she asked, turning her attention to the dog. It was safer to admire the cuteness of the canine than appreciate the sexiness of the man.

In answer to her question the dog licked her face and squirmed more in her arms. 'I should call you Slobber,' she said, tightening her grip. She dared another glance towards the road and saw Lawson returning with a massive bag of dog food in one arm and a bulging plastic bag in the other. 'Do you need any help?' she called.

He shook his head as he arrived beside her. 'Where shall I put all this stuff? I've got a bed for him on the back of the ute as well.'

Megan opened her mouth to tell him he could dump it all down where he was standing, but realised just in time how weird that would sound. The man had just given her a puppy, for goodness' sake: it would be rude not invite him inside.

'Um ...' She glanced behind her into the house.

It wasn't that she was scared of Lawson—after years of hanging out with undesirable types, it was easy to tell that this man could never be classified as such a thing—but her stomach turned over at the thought of bringing anyone into her private space. Closing the door would make them truly alone and she wasn't sure how to act around him. Around anyone.

You're being ridiculous. You can do this!

She could have a normal conversation without having a panic attack, couldn't she?

'I guess we can put everything on the kitchen table for now,' she said eventually.

He nodded. 'Righto. Lead the way.'

Megan forced her feet to step aside as she let him into the house. As Lawson marched inside like he'd been here a hundred times, she hesitated a moment about closing the door. What if he saw a clue as to who she was? She had no idea what, but then again, since when had fear or panic been logical?

Clinging to the dog like a child clutching its beloved teddy bear, she managed to close the door and then led Lawson into the kitchen.

He smiled at her as he dumped all the dog things onto the table. 'Last time I came in here, I was a little kid. We stopped to get an ice-cream, and it looked totally different. It closed not long after and I've been having a hard time imagining how you could live in the old general store but it looks as if you've been busy making it a home.'

She shrugged and slowly lowered the pup onto the ground, secretly pleased that he liked her house, secretly pleased he'd been thinking about her at all. 'It was already converted into a living space by the previous owners. I just cleaned it up a bit.'

He chuckled and gestured to the dog that was now tearing around the room like a headless chicken. 'And I've gone and brought you a hurricane to mess it all up again. You'll probably be cursing me by the end of the day.'

She tried to laugh but feared it didn't come out quite that way. 'He's gorgeous, thank you,' she rushed. 'Are you sure I can't give you any money for him?'

'Definitely not.' He shook his head and leaned back against the kitchen counter casually, making himself at home. For one split second she imagined that he *was* at home, that he was her guy and being there together was as natural as breathing. And then reality landed, reminding her of the unlikeliness of such a situation.

She rubbed her lips together, swallowed and racked her mind for something to say. Finally, she settled on, 'Hurricane. That's what I'll call him. Maybe Cane for short.'

'I love it.' He nodded his approval and then they both just stood there a moment looking at each other.

Feeling her cheeks heat again at the intensity of his gaze, Megan turned her attentions to Hurricane, who was still tearing round the kitchen, sniffing at everything. 'I wonder how long till he wears himself out?'

'Speaking of which,' Lawson pushed himself off the bench and straightened, 'I'll go get that bed for you. Back in a moment.' He strode past her and her lungs inhaled deeply as her nose got a whiff of *him*. Nothing like a posh, expensive cologne; no, Lawson smelled like the great outdoors with a hint of soap beneath, as if he'd scrubbed up before coming over.

Hurricane froze at the sound of the door opening and closing, and then bounded in the direction Lawson had left. The way his paws slipped and slid on the floorboards made Megan smile.

'Hurricane,' she called, hurrying after him. 'Come!'

He halted near the stairs and she thought, *Wow, he is well trained already*, but then he started to whine as he looked up to the second floor and she realised he hadn't stopped out of obedience. His ears were down and, as she picked him up and cuddled him close, she realised he was trembling.

'Do you feel that too?' she whispered, the hairs on the back of her neck prickling as she thought of the mysterious draught she often felt near the stairs.

At that moment, the front door opened again and in strode Lawson, carrying a big cushioned dog bed. 'It's a little large at the moment, but if his parents are anything to go by, he'll grow into it quick enough.'

He frowned when he heard Hurricane whining. 'Is he okay?'

Megan rubbed her lips together and glanced again at the stairs. Could it be that Lawson's son was right about the ghost? She almost asked if he too believed her house was haunted, but she swallowed the question just in time. Memories of the hallucinations she once experienced haunted her and, although it shouldn't matter what this man thought of her, she found she didn't want him to think she had a few screws loose.

'I think,' she said instead, mentally shaking her head of her silly thoughts, 'Hurricane didn't want you to go.'

'He's known me less than an hour. I'm sure he'll be fine.' Lawson put the bed down, shut the door behind him and crossed over to stroke Hurricane's head. He was so close she could see the dark stubble on his defined jawline and the view almost unbalanced her.

He frowned and for a moment she thought he'd caught her drooling or something, but then he glanced around them and rubbed a hand up his arm.

Megan's heart stilled. *Does he feel it too?*

But then he shook his head slightly and the grin reappeared on his face. 'Well, if you two are okay, I guess I'd better be getting back to the farm.'

'You don't want to stay for a coffee? Or a cool drink?' The question blurted from her mouth before she'd even contemplated asking it, almost as if an invisible force had compelled her to do so. Conflicted about whether she wanted him to accept or reject the invitation, her breath halted in her throat and her belly went rock hard as she waited for his reply.

He glanced down at his watch and she followed his gaze, admiring the taut tanned muscles of his forearm.

'I could probably squeeze in a quick drink,' he said.

Something inside her rejoiced and something else wanted to slap herself for such an invitation. Hadn't she retreated to Rose Hill because she wanted to fly under the radar? To refrain from making connections until any media attention was a distant memory and she'd put distance between herself and her past.

'But ...' Lawson raised his eyebrows and looked at her questioningly, 'if you've got other stuff to do, then ...'

'No,' she interrupted as she shook her head. 'Sorry, just got distracted there a moment. Come on back into the kitchen.'

Trying to ignore the far-too-fast beating of her heart, she pasted a smile on her face, turned and carried the puppy into the kitchen. She could hear and feel Lawson only a few feet behind. When they entered the room, she put Cane down again, but this time he cowered close to her.

'Do you want me to put the bed in here for now?' Lawson asked.

Megan nodded. 'Good idea. Do you want to try and settle Cane while I grab the drinks? Would you like a cuppa or some fresh orange juice? I'm afraid I don't have much else. Oh, and it'll have to be black coffee as I ran out of milk.'

'I'll have the juice then.' He grinned. 'Coffee isn't coffee without milk in it. If I'd known, I could have brought you some fresh from the cow.' Lawson dropped to his haunches and stretched a hand out to the dog, who immediately ran over to him, clumsy on his oversized puppy paws.

'Oh, are you a dairy farmer?' She didn't know why she was surprised—this was dairy country after all.

'Sure am.' He scooped up the puppy and carried it across to his new bed. 'We have a farm just outside of Walsh.'

'I guess that means you have to get up really early,' she said, cursing this blatantly stupid observation the moment she'd made it.

He chuckled. 'It sure does. But I grew up on the dairy, so I've never known anything different. Aren't you a morning person?'

'Not really, but I don't mind them so much around here.' She turned towards the fridge, happy for the opportunity to look away from him for fear something in her face might give away something about why she hadn't always liked getting up early.

'I reckon they're the best part of the day.' He rubbed his hand over the fluffy white puppy as he spoke. 'There there, little guy, that's right, snuggle up for a rest; you've had a big morning.'

As Megan retrieved the juice from the fridge, she said, 'You didn't think about getting the puppy for Ned?'

'Nah, we've already got two dogs, and if we get another, it'll be a Border Collie—they work well with the cows.'

'I see.' She poured two glasses of juice and then, realising Cane must be thirsty as well, she dug a dog bowl out of the plastic bag, filled that with water and placed it on the floor next to him. He immediately shoved his nose in and started lapping. Megan and Lawson laughed at the pup's antics as she took the glasses off the bench and passed one to him.

'Thanks,' he said, his fingers touching hers as he took it. Awareness skittered through her body and she hoped he didn't notice how affected she was by the simple brush of his skin against hers. It was embarrassing but hardly surprising considering he was the first real male interaction she'd had in years.

'Do you want to sit?' she asked, stepping back and pulling out a seat at the table.

'Sure.' He pushed himself off the floor, took the seat opposite her and lifted the glass to his mouth. When he put it down again, he smiled awkwardly at her.

Well, this is uncomfortable. Perhaps when he left she should make a list of possible conversation topics in case strangers landed on her unexpectedly again. He glanced around and his eyes fell on the orange cake she'd made that morning.

'Would you like a piece?' she asked, already standing up, happy at the prospect of something to do.

'Thanks. I never say no to cake.'

She smiled. 'In that case, you must take some home. I've been on a bit of a baking frenzy the last few days and there's only so much Archie and I can eat.'

'Archie?' he asked as she sliced off a large piece and placed it down in front of him. 'You met the old guy?'

'Yes.' She sat back down and, as Lawson ate and Cane fell asleep half-on-half-off his bed, she told him the chicken story. She began to relax; talking to him was a lot easier than she'd imagined.

'If all your cooking tastes like this,' Lawson said, patting his stomach, 'Archie is a lucky guy.'

She tried not to blush at his compliment. 'I'm glad you like it. How's Ned? Is he back at school now?'

Living the way she did, it would be easy for Megan to lose track of time, but she kept a calendar on the fridge and ticked off the days, so she knew it was Wednesday, the first of February.

'Yep—been back two days.'

'Does he like school?'

Lawson finished his mouthful and then nodded. 'Loves it. He takes after his mum, who was a bit of a nerd.' His smile told her this wasn't an insult and Megan's heart went out to him and Ned.

'I guess he got his gorgeous blond locks from his mother as well,' she said, glancing up at Lawson's dark hair.

He nodded and took another sip of his juice.

She swallowed. 'Ned told me his mum isn't around any more. I'm sorry.'

'Thanks.' He shrugged one shoulder and twisted the gold band on his finger, but didn't offer any further information.

Megan knew better than to pry. She didn't know this man from Adam and if he didn't want to talk about his wife, then so be it—there were plenty of topics she didn't want to talk about either. But that left her racking her mind for something to say again. She glanced down at Cane, now sleeping peacefully—no doubt garnering energy to keep her on her toes later. Oh well, it wasn't like she had much better to do. Then a thought struck and she snapped her head back to Lawson.

'I'll need to get him vaccinated, won't I?' Her pulse sped up at the prospect of having to take the dog into Walsh to the vet and having to hand over her name and contact details.

'Adeline, the breeder, said he's already had his first lot of injections, but he'll need the top up in a couple of weeks. There's a great vet in Walsh.' He paused a moment and then frowned; no doubt her panic was scrawled across her face. 'Is paying for that going to be a problem?'

'Oh, no,' she rushed to assure him, but she'd probably go to Bunbury where she'd have a better chance of remaining anonymous. 'I was just … wondering.'

Lawson nodded, then he pushed back his seat, the chair legs scraping against the floor. 'I really better be getting back to the farm. Thanks for the drink and for the cake.'

She summoned a smile and stood as well. 'Thanks for the dog.'

He shoved his hands into his pocket and offered her a sheepish grin. 'I know he's not a traditional house-warming gift, but I didn't want you to get lonely out here.'

'That's very sweet of you.' *Far sweeter than someone like me deserves.* She shook the thought from her head. 'Now, let me package you up some cakes and biscuits to take home to Ned.'

Lawson went to say goodbye to Cane as she put an orange cake and a batch of chocolate cookies into her only two disposable containers. She almost put them in some of the Tupperware she'd inherited from Granny Rose—knowing he'd feel obliged to bring them back—but that was tempting fate and she came to her senses just in time. Megan didn't trust herself around this far too gorgeous, far too lovely man.

'Thanks,' he said, when she handed him the containers. 'Tab's usually too busy making ice-cream to cook stuff like this and, although I have many skills, baking sadly isn't one of them.'

Megan's stomach clenched at his easy reference to another woman. 'Who's Tab?'

He smiled fondly. 'My little sister. She lives with Ned and me and is a bit of an ice-cream connoisseur. Luckily we have plenty of milk for her to experiment with.'

'Ah, I see.' Megan silently cursed her ridiculous relief at the knowledge that Tab was a relation, not his girlfriend. The sooner Lawson left the better, because having him so close affected her sensibilities.

'Right. Well, thanks again.' He tapped the containers and started towards the front door. She followed and Cane leaped up off the floor and darted in and out of their feet as they walked, making them both laugh.

'This really is a gorgeous old building,' Lawson said, looking up at the original mouldings on the ceiling as he stopped at the front door. 'They don't make shops like these any more.'

Megan sighed. 'So true. I'm enjoying the challenge of bringing it back to its former glory.'

He opened his mouth as if he were about to ask something but shut it again and shook his head slightly. 'I guess I'll be going now.'

She nodded. Lawson stepped forwards and put his hand on the door handle, but he still didn't make a move to go.

Instead, they stood there looking at each other for a few long moments and she swore her heart stopped beating all together. She barely noticed Cane jumping up at them as Lawson's eyes connected with hers. The chill from earlier had well and truly gone—there was something else fizzing in the air now. Something that terrified the hell out of her and at the same time aroused her like she hadn't been aroused in years.

Is he going to kiss me? Her tummy summersaulted in delicious anticipation. It seemed both possible and impossible and her tongue darted out of its own accord to lick her lips, her mind already two steps ahead, imagining the taste of his mouth on hers.

And then Cane barked and broke the moment. Embarrassed that Lawson might be able to read her mind, she stooped down to pick up the dog. 'Thanks again,' she said faux-brightly.

'You're welcome.' He smiled as he opened the door, then turned and hurried back to his ute.

Megan watched him go, her heart racing again, but Lawson didn't look back and she told herself that was a good thing. What on earth would she have done if he had kissed her? She didn't think she'd have had the wherewithal to resist, and yet kissing could lead her into all kinds of trouble. The fact she'd even contemplated it shocked her.

If it weren't for the warm, wriggly puppy in her arms and the blur of dust that kicked up off the road as he drove away, she probably wouldn't have believed what had just happened. She'd had some strange days in her life, but this one was up there at the top.

Despite the fact she now had a puppy, the house felt quieter than usual when she went back inside. The radio still chattered away in the corner, but it didn't offer the same comfort it previously had. She took Cane back into the kitchen and went through the bag on the table, retrieving a plastic pig-shaped chew toy and tossing it to him on the floor. She spent the rest of the day playing with Hurricane, puppy proofing the house and trying her darn best not to think any more about Lawson Cooper-Jones.

Chapter Six

Late in the evening with Cane tucked up on his bed downstairs in the kitchen and the door shut so he couldn't wreak havoc in the rest of the house, Megan climbed the stairs to her room and fell into bed. Her eyes were barely shut ten seconds before the dog's whines drifted up to her. She groaned and put the pillow over her head to try and drown out the noise. If she ignored him, he'd eventually settle.

Five minutes later she found herself heading back downstairs. The whining stopped the moment she opened the door. Cane skidded across the kitchen floor and jumped up at her knees, making eyes at her with that irresistible puppy face.

'It's not time to play. It's time to sleep,' she said in her firmest voice as she crossed over to the dog bed, stooped down and patted it. Cane took one look at his bed and darted out the door she'd forgotten to close behind her.

She scrambled to her feet cursing Lawson's name as she hurried after the puppy and found him in what had been the main shop area and would be her living room when she'd finished clearing all the clutter. In its current state it was a veritable playground for

a puppy, but it was nearing midnight and Megan was in no mood
to play. She caught the dog, who had a ball of her wool between
his teeth, and carried him back out and into the kitchen, where
she picked up his bed in her other arm and then took them both
upstairs.

As she navigated the stairs, Cane whined worse than ever and
struggled so much she almost dropped him, but he calmed down
once they were in her bedroom. She put his bed on the floor
next to hers and was surprised when he lay down on it without a
fuss. She climbed back into bed and rolled onto her side, her arm
hanging over the edge of the bed so she could stroke him while
he went to sleep.

A few hours later, creaking noises woke her again. No longer
scared of the sounds the house made, she reached down to check
for Cane. Panicking when she didn't feel him, she sat bolt upright
and fumbled to turn on her bedside lamp. As light spilled over the
room, her eyes came to rest on a furry little body at the end of her
bed and she let out a deep sigh. Cane looked sleepily up at her.
She stretched out her foot and stroked him with her toe. It was
probably a huge no-no to allow him to sleep in her bed, but quite
frankly she didn't care. She loved feeling him close and fell asleep
again with a smile on her face.

The next time she woke Cane was licking her face and light
crept in through the curtains. There'd be no getting him back to
sleep now.

'You're worse than a baby,' she told the dog as she pushed him
off her gently.

She dressed quickly, slipped her feet into thongs and then left
the room. As expected the pup charged after her but stopped a few
feet away from the top of the stairs and whimpered.

'Come on,' she called to him, 'time for breakfast.'

But he wouldn't budge.

His eyes were wide and his ears pressed flat against his head as he stared at the air between them. Could he see something? She remembered a cheesy horror movie she'd watched in her teens where the dog could see the ghost living in its owner's house.

She shivered. *Don't be ridiculous.* Even if there was a ghost, it hadn't given any indication it wanted to harm her. The three of them would just have to live in harmony.

'It's okay,' she told Cane, stepping back to scoop him up. He all but buried his head in her chest as they went downstairs, but happily bounded off into the yard for a pee when she opened the back door.

Although the garden was well fenced, she still didn't want to leave him outside alone yet. She'd had him less than twenty-four hours and already couldn't bear the thought of anything happening to him.

Megan waited until Cane had relieved himself, then ushered him back inside and into the kitchen, this time remembering to close the door behind them.

She filled his bowl with some of the dog food Lawson had given her, then filled the kettle, flicked it on and lifted the lid on her coffee tin.

'Oh disaster,' she exclaimed as she peered down at the near empty jar. She could do without milk, she could do without butter, but coffee? *Hell no.* Grocery shopping could be put off no longer.

'But what am I going to do with you?' she asked Cane, who'd found another roll of wool and wasted no time in unravelling it all over the kitchen. After his whining in the night and the destruction he left in his wake, leaving him home alone would be asking for trouble.

At that moment, she heard a noise out front and guessed it was Archie with her morning delivery of eggs. Although it went against all their unspoken rules, she hurried down the hallway and opened the door to see the old man and his black and white dog strolling back down the street.

'Archie!' she called, as her own dog darted out the open door and started towards them. She cursed and ran after him, glad she'd bothered to change out of her pyjamas.

He turned as she approached and his weathered mouth split into a grin. 'Well, hello there, missy,' he said, looking down at Cane, who was invading the old dog's personal space. 'And who is this?'

'Hi, sorry,' she panted as she grabbed Cane by his collar and scooped him off the ground. 'This is my dog, Cane. I got him yesterday.'

'Hello, little fella.' Archie reached out to rub the puppy's ears.

'Thanks for the eggs. I really appreciate them.'

'Well.' Archie patted his near-flat stomach. 'I appreciate the cakes.'

Megan smiled. 'I was wondering if you'd mind doing me a favour? You see, I need to get some groceries and things but I don't want to leave Cane home alone.'

'You want me to dog-sit?' Archie's lips quirked up in obvious amusement.

She nodded sheepishly, knowing it was a lot to ask a stranger. 'I'll be as quick as I can, but it's too hot to leave him in the car while I shop.'

'Of course.' He nodded and glanced down at his own dog. 'We'd love to look after the little tacker, wouldn't we, Buster? Do you want to bring him round to my place when you're ready? I'll make sure the chickens are locked in their pen.'

Relief flooded Megan that he hadn't suggested dog-sitting at her place. 'Thank you. I will. And good idea re the chickens.'

The arrangements made, Archie and Buster headed back up the road to the servo and Megan retreated into her house with Cane to make a shopping list.

At ten o'clock she clicked the leash onto Cane's collar and went outside to attempt their first walk. He tugged and pulled, darting in and out of her legs and wrapping the leash around them both, turning what should have been a two-minute walk into a ten-minute one.

At the roadhouse, she found Archie outside doing something with one of the pumps. It was the first time she'd seen any signs of life out the front, but then again, when she went for her run she always went the other way, and the rest of the time she spent inside or out the back of her house.

She felt a slight tremor in her stomach as Archie glanced up, stopped what he was doing and waved.

'Ah, my little charge is here. I must admit I'm quite excited.' The warmth in his voice helped to eradicate some of her unease. Besides, just because they were being neighbourly didn't mean they had to have deep and meaningful conversations.

'Thank you so much for doing this,' she said as he held out his hand to take the leash, Cane bouncing around on the end of it like an out-of-control yo-yo.

'No worries.'

'Is there anything I can get for you while I'm in town?'

Archie rubbed the side of his beard a moment. 'I could do with a few more packets of two-minute noodles. Chicken flavour. And a couple of litres of milk. I'll go grab you some money.'

'No, don't worry it.' Megan waved her hand in dismissal. 'I'll get them for you—consider it payment for dog-sitting.'

Archie winked. 'Deal.'

'Well, I guess I'll be off. I hope he behaves himself.'

He scooped Cane up into his arms and rubbed his head with his stubbly chin. 'I don't think puppies are supposed to behave.'

Megan laughed. 'If last night and this morning are anything to go by, I think you're right. I'll see you when I get back.'

* * *

As Megan neared the town of Walsh, her hands shook on the steering wheel. If it weren't for Cane, she'd have gone to Bunbury instead. But, not wanting to leave him with Archie too long, she swallowed her ridiculous paranoia that someone might recognise her. So far, she'd made acquaintances with both Lawson and Archie and neither of them had shown any signs of recognition. It wasn't like she was a TV star or anyone famous—maybe the media attention had been limited to Victoria, where her grandfather was best known.

Not wanting to think about media or the family that had disowned her, she focused on her surrounds, trying to pretend she was just an ordinary girl heading to the shops. About three times the size of the Rose Hill town site, Walsh was a beautiful, quaint little place—still relatively green, due to its southerly location, despite the time of year. Here the buildings had been looked after and she could only see one empty shop. Large painted wooden cows on either side of the road welcomed visitors and invited them to sample the local dairy produce. Megan couldn't help thinking of Lawson as she glanced at the passing cars and pedestrians strolling along either side of the street.

Of course he wasn't the only dairy farmer in the region, but he was the only one she knew, and the thought of possibly running into him both excited and terrified her.

With that thought, she parked her car near the IGA, took a deep breath and climbed out. She walked towards the entrance, holding her head high and her shoulders back, trying to carry herself like somebody who didn't have a ridiculous paranoia of strangers recognising them, somebody who had no past indiscretions to be ashamed of and just wanted to buy some damn groceries. As much as she wanted to walk up and down the aisles wearing her sunglasses like some kind of celebrity incognito, she pushed them up on top of her head and grabbed a trolley.

'Hi there.' An indigenous woman, with one kid in a pram and another one hanging onto her bright summer dress, smiled.

Her chirpy greeting almost made Megan jump out of her skin. Not wanting to appear rude and draw attention to herself, she forced a smile and managed a 'hello' in return as she pushed off down the first aisle. Thursday must be pension day, for there seemed to be people everywhere—far too many for a supposedly small town. And everyone else was just as friendly as the first woman—smiling and nodding hellos—so that she began to wonder about the logic of moving to the country. She'd thought she could hide out in deserted Rose Hill while things settled down, while people forgot, but maybe she'd have been better off in another city. Nobody noticed newcomers in the big smoke.

Moving as quickly as she could, she threw items into her trolley until she could fit nothing else and then headed for the front of the shop, where there were only three checkouts.

'Hey. How are ya?' asked the girl behind the counter as Megan began unloading her trolley.

'Good thanks,' she said, admiring the girl's bright pink hair and matching nose ring.

'You new to town?'

'Just passing through,' Megan said, not wanting anyone else to know she lived in Rose Hill.

The girl nodded towards her full trolley. 'You've got a lot of stuff for someone just passing through.'

She smiled politely. 'I'm buying some things for a friend as well.'

'I see.' Thankfully the checkout assistant was quiet for a while as she scanned the next few items, but when she came to the long-life milk cartons, she looked up in horror. 'You shouldn't buy UHT. Not when our local dairy farmers are struggling so much at the moment. We need to support the industry—buy fresh, buy local.'

Isn't that real milk as well? Doesn't it also come from cows? But, not wanting to get into a debate about farming practices with this woman, Megan picked up the six litres of fresh stuff she'd also bought—two for Archie, the rest for herself—and placed it on the checkout. 'I thoroughly agree, but I don't have room in my fridge to store all the milk I need.'

The woman raised an eyebrow. 'You drink a lot?'

'I cook a lot.' *And shop as little as possible, thanks to nosy parkers like you.*

'Fair enough.' She seemed content with this response and went back to scanning and packing, while Megan finished unloading. But she spoke again when she noticed a large bag of puppy biscuits. 'Ooh, have you got a puppy?'

'Yes.' Megan silently urged the woman to hurry the hell up.

'I'm sorry to interrupt,' said a voice from behind her.

Megan turned to see a tall pretty blonde in fashionable denim shorts and a pale pink polo shirt smiling at her.

'Did I hear you've got a puppy?' She continued before Megan had a chance to confirm this. 'I run puppy-training classes at the local vet every Saturday morning. You should bring your baby along.'

'She doesn't live here,' said the shop assistant. 'She's just passing through.'

'What a pity.' The woman sighed and then returned her attentions to her phone, which suited Megan just fine. All this inquisitive small talk was making her nervous.

'That'll be four hundred and twenty-three dollars and fifty-two cents,' stated the checkout girl once she'd tossed the last packet of two-minute noodles into a bag. 'Will you be putting that on your card?'

'No. I've got cash.' No way Megan was handing over a bank card with her real name on it. She couldn't be too careful, which was why she'd taken a few thousand dollars out of her account before moving to Rose Hill.

The woman raised her eyebrows as Megan handed over nine fifty-dollar notes and then counted it carefully before entering the amount into the till. She handed Megan her change, smiled and said, 'I'll just call Troy over to help you out to your car.'

It was on the tip of Megan's tongue to refuse assistance—she'd had enough exhausting small talk for one day—but she had a lot of bags and refusing help might make her seem weird. And weird solicited speculation, which she definitely did not want, so she smiled politely and said, 'Thank you.'

To her relief, Troy—a tall, lanky guy with bad acne who looked as if he should still be in school—wasn't a big talker: he loaded the bags into the back of her car without uttering a word.

Megan thanked him as he took her trolley, then she closed the boot and escaped back into her car. She slammed the door behind her and leaned back in the seat, closing her eyes for a moment to catch her breath. Whoever thought shopping could be so nerve-racking? She wasn't doing anything illegal but these days just going out in public made her feel like a criminal.

'But you did it,' she said as she started the car and allowed herself a small smile. *You spoke to people and nobody pointed their fingers or looked at you like you killed kittens for a hobby.* Progress. Victory. Maybe she wouldn't have to go to Bunbury every time she needed bread or milk.

As she reversed out the car park, her gaze caught on the sign for the café across the road. Her tastebuds watered at the thought of going in and sitting down, ordering a proper coffee and flicking through a magazine or something as she drank it. Such a normal thing to do, which felt like such a luxury to her. But would that be pushing her luck?

Remembering Cane back in Rose Hill made the decision for her. She needed to get back and relieve Archie. With a wistful glance at the café, she drove back out of town.

Chapter Seven

On the first Sunday of every month the Walsh Country Markets were held in the car park of the IGA, which of course didn't open on the Sabbath. Not that religion had anything to do with the opening hours of the town's shops—unless you classed sport as a religion, which most of the locals did. The markets, an initiative thought up by Adeline to showcase the town's talents and produce, were always well attended by residents and tourists alike and, if the vehicles lining the main street were anything to go by, this weekend had drawn the usual crowd.

Lawson parked his ute about half a kilometre up the road and went in search of Tabitha and Ned, who'd been in town early setting up her ice-cream stall. Once a month on market days, Funky came over to help Ethan with the milking so Lawson could do the calves and Tab could get into town. The youngest of five, Funky had chosen to become a builder more because there wasn't a job for him on the family farm than because he didn't love the lifestyle, so he was more than happy to help Lawson out whenever the need arose.

'Long time no see,' called a voice from behind him as he followed the noise of many voices and a local band up the road towards the markets.

Lawson turned to see Funky catching up. *Speak of the devil.* 'You didn't mention you were heading into the markets,' he said, as his best mate slapped him on the back.

'Gotta help man the sausage sizzle,' Funky explained and then inhaled deeply. 'And perhaps eat half a dozen while I'm there as well. Milking is hungry work.'

Lawson chuckled, his stomach rumbling at the thought of food. His morning Weetbix was hours back now and there was just something alluring about the aroma of freshly barbecued sausages and fried onions slapped on a slice of white bread. 'I'll come with you and get one for Tab and Ned too.'

The guys followed their noses to the sausage sizzle stall, run by the local firefighters, for whom Funky was a volunteer. In fact, half the men (and women) they'd gone to school with volunteered for the fire brigade, the SES or the St Johns ambulance sub-centre. Volunteering was just the way in small rural communities. Lawson had been a firie years ago, but he'd had to quit when Leah died because between Ned and the dairy he didn't have time for anything else. Also, he didn't want to leave Ned unnecessarily or put himself in danger's way; the kid didn't need to lose another parent. When Ned was older he'd volunteer again but for now he supported local causes by contributing to their fundraisers.

'Morning, boys.' Macca, a shire councillor, owner of the local agricultural supplies store and captain of the fire brigade, brandished a barbecue utensil in their general direction.

Beside him, his wife Suzie whipped off her apron and tossed it at Funky. 'Put this on, and then get behind here and make yourself useful. I want to go and check out the stalls.'

Funky caught the apron, held it up and read the writing on the front—*I'm still hot, it just comes in flashes now.* He raised his eyebrows, then shrugged and put it on anyway. It wouldn't be wise to argue with Suzie. As she headed off to look around, he helped himself to a bread roll, shoved in a sausage and took a bite.

Meanwhile Macca grinned at Lawson. 'What can I get for you this fine morning?'

Lawson dug his wallet out of his back pocket and gestured to the sausages. 'I'll take three, please?'

'How's things with you and young Ned?' the older man asked as he got to work fixing the order.

'Yeah, good,' Lawson said. 'Can't complain.'

''Tis true: no one listens anyway.'

They made small talk about the heat wave and how one had to be extra vigilant with livestock this time of year, and then Lawson thanked Macca for the food.

His hands full, he nodded farewell to his friend. 'See ya round.'

Already on his second sausage, Funky waved and spoke through a mouthful of food. 'Bye.'

'And don't eat all the profits.' Lawson called as he started towards Tab's ice-cream stall.

The various stalls were loosely categorised with food produce on one side of the car park and the arts, crafts and non-food items on the other side. In the middle there were some plastic chairs and tables for folks to sit and chat and a temporary stage set up on which the high school band played their unique blend of rock, pop and country music. It should have only taken Lawson about ten seconds to walk over to his family but stopping to talk to all the locals slowed him down.

'They better be for us,' Tab said, nodding towards the sausage sizzles in Lawson's hands when he finally arrived.

'Hey, Dad.' Ned glanced up briefly from where he was manning the money tin.

'I hope they're not too cold,' Lawson said as he passed Tab and Ned theirs and then finally took a bite of his own.

Tab shrugged. 'Still tastes good.'

'You been busy?' Lawson asked before taking another bite.

'We've been *so* busy, Dad—we've already sold out of salted caramel and popcorn.'

Tab nodded, a proud smile twisting her lips. 'And my new chocolate-orange flavour is proving to be a big hit too.'

Lawson wrapped an arm round Tabitha's shoulder and gave her a quick squeeze. 'That's awesome. I'm proud of you two.'

She'd saved hard to buy a refrigerated van and portable display cabinet so she could sell ice-cream at the markets and other local events. She definitely had a talent and, although he might be a little biased, the judges at the previous year's Royal Show had agreed. She'd taken out a top prize against some established ice-creameries and Lawson couldn't have been happier for her. After everything she'd been through, she deserved all her success.

'How were my babies this morning?' she asked, but a woman with two little kids yanking at her clothes came up to the stand before he could reply. Tab transformed before his eyes from little sister to savvy businesswoman. 'Would you like to try a sample?' she asked the trio.

The kids' eyes lit up. 'Can we, Mummy?'

'Of course.' The woman looked to Tabitha. 'We're staying in Harvey with my parents for the weekend and they've been raving about your ice-cream so we came all the way here to try it for ourselves.'

'We're sold out of salted caramel and popcorn,' Ned said, his expression solemn and apologetic, 'but I can recommend the Lolly Mayhem. It has popping candy that explodes in your mouth!'

While Tabitha and Ned took care of their customers, Lawson stepped back and ate his sausage, surveying the scene around them. For a small country town, they had almost everything covered here—you could buy fresh honey, homemade jams, local cheeses and meats, handmade clothes and jewellery, bric-a-brac, candles, funny wooden signs and paintings, just to name a few. He saw an elderly woman sitting at a table in front of the CWA stall a few metres away with an old black Labrador lounging at her feet and his thoughts immediately journeyed to Meg, wondering how she was going with her puppy. The whole idea behind giving her the dog was that it would set his mind at ease and stop him worrying about her being all alone out there in Rose Hill, but it hadn't exactly worked as planned.

'Earth to Lawson? Anyone home?'

'Huh?' He blinked and shook his head at the sound of Tab's voice and her hand waving in front of his face.

'Are you all right?' she asked, frowning at him.

He scrunched up the serviette he held in his hand and shoved it into his pocket. 'Sure. Why wouldn't I be?'

'You've been a little distant this last week—I've lost count of the number of times I've caught you staring off into space and I just did again. Are you worried about something? Did you hear the Baxters have just lost their milk contract?'

'Yes, I did.' If only it *were* the farm and current dairy industry crisis that had been occupying his mind. He sighed and tried to offer her a smile. 'I'm just tired for some reason, but I'm okay.'

'You know I'm always here if you want to talk—about *anything*,' Tab said, reaching out and squeezing his arm.

'Thanks.' He summoned a carefree smile, hoping she'd take his answer at face value. *Talking?* He wouldn't know where to start.

'Ethan!' Ned leaped up and around the table to greet their worker as he approached.

Lawson, happy for the distraction, lifted a hand in greeting. 'If I'd known you were coming into town I'd have given you a lift.'

Ethan shrugged. 'Was a last-minute decision. Had a craving for one of Tabby's ice-creams.'

'What flavour can I get you?' she asked, already picking up her scoop and rinsing it in her container of water.

Ethan turned to Ned. 'What do you recommend?'

Again, he espoused the virtues of the Lolly Mayhem and when Ethan decided to go with it, Ned asked if he could have one as well. He hadn't finished his sausage sizzle but it was the weekend.

'It's on the house,' Tab said when Ethan went to pay.

'Aw, thanks.' He took the ice-cream and was putting his wallet back in his pocket when Adeline came up to the stall.

'Hello, everyone,' she said, her smile lingering longer on Lawson than the others. 'Anyone want to buy a raffle ticket for the Progress Association?' The PA was another local pie Adeline had her fingers in.

'What's the prize?' Ethan asked.

'Ooh, it's a ripper this month. Two nights' accommodation for two people to a day spa retreat in Margaret River.' Again, she looked to Lawson as she said this.

'Nice idea but as if any of us could get away for two nights,' he mused.

'I'll take five tickets,' Tab said, stealing money from her ice-cream float.

'Who will you take if you win?'

She winked at Ethan as she took the tickets from Adeline. 'That's none of your business.'

'Good luck,' Adeline said, popping the coins into the top of her tin. 'What about you, Lawson? You want to buy some tickets?'

Had she not heard what he said a few moments earlier? He dug out his wallet, not because the idea of a spa retreat appealed in the slightest but because it was for a good cause. 'Give me five as well.'

She scribbled his name down on the tickets, tore off the stubs and then looked down at Ned as if she'd only just noticed him. 'Hello, Neddy. How's the puppy going? Have you given him a name yet? You know I'm happy to come out to the farm and help you with some training if you'd like.'

Ned looked up at her as if she were speaking a foreign language and Lawson's gut clenched. He hadn't mentioned Meg and the puppy thing to Ned or Tabitha—the latter because she'd read stuff into the gesture and Ned because he'd insist on going out to visit. But he'd been stupid to think he could hide something like this in a small town.

'What have you done with him this morning?' Adeline asked. 'He'll get up to mischief if left alone too long.'

At the same time Tab and Ned chimed in unison, 'What puppy?'

Lawson shoved his hands in his pockets and resisted the urge to whistle as he racked his mind for what to say.

'Lawson took one of my dogs on Wednesday,' Adeline explained, her tone sharp as she narrowed her eyes at him.

'You bought a puppy?' Ned asked, his mouth full of ice-cream.

Lawson didn't have the chance to reprimand him before Tab perched her hand on her hip and demanded, 'Well, if this is true, what on earth have you done with it?'

This felt like the bloody Spanish Inquisition. Adeline, Ned and Tabitha were all glaring at him as they waited for an answer. Ethan licked his ice-cream and looked on in obvious amusement.

'It's true.' Lawson looked to Tab and then to Ned. 'I did buy a puppy, but not for us.' He swallowed, drew his suddenly sweaty hands out of his pockets and wiped them against his shorts. 'I bought him for Meg, the woman Ned and I met in Rose Hill.'

Tab's lips transformed from a thin line into a wide grin. 'Oh, really?'

'You dark horse!' Ethan slapped him on the back in obvious approval. 'I thought you said she wasn't very keen on socialising. Hang on a minute, is she the girl who baked those cakes?'

'What cakes?' asked Ned.

Lawson had shared the cakes Meg had given him with Ethan for smoko over the last couple of days, knowing that if he'd brought them into the house, Tab would have wanted to know where they'd come from. He'd led Ethan to believe one of the old dears in town had gifted them.

He nodded in confirmation at Ethan.

Ethan grinned. 'That orange cake could give the CWA a run for their money.'

'Sounds like you have a bit of talking to do, big brother,' Tab said, not sounding cranky in the slightest.

The same could *not* be said for Adeline. 'You never said you were taking a puppy for a … a *woman*.' Hurt and surprise flashed in her eyes. Lawson felt a tiny pinprick of remorse—he didn't want to hurt Adeline—but perhaps if she thought there was something going on with him and Meg, she'd finally get the message that the two of them were never going to be more than friends.

'I didn't say I *wasn't*,' he countered. 'Is there a problem?'

'That girl sure can cook,' Ethan said, still stuck, as usual, on the food thing.

Adeline glared at him and then looked back to Lawson, her eyebrows raised expectantly. 'Of course there's a problem. I take great care finding good homes for my dogs and I don't feel comfortable with one going to a stranger.'

'Dad?' Ned tugged at his shirt. 'Can we go visit Meg and the puppy?'

Lawson ignored him. 'She's not a stranger. I've met her twice now and she fell in love with the puppy the moment she laid eyes on him. Relax, Adeline: she's a young woman living on her own in Rose Hill. You know how isolated that makes her. Your dog will have all her attention. He'll be fine, more than fine.'

'Having met someone twice, you can hardly give her a character reference.' Adeline sniffed and clutched the raffle tickets and tin close against her chest. 'What else do you know about her? Why *is* she living all on her lonesome in such a place?'

Lawson bristled, feeling defensive on Meg's part. 'I don't know. Not all of us waste so much time prying into other people's business.'

'Are you going to see her again? Are you going to check she's taking proper care of my dog?'

'I paid you for that dog, Adeline. It isn't yours any more. Now, if you don't mind, I've got to go buy some—' he glanced up and across the car park '—candles. See you later.'

Lawson strode off before she could say another word and didn't return to the ice-cream stall until she'd moved on.

'Dad,' Ned said the moment he arrived back, 'can we *please* go visit Meg?'

'No,' Lawson snapped. Ned was just as persistent as Adeline when he wanted something, but at least he had the excuse of childhood. 'Will you just stop asking?' There were enough voices in *his* head telling him to take another drive to Rose Hill, and he didn't like the way he felt not quite himself around Meg.

Tabitha raised her eyebrows, then leaned close and whispered, 'I'm not sure how I feel about you buying puppies for women I haven't even met.'

He rolled his eyes. 'Don't you start. Isn't a guy allowed to do a good deed without getting harangued about it from all directions?'

She smiled. 'Helping an old lady cross a road, buying someone a coffee when they've forgotten their wallet—those are good deeds. I'm not sure giving someone a purebred puppy is the same thing.'

Lawson scowled.

'Relax. I think it's sweet.' She scrutinised him. 'What I'm curious about is why you didn't see fit to mention it? Is Meg the reason for you looking off into space so much this last week?'

'Don't be ridiculous,' he scoffed. 'That is exactly why I didn't mention it. You're just as bad as everyone else in this town. You want life to be like one of your romance novels, but it's not.'

'Oh, trust me. I know it's not.' Tab turned away from him and plastered a smile on her face as Boots arrived with two of his kids in tow.

'Hey guys.' He wiped his hand over his brow as he grinned at Lawson, Ned, Tab and Ethan, who was now devouring his second ice-cream. 'It's bloody hot already. Tennille sent me over to get ice-cream for the kids, but I think I'll have one as well.'

'Good plan.' Tab gestured to the list of flavours on her little blackboard. 'What can we get for you?'

Again, Ned helped the younger kids make their selection, took the money from Boots and carefully counted out his change.

'Good kid you got there,' Boots said, nodding to Ned as he looked over at Lawson. 'Leah would be damn proud of the job you're doing.'

'Thanks.' He blinked his eyes, which suddenly felt gritty as he looked down at the top of Ned's blond head. How he wished Leah could see him now. He might have the odd parenting fail but most of the time he didn't think he was stuffing Ned up too badly and he hoped she would be proud of them both. But what would she think of him snapping at Ned, taking it out on their son when he was really annoyed at himself and others? Ned should be his priority above *all* else.

That thought sitting heavy in his chest, he vowed to make it up to him that afternoon. As Boots walked away with kids trailing behind him like ducklings, Lawson reached out and ruffled Ned's hair.

'Fancy a swim this afternoon? And then maybe I can whip your bum at a game of Mario Kart before the evening milking?'

Ned took a moment to answer and Lawson hoped he didn't ask about Meg again.

'Tell him he's dreaming,' Ethan said, piping up from where he'd been standing quietly watching. He couldn't pass up the opportunity to quote from his favourite Aussie film.

'He's right, Dad, I always beat you,' Ned said.

Lawson grinned. 'That, my son, sounds like a challenge too good to refuse.' With any luck a few hours playing mindless video games would take his mind off the whole Meg-Adeline-puppy debacle.

Chapter Eight

At half-past eleven on Monday morning, Megan was just sitting down with her crochet when a knock sounded on the front door. Cane immediately leaped up from where he'd only moments before settled on his bed, barked and shot in the direction of the sound. Megan put her needle, wool and half-finished purple and yellow tea-cosy down on the table and forced herself to her feet. Her heart stilled at the knowledge she had a visitor, but the panic didn't last half as long as it once had.

As she headed out of the kitchen and towards the entrance where Cane was jumping up and down and throwing his little body at the door like a maniac, a tiny flicker of hope sparked within at the thought that maybe Lawson had returned. But then, she shook her head and pushed that fantasy aside; it would more likely be Archie.

On Saturday when she'd delivered his milk and noodles and collected her dog, he'd invited her into his house for a coffee and she'd surprised herself by accepting. Despite the run-down façade of the road house, inside Archie's place was neat, clean and surprisingly homely. His walls were covered with beautiful, clearly Australian landscapes. Contrary to the reputation of artists, he seemed very organised and only one corner of his open-plan living space gave any indication that the paintings were his own work. A couple of easels displayed two half-finished canvasses and there were paints and brushes scattered across a high table between them.

Conversation had been easy, starting with discussing his art and moving onto the history of Rose Hill and the building Megan had bought. They hadn't discussed anything deep and meaningful but she discovered that Archie was employed by the Walsh shire as caretaker for the community-owned buildings in this obsolete community. Her house was one of the few privately owned buildings and when he'd mentioned he hadn't been inside it for years, she'd offered him an open invitation to come and take a look some time. She'd enjoyed their time chatting and sensed that, like her, he was happy to have another soul living not too far away, but would never become the type of neighbour to try and live in her pocket.

'Coming,' she called, feeling more normal than she had in a while as she neared the front door.

Having convinced herself the visitor would be Archie, on pulling back the front door she gasped at the sight of a blonde woman in a short red sundress. Cane, who had a lot to learn about becoming a guard dog, leaped excitedly up at the woman, whom Megan guessed to be selling religion or something else she didn't want. Her hackles rose—she'd thought she'd be safe from those types out here.

'I'm sorry, whatever it is you're peddling, I'm not interested,' she said, bending down and wrangling Cane into her arms before he made a run for it.

As she stepped back and went to shut the door, the woman thrust out her arm to stop it from closing. 'Oh, I'm not selling anything,' said the blonde, smiling so widely Megan thought her facial muscles must hurt. 'I'm Adeline Walsh and I've come to welcome you to Rose Hill.'

The woman looked vaguely familiar and Megan tried to work out why. 'You live in Rose Hill as well?'

The other woman laughed as if this was a ridiculous thought, somehow stepping inside as she did so, despite not being offered an invitation. 'God no, I live in Walsh. As you can probably guess by my name, my ancestors were one of the town's founding families. My great-grandmother, Penelope, was an Elverd before she married Henry Walsh—the Elverds and the Walshes have a long history in this area.'

'Right.' Megan didn't know what this had to do with the price of eggs, never mind with her, but she got the feeling she was supposed to be impressed. Her stomach tightened as Adeline stood just inside the door and gazed around. 'Nice to meet you,' she lied.

Would it be rude if she manhandled this intruder back outside and shut the door in her face?

Adeline reached out and fluffed up Cane's fur. 'I had to come and check on my baby.'

Baby? It took a moment for Megan's brain to click into gear and then she realised why Adeline looked familiar. 'You're the woman I met at the supermarket,' she blurted. 'The one who trains the puppies. Are you also the breeder? Lawson's friend?' The pressure in her chest released a little—perhaps Adeline did have a logical reason for stopping by.

'Oh.' She laughed and gave Megan a knowing look. 'We're a little more than *friends*, but yes, I bred this gorgeous little bundle. His parents are Australian prize-winning pedigrees.' And with these words, she turned and headed not back *outside* as Megan would have liked, but further into her home.

Megan placed Cane down on the floor—he took a wide berth around the stairs and bounded after Adeline—and followed reluctantly.

'How long have you been living here?' Adeline asked as she paused at a side table. She looked through the books Megan had stacked there, not bothering to put them back neatly.

'A couple of weeks,' Megan replied.

'Shall we have a drink?' Adeline asked. 'I make it a point of getting to know the new owners of my dogs and I can just tell we're going to be fabulous friends.'

Funny, Megan wasn't getting that feeling at all. 'I don't have much to offer you I'm afraid,' she said, but Adeline, already making her way into the kitchen, didn't appear to hear.

As she and Cane followed her in, Megan glanced longingly at her crochet sitting on the table and decided next time some random stranger came knocking at her door, she'd hide under the bed. Whether Adeline was genuine or not, Megan wasn't in the market for friendship any more than she was for a relationship. Both things would eventually mean baring her soul and doing so would likely ruin the bond, so what was the point starting anything in the first place?

'Can I get you a cup of coffee or a glass of cold water?' Megan offered. 'I'm sorry, but I really don't have anything else.'

Adeline's smile grew wider. 'I'd love a cup of tea.'

Did I offer you that? Megan swallowed her irritation as her guest pulled out a chair and dusted it with her fingers. Seemingly satisfied that it was clean enough, she turned to sit down, but just as she was about to connect, the seat moved backwards and Adeline crashed ungracefully to the floor.

If Megan hadn't seen it with her own eyes, she wouldn't have believed it. It was as if an invisible force had played that cruel old trick on Adeline.

'Are you okay?' She rushed forwards, trying to stifle a laugh and offer the other woman a hand up as Cane bounced all over her in excitement at this new game.

Adeline blinked, shook her head, then allowed Megan to assist her. 'Don't know what happened there.' She laughed nervously as she stood and rubbed her backside. Her faux smile well and truly vanished, this time she held on firmly to the chair as she lowered herself into it. 'Now, where were we? Cup of tea?'

'I'm sorry, but I don't drink tea so I don't have any.'

Adeline's eyes widened as she looked from Megan to the dozen or so finished crocheted tea-cosies on the other end of the table. 'You crochet tea-cosies but you don't drink tea?' She sounded incredulous, as if doing such a thing were a mortal sin. What would she think if she knew some of the other things Megan had done?

She shrugged, annoyed. 'My grandma collected teapots and she taught me to crochet. I just like tea-cosies I guess.'

Adeline reached across to pick a black and white example with a crocheted dog on the side. 'They are cute in a retro kind of way,' she admitted, managing to make the compliment sound condescending. 'These would be very popular at our ...' Her voice drifted off as if she'd suddenly changed her mind about saying something.

'At your what?' Megan prompted.

'Oh, nothing.' Adeline dropped the cosy as if it were a dead rodent and waved her hand in dismissal. 'Do you sell them?'

'No. I just enjoy making them.' Which was true, although not the whole truth. Crocheting was therapeutic—sometimes when the sadness and grief of losing her loved ones started to overcome Megan again, she simply needed something to occupy her mind. Crochet and exercise were safer than the alternatives. And if making endless tea-cosies stopped her seeking other comforts, so be it. Crocheting also helped her feel close to Granny Rose, as she'd been the one to teach her in the first place. 'Do you crochet?'

'No.' Adeline shook her head. 'But I knit for the church's winter appeal. We make jumpers and beanies for homeless people. If you also knit, I could drop you round a pattern—we'll be starting the appeal again soon and we can never make enough.'

Of course someone like Adeline would do something worthwhile in her *free* time. And Megan *would* like to help, but she didn't want to give Adeline any excuse for a return visit. She couldn't quite put her finger on it but something about this woman left Megan feeling cold.

'That sounds great, but maybe I could pick up the pattern next time I go into Walsh to shop. It'll save you a trip. Now, can I get you coffee or water?'

Adeline frowned. 'I would have said it was too hot for coffee, but these old buildings are really good at keeping the heat out, aren't they?' She rubbed her upper arms.

Megan made no comment as she retrieved two mugs from a cupboard.

'What are your plans for the store?'

'What do you mean?' *Hurry up, kettle*, she willed. The faster she made the coffees, the faster they could drink them and the faster whatever this was could be over. Entertaining Lawson and Archie was one thing because they were guys and in general guys didn't pry, but she got the feeling Adeline could be very good at prying.

'Well, this is a very large place for one person to live.'

'One person and a dog,' Megan pointed out.

Adeline didn't act as if she'd even registered Megan speaking. 'Why *did* you decide to move here? What are your plans for the building? It's going to take a lot of work to fix and clean it up.'

Megan took a lesson in fake smiling from her visitor and plastered one on her face. 'Do you want sugar in your coffee?'

'No, thank you.'

You probably think you're sweet enough, Megan thought as the kettle whistled. 'So how long have you been breeding Maremmas?' Adeline wasn't the only one who could ask questions but Megan hoped she could be distracted by the lure of talking about herself.

'This little guy ...' she tugged her shoe out of Cane's mouth '... is from my third litter. What did you decide to call him?'

'Cane,' Megan said as she put the coffees down on the table and sat down opposite Adeline. 'Short for Hurricane.'

'Interesting.' Adeline's expression showed her distaste.

Megan couldn't help herself. 'It was Lawson's suggestion actually.'

'Oh?' Adeline raised one eyebrow and her mug to her lips.

'Yes, when he first brought Cane over, the puppy wouldn't stop running around and Lawson joked he'd delivered a hurricane. I liked it.'

'Well,' Adeline cleared her throat, 'as much as I adore Lawson, I do hope he knew what he was doing bringing you a puppy. Maremmas are energetic dogs and they need a firm hand or they'll easily become out of control. I strongly recommend you coming to my puppy-training classes. It'll give us a chance to catch up again too.'

Neither idea appealed. 'I'll give it some thought,' she lied, 'but honestly he hasn't been much trouble. I love to run so we've been getting out every morning and—'

'I hope you're not over-running him. It's a fine line with puppies.'

Speaking of fine lines, Megan formed her mouth into one, her irritation at having Adeline in her home growing by the second. 'Thank you for your concern, I'll be careful.'

'If you have any problems, don't hesitate to give me a call though. I'm happy to help.' Adeline scooped a business card out of her handbag and laid it on the table.

'Thanks,' Megan said.

'So, what brought you to Rose Hill?' Adeline asked again and it was clear she wasn't going to give up.

'I have had some family tragedy over the past few years, culminating with the death of my grandmother a few months back. I needed a tree change.'

'Strange place for a tree change.' Adeline rubbed her lips together and put down her mug. 'Won't you get bored out here?'

'As you said, there's a lot of work to do on this building; that will keep me busy for a while.'

'No offense,' Adeline began, telling Megan that what she was about to say would indeed be offensive, 'but have you really thought this through? Even if you renovate the old store into a palace, what are you going to do with it? Since the bypass was put in, hardly anyone comes through even Walsh, let alone Rose Hill, so it's not exactly good real estate.'

Megan hadn't really thought past doing the building up. Quite frankly, she'd paid so little for it that she didn't really care what happened to it once she was ready to move on. She just needed a project to stop her going insane for the time that it took for people to forget. When she'd seen this old place on the internet, she'd contacted the real estate agent before she could talk herself out of it.

'I've got a few ideas,' she said, 'but I'm not really ready to talk about them yet.'

Adeline glanced around again. 'They say this place is haunted, you know.' She added quickly, 'Not that I believe in ghosts.'

'Don't you?'

'You're not telling me you *do*?'

Megan thought about the coolness on the stairs and the way Cane didn't want to go anywhere near it. She thought about the noises in the night and the chair moving out as Adeline had tried to sit down. 'Of course not.' She laughed.

At that moment the light bulb dropped from the ceiling and crashed against Adeline's mug. They both startled at the noise as glass shattered across the table. Cane froze, then rushed to cower and whine under Megan's chair. Adeline pushed back her seat and stood, snatching her bag off the floor and clutching it against her chest.

'Well, look at the time.' Her gaze darted around the room, everywhere but at the face on her shiny gold watch. 'Things to do, people to see. I'll be sure to tell Lawson you and Cane are doing well.'

Adeline didn't offer to help clean up the mess; Megan didn't care. It had probably been a weird freak-episode—the light fitting was ancient and she hadn't had to replace that bulb yet—but if there were a ghost, Megan would love to thank her for spooking Adeline into a hasty departure. She stifled another giggle as she scooped Cane up from under the chair, then followed her unwanted guest as she hurried down the hallway.

Adeline wrenched open the front door, rushing out as if the building were on fire.

'Nice meeting you,' Megan called, waving Cane's little paw at his rapidly departing breeder.

Adeline climbed into her expensive-looking four-wheel drive and then skidded on the gravel at the side of the road as she pulled away without even a backwards glance. Megan hoped she'd been spooked enough not to consider returning.

Aside from her looks, Megan couldn't understand what a lovely guy like Lawson could see in Adeline, but they were obviously friends and, if Adeline could be believed, perhaps a lot more than that. Was that the real reason Megan had not taken to her? She was jealous?

She sighed sadly as she closed the door and put Cane back down on the floor to continue wreaking havoc. On her way back into the kitchen to resume crocheting her useless tea-cosies, her eyes fell on the books Adeline had messed up ... only now they were back in a neat pile.

Megan shivered as she glanced at the book on the top. All of them were from a couple of boxes she'd found among the previous owners' junk and although she hadn't paid much attention to the titles before, she felt certain she'd never seen this one. Her hand quivering a little, she reached out to pick it up—*The Ghost and Mrs Muir*. She'd never given much credence to the notion of ghosts, but the longer she spent in this house, the more she started to wonder.

Chapter Nine

Lawson wiped the sweat from his brow and then reached for the next calf in the queue to be tagged. It was barely eleven am and already he'd worked as many hours as some people did in a day. Normally he liked hard work but even in the shade it felt about a hundred degrees, and he'd been fantasising about skiving off work and jumping into the swimming pool beside the farmhouse. His phone vibrated in his pocket and he yanked it out, glad of the distraction until he saw the school's number on the screen.

He cleared his throat as he swiped to answer. 'Hello?'

'Hi Lawson, it's Beck calling from the school. How are you?'

'Fine thanks, Beck. What can I do for you?' He tried to tell himself she didn't sound panicked so he shouldn't either, but a call from the school in the middle of the day always worried him. 'Is Ned okay?'

'He's feeling a little off,' she said. 'I've got him here with me in the office and I don't want you to worry, he doesn't have a temperature and he hasn't been physically ill, but he's not his usually chirpy self. Do you think you could come and collect him? He might just be over-tired and need a little rest.'

'I'm on my way,' Lawson promised before disconnecting. He called across to Ethan, who was just coming back after returning the last lot of calves. 'I've got to go get Ned from school. Will you be okay to finish up here?'

'No probs, boss. I am the Nightrider. I'm a fuel-injected suicide machine. I am the rocker. I am the roller. I am the out-of-controller. And I have it all under control.'

Lawson raised an eyebrow and shook his head.

'Is Ned okay?' Ethan asked.

'I hope so,' Lawson replied as he headed off in the direction of his ute. The keys were in the ignition where he always left them and, as he started the vehicle and drove off, he thought back to that morning. Ned hadn't shown any signs of illness as far as he could remember, but then again, if he'd learned anything in eight years of parenthood, it was that kids could go from healthy to pretty damn sick in a flash. Tab would have happily gone into town to collect Ned but another thing Lawson had learned was that if Ned was really ill, no one but him would do for comfort.

The calves could wait but his boy couldn't.

He drove through the main street of town and then turned into the school, which was located at one end just before the *Thank You For Visiting Walsh* sign. As it wasn't recess or lunchtime, the playgrounds were empty and the whole place almost eerily quiet. He walked briskly towards the front office building, which also doubled as the staff room and sickbay.

'Hi, Lawson.' Beck, who'd been the school receptionist for longer than he could remember, rose from her swivel chair.

He nodded a quick hello and then turned straight into the room off the office, which he knew held a bed and the school's first aid cabinet. Ned lay atop the mattress, curled up in a ball and hugging the pillow to his chest. For all his talk about growing up lately, he looked small and vulnerable, and Lawson's heart squeezed as he rushed over to him.

'Hey, little buddy. What's up?' He pulled him into his arms and put his hand against Ned's forehead. 'You not feeling well?'

Ned looked up at him, his eyes wide and a little red. 'I just wanted to see you.'

'I'm here now. Let's get you home.' He scooped Ned up and carried him back into the office, where he signed him out, picked up his school bag and thanked Beck for looking after him.

'It was my pleasure.' She smiled and waved. 'Get better soon, Ned.'

'Thanks, Mrs Sampson,' Ned said before burying his head in Lawson's chest.

He frowned as he carried his son to the car and deposited him in the passenger seat. 'What's up, buddy? Where don't you feel well?' Should they stop in at the doctor's surgery on the way home?

Ned looked down at his shoes.

'Is it your head? Your tummy? Do you feel like you might vomit?'

'No.' He shook his head. 'Sorry, Dad, I'm not sick, I just didn't want to be at school any more.'

'What?' Lawson was more surprised than angry. 'But you love school.'

Ned took a breath. 'Some of the kids have been saying mean things to me.'

What the?! Lawson's hands formed fists as he glanced back at the school. He usually didn't have a violent bone in his body but if some little brats were being cruel to his son, they'd better watch out. Taking a deep breath, he looked back to Ned. 'Who? And what kind of things?'

Ned hesitated a moment, then, 'Tate and Levi Walsh. They said they don't want to play with me because I don't have a mum.'

'What? But you guys have always been good friends. That's just ridiculous,' Lawson scoffed, then realisation dawned. Tate and Levi were twins and, according to the bush telegraph, their parents—Adeline's brother and his wife—had just separated after their father had been found in a compromising position with their farm hand. He guessed the kids were feeling insecure in their own home situation and were trying to make themselves feel better by making others feel bad. Not that this was an excuse. Should he try and explain it to Ned?

'I told them I do have a mum, she's just in heaven.' Ned let out a long sigh far too big for his little body. 'I'm sorry for interrupting your work.'

'Hey, it's all right.' Lawson hugged him tightly before pulling the seatbelt across his body and clicking it into place. 'But if you're not feeling ill, how about we go get one of those spider drinks you like from the café and a big piece of Mrs Mac's apple pie to share?'

Ned's eyes lit up. 'Seriously?'

Lawson nodded. 'Seriously.'

By the time they arrived at the café, Ned looked so much better that Lawson wasn't sure whether to mention the Tate/Levi thing again or just wait and see if there were further developments. He'd send an email to Mrs Warburton later, explaining what had happened and asking her to keep an eye on things.

'Well, isn't this a surprise?' Mrs Mac, who'd been a friend of Lawson's mum and had inherited A Country Kitchen from her own mother, wiped her hands on her apron and beamed at the two of them from behind the counter. 'You're not skiving off school are you, young Ned?'

He looked to Lawson for help.

Lawson put a hand on his shoulder. 'Ned hasn't had the best day but it's nothing one of your famous lemonade spiders and a piece of apple pie won't fix.'

'Got it.' Mrs Mac tapped the side of her head where she kept orders no matter how big they were. 'And what can I get you to drink, Lawson?'

He contemplated a moment, then, 'I think I'll have the same.'

'Splendid.'

Lawson tried to pay but she waved his hand away. 'This one's on the house.'

'Thank you,' said he and Ned in unison.

'Take a seat, gentlemen, and I'll bring your order out to you in a moment.' Mrs Mac turned and bustled back into the kitchen.

'Where shall we sit, Dad?'

'You choose,' Lawson said, looking over the near-empty café. Within the next hour the place would fill for the lunch rush— there wasn't anywhere else in town except the servo to eat—but they should be gone by the time it got really busy.

Ned grabbed his hand and dragged him over to a table in the corner by the window. Tab had schooled him in the fun of people-watching and they often played this game where they'd choose a random passer-by and make up a history for them. In the absence of his sister, Lawson guessed he'd have to take part.

'Hey look,' Ned said.

Lawson followed the direction of his finger, expecting to see the first victim for their game, but instead he almost fell off his chair at the sight of Meg from Rose Hill coming towards the café. Her long, dark mahogany-coloured hair fell in two curtains on either side of her face and he didn't know how she could bear it like that in the heat, but it had to be the prettiest thing he'd ever seen. He imagined what it might feel like to run his hands through.

'It's Meg!' Ned cried out, as if Lawson needed any reminding.

He couldn't tear his eyes away and he held his breath as he wondered whether she would come inside or keep on walking.

He'd been trying not to think of her, had brushed the conversation off when Tabitha tried to talk about her and had been ignoring Ned's pleas to take another trip out to Rose Hill, but he'd be lying to himself if he said he didn't want her to come into the café.

'She's coming in,' Ned shrieked, leaping off his chair and heading for the door before Lawson could think to pull him back.

He looked down at his attire, cursing the fact he hadn't at least cleaned up a little before he'd high-tailed it into town. As Meg opened the door, Lawson surreptitiously lifted his arm a little and sniffed. Why hadn't he thought to spray some deodorant over his farmyard aroma?

Because you usually don't give a damn what you look or smell like.

'Meg!' Having obviously forgotten about using his inside voice, Ned threw his arms around her the moment she stepped through the door.

'Well, hello!' Her arms went around Ned and she patted his back as she looked over the top of him and her eyes met with Lawson's.

When he smiled and lifted a hand to wave, she copied the gesture, looking as surprised to see them as he was to see her. Lawson mentally shook his head at how stupid this was—the size of Walsh meant it wasn't unusual to run into someone you knew in town. Meg might not live there, but considering the lack of shops and facilities in Rose Hill, she may as well.

'Come sit with us,' Ned demanded, letting her go only long enough to grab her hand. He started tugging her towards their table.

She laughed. It was such a beautiful sound Lawson felt it rippling through his body, awakening parts of him he'd thought were near-on dead. 'I was only going to get a takeaway.'

'Aw, no, *please* come and sit with us.' If he hadn't been only eight years old, Ned's desperation would have been embarrassing.

Rachael Johns

Meg looked to Lawson questioningly.

He swallowed, found his voice and gestured to the empty chairs at their table. 'You're more than welcome.'

'Mrs Mac?' Ned called through to the kitchen. 'Can you come and take Meg's order?'

Lawson couldn't help laughing as Mrs Mac reappeared.

'I'm sorry,' she said to Meg, 'I mustn't have heard the door open.' She looked from Meg to Lawson and back to Meg, her gaze dropping to where Ned clung to her hand, and her eyebrows rose. You didn't have to be a genius to know what she was thinking. As much as he adored Mrs Mac, she wasn't known for her discretion and he could already hear the rumours that would be circulating Walsh within a couple of hours. 'What can I get you?' she asked Meg.

'I was going to get a coffee,' Meg said, 'but after walking up the hill from the IGA car park, I'm thinking a cool drink might be a better idea.'

'You should get a spider,' Ned suggested. 'They're the best.'

A smile bloomed on Meg's previously uncertain face. 'Oh, I used to love them when I was a kid. Can I have a Coke one, please? That way I still get my caffeine hit.'

'I like your thinking,' Mrs Mac said, tapping the side of her head. 'By the way, I'm Beverly. Lovely to meet you.'

'You too. And I'm Meg,' she said, digging her purse out of her bag to pay.

Again, Mrs Mac shooed her money away. 'Oh no, this one's on the house as a welcome to the area. I assume you *are* a newcomer.'

Lawson didn't know how she managed to stay in business giving away all these freebies.

Meg nodded. 'Thank you. That's very kind of you.'

After another assurance, Mrs Mac retreated again and Ned achieved his goal of dragging Meg to their table.

Lawson stood to pull out a seat for her. 'Hi there.'

'Hi.' She hesitated a moment before sitting down, as if second-guessing her decision. She seemed kinda jumpy and had been the same the two times they'd met, although she'd relaxed a little towards the end of his dog visit. Maybe she was jumpy because of the moment they'd shared right before he left her place. Did she think he might overstep the mark and try and kiss her if she sat with them?

It would be funny if the thought hadn't actually crossed his mind.

'Thank you,' she finally said, dropping her bag to the floor and lowering herself into the seat.

Lawson worried they might not have anything to say and that awkward silence may descend upon the table, but then Ned opened his mouth.

'How's your puppy, Meg? Where is he? Did you bring him to town?' As Ned bombarded her with questions, he glanced down at her handbag as if maybe she were hiding Cane in there.

'He's doing well.' She half-laughed and then looked over to Lawson. 'Thank you again for giving him to me. He's been such wonderful company.'

Her eyes were almost translucent blue—like nothing he'd ever seen before—and although you couldn't call her classically beautiful, she invoked sensations inside him no one had done in a very long time. Lawson suddenly realised it was his turn to speak and that staring at her as he was might be quite unsettling.

'He's not causing too much trouble then?' he asked.

'I didn't say *that*.' She smiled properly this time and her see-through eyes shimmered.

'Is he naughty?' Ned asked, leaning forwards and planting his elbows on the table, clearly excited by this idea.

'Let's just say I came in to town because I decided to invest in some baby gates and stock up on toilet paper, even though I thought I bought plenty on the weekend.'

'Oh no.' Lawson closed his eyes a moment. 'What did he do?'

'Somehow in the five minutes I was having a shower this morning, he managed to get a hold of the bulk pack of toilet rolls I bought and tear the whole lot of them to shreds. As if that wasn't enough, he also found the roll on the wall, grabbed the end and ran through the whole house with it.'

Ned cackled, finding this hilarious, but Lawson's mind was stuck on the image of Meg naked in the shower. He gulped. 'Maybe he's been watching too much TV.'

When Meg's expression remained blank, he elaborated. 'You know the advert with Labrador pups and toilet paper?' He shook his head. 'Never mind, it's probably not even on any more.'

'I remember it.' Meg smiled and their eyes met again, but before either of them could say anything else, a young waitress Lawson hadn't seen before arrived at their table with a tray.

'Hi guys.' She grinned as she unloaded their drinks and the apple pie. 'I brought you three spoons. Enjoy.'

'Thank you,' they all said at the same time.

'I haven't had one of these for so long.' Meg twirled the straw between her fingers and then leaned forwards to take a sip.

Lawson dragged his own glass towards him. 'I hope they're as good as you remember.'

Ned devoured the ice-cream in his drink with his spoon first and then drank the rest of it in ten seconds flat, making impolite noises through the straw when he reached the bottom.

'Ned.' Lawson tossed him a reproachful glare and then shrugged apologetically at Meg. 'I do teach him manners, I swear.'

She chuckled and then grinned at Ned. 'You're just enjoying it, aren't you?'

He nodded, then leaped up from his chair. 'I need to go to the bathroom,' he announced loudly, before rushing off to the conveniences at the back of the café.

'It's like everything goes right through him,' Lawson said, and then silently cursed the fact he was telling Meg about his son's toilet habits.

'He's a pretty cool kid. Why isn't he at school today?'

Enjoying Meg's surprise company, he'd almost forgotten what had brought them into the café. 'I got a call from the school saying he wasn't feeling well,' he said, keeping his voice low. 'But he's not sick; he told me some kids at school were teasing him about not having a mum.'

'That's awful.' She was silent a moment, then added, 'I lost my parents at seventeen and most of the girls at the school I went to were really nice but some were downright nasty.'

'You lost both your parents at the same time?'

She rubbed her lips together and nodded. 'Yes, and also my younger brother. I was on school study camp, prepping for our final exams. At home, there was a house fire in the night, it started downstairs and they were all upstairs asleep. None of them survived.'

'God.' Lawson had been on the receiving end of pity due to the loss of his own mother, but suddenly he was grateful he'd lost just one parent. How do you ever come out the other side of something like that? 'I can't even imagine how hard that must have been.'

'It was a dark time in my life,' she admitted, glancing down at the table.

He shook his head—thinking that was probably an understatement. When he lost his mum, he thought his world was going to end. If it hadn't been for Leah … 'Who did you live with after that? Did you have some kind of support system?'

'I went to live with my mum's folks. They were great but I pretty much shut them and everyone else out of my life for a while.' She shrugged. 'Anyway, kids can be cruel, but Ned's lucky he's got such a great dad.'

Lawson could tell Meg was trying to divert the conversation from herself again and, not wanting to upset her, he nodded. 'I'm trying to remember they're just kids, but I gotta be honest, I thought about storming into the school and knocking their heads together.'

'I don't blame you. Is this the first time anything like this has happened?'

'I think so. And Ned seems to have perked up since we left school. Tomorrow he'll probably be best mates with the boys again. That seems to be the way of eight-year-olds.'

Meg nodded. 'I vaguely remember being that young.'

She spoke as if she were a hundred and two but at a guess he'd put her around twenty-five, about Tab's age.

The bathroom door slammed, indicating Ned was on his way back out. 'Another thing about eight-year-olds is that they seem incapable of doing anything without noise,' Lawson said as his son returned.

'They have a lot in common with puppies.' Meg took a sip of her drink, her smile visible around the straw.

Ned immediately made a start on the apple pie. He dug the spoon in, then shoved it into his mouth, which he opened seconds later as if about to speak. Lawson gave him a warning look, so he zipped his lips.

'What's your dog called?' Ned asked once he'd finished his mouthful.

'Cane, short for Hurricane,' she said, then glanced fleetingly at Lawson again. 'Your dad named him.'

'That's so cool. What other naughty things has he done?'

Meg smiled and entertained them for a little while with more stories of Cane's adventures—shoes he'd buried, wool he'd unravelled and furniture he'd tried to massacre. 'Lucky all my stuff is secondhand,' she finished.

'I'm sorry.' Lawson shook his head and ran a hand through his curls. 'I probably should have asked whether you wanted a puppy before I delivered him.'

'He has to have been the most unexpected gift I've ever received,' she admitted, 'but he's also the best. I still feel guilty for not paying you for him.'

'If your puppy is so naughty,' Ned interrupted, 'aren't you scared to leave him at home alone?'

'Terrified,' Meg said, grinning. 'Which is why I've left him with Archie.' She glanced at her watch. 'I'd better be getting back there soon to relieve him.'

Ned's eyes grew wide. '*Crazy* Archie?'

'I'm sorry to disappoint, Ned, but I don't think he's all that crazy. Well, no more than the rest of us anyway.'

'Are you spending quite a bit of time with him then?' He should be relieved that she had someone looking out for her in Rose Hill, but instead he felt oddly jealous. At least that's what he thought caused the weird tightening in his gut. And if she wasn't alone, he couldn't use that old worrying-about-her excuse to explain to himself why he couldn't stop thinking about her.

'Not that much, but I think I mentioned he gives me eggs daily and in return I've been cooking a bit for him? Between you and me, I think he lived on two-minute noodles and eggs before I arrived.'

'Want some apple pie?' Ned asked, pushing the plate towards her. There wasn't much left.

'No, thanks,' she said, and then, as the door of the café opened, she spun her head quickly to look around.

A bunch of local seniors came in and their eyes immediately zeroed in on the three of them. He lifted a hand to wave at the ladies, knowing later he'd have to field questions about who she was and why they were together.

Meg stood so suddenly her chair legs scraped against the floor.
He frowned up at her. 'Are you okay?'

She nodded and hitched her bag over her shoulder, but her eyes
were as wide as if she'd just seen a ghost. 'Well, thanks for the
company, boys, but I better be getting back to Cane.'

They'd been sitting here for almost twenty minutes but it
didn't seem nearly long enough. Lawson had enjoyed talking to
her and listening to her tales of the dog. The words 'Could I see
you again?' lingered on the end of his tongue. It had been so
long since he'd asked anyone out—the first and last time he'd
ever really done anything of the sort was asking Leah to the Year
Ten dinner dance. His hands and heart had been shaking so hard
he'd barely been able to speak, but to his immense relief, she'd
said yes almost before he'd finished asking. They'd pretty much
started dating after that and it hadn't been long before his mates
had been joking about them being an old married couple. He
didn't care—with Leah at his side, he'd felt like the luckiest boy
in the world.

The fingers of his right hand drifted to the gold band on his left
and twisted it around. He didn't want to ask Meg on a date; he just
wanted to get to know her a little better.

'Can we come to your place and see Cane?' Ned asked, leaping
off his seat and knocking over his empty glass.

Lawson reached out to stop it rolling off the table. 'Ned, it's
rude to invite yourself somewhere,' he said, secretly jealous of his
son's ability to just come straight out and ask whatever he wanted.

'Oh.' Meg blinked and hesitated a moment. Then, 'It's fine. Of
course. I'm sure Cane would love to play with you.'

'Great. Come on, Dad, let's go.'

As much as Lawson found himself wanting to go along with
this unexpected turn of events, he had responsibilities and jobs
that couldn't be put off. Coming into town to pick up Ned and

stopping at the café had already put him behind—and it was only a couple of hours until milking.

'Sorry, mate, but I've got to get back to the farm.' He swallowed the lump in his throat as he looked to Meg and managed to add, 'Maybe another time?'

'Sure.' She nodded a few times in quick succession. 'How about you guys come out for lunch on Saturday? That's if you don't already have plans. Of course, Adeline's welcome as well.'

'Adeline?' *Why the heck would I want to bring her?*

'The dog breeder?' Meg clarified. 'Isn't she your girlfriend?'

'No, she's not,' Lawson said emphatically, while Ned started to laugh. He shot his son a glare and then turned back to Meg. 'You've met her?'

'Yes. She came out to introduce herself and check on Cane.' Meg's brow creased slightly. 'I thought she'd have told you.'

'No. She didn't.' His jaw clenched—he wasn't sure why but he didn't like the idea of Meg and Adeline chumming up.

'I'm sorry. She led me to believe you guys were together and she definitely said she'd mention her visit.'

'Never mind.' Lawson shook his head, trying to banish Adeline from it. 'Saturday it is then. Can we bring anything?'

'No, just yourselves. Oh, and your sister is more than welcome as well.' She smiled down at Ned and then, without another word, turned and hurried out of the café.

Chapter Ten

For ten seconds post waking up on Saturday morning, Megan didn't panic. She woke to the early-morning sun and a breeze that already carried a hint of the heat to come wafting in her through her open window and smiled at the sweet smell of summer. These days something as simple as sleeping with a window open brought her so much joy.

Then, the significance of the day dawned and she became incapable of thinking about anything except Ned and Lawson arriving in a few hours. She sat bolt upright, waking Cane, who'd been slumbering like the dead at her feet, and then scrambled up to start getting ready. As she carried the dog down the stairs—a feat she wouldn't be able to do forever—she asked herself some very pertinent questions.

What had she been *thinking* inviting Lawson and his son for lunch?

It had been daring enough sitting down with them in the café like it were a normal thing to do, but asking them to her place? *Utter madness.* When she'd moved to Rose Hill, there hadn't seemed any point connecting the landline and a mobile phone felt like a waste of money, but right about now, not having a means to contact Lawson had knobs on. If she had a mobile, she could text some excuse to him about coming down with some highly contagious disease and needing to be quarantined.

Mumps? Chicken pox? Bird Flu? Ebola?

The words rattled around in her head like pretend ammunition in a real fight. She didn't have a phone and thus had no way of calling Lawson and cancelling their arrangement.

Stifling the urge to throw up, she deposited Cane at the bottom of the stairs. He made a beeline for the back door and, as she opened it for him, she heard the whistling of her kettle in the kitchen telling her the water was boiled. Only she hadn't switched it on. Her stomach did a little flip as she went into the kitchen to make her coffee and found her favourite mug waiting beside the kettle. The first time this had happened the day following Adeline's visit, Megan had thought little of it, assuming she'd filled the kettle and put out her mug the night before. She'd put the timely boiling of the water down to faulty electrics.

But the next day when the same thing had happened, she'd felt a quiver down her spine. The third day she'd had to acknowledge that either she was becoming very forgetful and desperately needed the services of an electrician, or she and Cane weren't the only ones living in her house. That's if you could call a ghost living. Which, technically, she guessed you couldn't. *But ...* semantics.

'Thank you,' she said, picking up the kettle and pouring hot water into her mug. 'I'm in dire need of this coffee today.' Her hands shook as she scooped up some coffee granules and stirred them into the water. 'I have a hot guy and his young son coming to visit and I have no idea what we'll talk about.'

The breeze from the open back door made the kitchen curtains move a little.

'What would you talk about to such a man? Did you ever have a beau? What did you guys talk about? Not that Lawson is my beau or anything.' The thought was laughable but Megan didn't laugh.

'I'm going to make quiche for lunch and some salads,' she said as stirred in the milk. 'Do you think kids like quiche? I used to like it when I was little but then some children are really fussy, aren't they?'

Funny, but talking to the ghost had settled her nerves slightly. She just wished the ghost would talk back.

'What's your story? How long have you been here?' she asked, leaning against the kitchen bench and taking the first sip of her coffee.

When, after a few moments, there was no reply, she sighed and took her coffee out to the back verandah and sat down on the step to watch Cane tearing around the yard. She had no appetite for breakfast and so after she'd finished her drink and Cane had finished his shenanigans, she went inside to start cleaning and cooking for her guests.

* * *

Just before midday, the sound of a vehicle outside announced the arrival of her visitors and Megan's anxiety returned with a vengeance. She glanced in the hallway mirror, hoping it didn't look like she'd gone to too much trouble. For the first time since she'd come to Rose Hill she was wearing make-up and a denim skirt instead of her usual shorts. She ran her fingers through the ends of her hair, which she'd washed and blow-dried that morning, and then took a deep breath before going to open the front door.

Although she'd spent hours preparing for the visit, nothing could prepare her for her physical reaction when Lawson stepped out of his ute, ran a hand through that crazy hair of his and glanced up to see her standing on the porch. As their gazes connected, her belly didn't just flop, it did freaking gymnastics for Australia. He wore khaki shorts to his knees, a navy polo shirt and black thongs that on him looked far sexier than she'd ever given thongs credit for.

She lifted a hand to wave and opened her mouth to say Hi but the sound didn't even come out.

'Hey there,' Lawson called as he reached into the back of his ute to retrieve something.

Ned raced towards her and threw his arms around her again in the exact same way he had in the café. 'Hi, Meg!'

She found her voice, 'Hello,' as she stooped a little to hug him back. It felt so weird to have such an immediate connection with another human being. Weird but nice.

'Where's Cane?' he asked, bouncing up and down in much the same way the dog did when he was excited.

'He's out the back.' Megan had barely finished uttering this sentence before Ned headed into her house as if he'd been there a hundred times before. She laughed and tried not to feel nervous—there was nothing Ned or Lawson might see that would give them clues to her past life and it wasn't a crime to have people round for lunch.

Lawson chuckled as he stepped onto the front porch. 'Someone's a little excited.' Then he leaned forwards and brushed his lips against her cheek. 'This is for you,' he said, holding up a bottle of milk. 'Straight from the cow.'

'Wow, thanks.' Her fingers closed around the cool bottle and she hoped holding it would help lower her body temperature, which had skyrocketed the moment his mouth had touched her skin. It was the most chaste kiss she'd had in her life, but her hormones had been so deprived of human contact that they went wild. 'I don't think I've ever drunk milk this fresh.'

'You'll probably find it tastes a little different from the milk you usually drink, but if you just have it in coffee or use it for cooking, you might not notice. I know milk isn't the most conventional gift, but Mum always said that you never show up as a guest at someone's house without bringing a gift of appreciation.'

'Said?'

Lawson nodded. 'You, me and Ned all lost our mums far too young. Speaking of Ned, I reckon we should go see what mischief he and Cane are up to, don't you?'

The knowledge of this common ground helped ease Megan's nerves a little. He might be a country boy, and she might have been raised in the inner suburbs of Melbourne, but losing a parent hurt like hell no matter who you were. Not to mention he'd lost his wife as well.

'Good idea,' she said, turning and holding the door open for him. 'Your sister couldn't make it?'

'No. Tab is selling her ice-cream at a community event in Harvey today but she said to say thanks for the invitation and she hopes to meet you very soon.'

'I hope so too,' Megan lied as she started down the hallway. Part of her would love to meet Lawson's sister because everything about him piqued her curiosity, and if Tab were half as cool as he and Ned, she'd be a great person, but at the same time it was a relief (and safer) not to have to make another acquaintance. The more people she got to know, the more people she would have to lose and she was fed up with losing people. It was easier not to get close in the first place. She'd broken her own rules by inviting Lawson and Ned to lunch, but she'd just have to tread carefully.

He followed her into the kitchen where she popped the milk bottle into the fridge.

'Can I get you a drink?' she asked, deciding to forget about the fact she shouldn't be entertaining and try to enjoy the company while she had it. 'Coffee, juice or soft drink? I have Coke, Fanta and lemonade.' After making this crazy 'date' with them in the café, Megan had returned to the supermarket and bought a variety of treats she'd never buy for herself.

'I'll start with water,' he said, hitting her once again with that potent smile. Every time he flashed it, she got a jolt to her nether regions.

'Right, water.' She turned to grab a clean glass off the sink and then went to the fridge to get out the jug. 'Shall I pour one for Ned as well? I thought we could eat out on the back verandah. It's not too hot in the shade today.'

'Sounds good. Is there anything I can do to help?'

'No. Why don't you go out the back and check on Cane and Ned? I'll grab the drinks.'

Lawson retreated and a few seconds later Megan heard squealing. She peeked around the curtain and saw him holding a grinning Ned by his ankles, swinging him from side to side. Cane danced around them both, having a ball as well. A pang of loneliness and longing gripped her; growing up she'd always dreamed of having a big family, but now such a thing seemed like an impossible fantasy. The type of man she'd like to settle down with probably wouldn't want the likes of her.

She let the curtain fall back and sighed, noticing her hands were shaking. And then, she felt a presence behind her as if someone had come into the room. Her heart in her throat, she spun around but of course she was alone.

It's all right. Stay calm.

These words came into her mind but, although she heard no sound, it was as if someone else had spoken them.

Megan took a deep breath, forcing the air in and then out of her lungs. Shaking her head, she turned back to the task at hand.

'Drinks,' she called out a few moments later as she emerged onto the back verandah.

Cane bounded over to her, followed by Lawson and Ned, who already looked a little red. He wore a cap on his head and she hoped he was wearing sun-cream as well, but bit down on the impulse to ask, as it wasn't any of her business.

While the dog lapped water from his bowl, Ned downed almost an entire glass of water. 'I love Cane,' he announced when he'd finished.

'I think he likes you too. I do take him out for runs, but he never seems to use up his energy.' She glanced over at Lawson, who was also drinking. 'Are you guys ready for lunch?'

'I'm starving,' Ned announced.

Lawson nodded as he put his empty glass down on the plastic table.

'Right then, I'll be back in a second.' She went inside, took the quiche out where it had been keeping semi-warm in the oven and once again felt as if someone was behind her watching. Assuming she was imagining things again, she almost dropped the dish when she turned to find Lawson standing only a foot behind her.

'Sorry,' he said, reaching out to steady her hands. Of course his touch did no such thing. 'I know you said you didn't need any help but … I couldn't just sit out there letting you do everything. Here let me take that.'

'Thanks,' Megan managed as he took the quiche from her.

'Anything else I can carry?' he asked.

She gestured to the stack of three plates on the table. 'If you grab them, I'll bring the salads.'

The cutlery was already outside on the table and within a few minutes the three of them were sitting down to eat. Cane sat at their feet ready to pounce on any falling scraps.

'This is really yummy, Meg,' Ned said, after swallowing his first mouthful of quiche.

Thank God. 'I'm glad you like it. And I've made jelly slice for dessert.'

Both Ned's and Lawson's faces lit up at this announcement and Megan couldn't deny the buzz that shot through her. Although she'd been cooking for others for the last few years, doing so had brought none of the satisfaction she felt right now.

'So, tell me about the life of a dairy farmer,' she said, leaning back in her seat, beginning to relax a little.

Lawson snorted. 'It's not that exciting—we get up before the sun and work until after it goes down—but I wouldn't want to do anything else.'

'Does your father work on the farm with you and your sister?'

'Gramps married Sandra, and they live in Bunbury. Sandra doesn't like cows so he tired early,' Ned informed, before shoving another mouthful in his mouth.

By 'tired', Megan guessed he meant 'retired'. She hid a smile as Lawson elaborated.

'Ned's right. It's just us and Tab on the farm now.'

'And Ethan,' Ned exclaimed.

'Yes, Ethan's our worker, but he's part of the family these days. Dad did work up until a couple of years ago, but he had a heart attack that freaked out his new wife. She convinced him to move with her to be closer to medical facilities.'

'I guess that makes sense, but you guys must miss him.'

Lawson shrugged. 'To be honest, Dad changed after my mum died. She had ovarian cancer and it wasn't easy on any of us, but trying to keep the dairy running, look after me and Tab and take care of Mum, who was in and out of hospital in Perth, took its toll on him. He became a shadow of the man he once was. Life is a lot easier for Tab and me not having to consult with him about every little thing.'

'I must admit I don't know much about the dairy industry.' She wondered if cancer had been what had taken Ned's mum as well, but now didn't seem the moment to ask.

'You'll have to come out and help with milking one day,' Lawson said. 'That's if you don't mind wearing ugly gumboots and aren't afraid of a little cow shit.'

'Language!' Ned said and they both laughed.

Megan *wasn't* afraid of a little poo but as much as she'd love to see Lawson in his element, she remembered her determination not to get too close and, ignoring his suggestion, gestured to the water jug in the middle of the table. 'Anyone like a refill?'

'Yes, please.' Ned pushed his glass towards her and she filled it again, hoping no one noticed her hand still shaking a little.

'How many cows do you have?' she asked before lifting a fork-ful of potato salad to her mouth.

'Just over four hundred milkers but it's calving season at the moment, so we've got another two hundred babies with more arriving every day.'

As they finished their quiche and salad, Megan asked him more questions about the farm. She was genuinely interested but she also didn't want to leave an opportunity for awkward silence, or worse, for him to start prying into *her* background.

'There's been lots in the media lately about big supermarkets killing the dairy industry. Has that been a problem for you guys?'

'Yes and no. The price cuts have affected everyone, but we're lucky enough to supply one of WA's big milk companies and a few years back when things were pretty dire, it was get bigger or get out. We decided to get bigger. Sadly though some of the smaller dairies in the region are doing it tough at the moment.'

'Dairy farming doesn't sound like it's for the faint-hearted,' she said.

Lawson chuckled. 'I don't think any type of farming is for the faint-hearted.'

'Meg? Does Cane like water?' Ned asked, when he'd all but scraped his plate clean and must have been getting bored with the shoptalk. 'Can he and I play under your sprinklers for a bit?'

She looked to Lawson for clarification.

'If Meg doesn't mind, it's fine with me. But not for too long— we don't want to waste water or for you to get burned. Go out to the ute and get the sun-cream so we can top you up.'

'And if you move the sprinkler near the fruit trees, the water won't be wasted,' Megan suggested.

While Ned retreated back through the house, she stood and began clearing the table.

Lawson also pushed back his seat and started to help. 'Thanks for lunch. It was delicious.'

'It was my pleasure.'

They carried everything inside and then he started to fill up the sink.

'Oh, I'll do that later,' she said. 'Let's go sit outside and watch Ned and Cane.' The thought of being alone in the kitchen with Lawson made her jumpy. It was one thing chatting to him when his son was chaperone, but spending time alone with a guy like him would be a dangerous thing to do considering she could never allow herself to act on the attraction she felt for him.

At the sound of Ned thundering back down the hallway, Lawson smiled. 'I better go out to help him or there'll be more sun-cream on your back verandah than on him.'

Megan laughed, dumped the dishes in the sink to soak and then followed him out. Ned had stripped down to only his jocks and while Lawson lathered his skinny limbs in cream, she went to turn on the sprinkler. She'd only used it a few times in the evening and so far Cane had always been inside. The moment the water shot into the air, he launched atop the sprinkler as if he needed to defend them from it. Seconds later Ned joined him.

The sounds of Cane yapping at the water and Ned laughing rang out through the yard. Such an innocent, sweet sound. Megan smiled as she went over to join Lawson. He lowered himself onto the top step and patted the space beside him. Her heart skipped a beat at the thought of being so close, but she'd look silly (and rude) if she refused.

'So, are you going to tell me what brought you to Rose Hill?' he asked as she sat down beside him.

I'd rather not. But, after the questions she'd been firing at him, it was only fair that he asked some of his own. And following Adeline's visit, Megan had spent many an hour in bed at night conjuring up answers to this question.

She was a widow—her husband had recently died and her old life held too many awful memories. Lawson would certainly understand that kind of heartache. But how could she tell him such a thing when he really had lost a spouse?

She was running from an abusive partner.

Her boyfriend had betrayed her.

Something about unrequited love perhaps?

However, while the thought of telling tales to Adeline or other strangers didn't bother her that much, lying outright to Lawson didn't sit well—not when he'd been so kind to her. But neither could she bring herself to tell him the truth. That would defeat the purpose of coming to Rose Hill to try and reinvent herself. Perhaps she could come up with a history that was based on truth but left out the unsavoury parts?

'You know how I told you my parents and brother died in a fire?' she began.

He nodded, his gaze trained unnervingly on her.

'And,' she swallowed, 'then I went to live with my grandparents. Well, a year ago my granddad died and my grandmother was lost without him and passed away not long after. They'd helped me through some tough times but without them there any more, Victoria no longer felt like home.'

'Didn't you have other family and friends? What about your father's parents?' he asked.

My father's parents all but disowned me. I'm dead to them. Again, she didn't go the radical honesty route. 'We've never been that close and I felt like I needed to get away for a bit. I've always loved old buildings and so I decided maybe I could buy something to do up. Give myself a project and a change of scenery. I spent days looking on real estate websites for a house I could afford. I stumbled across Rose Hill and fell in love with this old place on sight—it probably sounds stupid but my Gran's name was Rose and I felt like somehow she was connected to it.'

'It doesn't sound stupid,' he said, moving slightly so that his knee touched hers.

'I know Rose Hill is isolated but this building has a lot of potential. I got it cheap, and I thought maybe I could restore it to its former glory.'

'It's a gorgeous old building,' he agreed, 'but what do you plan on doing with it after that? Not to be rude or anything, but you're right about Rose Hill being isolated. I'm not sure the resale value will be much more even after you're finished.'

Although this was basically exactly what Adeline had said, his tone was different and his observation didn't irritate her the same way.

She laughed nervously as she racked her mind for a logical-sounding answer. Inviting him and Ned there for lunch had been a very *bad* idea. How had she ever thought she could hold a normal conversation with anyone, never mind someone as hot and physically distracting as Lawson?

You want to open a tea room and sell arts and crafts.

Megan blinked as once again words landed in her head as if a voice that wasn't her own had spoken them. *A tea room?* She didn't even like tea.

'I'm sorry,' Lawson said. 'That was rude of me and —'

'I actually want to open an old-fashioned tea room,' she found herself saying. 'One that does morning and afternoon teas and light lunches, but also sells local arts and crafts.' Even as she said this she was starting to visualise how perfect such a place could be. She could use the front part of the building, which used to be the general store, as the café/shop and still be able to live out the back and upstairs. She might even be able to convince Archie to let her showcase some of his amazing paintings. If she managed to train Cane not to wreak havoc wherever he went, he could lie out the front on the verandah as the tea room's mascot.

'I know it might seem like Rose Hill is off the beaten track but I've heard of and even visited a few places in Victoria that are just as isolated and work well. Of course it might take a while to build up a reputation but—'

'I think it's a great idea,' Lawson interrupted, glancing back inside through the fly-screen door as if seeing what it could look like once she'd finished.

'Really?'

'Yes. You might be off the beaten track like you say, but you're not too far from civilisation, and people sometimes like a drive in the country. I've got a friend who farms in Goomalling and there's this pub about a fifteen-minute drive from town in a tiny place called Jennacubbine. Nothing else there, but it does a roaring trade.'

Megan couldn't help grinning. Could she really imagine something like that for herself? Even if the tea room never eventuated, the idea had at least given her something to talk to Lawson about and a believable reason for buying a rundown building in a supposed ghost town.

'And,' he added, 'there are plenty of folk around here who do wonderful arts and crafts, so if you offer to sell their stuff in the shop for a commission, they'll help spread the word.'

'That would be wonderful.' She let the fantasy take root and tried to ignore the reality that such a thing would mean getting to know more people.

'Do you plan to do most of the renovations yourself?' Lawson asked.

'Yep. I've made a start and once I get rid of all the clutter I inherited, the big repairs won't actually take that long—and I've done similar work before.'

She gestured to the pile of junk that was rapidly turning into a mountain at the other end of the verandah. She needed to take it to the tip some time but was holding off until the weather cooled down as she'd only be able to fit a small amount in her car each time.

'For your job?' he asked.

She could tell he was trying not to sound sceptical.

'Yes, I've done a little cabinet making in my time.'

'Wow. A woman who can fix things. I'm impressed.'

Megan's cheeks flushed a little at his words, but she wondered if he'd be so impressed if he knew where she'd learned the trade. She forced a smile and kept her reply light. 'I'll have you know women can do most things as well as, if not better than men.'

He laughed and held up his hands in surrender pose. 'Hey. No arguments here. My sister proves that every single day. I was just teasing.'

'You guys sound close,' she said, grabbing onto the opportunity to talk about him again.

'We are. Tab's four years younger than me and when we were kids, Mum used to call her my shadow. I pretended to be annoyed by her,' he admitted, 'but I secretly liked her company and then when Mum got sick we really grew close. Tab's had her own hardships, but she's always remained upbeat and positive. Without her, I'm not sure I'd have coped raising a kid alone.'

She was about to ask how old Ned had been when they'd lost his mum, but Lawson got in first.

'What about you?' he said. 'Was your brother older or younger than you? Were you guys close?'

For a second her heart froze as she wondered how he knew about Tim, but then she remembered she'd mentioned the fire when they were in the café. 'He was two years younger,' she said, suddenly struggling not to cry—this conversation was so downbeat. 'And we fought like crazy, but when he was no longer there, I felt like I'd lost a part of myself.'

'I'm so sorry.' Lawson reached out his hand and took hold of hers. He squeezed ever so gently and then let it go again so quickly she almost wondered if she'd imagined the gesture.

'Do you believe in ghosts?' she asked, in a drastic attempt to redirect the conversation and calm her hormones.

'I'm not sure.' He shrugged and his lips quirked up at the corners. 'Why? Is the old house getting to you?'

This was it, where she admitted the bizarre happenings and Lawson decided she must be mentally unstable, which was perhaps closer to the truth than she wanted to admit, but she felt the need to get it off her chest anyway. And it would probably be a good thing if he took his child and ran.

'I didn't before I moved here, but things have been happening and I've been getting weird sensations that I can't explain away.'

'What kind of things?' The way he asked, as if he really cared, made certain parts of her quiver. Or that could just be the afteraffects of him touching her hand.

'Well, for starters, it's always cold near the stairs—even when it's scorching outside and I'm sweltering in the rest of the house—and Cane hates going anywhere near them. I have to carry him up and down to my bedroom and the rest of the time he takes as wide a berth as possible around them.'

Lawson raised an eyebrow but she went on.

'Sometimes furniture and objects move of their own accord.' She thought of *The Ghost and Mrs Muir* at the top of her book pile and way the chair had moved out from Adeline, but decided not to bring the other woman into the conversation. 'I hear noises outside my room at night and now every day when I wake up … This is gunna sound crazy, but the kettle is always boiling for me when I walk into the kitchen.'

'A helpful ghost?' His slight smile exploded into a full-on grin. 'That sounds like my kind of spirit. Do you think your ghost has a friend they could send on over to my place?'

She laughed. 'I could maybe explain away any of these things on their own, but when I add them all up, I start to feel like I'm living on the set of some gothic movie.'

'I'm not sure the kettle thing can be explained away.'

'Well, thank you. That's very kind of you—you could just say I'm delusional.'

'That wouldn't be very nice,' Lawson said, his deep voice combined with his warm smile making Megan blush.

As if Cane could feel the heat rising in her body and decided she needed cooling down, he chose that second to run over and shake his wetness onto them. Any moment she may or may not have been imagining between herself and Lawson was broken as they shrieked and leaped up from the step.

'Oh my God! Cane, stop!' she ordered, holding her hands out to try and stop the puppy as he bounded after her up the few steps and tried to jump up at her legs.

Ned ran over to join them, laughing so hard he was snorting through his nose. Lawson leaned forwards, grabbed onto Cane's collar and yanked him away from her. 'Sit,' he ordered, his voice kind but stern.

To her surprise, Cane dropped to his haunches, subdued.

'Thanks,' Megan said, trying to catch her breath, hoping her now-soaked T-shirt wasn't giving Ned and Lawson an eyeful. 'I'll go inside and get us all some towels.

As she raced inside to the bathroom, she swore she heard faint laughter coming from the stairs, but she ignored it, grabbed three towels and headed back outside.

'Here,' she said, tossing a towel at Lawson and then unfolding another and wrapping it around Ned's shoulders.

She turned back to see Lawson had stooped down and was drying Cane rather than himself. 'There there, little guy,' he murmured softly as he rubbed Cane's previously white fur.

At this sight another lump formed in her throat. 'That towel was supposed to be for you,' she said, holding hers out to him. 'Here, you have this one.'

'Nah, I'm fine,' he said, and then he stood again and in one swift movement whipped his T-shirt over his head. 'I'm not that wet and this will dry in no time if I hang it on the chair here.'

Megan could barely register his words. Every cell in her head was distracted by the perfection that was Lawson's tanned, chiselled chest. She swallowed, knowing full well she was staring but unable to look away as her gaze travelled from his broad shoulders downwards. He had just the right smattering of hair across his chest—enough to be sexy without being creepy—and her eyes followed the trail down to …

Oh my! She snapped her head up when she saw the bulge in his shorts. She'd thought she'd been blushing earlier, but now her cheeks were scorched and they weren't the only part of her on fire.

Thank God Ned was there or who knew what kind of craziness might have erupted inside of her at this more than pleasant visual. After years with only women for company, seeing Lawson standing in front of her bare-chested was like emerging into a rainstorm on the other side of a long drought.

She brought the towel up to cover her head, pretending to dry her hair, whereas in reality she just needed a moment.

'Right,' she said finally, when she'd almost given herself a headache from rubbing too hard. 'Now that we're all dry again, who wants some jelly slice?'

Chapter Eleven

'Yes, please,' Ned said as Meg turned and all but fled into the house.

Lawson's heart was racing at the sight of her hardened nipples clearly visible through her wet white T-shirt. Feeling a sudden tightness in his shorts, he glanced down and instantly regretted ripping off his shirt, which may have slightly covered his embarrassing hard-on. Geez, he couldn't remember the last time that had happened in polite company. Gripping the back of the plastic seat and trying to think non-sexual thoughts, he cleared his throat and turned his mind to parenting.

'Ned, put your clothes back on.' He sounded far more gruff than he'd intended.

'What do you think I'm doing, Dad?' Ned asked as he pulled his shorts up over his narrow hips and gave him a bemused smile.

'Right.' Lawson nodded. 'Good boy.' He grabbed his own still damp T-shirt and yanked it back on over his head. Taking it off in the first place had been a stupid move, but he had to admit, he'd liked the way Meg's gaze had raked over his body. It was her look of appreciation as much as her wet shirt that had inspired his raging erection and he knew he wouldn't be able to get it out of his head for quite some time.

'Come on, Dad, let's go get that slice.' Ned, who'd dressed much faster than he usually did, grabbed his hand.

'I'm coming,' he said, following his son and Cane back into the kitchen.

Meg wasn't there, but seconds later footsteps sounded behind them and she appeared again, wearing a new *dry* T-shirt. Once again their eyes met in shared acknowledgment of what had happened between them outside. They might not have touched each other but the way she'd looked at him had almost the same effect.

'Do you guys want to eat in the lounge room?' she asked, her voice a little *too* chirpy. 'We can take dessert in there and maybe play a game of Uno or something.'

'I love Uno,' Ned said, 'but I gotta warn you, Dad cheats.'

'Is that right?' Meg laughed and the tension in the air dissipated.

'I do not,' Lawson exclaimed, jokingly reaching out and cuffing Ned's ear.

'I'll be watching both of you,' Meg said as she crossed the kitchen, opened the fridge and pulled out a plate of jelly slice. The sweet smell wafted his way and Lawson reckoned he'd never be able to eat anything jelly again without thinking of her.

'Where are the cards?' Ned asked, his eyes wide as he gazed at the slice.

'I think they're in a box next to the fireplace,' she said and Ned was off, Cane racing behind him.

'Uno is pretty hard to play alone,' Lawson said more for something to say than any other reason.

She smiled and held the plate of slice close. 'It was one of the many games I inherited with the house. The rest of them are there too—I hadn't put them out the back with the stuff for the tip because it seemed a shame to throw them out. Do you and Ned play many board games? You can have them if you like.'

'We should play more than we do. These days we tend to spend more time on the Xbox.'

Meg chuckled and then gestured to the fridge. 'Do you want to grab some drinks?'

He retrieved a jug of water and three glasses, then followed Meg into the living room. They sat on the floor around a few milk crates she'd put together to make a coffee table and devoured half the slice before they even started the first round of Uno. Cane—his nose sniffing like one of those airport customs dogs—tried fluttering his puppy dog eyes at all of them to no avail.

'Sweet stuff is bad for dogs,' Ned informed him. 'But really good for humans.'

Again they all laughed. Cane gave up and sulked his way under the table. Within minutes he was snoring loudly on the floor, totally oblivious to the laughter and accusations of cheating above him.

'Uno,' Meg shouted, pressing her last card against her chest as if it were a winning lottery ticket.

Lawson raised a bemused eyebrow. He'd thought his sister competitive at card games but she had nothing on Meg. It was strangely attractive.

'Draw four!' Ned slammed his card down on the pile and hit Meg with a take-that look. 'Yellow.'

'Aw, you play a mean game of Uno, Ned Cooper-Jones,' she said as she leaned forwards and picked up four new cards.

Ned chuckled like the villain in a Disney movie and Lawson found himself smiling harder than he had in a long time.

They played eight rounds of the card game—Ned won four, Meg three and Lawson one—before Ned decided he'd had enough. 'Can I explore your house?' he asked, already scrambling to his feet.

'Sure, go ahead,' Meg said, 'Just be careful on the stairs.'

'I will,' Ned promised as he dashed out of the room, Cane springing to life and hurtling after him.

'Because of the ghost or because stairs in general can be dangerous?' Lawson asked, trying to keep things light now he and Meg were alone again.

'Are you mocking me?' Her mouth went up on one side.

'No. I'm definitely not,' he said, shaking his head.

A little nervous at being alone with her after the wet-dog-wet-shirts incident, Lawson spoke again to avoid any awkwardness. 'You're not scared here all by yourself, are you?'

'Thanks to you I've got Cane. Not that he'd be much help if the ghost was a bad sort—as I said, he's terrified of her—but so far the spirit or whatever she is hasn't tried to do me or him any harm.'

'You think the ghost is female?'

She shrugged. 'Yes, I guess I do. I hadn't really thought about it but I just feel that she is. I'd really love to find out more about her.'

'What about seeing if you can get access to the Rose Hill historical society?' he suggested, getting caught up in her enthusiasm. 'I'm not sure what's left there these days but the one in Walsh opens every second Wednesday for tourists and keeps stacks of local information. You might find some old newspaper articles about this building or some photos or something.'

'That's a great idea.' Her face lit up in one of those smiles that sparked something warm inside him. 'I'll ask Archie about it.'

'Good idea,' he said. 'Now, shall we go see what Ned and Cane are up to?'

'Another good idea.' She smiled and pushed herself to her feet.

They found Ned at the bottom of the stairs, trying to lure Cane up.

'Cane doesn't like going upstairs,' Meg said, going over to him and lifting him into her arms. She glanced at Lawson but didn't mention the ghost thing to Ned and for that he was grateful. Ned had enough of an imagination as it was and he didn't need any encouragement or neither of them would ever get any sleep again.

'Go ahead.' She nodded up the stairs as she repositioned Cane. Lawson held out his arms. 'Here, let me take him.'

Meg gave him the rapidly growing puppy and then followed Ned up the stairs. When Lawson got to the top and Cane struggled to be free, he set him on the landing and caught his breath. 'What are you going to do when Cane is too big for you to carry?'

'I'm hoping by then he'll either be over his fear or he'll be happy enough to sleep on his own downstairs. But hey, who needs a gym workout when I have him?' To prove her point, she held up one arm like a muscle man and he laughed while also admiring the slender curves.

They ambled through the rooms upstairs, talking about Meg's plans for the building while Ned investigated every nook and cranny. The time passed incredibly fast and it felt way too soon when the alarm on Lawson's mobile beeped. He wanted to switch it off and forget about it as he'd enjoyed their time together much more than he'd ever imagined possible, but the cows would wait for no one and it wasn't fair to leave all the hard work to Tabitha and Ethan.

'Is everything okay?' Meg asked, nodding towards his mobile as he silenced the alarm.

'Yes, that's just my alarm reminder. I've got to get home to get the cows ready for milking.'

'Aw, Dad,' Ned whined from where he'd been playing Narnia in the back of an empty wardrobe in one of Meg's spare rooms. 'I wanna stay here.'

You and me both. 'Unfortunately we can't always get what we want in life, mate, and we don't want to outstay our welcome.'

'Yes, we do!'

Meg laughed, then looked to Ned. 'I'm glad you enjoyed yourself. I was worried you'd get bored here. How about I box up the rest of the jelly slice for you to take home?'

An expression of indecision crossed Ned's face as he deliberated whether more slice was worth backing down for. 'Okay,' he said eventually. 'That would be good.'

Lawson gave his son a stern look. 'Yes, please, Meg, that would be lovely.'

'Yes, please, Meg, that would be lovely,' Ned echoed.

Lawson saw her hiding a smile. He probably should reprimand Ned's cheekiness but he couldn't help smiling as well.

Downstairs, Lawson put Cane down and followed Meg and Ned into the kitchen. She piled the slice into a plastic container and then handed it to Ned. 'Don't eat them all at once.'

'Don't worry, *he* won't let me,' Ned replied, jerking his head towards Lawson.

'Be careful,' Lawson warned, 'or I won't let you have any at all. Now, what do you say to Meg?'

Ned looked slightly chastised. 'Thanks for the jelly slice, Meg, and thanks for having us over for lunch and thanks for letting me play with Cane and thanks for letting me look around your haunted house and thanks—'

'Okay, okay, we get the picture.' As Meg laughed, Lawson placed his hands on Ned's shoulders. 'We need to make a move.'

He was as reluctant to leave as his son, but he forced his feet to move and the three of them walked towards the front door with Cane darting between them. Meg clipped a leash onto the pup's collar as she opened the front door and then they were standing there on the porch as if in limbo between two worlds.

'Thanks so much for lunch,' he said, shoving his hands in his pockets and fiddling with his wallet and keys.

'It was my pleasure,' she replied, her hand drifting up to tuck her hair behind her ear.

With Ned on his knees giving Cane a lengthy hug goodbye, Lawson found himself standing awkwardly on the porch like some teenage boy at the end of a first date. Only this wasn't a date and he wasn't a teenage boy. Time seemed to stop but his heart was tick-tocking away inside him like a clock on steroids.

Finally, Ned looked up and broke the silence. 'I thought we were in a hurry.'

'Right.' Lawson blinked and yanked his keys out of his pocket. 'Thanks again,' he said, before leaning forwards and brushing his lips against Meg's cheek. He could taste the soft sweetness of her skin on his lips and the yearning to taste more of her invoked a whole host of complicated feelings inside of him.

'You're welcome,' she whispered.

'See you soon,' Ned said, as he grabbed hold of Lawson's hand and tugged.

With a final nod of his head, he turned and walked with Ned over to his ute. He climbed inside and, as he started the vehicle, lifted a hand to wave goodbye, but Meg had already gone back inside.

* * *

Later that night, when Ned had fallen asleep in front of the TV while watching *Minions* and been half-carried, half-led off to bed, Lawson sat out on the front verandah with Tabitha, each of them nursing a beer.

She dropped her knitting in her lap for a moment to take a sip of her beer. 'So,' she said, when she picked it back up, jammed the stationary needle under her short arm and started the next line, 'are you going to tell me about your day?'

Lawson raised an eyebrow. Over dinner Ned had given an elaborate account of their afternoon—what Meg had made for lunch, the water fiasco, the jelly slice, the Uno, the exploring of the house. 'I thought you heard it all from Ned.'

'Yes, and reading between the lines he has quite a little crush on your new friend, but to be honest, I'm more interested in *your* feelings. You've been very quiet this evening.'

'That's because I couldn't get a word in with Ned.' He took another gulp of beer, but it didn't bring its usual satisfaction.

'Well, Ned isn't here now,' Tab said pointing her knitting around the verandah as if to prove her point, 'and I'm all ears. Tell me about this Meg. And don't give me any bullshit—this is me you're talking to—and I can tell she's got under your skin.'

He sighed long and hard. 'I like her, Tab.'

'I knew it!' Her voice pierced the otherwise silent night air as she cracked a smile and leaned forward in her seat. '*And?*'

'And what?'

She rolled her eyes and shook her head. '*And ...* what is it you like so much about her?'

Heat rushed to his cheeks as he recalled seeing her nipples through her wet top. Hopefully the dim lighting under the verandah meant Tab didn't notice because there were certain things he didn't want to admit to his little sister.

But it wasn't just a physical thing with Meg.

He liked the way she laughed and the non-condescending way she interacted with Ned. Her competitiveness during Uno had turned him on almost as much as the wet-T-shirt episode had. Her cooking not only made his taste buds sing but satisfied his soul, and it wasn't the only thing she was good at—the progress she'd made on the house in such a short time showed she had plenty of skills in other areas. He admired the guts she obviously possessed to be able to move to a near-deserted town and her ambition to start a business there, which wouldn't be an easy feat. He found her interest in rather than fear of the possibility of a ghost fascinating, so much so that she'd made him contemplate the existence of something he definitely hadn't believed in before.

And maybe all these things were what terrified him so much. Physical attraction—however surprising—he could deal with, but actually liking another woman enough that he wanted to spend time with her felt like a massive betrayal to Leah.

'Earth to Lawson!' Tab waved her knitting needles at him. 'We're supposed to be having a conversation here.'

'I'm sorry. What was the question again?'

She chuckled. 'What's Meg like?'

'She's kinda quiet, but interesting. She's got these plans to start a tea room in the old building and sell local art and craft there as well.'

'Sounds like quite an ambition. Most people who want to start a business would choose somewhere a little more populated.' Tab took another sip of her beer. 'I wonder if she'd like to sell my ice-cream in her shop?'

'She's a long way from opening, but that's a good idea. You should ask her.'

'Maybe I will. I must admit I'm itching to meet the woman who can make you blush.'

Dammit. She'd noticed. He blushed again and Tabitha laughed. 'So, what else did you talk about?'

He told her about the mention of a possible ghost and about how Meg had lost all her family at once in a horrible fire. 'She was close to her mum's parents, but then they died close together as well recently.'

'Geez, that's a lot of crap for one person to deal with. But surely she had friends to help her through it. Did she mention a boyfriend?'

Lawson shook his head. He'd been desperate to ask this and so many other questions, but Meg came across as a very private person and, at the risk of sounding like a journalist or a detective and scaring her off, he'd swallowed almost all of them.

'Never mind. That'll give you something to talk about next time you see her.'

When he didn't say anything, Tab added, 'When *are* you going to see her again?'

'I don't know. We didn't make any arrangements.' And he'd been kicking himself ever since.

'So, you had lunch at her place and then left without so much as offering to repay the favour and have her out here for a meal?' Tab shook her head. 'Lawson, Lawson, Lawson, where are your manners?'

'I was flustered,' he admitted. Why didn't the woman have a mobile phone? Then he could send her a casual text thanking her for lunch and asking if she wanted to grab a bite to eat in the café again one day. The thought made his heart race and his palms sweat, longing and nerves whirling together.

'It's understandable that you feel unsure about this,' Tab said, nodding at his hand. He looked down and realised he was twisting his wedding ring again. 'It's a big move thinking about seeing someone new, but you're allowed to feel attracted to someone else. Hell, you're even allowed to fall in love again.'

A bitter taste came into his mouth at this alien thought.

Tab smiled at him. 'Leah was one of the best women I've ever known—she was loving, kind, warm, generous and selfless, which means I know she'd want you to be happy. See where things go with Meg, have a little bit of fun. I'm sure Leah would want you to be having fun.'

Oh Leah. Why did you have to go and get yourself killed?

Everything would have been so much easier if she were still there. He wouldn't be a single dad and he wouldn't have to contemplate whether or not he was ready to start dating again.

'In fact,' Tab added, her tone wary, 'do you think perhaps it's time you took that ring off?'

He ignored her question and instead tried to think of a pretext to drop by Meg's place again. Unwittingly, he'd already used the old 'flat tyre' excuse and he couldn't exactly buy her another puppy.

'I know!' He leaned forwards, excited. 'Meg's got all this junk piled up on her back verandah that she needs to take to the tip. I could go over and offer to help her with it.'

'Yeah,' Tab nodded her head slowly, 'taking a woman to the tip. That's a great date. You *are* out of practice, aren't you?'

He sighed and flopped back in the chair. 'To be fair, I don't think I was ever *in* practice.'

She snorted and took a sip of her beer.

'Well, Miss Dating Expert,' he asked. 'What do *you* suggest?'

'Hey, I may not go on many dates ...' When he raised an eyebrow, she clarified '... okay, *any* dates, but I'm a woman and I know if I wanted to get to know a guy better, a trip to the local tip would be pretty much at the bottom of my list. Why not go over there one lunch time with a picnic basket?'

'No. Way too romantic. I just want to get to know her a bit better but I don't want to give her the wrong idea.'

'And what would that be? That you think she's hot and want to get in her pants?'

'Tabitha!'

'Forgive me for straight-talking, big brother, but that's what two people do these days when they like each other.'

He shrugged one shoulder, feigning a nonchalance he didn't feel. 'That may be a fact but I have no idea if Meg feels anything for me anyway.'

And he didn't want to embarrass himself (or her) by making a move if she didn't. Then there was the worry that he was so out of practice that if he and Meg did take things to the next level, he'd not be able to last long enough to bring her any pleasure. He shifted in his seat at the thought.

Not a concern he planned on voicing to his sister.

'Then find out,' Tab urged. 'I'm not suggesting you propose to the woman—but if you enjoy her company, then make the time to get to know her better, take things slowly and if something more than friendship develops, well, that's a bonus.'

'What about Ned?'

'What about him?' She shrugged. 'It's obvious he likes Meg almost as much as you do.'

'That's exactly what worries me. Where will it leave him if he gets attached to her and things don't work out? I don't want to get his hopes up.'

'Then don't.' As usual Tab was the voice of reason. 'Get to know her separately to Ned as well and then when he's around make sure you keep things purely platonic until you're certain they're going places—that way it's only your heart on the line. And Meg's. But you two are both adults and sometimes you have to take risks to reap rewards.'

She yawned and put down her knitting. 'All this serious talk is making me tired. I think I'm going to call it a night. Unless there's anything else you need to get off your chest?'

He shook his head and lifted his beer to his mouth but found it empty. It was only just after nine pm but that was practically midnight to a dairy farmer, so instead of another drink he opted for bed as well.

'Thanks, Tab,' he said as they both pushed themselves out of their seats. 'I appreciate the chat.'

'No worries.' She closed the gap between them and hugged him hard. 'That's what little sisters are for. You can thank me by making me best man at your wedding.'

He laughed as she pulled away and picked up her knitting. 'It's a deal, although I think you might be getting a little ahead of things.'

He still wasn't sure whether he was ready, or had enough courage, to even ask Meg on a first date, never mind to get down on bended knee.

Chapter Twelve

Sunday morning after taking Cane for a run and finishing her chores, Megan forwent her crocheting and book in favour of a stroll down the road to visit Archie. Ever since Lawson had suggested checking out the Rose Hill Historical Society, it had been pretty much all she could think about—that and Lawson Cooper-Jones himself. Last night it hadn't only been the noises downstairs keeping her awake; her imagination had been far too active with thoughts of Lawson's bare chest to let her sleep. Logically she told herself it was a good thing he hadn't made arrangements for them to catch up again, but she couldn't help wishing he had.

She sighed as she clipped Cane's leash onto his collar, closed the front door behind them and started down the path towards the service station, carrying a meat pie she'd baked for Archie's lunch. It was so still and quiet in Rose Hill but as she got closer to his place she could hear the clucking of his chickens and the occasional crow of his rooster, which didn't appear to have any sense of time.

'Hello,' she called, as she let herself in through the side gate. Archie had told her to do this after her second visit as he said sometimes he got so enthralled in his painting he wouldn't notice if the petrol pumps exploded.

Buster met her and Cane with a half-hearted bark and then led them towards the back door like some kind of furry butler.

'Hello, luv,' Archie said, appearing in the doorway. His gaze dropped to the pie dish she was carrying. 'Geez, that smells good. You truly spoil me, you do.'

She smiled as she handed it to him. 'It's my pleasure, but I might have an ulterior motive today. I've come to ask you a favour.'

'Is that right?' He hit her with his weathered grin and then stepped aside to let her into his house. 'Need more dog-sitting?'

'Not this time.' She chuckled. 'I was wondering, is the old historical society building one of the ones you look after?'

He nodded. 'Yeah, it's in the original post office. Why?'

'I'm wanting to do a little research on my house and someone suggested I might find the information I'm looking for there.'

'What exactly *are* you looking for?'

She got the feeling Archie wasn't the type to believe in the supernatural but she told him anyway. 'I think there's a ghost in my building and I'd like to find some more information about her.'

As suspected, he found this highly entertaining.

'Well?' she said when he'd finally regained his composure. 'Is that a yes or a no?'

'If you want to waste your time investigating the paranormal, then go ahead.' He crossed over to his kitchen where bunches of keys hung on a row of nails and plucked one off. 'But I gotta warn ya, that building is full of old junk. The shire wouldn't let me turf any of it—now everything is covered in a layer of dust and I shudder to think how many spiders have moved in.'

'I'm not afraid of a little dirt and I can handle spiders,' she said, taking the key he offered. 'Thank you.'

'No worries. Do ya want me to keep Cane for ya while you're sniffing around there?'

'Oh, that would be great. Are you sure it's no trouble?'

'Not at all.' He gestured behind him. 'All I'm doing is a little painting.'

Megan looked over in the direction of his easel. 'Can I have a look?'

'Sure. Be my guest.'

'This is amazing,' she said a few moments later as she gazed down at a painting of Buster. 'It's almost like a photo. You have a real talent. Do you sell your work anywhere?'

He laughed as if she'd just asked if he sold his paintings in outer space. 'They're nothing special. Who'd wanna pay to have my mess hanging on their wall?' Still, the colour in his cheeks gave away the fact he was tickled by the idea.

'I'd buy one,' she said.

He laughed again and gestured to a pile of canvases leaning against one wall, which reminded her a little of her mountain of finished tea-cosies. 'Sweetheart, you can have as many as you like.'

She smiled. 'Thank you. Once I've got my house ready to hang things, I'm going to take you up on that offer. But I insist on paying you.'

He raised one bushy eyebrow. 'In that case, how much do I owe you for this pie?'

She ignored that comment—a pie and a painting were hardly the same thing—and held up the key. 'Thanks for this. If you're sure you don't mind looking after Cane, I'll go get started.'

Archie dipped his head. 'You have fun and don't get bitten by any nasty arachnids.'

Megan shuddered, and took a detour via her place to get some insect spray. She may have said she could handle spiders, but by handle, she meant covering herself in a biohazard suit and nuking a five-kilometre radius with spray.

Then, can in hand, she headed up the three steps of the tiny colonial-era building that had been the original Rose Hill post office, replaced in the late sixties by another building, which also now stood empty. When she finally managed to shove open the stiff door, a terrible smell hit her so hard she took a step backwards. She screwed up her nose at the thought of how many dead rodents could be decaying in there—never mind live ones. She should have bought air-freshener as well as insect spray.

Covering her nose, she ventured into the building and felt around for the light switch. Heavy black blinds covered the windows, but before she opened them she wanted to make sure there weren't any spider webs in her way. *Bingo*. She flicked the switch but, although it made a noise, no light was forthcoming.

'Dammit.'

Holding her breath and her arm out in front of her to alert her to any cobwebs, she crossed over to the first window, making sure not to step on any of the piles of old papers on the floor. She tugged the first blind and it shot up. The sun blinded her as it flooded into the room and the dust that had been settled for goodness knew how long puffed up in her face. She coughed and spluttered and then turned around.

'Oh. My. God.' She almost forgot about the smell, the dust and the possibility of spiders as she surveyed the scene.

Archie hadn't been kidding—the small building was jam-packed with stuff. There were tables in the middle of the room with papers scattered across them as if someone had finished working for the day and never returned. Bookshelves lined one wall with old books and various other historical relics. Faded black and white photos covered the other walls, but there were also archive boxes and piles of what looked like old newspapers all across the floor.

She wouldn't call any of this junk like Archie had but sorting through the treasure trove would be a mammoth task. It might be easier to hire a spirit medium to come take a look around her house, but she had absolutely no faith in finding any such person who was authentic. Besides, she had all the time in the world and sorting through this historical gold would be a nice break from the clearing and fixing up at her place.

'Argh!' She squealed and jumped back as something dropped from the ceiling and onto her shoulder. Archie hadn't been kidding about the spiders either. She flicked the little black creature off her and aimed the fly spray at it. Once it was drowned, she continued around the room, blasting all the corners and crevices.

Covering her nose again so as not to inhale the insect killer, Megan opened all the blinds and windows. Leaving anything still breathing to wither up and die, she dashed back to her place for a scented candle and her vacuum cleaner. Only when she went to plug it in did she realise the light bulb wasn't blown—it hadn't worked because the electricity wasn't connected any more.

Feeling defeated, she lit the candle and then pulled out an old wooden chair, scrutinised it for spiders, sat down and picked up a newspaper off the top of the nearest pile.

Rose Hill Gazette, 15 February 1969

Thinking she needed a much earlier edition, she almost discarded the newspaper, but then she realised she had no idea how old her ghost was. Or rather how long ago said ghost had died. She didn't have a name or anything to go on except that the person had obviously had something to do with the old general store, so she guessed that was where she needed to concentrate her efforts.

The question was, she thought, as she once again surveyed her surroundings, where the hell was she supposed to start?

Chapter Thirteen

Lawson rapped on the door of the old general store and then stood back, his stomach churning as he waited for Meg to answer it. He expected to hear Cane bark and then the approach of footsteps, but after the echo of his knock died down he was met with only silence. A tiny part of him felt relieved—he'd attempted to make further contact with Meg but she wasn't there. Perhaps this was fate's way of telling him it wasn't meant to be.

But a *much* bigger part of him felt bitter disappointment.

He'd thought about little but her since driving out of Rose Hill on Saturday afternoon; however, due to a combination of wanting to play things cool and being paralysed with nerves, he'd waited three full days before venturing to Rose Hill again. All the way there he'd been going over and over in his head what he could say to her but the thought had never crossed his mind that Meg might not be here when he arrived.

Perhaps she's in the shower and can't hear me. That prospect brought a visual that left him more hot and bothered than if he were standing out beneath the scorching midday sun. No, if she were in the shower, Cane would still be inside to bark his head off at the sound of an intruder.

An intruder! Could something bad have happened to her?

Panic quickened Lawson's heart rate as he deliberated for all of two seconds before trying the door knob. Finding it locked, he attempted to peer in through the ridiculously dirty glass, but he couldn't see a damn thing. While he didn't want to intrude on Meg's privacy, he ventured further round the side and saw a rusty hatchback sitting out of sight.

So where is she?

As his anxiety gathered momentum, he told himself there had to be a simple explanation. She was taking Cane for a walk. *In the middle of a hot summer day?* Or she was visiting Archie again. But even as he reasoned that, he started having visions of her lying on the floor injured, or worse, having been taken advantage of: a single woman all alone in such a place.

As he glanced around for something to break a window, he looked down the street and his anxiety eased when he saw the door of the old historical society wide open. He'd been too focused on getting to Meg's place to notice the open door on his way into town.

A slow smile spread across his face at the realisation Meg must have taken his suggestion to do some research there. He started jogging across the road towards the building—his worry that something may have happened to her had all but eradicated his nerves and now he just wanted to see that she was okay.

He found her sitting amongst a pile of old newspapers, books and boxes, so engrossed in whatever she was reading that she didn't even look up as he arrived in the doorway. A serious expression creased her brow and her long hair was tied up in a ponytail—the first time he'd seen it all off her face, giving him full view of her pale, slender neck. *Man, she's gorgeous.* He couldn't remember the last time he'd been so happy to see someone other than Ned. He let out the breath he'd been holding as relief poured through him, but with such relief came the knowledge that opening his heart to someone again would also open him up to the possibility of more loss, more heartache and more grief.

He barely knew Meg yet already the thought of something bad happening to her terrified him. If he were sensible he'd retreat now—sneak away again without her ever knowing he'd been there. But, as much as he didn't want to go through the loss of a loved one ever again, spending time with Meg had made him feel more alive than he had in a very long time and he liked the feeling. He didn't want to spend the rest of his time on earth not living because he was too scared of getting hurt. And he guessed Tab was right—Leah wouldn't have wanted that either.

He cleared his throat. 'Hi, Meg.'

Her head snapped up and she pressed the faded newspaper against her chest. 'Oh my goodness. You scared me half to death.'

'I'm sorry.' He took a step into the building, which looked like something out of an office horror movie—*Revenge of the Dust Motes.* 'I didn't mean to.'

'What are you doing here?' She didn't sound disappointed, just surprised.

'I came to help you with your junk.'

'My *junk*?'

He silently cursed—Tab would be laughing her head off if she were a fly on the wall right now—and swallowed. She'd been right, the tip idea was ridiculous, but in lieu of a better plan he tried to explain. 'What I meant was I thought you might like some help with all that clutter on your verandah. I could get rid of most of it for you in a ute load to the tip.'

'Oh.' She blinked and wiped a hand over her brow. It *was* stinking hot in there. 'Thanks. That's really kind of you.'

'I saw the door open here and guessed you must be doing some research.' He gestured to the newspaper in her hand. 'But I can see you're busy, so if now's not a good time I can go, or maybe I can clear the rubbish without you.' Although the latter would defeat the purpose of going on this trip to the tip specifically in order to get to know her better. Realising he was babbling—it had been so much easier talking to Meg when Ned was with him—he shut his mouth and glanced around. In addition to the newspapers and books and stuff there was so much dust, and cobwebs, and a smell that surely couldn't be good for her health.

As if reading his mind, she said, 'I've tried to air the place by opening the windows in the mornings and I've swept and dusted a bit, but the electricity isn't connected so I haven't been able to vacuum and, to be honest, I keep getting distracted by all this information.' She held the newspaper she'd been reading out to him. 'Check out some of the articles in here. It's hard to believe they are describing Rose Hill. It sounds like it was once such a thriving community.'

He took the newspaper and glanced down at the photos of some local ladies all done up for the races—dresses just past their knees, pearls around their necks and boater hats they were holding tightly to stop from flying off in the breeze. 'I remember my grandma mentioning that when she was a girl they used to come to Rose Hill for the races every January. Looks like it was lots of fun.'

'Is your grandma still alive?'

'Yep. Although she's not very well, so she lives in the local nursing home.' He leaned back against one of the tables. 'Have you found anything useful yet?'

She sighed. 'If you mean to do with my ghost … not one tiny thing. I decided to start with these old newspapers because I figured if there'd been a tragic accident or a murder, it'd be reported in the local newspaper, but I keep getting distracted by other articles.'

He forced a laugh, despite the fact the words *tragic accident* and *murder* had his mind skipping to Leah. Yep—her death had been all over the papers, but that wasn't something he liked talking about.

'Far out, it's hot in here,' he said, lifting his shirt a little as it was starting to stick to his skin. 'It feels even hotter than it is outside.'

'I know.' Meg picked up a bottle beside her and sighed. 'I'd offer you some water but it looks like I've already drunk it all. I've been coming in here early in the morning and then leaving when it gets hot the last few days, but I lost track of time today. All this history is fascinating but it's a massive time-suck.'

'You need a fan in here at least.'

She shrugged one shoulder. 'Even if I had one, it wouldn't be good without electricity.'

'Ah, right.'

'Did you really come all the way over here to help me get rid of my junk?' she asked, a twinkle in her eye.

He nodded, suddenly realising he could have used the simple excuse of bringing back her Tupperware.

'Well, in that case,' she pushed herself to a stand, 'let's get out of here.'

He blinked, way more excited by the prospect of a trip to the tip than he should have been. 'You're finished here?'

'I don't know if I'll ever be finished, but I'm not going to look a gift horse in the mouth. If you and your ute are available for a tip run, then I'll be eternally grateful. Who knows how long it'll take me on my own?'

'The good thing is my ute has air conditioning,' he told her.

She half-moaned as she wiped her brow with the back of her hand again. 'Now you're talking.'

As they stepped outside, Meg locked the door behind them and Lawson noticed something was missing. Or rather someone.

'Where's Cane?' he asked, surprised he hadn't noticed the absence of the hyperactive pup before now.

'He's with Archie,' she explained. 'He offered to look after him while I sort through this stuff, so he's been spending a few hours there the last few days. I think Buster, Archie's old dog, is secretly becoming quite fond of Cane and he's definitely teaching him some manners.' She glanced at her watch. 'I really lost track of time today. Poor Archie. Do you mind if I go grab him now?'

'Of course not. Do you want me to come or shall I start loading the ute?'

She rubbed her lips together a few moments as if contemplating the options. 'I'll walk back with you first and grab some cookies for Archie and then I'll go get Cane.'

He nodded and, as they started walking towards the general store, Lawson was all too aware of Meg's hand swinging beside him. He fought the urge to reach out and hold it.

'Who taught you to cook?' he asked, in an effort to distract himself. As much as his hormones berated him, he planned on taking things slow with Meg and getting to know her better before complicating their relationship. He didn't just have himself to think about these days.

'My mum and my Granny Rose. They were always baking something or other. My brother and I would play this game when we walked home from school, trying to guess what Mum would have cooked for afternoon tea. There was always some cake or biscuit or slice. Did your mum cook?'

'Of course.' He smiled, thinking fondly of his mother. 'She was your typical country farmer's wife—she was busy from before dawn till after dusk. She worked on the dairy with Dad, volunteered on every local committee, looked after us and still managed to have a clean house and a home-cooked meal on the table every night. I blame her for the fact I'm totally hopeless in the kitchen.'

'You can't cook?'

'I didn't say that. I make a mean beans on toast, my cheese jaffles are to die for and, unless you're a fussy Irish bugger, I'm great on the barbecue too.'

'Fussy Irish bugger?' she asked, her tone amused.

He told her about Ethan and the fact he thought Aussies couldn't barbecue to save their lives.

'He sounds like quite a character.'

'That is an understatement,' he said as they arrived at her place.

Meg opened the door and the moment they stepped inside they were hit by a waft of cool air. Their gazes met and he raised an eyebrow. These old buildings were built to keep the heat out much better than modern buildings, but this was a different kind of cold and Lawson shivered.

'I honestly believe there's someone here,' Meg said on a sigh. 'I just wish we knew her name at least.'

'We'll find it,' he said. It was hard to stand there, feel that presence and not believe. He found himself as curious as Meg. 'You know, I could ask my grandma if she remembers any tragic deaths in Rose Hill. She's eighty-four—if it happened in her lifetime I guarantee she'll know about it, and even if your ghost was before her time, she might have heard of something.'

'Would you?' She rubbed her hands up and down her arms—they'd gone from sweltering to goose bumps in less than ten seconds. 'Thank you.'

'You're welcome.' The best thing about this idea was that whether or not Gran had any information he'd have the perfect excuse to come back.

'I'll go get some cookies for Archie and then I'd better collect Cane. Can I get you a cool drink or anything?'

'A glass of water would be great.'

They went into the kitchen and, while Lawson poured them both drinks from a jug in the fridge, she piled some delicious-smelling chocolate chip cookies into a container. He couldn't help but inhale deeply at the scent. She caught him, laughed and tossed one through the air towards him.

'Thanks.' He caught it and took a bite, marvelling that it tasted even better than it smelled. 'What's your secret?' he asked when he'd finished a mouthful.

She held Archie's container close to her chest. 'What do you mean?'

'The cookies. They look like simple chocolate chip but they taste way better than any cookie I've ever had before.'

She grinned at the compliment and cocked her head to one side. 'I could tell you but ...'

'Then you'd have to kill me?'

She laughed. 'Something like that. I'd better get these to Archie.'

He nodded and resisted the urge to beg her for another. 'Is everything outside at the end of the verandah for the tip?'

'Yep. I've kept anything I think that might be good enough to donate to the Salvos or use here in one of the spare rooms.'

'Righto. I'll get started then.'

As Meg headed up the street to collect Cane, Lawson went outside to assess the clutter. Most of it was pieces of broken furniture, rotten rugs and shelving obviously left over from the general store. He was carrying the second load round the house and tossing it onto the back of his ute when she and Cane returned.

'Wow—you work fast,' she said as Cane yanked on the lead in his efforts to get to him.

Lawson smiled and placed a three-legged chair on the tray. If he wanted to prolong his time in Meg's company he should probably be less efficient. 'Hey there, little guy.' He bent down and ruffled Cane's fur as the pup jumped up at his knees. Then he looked back to Meg. 'Is *all* this stuff left over from the previous owners?'

She nodded. 'I was so eager to move in, I stupidly agreed to clear it all out myself. Of course I didn't realise just how big a job it was and that all this stuff was hiding just how much the building is in dire need of improvement. Rookie mistake, I guess.'

'It's not as bad as it looks,' he said, trying to encourage her.

She laughed. 'I like your positive attitude. I also like a challenge. I'll just tie Cane up while we load the ute.'

For the next twenty minutes they walked back and forth from the back verandah to his ute carrying armloads of stuff, smiling and making small talk as they passed each other en route. Loading junk onto his ute should not be so much fun—he was almost disappointed when they could no longer fit anything else in.

And then he remembered he still had the drive to the tip and back to look forward to.

Chapter Fourteen

Megan's hand shook as she clicked her seatbelt into place. What was she thinking spending time alone with Lawson? The heat had gone to her head and, if she were honest, the idea of a little bit of human company after all that history stuff had been too good to resist. A little voice in her head asked her if she'd feel the same if the company was Adeline's, but she told said voice to take a hike.

It soon became apparent that her nerves at being alone with Lawson in the confined space of his ute were unwarranted. For *one*, it was only a ten-minute drive to the tip, which he told her was located almost exactly in the middle of the three towns that made up the shire of Walsh—not that Rose Hill classified as a town any more. For *two*, Cane sat squished between them as chaperone and 'sat' wasn't really the right word. He bounced around so much Megan worried he might wet himself with the excitement of a new adventure. For *three*, they managed to find plenty to talk about, starting with her teasing him about his music tastes. The moment he'd turned the key in the ignition, the Dixie Chicks blasted from the stereo and it was on a CD, not the radio.

'Nothing wrong with country music,' he argued, as, still laughing, she'd rifled through his glovebox to find a whole host of similar CDs, many of which were bands she'd never heard of. She wondered if they'd been favourites of his wife.

'Who are The Sunny Cowgirls?' she asked, as she glanced down at the photo of two blonde beauties.

'A couple of Aussie sisters. They grew up on a farm somewhere in Victoria I think and their lyrics about living in rural Australia are spot on. And funny.'

She raised an eyebrow.

'Hey, don't mock 'em until you've tried 'em,' he said, nodding towards the stereo.

Megan replaced the Dixie Chicks with a song called 'Drinking Down Our Pay'. She couldn't help laughing as she listened to the lyrics and had to concede their sound wasn't at all that bad either.

'What kind of music do you listen to?' Lawson asked, as Cane finally settled down with his head in her lap.

She stroked his fur absentmindedly. 'I'm more a rock kinda girl. A little alternative though.' Truth be told she'd lost track of what some of her favourite groups were doing the last few years, and since she'd been in Rose Hill, she'd been listening mostly to talkback on the ABC. She hoped he wouldn't ask her to name any recent hits.

'What? Bands like Muse? Stone Roses? The Wombats? Or are we talking Red Hot Chili Peppers?'

'I'm impressed.'

'Just because I like a little bit of country and pop, doesn't mean I can't appreciate other types of music. I'm an all rounder.'

Somehow talk of music turned to talk of TV shows and by the time they arrived at the tip, Megan had discovered they had more in common than she'd initially imagined.

'Well, here we are,' Lawson said, winding down his window to speak to the guy who ran the place. 'Hey, Tommo. Just got a load of general rubbish.'

'Don't we have to pay?' Megan asked as they drove on.

'Yes, but I've got an annual pass.'

'I can't ask you to pay for me,' she said, feeling nervous and uneasy all over again.

'Relax,' he said as he search for somewhere to park, 'I've already paid for the pass and you using it won't stop me using it later.'

Knowing that objecting too much would be rude, Megan swallowed and said, 'Thank you.'

They climbed out, leaving Cane in the ute, as there was no safe place to hook his leash on the ground. He whined while they unloaded the tray, poking his head out the half-open window and giving them puppy dog eyes every time they walked past, so they gave him a quick walk around the ute when they were done.

'This is heaven for him,' Megan said as he sniffed at something on the ground.

'It's heaven to Ned as well.' He smiled as he mentioned his son.

'Really?'

'Yep. Ned is a little bit of a hoarder,' he said as they got back into the ute. 'One man's junk is definitely his treasure—he likes to make things out of old stuff he finds, so I tend to try and do any tip runs when he's not around, or we're liable to bring home more than we dump.'

'How is Ned?' she asked, as she picked up the water bottles she'd brought and handed one to him.

'He's good,' he said and then took a long sip.

'No more problems at school, then?' Megan asked and then drank from her bottle, relishing the cool liquid as it slid down her throat. She clicked her seatbelt into place and grabbed hold of Cane as he tried to climb onto Lawson's lap.

Lawson shook his head. 'It's only been a few days, but he hasn't said anything again and he seems happy enough. I think the kids who teased him are not feeling very settled about their own family life. Their parents are in the middle of a messy break-up, but still no excuse to tease Ned about his mum though. He already beats himself up a bit that he can't remember her.'

This was Megan's chance to ask about his wife. 'How old was he when his mother died?'

'He'd just turned four.'

A lump formed in her throat. 'That's heart-wrenching,' she said. 'For you and him.'

'I won't pretend it was a walk in the park but without Ned I don't think I'd have coped well at all.' Although he had his hands on the steering wheel, he lifted his fingers slightly and glanced down at his ring. It was clear he still struggled with his loss and she resisted the urge to reach over and place her hand on his in a show of comfort.

'How long had you been married?' She wanted to ask if it had been a shotgun wedding, but bit her tongue, unsure if she'd already crossed an invisible line.

He took a moment and then said, 'Five years.'

Not a shotgun wedding. 'Wow, you must have got married young.'

Although Lawson kept his eyes on the road ahead, she glanced over and saw his expression tinged with sadness. 'I'm sorry,' she rushed. 'It's none of my business. You don't have to talk about it if you don't want to.'

'We met in high school. Her family moved to town when we were both fifteen and I knew from the moment Leah walked into the classroom she was special. She was my first love, first a lot of things.' He blushed as he said this, which Megan found endearing. 'She didn't start out a country girl but she grew into one and loved hanging out on the farm. She was so full of life and good at schoolwork, but also loved sport. It sounds stupid now that I'm older, but I proposed on her eighteenth birthday. Everyone thought we were insane getting hitched so young and then when Ned came along, my mates joked that my life was over.'

But it was clear from his voice and the smile on his face when he talked about his wife that he hadn't given a damn what they'd thought and he'd probably do it all over again if he got the chance.

'She sounds like she was a very special person,' Megan said.

'She was.' He cleared his throat and glanced again at his ring finger before looking up and flashing her a smile. 'What about you?'

'What about me?' Megan asked, her heart seizing up a little. She felt much more comfortable talking about *his* life.

'You been married before?'

She snorted.

He laughed. 'I'll take that as a no; but you must have had some significant other in your past. You can't have got to—what are you? twenty-five?—without some smart guy trying to have his wicked way.'

Some *wicked* guy would be more accurate. She shuddered when she thought about how much of herself and how much of her life she'd given to such a man. The only consolation was that he'd somehow managed to overdose in prison a year later and would therefore never be on the streets again to hurt more innocent people. Or come after her.

'Good guess. I am twenty-five,' she said, trying to keep her voice light, 'and despite my grand old age, I haven't had any great romances in my life. How old are you?'

'I'm almost thirty but some days I feel like I'm about a hundred and five.'

She laughed, totally able to relate. The things she'd experienced aged a girl, so that she doubted now she'd have much in common with women her own age, even if she had such friends.

'However, today, hanging out with you, I don't feel quite so old. Thanks for entertaining me for a few hours,' he said and she glanced out the window and saw they were almost back in Rose Hill.

Although the mood on the return journey had been more sober than on the way to the tip, Megan had enjoyed every second of her afternoon with Lawson. 'You have a strange idea of fun,' she joked, 'but I'm grateful for that. It'll be nice to be able to sit out on the back verandah without having to look at all that junk.'

'Once you've done more clearing, I'll be happy to help again,' he said as he pulled into the kerb at the front of her house.

Taking hold of Cane's leash, she turned in her seat to look at Lawson. 'Want to come in for a drink before you go?' She justified the invitation by telling herself it was wrong not to ask after the good deed he'd done her. And now she knew he was still head-over-heels for his wife, perhaps it wasn't so dangerous to get to know him better.

He deliberated a moment and she swore he wanted to say yes, but finally he shook his head. 'I've got to get back to work, but are you planning on doing more research in the historical society?'

'Yes.' As daunting as the task seemed, she didn't plan on stopping until she'd found information about her housemate.

'Then I've got a generator I can lend you, which will give you enough power to vacuum up all that dust. It can't be healthy breathing it all in. And it'll also mean you can either plug in a fan during the day, or make the lights work so you can go there when it's cooler in the evening.'

'Oh, that would be wonderful. Are you sure you can do without it?' The thought made her happy not only because it would make her research so much more pleasant, but also because it meant she'd see him again. 'Would you like me to come to your place to pick it up?'

Lawson shook his head. 'It's quite heavy and dirty. I'll get Ethan to help me. Would it be okay to drop it round tomorrow?'

'Of course.' It wasn't as if she had a full diary. She planned on taking Cane into Bunbury for his second lot of vaccinations soon, but aside from that, her schedule was a blank canvas.

'Awesome. I'll see you both then.' And with that he reached out and ruffled Cane's fur. Megan watched his fingers as he did so and couldn't help imagining what it might feel like to have them touching her.

'Yep, see you then,' she said, grabbing hold of Cane and opening the car door before this very sexy, very lovely man noticed her blushing.

Chapter Fifteen

Feeling a little deflated, Megan headed back from the historical society to her house just before midday on Friday.

'Nothing yet,' she called into the seemingly empty house as she closed the door behind Cane and herself. 'Want to give me any hints? Any clues where to look?'

When there was no reply—no wafts of air brushing past her, no strange noises, no doors opening and closing—she laughed at herself. Maybe her search was futile. Was she imagining a presence that wasn't really there because she was desperate for company?

Perhaps that was her other reason for being in a funk today. Lawson had, as promised, delivered her the generator the day before and they'd spent another lovely few hours together. He'd set it up for her, helped vacuum and dust and, just like the tip-stuff the day before, cleaning had never been so much fun. When they were finished and the historical society no longer required a warning sign on its door, they'd shared a cool drink and more bickies. He'd kissed her on the cheek when he left—the kind of kiss he'd give his grandmother or his sister—but that simple gesture had made every last inch of her quiver.

He hadn't made plans to come back and see her. This was a good thing, so why had she spent all night, lying in bed, trying to come up with ways to engineer another meeting?

Annoyed at herself, she shook her head as she headed down the hallway. She let Cane out to go and dig holes in the yard—luckily she didn't really have a garden for him to destroy—and then she headed into the kitchen to throw something together for lunch. Cooking usually brought her immense joy, but today she couldn't be bothered to put much effort in simply for herself, so a toastie would have to suffice.

As she waited for her sandwich to toast, someone rapped on her front door and she almost jumped out of her skin. It took a second for her heart to jumpstart itself and then it raced off with the thought that maybe Lawson had come back. Perhaps he had news from his grandmother about significant deaths in Rose Hill. Ridiculous hope filling her heart, she ran a hand through her hair and then whipped her lipgloss out of her pocket. Already at the front door, Cane jumped up at it and barked as she walked towards it. She paused momentarily to glance in the hallway mirror, apply said gloss and pinch her cheeks to make her look less like a corpse.

Since Lawson's second unexpected drop-in, she'd started making more of an effort with her appearance in the morning. Nothing OTT but she made sure her T-shirts matched her shorts, she actually brushed her hair and may have started using tinted moisturiser as well.

Yet, as she approached the door her heart sank: she could tell from the silhouette—just visible through all the dirt on her still un-cleaned glass—that it wasn't him, or Archie. They were both over six foot and this figure was much closer to her own five and a half.

Could it be Adeline again?

She cringed at the thought, but then noticed that this person had much darker hair. The knock sounded again. Whoever it was, they were damn persistent.

Megan contemplated not answering but if she could see the shadow of her visitor, then likely they could see her as well. She opened the door a fraction, ready to send whoever this was on their way.

'Hello,' said the brunette as Cane jumped at her. She laughed and bent down to stroke him. 'Cute dog.'

Damn puppy is a pathetic guard dog, Megan thought for the umpteenth time as she scrutinised the woman. There was something vaguely familiar about her but she couldn't put her finger on it.

'I'm Tabitha Cooper-Jones. Lawson's sister.' The woman offered out her hand, which Megan accepted as her words registered. Lawson and this woman had the same deep brown eyes.

'I'm sorry to just drop by like this,' she continued, 'but I thought it was time to meet the mystery woman my brother and nephew can't stop talking about.'

Megan took an instant liking to Tabitha and not simply because what she said about Lawson made her pulse race with excitement. She also had a warm, genuine smile that reached right to her eyes and she only had *one arm*. Megan tried not to stare, searching her mind for any recollection of Lawson ever mentioning this. He'd spoken fondly of how capable his sister was and said she'd been through some tough times but surely she'd have remembered if he'd said Tabitha was an amputee.

'Well, hi there,' she managed, forcing herself to look at Tabitha's face rather than her arm. 'It's lovely to meet you.'

Tabitha laughed and lifted the stump that finished where her elbow should be. 'I'm guessing Lawson didn't mention he calls me the one-armed bandit?'

Megan swallowed and shook her head. 'I'm sorry—I didn't mean to stare.'

'Ah, don't worry about it. People always do at first.' She glanced down at the arm in question and then looked back up to Megan. 'When I was sixteen I had a lump there about the size of a golf ball but our local doc thought it was tennis elbow, so I popped a hell of a lot of painkillers and kept going about my business. Then one day a year later, I went to see a locum and he sent me off for scans. Turns out my tennis elbow was actually a sarcoma. A surgeon tried to remove it, but said it could come back. He was right and just after my eighteenth birthday, I had my amputation.'

Holy shit. What did you say to a story like that? She didn't think such medical misdemeanours as Tabitha had described could happen in this day and age. *I'm sorry* seemed vastly unsatisfactory.

'It's okay,' Tabitha said, as if she could sense Megan's discomfort. 'I was one of the lucky ones. This type of cancer only ever attacks females under twenty-one and the poor girl that was diagnosed right after me passed away. I may only have one arm, but at least I'm alive, right?'

'Yeah, of course. Would you like to come in for a drink?'

'Thanks. That would be great.' Tabitha pulled a paper bag out from where it had been wedged under her arm and held it high out of Cane's reach. 'I brought lunch. I don't know if you've had a chance to sample the wares of the Walsh bakery yet, but their sausage rolls are to-die-for.'

Cane whimpered and Megan smiled. 'They certainly smell like it. Come on in.'

As Tabitha stepped inside, Megan closed the door behind them and then led her down the hallway.

'This is such a great old building,' Tabitha said, glancing up and around her as they walked.

'You've never been here before? Lawson said he remembers the shop from when he was a kid.'

Tabitha shook her head. 'There's five years between us and although we might have come when I was little, the general store closed before I was old enough to remember.'

In the kitchen, Megan got out two plates and put them on the table. As she went to the fridge to fetch drinks, Tabitha put the sausage rolls onto the plates and exclaimed at all the tea-cosies.

'Oh wow, these are gorgeous,' she said, reaching out and picking up a black one that had bright yellow sunflowers as a decoration. 'You make them?'

Megan nodded as she sat down at the table, waiting for Tabitha to make her feel silly like Adeline had. 'Crocheting relaxes me.'

'Me too,' Tabitha said, 'although I'm nowhere near as good as this. And you must be fast too.'

It wasn't the compliment that stuck with Megan. 'You crochet too?' she asked, failing dismally at hiding her incredulity.

Tabitha laughed—she was clearly such a good-natured person. 'Yes, not only a one-armed bandit but a one-armed crocheter. Among other things. I knit more than I crochet though. It took me a while to get used to it—learning to tie shoelaces again required a lot of patience and putting on bras was a challenge for a few years—but I'm a pro these days. The only thing I truly miss from my two-armed days is playing the guitar.'

Megan's heart squeezed. 'Had you played since you were a kid?'

Tabitha nodded. 'Mum played it too. And the keyboard. She was an awesome singer as well and I used to help her round the farm and the kitchen and we'd always be singing something. She taught me to play the basics of the guitar but when she got sick and couldn't do it any more, Dad paid for professional lessons.'

'Did you play yourself or in a group?' Megan felt a little rude asking all these questions, but it seemed better than offering sympathy. Tabitha didn't seem the type to want pity.

'Ever heard of Ryder O'Connell?' Tabitha smiled as she said this. Everyone had heard of Ryder O'C. He was only the most successful male solo musical artist in Australia at the moment. Or she should say *from* Australia, as he'd made it big time overseas as well.

'Of course. Why?'

'Before he went solo, he was in a duo with me. He was the brother of one of the girls I went to school with in Perth and we kinda had a thing. On *and* off stage.'

'No way. You and Ryder were a couple?'

'Ah ha.' Tabitha cocked her head to one side. 'It's my claim to fame. I thought we were in love, but Ryder couldn't cope when I lost my arm and couldn't play guitar any more. We broke up. He went solo and became a massive success without me. Guess I don't really blame him. We were only kids and who knows how long we'd have lasted or whether we'd have got anywhere in the music industry together, but it kinda sucks to have your ex-boyfriend splashed all over social media.'

'I can imagine.' Megan sympathised.

'Are you on Facebook?' Tabitha asked.

Megan shook her head.

'Me either. Waste of time if you ask me. Too many people looking at their phones instead of the world around them these days.' Tabitha spoke as if she were a senior citizen, whereas Megan knew from what Lawson had said that she was the same age as her.

They talked as they ate and Tabitha had been right about the sausage rolls. The pastry was perfectly flaky and the meat more flavoursome than usual. They lamented more about social media. Megan had to pretend she knew more about it than she did. Access to the internet was just one of the many things she'd been denied over the last few years, but unlike fresh air and freedom, she found she hadn't even missed it. They moved on to talking about the house and when Tabitha asked about the mystery ghost, Megan relayed her frustration at not finding anything so far. They whined about ex-boyfriends—Megan didn't give much away but discovered Tabitha had almost as little experience as she did.

'Most men don't know what to do with a one-armed girl-friend,' Tabitha joked, but Megan could tell this upset her more than she let on.

The conversation quickly moved on.

'Lawson said you want to open a tea room slash art and craft gallery here? I think that's a great idea.'

'Thanks.' Megan smiled, it was great to know people had faith in the idea that had landed in her head out of nowhere. Problem was, she might be able to cook and craft, but she didn't know the first thing about opening or running a business.

Finally, they gushed over Cane—who, despite trying to jump up at them and steal their lunch, they both agreed was one of the cutest dogs either of them had ever known. 'It's hard to believe someone as irritating as Adeline could breed something quite as adorable as him,' Tabitha said, feeding him the last bite of her sausage roll. 'I hear she paid you a visit.'

Megan nodded. If she liked Tabitha before, her less than glowing opinion of Adeline only made her like her more. They shared a laugh and then Tabitha said, 'I shouldn't be so cruel. She means well and she does a lot for our little town, but it's embarrassing the way she throws herself at Lawson.'

Megan swallowed, willing her cheeks not to turn beetroot at the thought of throwing *herself* at Lawson. She'd love to ask Tabitha more about him, but didn't want to sound too interested. She *was* interested, but she knew she *shouldn't* be.

'Can I get you another drink?' she asked, trying to distract her thoughts and Tabitha's.

Tabitha sighed, glanced at her watch. 'As good as that sounds and as enjoyable as chatting to you has been, I should probably head home and see to my babies.'

'Babies?' What else had Lawson left unsaid?

Tabitha smiled. 'Our calves. I feed them twice a day, and at this time of the year, there's a lot of mouths to feed. You should come out and see them some time. I challenge you not to fall in love with them.'

Falling in love with cows wasn't what Megan was worried about.

'Why don't you come one day this weekend?' Tabitha said before Megan had a chance to say anything. 'We can have a barbecue and I'll make some salads.'

Every cell in Megan's body wanted to accept this invitation but her head told her to come up with a good excuse. She liked Tabitha and her brother. Conversing with them was easier than she'd imagined, but spending more time with them could be risky. Getting close to anyone would mean she'd eventually have to open up about her past, and that thought made her chest grow tight. These lovely people likely wouldn't be so welcoming if they knew what kind of person she'd been. Their rejection would hurt, therefore it would be easier to avoid developing a friendship in the first place.

'That sounds great,' she said, offering Tabitha a regret-filled smile, 'but I'm busy this weekend.' Hearing how ridiculous that sounded to her own ears, she quickly added, 'I'm catching up with an old friend.'

She hated lying but what else could she do? This way she was protecting the Cooper-Jones family as well as herself.

Tabitha blinked. 'Oh, okay. Maybe another time. The invitation is always open.'

She stood to go and Megan had to physically restrain herself from grabbing out to hold onto her a little longer. She'd had such a fun afternoon, experiencing a glimpse of what life could be like with a good female friend.

'You know,' Tabitha said, glancing again at the pile of tea-cosies, 'this might not be your thing at all but we have these country markets in Walsh. They're usually once a month but in February we're having two because we get good crowds in the summer. Anyway, what I'm trying to say is, if you'd like to sell some of your awesome crocheted items and maybe make some pocket money, I could get you a stand for our next markets, which is not this Sunday but next.'

'You think people would want to buy my tea-cosies?' Megan asked, incredulous. The thought of selling her efforts hadn't crossed her mind.

Tabitha nodded. 'Sure they would. The market-goers love stuff like that. Do you have any teapots we could use to display them? If not, we might be able to find some in the local op shop. What do you say?'

The way Tabitha said 'we' as if they were in this together gave Megan such a buzz. She hadn't had anyone in her corner since her grandma died. And it would be nice to see her crocheting go to good homes, rather than sit gathering dust in hers. There was also the bonus of making a little cash in hand. Her tummy twisted a little at the thought of everything Tabitha's suggestion would involve—meeting and talking to new people—but she was feeling brave and found herself accepting the offer.

'Do you think I can get a table at this late notice?'

'Don't you worry about that.' Tabitha waved her hand. 'I'll sort it out and if not, you can set up at the other end of my ice-cream stall. I'll be in touch.'

Two seconds later, she spoke again. 'Hang on, did Lawson say you don't have a phone?'

Megan nodded, feeling silly about this decision and deciding she'd buy a pre-paid mobile when she went to Bunbury, which she'd do on the weekend so she hadn't been lying about being busy.

Tabitha waved dismissively again. 'Never mind. I'll sort out the table and then I'll drop by next week to confirm. Or I'll send Lawson.'

'Okay, thank you.' As much as Megan liked Tabitha, she couldn't help wishing and hoping that she would send her brother.

Oh dear … She could feel it in her bones. She was headed for trouble.

Chapter Sixteen

Lawson wasn't stupid. He knew Tabitha had given him an excuse to go visit Meg but he also had a super-duper one of his own. When he and Ned had visited his grandmother on the weekend, he'd picked her brain on the history of Rose Hill. She vaguely remembered a young woman dying tragically in a shop in Rose Hill when she was a little girl, but couldn't remember who, which shop or any of the details.

Penelope, Adeline's grandmother, had been sitting in her recliner nearby at the time. She'd made some sort of moaning noise and opened and closed her mouth as if she had something to add, but since her stroke she hadn't been able to communicate in a manner that anyone else could understand. Poor old woman; Lawson felt for her—it must be hell on earth to be stuck in a body but no longer able to control it. And he couldn't help being disappointed for himself and Meg as well—at the very respectable age of a hundred, he reckoned somewhere in the deep crevices of her mind, Penelope might have exactly the information they were looking for.

Still, his grandmother had given him a time period and it was with this knowledge that he drove excitedly to Rose Hill on

Monday morning. It had only been a few days since he'd seen Meg but he'd raced through the tasks following milking, desperate to visit her again.

When he finally arrived in Rose Hill just after ten o'clock he saw the door to the old historical society already open. He parked out the front and leaped the few steps onto the tiny verandah.

Meg smiled up at him from the floor where she sat, leaning against a desk, a massive pile of faded newspapers on either side of her. She looked even more beautiful than usual, with the pedestal fan aimed against her blowing her hair and the sun shining in through the open window, framing her head like some kind of angel. A mahogany-headed angel.

'Hi there,' she said 'Have you come to tell me yay or nay about the markets?'

'Yes,' he said a little emphatically as he stepped into the building. 'It's a yay. Tabitha has registered you for the stall next to hers. You can set up from seven-thirty and the markets open at eight. We've got a fold-up table you can borrow if you want? And Tabitha said to say she's sourced teapots.'

'Wow. That's wonderful, thank you. I've been spending the evenings crocheting some other things, so I don't only have tea-cosies to sell. But I'm scared they're a little naff.'

'People love stuff like that round here. You'll be a hit, I'm sure.'

She blushed a little, her cheeks now a few shades lighter than her hair. 'Thanks.'

'Looks like you've been busy.' He nodded towards one pile of newspapers. 'Make any breakthroughs yet?'

She sighed sadly and shook her head. 'I'm wondering if I'm wasting my time, but I can't seem to stop. I keep telling myself it's time to go home and do something productive, but then I convince myself just five more minutes.'

He grinned. 'You want some help?'

She looked sceptical. 'You've got nothing better to do than help me with my silly mission on this lovely warm day?'

In reply, he dropped to the floor beside her. Truth was he had plenty to do—with farming there was always something to do and never a chance to get bored—but despite the sweat already beading on his forehead due to the oven-like room, he couldn't think of any place he'd rather be. 'It's not a silly mission.'

'Well, thanks.' She gave him a quick smile and explained her process, starting by pointing to the smaller pile of newspapers. 'These are what I've already been through this morning and this pile is still to check.'

He picked a newspaper off the top of the un-checked pile and glanced at the date. 1944. 'I spoke to my gran on Sunday,' he said. 'She remembers a tragic death when she was a little girl, so maybe we should be looking in the late thirties. Have you found any from that era? I wonder when the paper first started?'

'In 1922, with the last edition printed in 1976, but I haven't gone through any from the thirties yet. And unfortunately I've come to realise there are a lot of issues missing. You know what amazes me?' It was obviously a rhetorical question. 'How a small town like Rose Hill had such a vibrant little newspaper. And there were so many social events happening in and out of town.'

He nodded. 'These days the community newspaper in Walsh only comes out once a month and they struggle to get content. Not that there isn't plenty happening these days; it's just nobody can be bothered reporting on it.'

'1930s, you reckon?' she said, pushing to her feet. 'I think I have a pile over here from back then.'

Standing, she arched her back in some kind of stretch, which pushed her breasts forwards, and Lawson almost swallowed his tongue. Then, oblivious to his gawking, Meg crossed the room and grabbed a stack of yellowed papers from one corner of the

room. She returned and dumped them on the wooden floorboards between them. 'Let's hope you and your grandmother are
my lucky charms.'

He grinned as he plucked a newspaper from the pile, leaned
back against the desk and got to work. The way he felt right now,
he'd be more than happy to be her lucky charm.

They sat alongside each other on the floor, reading in compan-
ionable silence and only occasionally pausing to share something
sad or amusing. Lawson's body was all too aware of how close
Meg was to him and if he had a little more guts and it wasn't so
stinking hot in here, he might have made a move, but what if he'd
read things wrong? He didn't want to freak her out. Right now
he was simply happy spending time with her and getting to know
her better. His hormones would just have to learn some patience
while he laid the groundwork.

With that thought, he discarded one newspaper and reached
for the next one.

'Bingo!' he said as his gaze came to rest on the front page heading: *FATAL TRAGEDY AT GENERAL STORE*

'What?' Meg asked, leaning towards him. Then she gasped in
excitement. 'Oh my God.'

They sat in silence a few moments reading the rest of the
article.

Then Lawson said, 'Reading between the lines, I reckon they
think she killed herself.'

Meg vigorously shook her head. 'No, it can't be. I know it
sounds like that but they've gotta be wrong. If someone commits
suicide, they've chosen to end their life and leave the earth, so
why would they linger for almost eighty years more? It doesn't
make sense.'

Lawson frowned. She had a point, but then what did he know
about the way a ghost's mind worked? Until a few weeks back,

he'd have adamantly argued that he didn't even believe in them. 'Maybe … she … changed her mind. After the event?'

Megan considered this a moment but her brow furrowed and her shoulders slumped. She'd come to have an affinity with the ghost and he could tell she didn't want to believe that her new friend had made the decision to end her life.

'How'd she die?' Megan asked.

Lawson started to read down the article. 'It says she jumped over the stair railing to her death.'

He shivered as their eyes met. He knew she too was thinking about the undeniable coolness that surrounded her stairs, but then she let out a long, deep sigh.

'It is definitely not the way I'd do it.'

'No?' He tried not to smile. 'How would you commit suicide?'

She replied without a moment's hesitation. 'I'd take an overdose of barbiturates. Most painless, hassle-free way as far as I can tell, but, if I was going to jump, it would be from a far greater height than the second floor of a building, so that I was certain of success.'

Despite the temperature in the building, a chill prickled his scalp. Even in his most darkest hour, Lawson had never contemplated taking the easy way out—perhaps because of Ned or because he knew Leah would have been so disappointed in him—but he got the feeling Meg had given it serious consideration. He wanted to know what could have happened to her to make her think of such a thing. Was it right after the deaths of her family? Just as he summoned the courage to broach this topic, his mobile rang.

He cursed silently and would have ignored it had it not been the ring tone he used for Ned's school. His heart leaped in the way it always did whenever the school called and he dug the phone out of his pocket. 'I'm sorry. This is the school. I have to answer it.'

'Of course.' She took the newspaper from him, turning her attention once again to the contents on the page.

'Hello, Lawson speaking.'

'Hi, Lawson, it's Carline Saunders, here.' *The principal?* He'd been expecting Beck again or Ned's teacher. 'I'm afraid Ned has been involved in an incident at school and has seriously hurt another student. I'm going to have to ask you come in so we can discuss this.'

He couldn't believe his ears. Ned had never been in any kind of strife at school before. 'What did he do? How serious?'

'I'd rather talk about it in person,' said the principal, making Lawson feel as if *he* had done something wrong. 'Ned is in my office now and he's distraught. Can you come as soon as possible?'

Lawson felt like he'd swallowed a brick. If Ned had hurt some other kid, he must have been provoked pretty badly and he wanted to get to the bottom of it. At the same time, he wanted to kick the corner of the desk and sulk like a two-year-old denied cookies. He and Meg had finally stumbled across something interesting and he had to leave.

'I'll be there in fifteen minutes.'

'Is everything okay?' Meg asked when he disconnected.

'No.' He shook his head as he stood. 'Ned's got into some trouble at school. I'm sorry but I have to go.'

'Of course.' She scrambled to her feet. 'I hope he's okay.'

'Thanks. So do I. See you soon.' He kissed her on the cheek, then stalked out of the building, his fingers curling into fists as he headed for the ute. Those friendly kisses were no longer enough, but now wasn't the time to try anything more.

* * *

A solemn-faced Beck led Lawson into the principal's office. She smiled sympathetically and patted his arm as she announced his arrival to Carline Saunders, before retreating quick smart.

'Good morning, Lawson.' Carline stood from behind her desk and gestured for him to sit in one of the two chairs opposite.

Ned sat in the other chair, his arms folded across his chest and a very un-Ned-like scowl on his face. He glanced quickly up at Lawson and then dropped his gaze back to his feet, which dangled over the edge of the chair.

'Hi, Ms Saunders,' Lawson managed, resisting the urge to pull Ned onto his lap as he lowered himself into the seat. 'What's going on?'

The principal sat back down, planted her elbows on the desk and then folded her hands as if she were about to pray. 'Ned and Tate Walsh got into a little bit of a disagreement today and it ended with Ned punching Tate in the face. Your son has a good swing on him, I'm afraid, and it appears he may have broken Tate's nose.'

Lawson glanced to Ned and back to the principal, opened his mouth, closed it again. He was speechless.

'And unfortunately,' Carline continued, 'Ned is refusing to apologise for his actions.'

He raised an eyebrow and turned his whole body to face his son. 'Ned? Is all this true?' It wasn't that he didn't believe Carline but he had to hear Ned's side of events.

Ned simply nodded once, none of his defensive body language lessening.

Okay, then. Lawson swallowed, feeling totally unqualified for this situation. If Leah were still alive he guessed she'd be the one sitting in that chair and she'd know how to handle this.

'I think you'll agree that no matter what happened between the two boys there is no excuse for violence,' Carline said.

Lawson nodded. 'Of course, but—'

She cut him off. 'If Ned showed some remorse, the punishment might be different, but, as things currently stand, I'm going to suspend him from school for the remainder of the week so he can think long and hard about his actions. I want the other students to get the message that violence will not be tolerated in our school.'

'You're going to suspend him? Isn't that a little harsh considering he's only eight and this is his first offence?' Lawson couldn't help feeling frustrated at what it would mean for himself. With Ned at home, he couldn't sneak off and spend time with Meg.

Carline nodded. 'Unless he's willing to apologise to Tate.'

Lawson looked to Ned again as he remembered that Tate and his brother had been the one to upset him before. 'Hang on, why did you punch Tate?'

'Cos he was teasing me about not having a mum again.' Ned sniffed. 'I'm not sorry, so I won't say I am.'

Lawson opened his mouth to address this but Carline got in first. 'I assure you, Lawson, that I do not tolerate bullying any more than I do violence and Tate will also receive a suspension for his actions, but I'm standing my ground on this decision. I don't want the other children to think this kind of behaviour is acceptable. I've asked Ned's teacher to get some work organised for him and email it to you this afternoon.'

She stood, making it clear this meeting was over, then glanced down at Ned. 'I know this is out of character for you, Ned, so I hope that when you come back to school next week we can put this unfortunate incident behind us and learn together to work out alternative ways to deal with conflict. I promise you, Lawson, that this is something we'll be focusing on with all the children, in all the classrooms. Now, I must go see Tate and his parents at the hospital.'

'Please tell the Walshes that I'm sorry,' Lawson said, silently adding that he'd be talking to them himself later. Then he grabbed Ned's hand and all but dragged him out to the car park. Anger coursed through his body—anger at Tate, anger at Ned, anger at Ms Saunders, anger at this whole damn situation.

The moment they were in the ute, he turned to Ned. 'What the hell was that about?'

Ned blinked and then started to cry. Lawson immediately felt remorse for his harsh words and tone.

'Hey, buddy.' He reached out and pulled his son into his arms. 'It'll be all right.'

He simply held him for about five minutes as Ned sobbed and then they spent the journey home having the conversation that had to be had. Ned calmed down and told Lawson that Tate and Levi just wouldn't let up about him not having a mum, how she mustn't have loved him enough to live.

'Well, that's just ridiculous logic,' Lawson said. 'What about Harry Potter's mum? She died but she loved him so much her love *saved* him. And trust me, I knew your mum better than anyone and she loved you more than God loves the whole wide world.'

Ned's lips quirked up at the edges.

Lawson decided to speak plainly. 'Look, when people do or say bad things, there's usually a reason and I think Tate and Levi are going through a bit of a tough time at home. Their parents have decided not to live together any more and Tate and Levi are probably feeling unsettled, not knowing who *they* are going to live with or what their lives will be like. That's not an excuse but bullies usually pick on people to make themselves feel better, so we should feel sorry for them and forgive them. Violence is never the answer—you know that right?'

'So have you forgiven the person who killed Mum?' Ned asked.

Lawson's grip tightened on the steering wheel and he hoped Ned didn't notice. He would never forgive that lowlife for taking Leah's life and robbing him of a wife and Ned of a mother. Hopefully he'd rot in prison before he came up for parole.

'Yes, I have,' he said, knowing that it was the right thing to say. He didn't want his anger and bitterness to affect Ned and lead him to live a resentful life. 'The man who killed your mother had big problems of his own and, although that doesn't make what he did right, it makes me realise that he didn't do it to hurt us. Losing your mother was a tragedy but what would be an even bigger tragedy would be holding onto my anger and letting it affect how I live. Your mum wouldn't have wanted that and she wouldn't have wanted you hitting Tate either.'

'I know.' Ned made a face. 'Do I have to say sorry to him?'

Lawson sighed. 'It would probably be the right thing to do, but I'm going to leave it up to you to make that decision.'

Ned nodded. 'I'll give it some thought.'

Lawson smiled at how mature his little man sounded. 'And while you're home this week,' he said, 'don't expect to be lying around playing Xbox and watching TV. When you're not doing your schoolwork, you'll be helping me around the farm.'

Ned groaned, but Lawson knew working around the dairy wasn't punishment at all in his eyes.

As he turned the ute into the farm's long gravel driveway, his phone beeped, signalling a message. He waited until he'd stopped the vehicle to check, glancing down at the unknown number as Ned leaped out.

I hope Ned is okay. I forgot to tell you I finally have a mobile now. Thanks for all your help with the ghost. Meg.

As Lawson stared at the message, he started to smile. Meg had a phone! He'd almost forgotten giving her his number that very first day, and he couldn't remember ever being so excited by a text message before. Although having her number meant he no longer had an excuse to just drop round, at least in the days ahead where he couldn't go see her because of Ned, he'd be able to message, or even phone her, to ask if she'd found anything more about the dead girl.

Any excuse to hear her voice again.

Chapter Seventeen

The next few days passed faster than all the days Megan had been in Rose Hill before. Following Lawson's sudden departure, she studied the article he'd found as if it were a text book and she were about to sit the most important exam of her life.

The woman who'd supposedly thrown herself from the top of the stairs was called Eliza Jane Abbott. She was twenty-one and the daughter of the general store owners, Isaac and Mary Abbott, who had no other children. She was described as a free spirit, had apparently been caught in a local horse race disguised as a man and often won card games at the local pub. The article was part news report, part obituary, and the writer, obviously not a fan of Miss Abbott, described her shenanigans as not becoming of a lady.

But no matter the opinion of the writer, it didn't sound as though Eliza had a care in the world for what other people thought of her and she certainly didn't sound like the kind of person who would want to kill herself. Then again, Megan knew from personal experience that life could change you in an instant. If Eliza had taken her own life, there must have been a damn good reason. And if she hadn't, then somebody had killed her.

186

Clutching the newspaper to her, she'd collected Cane from Archie's and then hurried home.

'Eliza?' she called, as she stepped inside the building. 'Eliza, are you here?'

She walked toward the stairs as she spoke and then she froze, waiting.

Talk to me, please.

Just as she was about to give up and go make herself a cup of coffee, the lights flashed on above her. And then immediately flashed off again. A chill swirled around her and Cane let out a high-pitched yowl, before running away into the lounge room.

'Eliza?' This time Megan whispered as goose bumps sprang up on her skin. 'Did you kill yourself?'

The strangest thing happened next. A loud clattering came from the kitchen. She hurried after the noise, turning into the room to find a pile of dishes had fallen from the drainer to the floor and smashed.

'I'm sorry, Eliza,' she said. 'I didn't mean to upset you. I don't believe you committed suicide.' Her heart squeezed and she wished she could hug the spectre, which she strongly felt was in her presence.

Instead, she said, 'I'm going to find out exactly what *did* happen to you, I promise.' She didn't know if this would help the ghost feel more settled, but she felt a deep need to do something.

Always one to keep her promise, Megan threw herself whole-heartedly into this task for the rest of the week. She neglected the house—reasoning there was no rush to de-clutter and renovate—choosing instead to spend her time researching during the day and crocheting for her weekend stall. Had there not been Eliza to think about, she might have felt more nervous or even decided to back out of the Walsh Country Markets, but she felt as if Eliza wouldn't be the kind of person to hide herself away and she wasn't sure if she wanted to be any more either. At nights, while she crocheted and Cane slumbered at her feet, Megan spoke to Eliza, certain she could feel her presence. It was more comforting than she'd ever imagined that of a ghost would be.

During the days, Cane spent some of the time lounging around the historical society with her—when she was quietly working, he tended to sleep the time away—and at other times he went to Archie's to play with Buster. Archie showed amused interest in her findings, but nowhere near as much as Lawson, with whom she'd been in frequent contact since sending him a text message.

He'd texted back almost immediately, filled her in on the Ned school drama and asked her how she was feeling after the discovery of the suicide article. These couple of messages had grown into hundreds more, so that she was going to need to go buy more credit for her pre-paid mobile. After two days of messages, he'd called Wednesday night and they'd talked for over an hour. Just the memory of that conversation (and the one that had followed on Thursday night) made her smile.

She'd told him about the few photos she'd found of Eliza—most of which were with other people and, unfortunately, unlabelled. She'd been working her way through them trying to put names to faces, which was an arduous task. The historical society had an abundance of information but there didn't seem to be any system to any of it. It wasn't like the historical societies she'd visited with her grandmother long ago in some small towns in Victoria—most of them were like mini-museums, their artefacts categorised in library-type perfection. Lawson had apologised for not being able to help her but she'd told him not to be so silly. He had a job and a son to think about and she respected that. He didn't owe her anything, but she had to admit she often lost herself in a daydream thinking about what might happen if they were left to spend more time alone together.

When she was with him, she sometimes forgot herself for a moment. She started to let go, as if he were just a guy and she were just a girl and flirting with him was totally normal and acceptable.

Their long conversations didn't only revolve around Eliza. They talked about the dairy, about Ned, about Cane; their childhood memories and funny anecdotes from the past. Megan had got good at conversing about the past without giving away any suspicious details. And talking to Lawson on the phone seemed safe somehow. It felt wonderful to have a friend and she kept reminding herself that was exactly what they were. Although her insides might quiver every time she heard his voice or even thought about him, the way he always fiddled with his wedding ring told her he was clearly still in love with his wife and that meant her stupid crush was also safe. Just because Lawson was male didn't mean their friendship was any different from hers with Tabitha, or so she kept telling herself.

With that thought, Megan yawned and glanced at her watch. It was Friday afternoon and she was making dinner for Archie to say thank you for being such a good sport about Cane, so she really needed to make a move.

Just five more minutes, she promised herself and then turned back to the pile of photos she'd been sorting through. The next few held nothing of interest, and she was just about to call it a day when her gaze fell upon a photo of her building. She brought it closer and saw a line of people waiting for their turn at full tables on the front verandah, and a blackboard saying: *Grand Opening: Eliza's Tea Room*.

Her heart skipping a beat, she clutched the weathered black and white photograph to her chest as a shiver scuttled down her spine. Goose bumps sprouted all over her arms. So *that's* where the idea for the tea room had come from. It looked as if Eliza had planned on serving afternoon tea on the verandah of the general store, proving herself to be a businesswoman looking for ways to bring in more profit for her family. Megan turned the photo over and saw that the date was only one day before Eliza's death. This only made her more certain that Eliza hadn't committed suicide—what could have happened in such a short time to take her from a new business success to giving up so completely?

Although she had no idea of the answer, she couldn't wait to tell Lawson about this latest development.

But tears prickled at the corners of her eyes as she thought of this unfulfilled dream. What had happened to the tea room after Eliza's death?

These thoughts circling her head, Megan got up, locked the historical society building and went home to cook up a feast for her and Archie's dinner. She glanced at her watch, contemplating calling Lawson immediately, but he'd be smack bang in the middle of milking and so she settled on a message instead: *Found spooky information about Eliza.*

He replied almost instantly: *Sounds intriguing. Can't wait to hear all about it.*

Feeling buoyed with her discovery and the prospect of talking to Lawson on the phone about it later, Megan threw herself into preparing a good, healthy, delicious meal for Archie. She'd seen what he usually ate—eggs, cheap biscuits, microwave pies and two-minute noodles—and she was on a mission to improve his eating habits.

Just before six pm, she carried a big tray of lasagne, some homemade garlic bread and two salads over to the old servo. Archie had told her he didn't do vegetables, so unbeknownst to him she'd hidden some in the lasagne—but she also reckoned if he'd just give her coleslaw and tomato salad a try he'd be hooked.

'Looks like you've made enough to feed an army,' he said by way of a greeting when she arrived.

While Cane greeted her in his usual enthusiastic manner, Archie took the two salad bowls off the top of the pile precariously balanced in her arms.

'You can keep the leftovers for dinner over the weekend,' she told him.

Archie fed the dogs outside, while Megan made herself at home in his surprisingly clean and tidy kitchen, serving the lasagne onto plates. Knowing he likely wouldn't try the salad on his own, she put a large serving on each of their plates and then set the garlic bread down in the middle of the table.

'I'm sorry I don't have any wine or beer to offer you,' Archie said as he came back into the house, 'but the water's been in the fridge all day.'

'Sounds perfect,' Megan replied with a smile. She couldn't remember the last time she'd had alcohol.

It was the first time they'd actually sat down together and shared any of the food she'd brought, but judging by the way he'd gone to the effort to set his small plastic table, she guessed he was as happy with her company as she was with his. Thank God she'd discovered she was quite fond of her lone neighbour.

'I told you, I don't eat vegetables,' Archie said, sitting down in his seat, picking up his fork and prodding a cherry tomato like it might jump off his plate and bite him on the nose.

Megan smiled. 'I'll be offended if you don't at least try after all the effort I went to make those salads.'

'What makes you think I care about offending people?' Archie replied, with a cheeky grin.

'Do it for yourself then. If you don't start eating better and looking after yourself, you'll have a heart attack.'

He shrugged as if this idea didn't much bother him, but he popped the tomato into his mouth nevertheless.

She knew better than to think he might actually admit to liking it, but the evidence spoke for itself. Archie all but scraped his plate clean of lasagne *and* salad.

'Can I get you a cuppa?' he asked when they'd finished eating.

'That would be great.' She stood to start clearing the table.

'Leave the mess,' he said. 'I'll clean up later after you're gone. In my house, the rules were always whoever cooks doesn't have to clean.'

This was the first time he'd made any reference to any kind of family—until now their conversation had revolved mostly around Cane and Archie's menagerie of animals. Once Archie had made the coffees and they'd sat down in his lounge room with a container of cookies she'd given him earlier in the week between them, she broached the subject.

'Where'd you live before Rose Hill?' she asked, knowing she was giving him tacit permission to ask her some questions of his own.

'I was a tenant of the Department of Corrective Services,' he said.

Megan blinked. *That* she hadn't been expecting. She didn't know why she seemed so surprised, but perhaps it was his art. She'd pegged him as a quirky, hermit artist, not someone more like, well, herself. 'Why? What did you do?' She blurted before remembering the rules. 'I'm sorry, that's none of my business.'

Archie chuckled. 'I wouldn't have mentioned being inside if I wasn't willing to talk about it.' He took a sip of his coffee and started to talk as if he were telling a child a fairytale. 'About twenty-five years ago, I was a respectable businessman, but then I made some less than smart decisions and got myself and my family into a lot of debt. I drowned my sorrows and then one day I drove my wife and two kids—they were ten and twelve at the time— home from the pub where we'd been celebrating her birthday.

Katy, that was my wife, insisted I'd drunk too much to drive but I got angry and told her to stop being a nag. I made them all get into the car and then less than a kilometre from home I drove us all into a tree.'

Megan couldn't help gasping—the way he said it, it almost sounded like he'd meant to do it.

He answered her next question before she asked it. 'My wife and our daughter died on impact. I went to prison and my son went to live with my wife's family. That was the last time I ever saw him.'

'Shit.' No matter how bad Megan's losses had been, she never failed to be affected by other people's. Maybe her own grief and heartbreak made her even more attuned.

'Did you ever try to make contact with your son ... after you got out? Didn't you want to get him back?'

Archie nodded and spoke gruffly. 'Course I did, but he didn't want to be with me after what I'd done to his mum and sister. I wrote to him from prison and I wrote to him for years after. He's an adult now and I don't blame him for not wanting anything to do with me. I can say I'm sorry a hundred times but he'll never forgive me and I can understand, because I'll never forgive myself either.'

'So how'd you end up here?'

'Saw an ad in *The West* for a caretaker. Didn't know if they'd want me with a criminal record but I guess they didn't find any-one better. If I'd had my way I'd still be in prison—no amount of time served will ever be enough. I'd have killed myself but that seemed like a cop out. I deserve to spend every day for the rest of my life reliving that awful moment and being punished for my stupid mistakes.'

Megan nodded. She understood. She too had briefly contem-plated suicide but had decided against that option for a number of reasons. As Archie said, it seemed like an easy solution and she didn't deserve easy when she had no one to blame for her mistakes but herself. Also, somewhere deep inside, she believed she should try and make amends, try to be a better person, live a better life, because she'd been given a second chance. There'd been plenty of others like her who never got that chance.

'You don't look particularly freaked out by my story,' Archie said, breaking her thoughts. He paused a moment, then added, 'It's because you've been there as well, haven't you?'

Megan glanced down at the floor as she reached out and ran her fingers through Cane's fur; she didn't need to ask what he meant by 'there'. He'd obviously seen something in her he recognised—prison left its mark on everyone, but not everyone could see it.

'Don't worry, missy, your secret's safe with me. You don't have to tell me what happened.'

But she wanted to. She hadn't talked about it for so long that being able to tell someone who would understand and not judge felt like a lifeline.

'My parents and brother died in a fire when I was seventeen and I didn't handle my grief well,' she confessed, her voice not much more than a whisper. 'I stuffed up my final school exams, then got in with a really bad crowd and made some terrible decisions. I started smoking a bit of weed to try and numb the pain, to deal with my grief. It worked at first—when I was high I felt as if I could cope, I felt good, almost happy. But after a while I needed more and I got into ice—that nearly destroyed me.'

Archie gave her a nod of encouragement but he didn't say a word. He didn't ask questions; he just let her get what she needed to off her chest.

'It was an expensive habit—I couldn't hold down a job because I was too unreliable, but I lived rent-free with my grandparents and had money from my parents' estate to feed my habit. It wasn't a lot but if I hadn't squandered it on drugs, I would have had a roof over my head and enough money to help me get through university, although by then I was too messed up to even contemplate study. I lived from one hit to the next and I was generous because I didn't give a damn about myself. I thought I had good friends but in hindsight I know they were nothing but users, addicts just like me, unable to think about anyone but themselves. After a few years my money ran out and most of them disappeared, but surprisingly my so-called boyfriend at the time didn't abandon me. Instead, he told me he had a sure-fire plan to finance our next hit.'

She told Archie everything, didn't leave out one sordid detail, and when she was finished she felt lighter than she had in years.

'I was sentenced to four and a half years, which was about the harshest anyone has ever been sentenced for being an accessory to such a crime, but you see, my dad's father is a supreme court judge, so the system came down hard on me. They made an example of me.

'Inside I had to go cold turkey on the drugs and, although that time was excruciating, going to prison was basically exactly what I needed. By the time I finally got counselling and was offered drug treatment, I'd been through the worst and I knew I never wanted to go back to that place ever again. In prison, I kept to myself because I was so terrified of getting back in with people who would test my resolve. I threw myself into working hard, studying, exercise, anything on offer to keep my mind off the cravings. It wasn't easy—and I wouldn't wish that kind of sentence on my worst enemy—but it taught me to appreciate life, to appreciate my second chance. I looked forward to getting out and starting again, but I was totally naïve on that front.'

Finally Archie spoke. 'Life had moved on? Left you behind?

She sighed. 'My grandfather's position meant my case had got a lot of publicity at the time and some journalist latched onto the story of me getting out. My face was on the front page of every Victorian newspaper.'

'Geez.' Archie gave her a wry smile. 'It's a pretty face but not the kind of publicity anyone wants.'

'Damn straight. Any friends I had at the time of my parents' and brother's deaths no longer wanted anything to do with me and no way I wanted to track down any associates from my drug days. Once an addict, always an addict. I started looking for work but of course, even if I'd had experience, no one wants to hire a convicted criminal. That was disheartening but the worst of it was that I couldn't even walk down the street without some-one recognising me. I'd been out three months when I decided enough was enough. Being in Melbourne wasn't working. I came here—I figured it would be unlikely anyone would know me in a town where no one else lived.'

'Apart from me,' Archie said with a chuckle.

'Well, yes, apart from you.' Despite feeling wrung out from sharing her story, she couldn't help but smile. 'The real estate agent failed to tell me about you though.'

Archie smiled sadly. 'What did your grandfather, the judge, think of all this?'

'He and my grandmother disowned me; they've made it clear they want nothing to do with me.'

'And they're your only family left?'

'Yes.' Megan sniffed. 'Both my parents were only children so I don't have aunties, uncles or cousins. My mother's parents took me in after the fire and despite all the hell I put them through, they never once gave up on me. Gran and Grandpa visited me in prison, until they died. Grandpa had a heart attack last year and Granny Rose had a fall like three weeks later. She didn't have it in her to …' Meg's voice failed her; for a minute that grief felt brand new again.

Archie sighed. 'No doubt you've had it tough, kiddo. And I understand you're scarred from your many awful experiences, but you're young and I can see you're a good soul. You lost your way for a while, but you had good reason, and you deserve a fresh start. However you may feel, that man's blood is *not* on your hands. I hate to see you locking yourself up in this shithole. You may as well still be in prison.'

Her life in Rose Hill didn't feel like a prison to Megan. She had a wonderful freedom out there with none of the temptation to return to the dark side. But she suddenly realised she didn't want to end up like Archie, all cut off from the world with nothing but the company of pets (and ghosts).

'That's nice of you to say,' she said, 'and I'm not locking myself up. I'm doing the markets on Sunday, aren't I? And I told you, I've made a few friends.' Warmth filled her as she thought of Lawson, Tabitha and Ned, and of course Archie himself. 'But I must admit I'm terrified of what they'll say when I tell them about my past. About who I really am.'

'Then don't tell them. As you said, it's the past. Don't let it define your future. You've been clean four and a half years, that's something to be proud of.' Archie reached over and took her hand in his old, papery one. 'You are a kind, warm-hearted, lovely girl and anyone would be lucky to be your friend.'

'Ditto,' she said.

He chuckled. 'I haven't been called a lovely girl in a long time. Now, enough of this sombre conversation: what's the latest on your ghost?'

Chapter Eighteen

'Good night, little man. Sleep tight; don't let the bed bugs bite.' Lawson bent down to kiss his son on the forehead.

As he straightened again, Ned said, 'Can you lie with me while I fall asleep, Dad? Please?'

Inwardly Lawson groaned. Since Meg's message that afternoon, he'd been counting down the hours and minutes until Ned was in bed and he could call her. It wasn't just that he was curious to find out what she'd discovered about their ghost—he wanted to hear her voice again. For two nights in a row now, they'd talked for hours past his usual bedtime. He should have been exhausted during the day but he'd had more energy than he'd had in a long time. That afternoon Ethan had even caught him whistling.

'Sure, little man, slide over,' he said, trying to curtail his disappointment as he kicked off his thongs, climbed in beside Ned and drew him in for a cuddle.

For years, he'd needed the comfort of his son's little warm body as much as Ned had needed him. Holding onto him had always made him feel somehow close to Leah, as if she lived on in their little boy. And she did—he often saw her smile reflected in

Ned's, heard her laugh when he did—and it always made the day brighter. But although he'd always love Leah, and their son would always take precedence over anything and *anyone* else, Ned wasn't quite enough any more.

Just thinking like this filled Lawson with guilt, but he craved a different kind of companionship.

'What vegetable would you be, Dad?'

'What?' Lawson blinked.

Ned sighed as if frustrated by Lawson's lack of comprehension. 'If you were a vegetable instead of a human, what would you be?

He loved hypotheticals and often asked random questions; they could be anything from deeply philosophical to just plain out there like this one. Lawson loved his enquiring mind, but right now, he wasn't in the mood to answer anything.

'I dunno, maybe a tomato.' It was the first vegetable that came into his head.

Ned laughed. 'For one,' he said, 'tomatoes are fruit and two, you are much more like a carrot—you're tall and strong and everyone likes you.'

Lawson grinned. 'That's nice of you to say but, as fascinating as this conversation is, it's time to get some rest.'

'I'm not really tired,' Ned confessed in a matter-of-fact tone.

Lawson could have screamed. 'Well, I am,' he lied.

'I could read you a bedtime story if you want or go make you some warm milk?'

'No thanks. I'd rather you rest. Let's have a quiet competition.'

Generally if Lawson suggested a quiet competition they'd both end up falling asleep eventually but often Lawson beat Ned to it. Tonight he was determined to keep his eyes open and outlast his son. He lay still beside Ned, listening to his breathing, until finally, after what felt like hours, the sound changed and he knew he'd fallen asleep.

He manoeuvred himself off the bed, then tiptoed out of the room. As usual Tab was sitting out on the back verandah knitting, Bonnie and Clyde sprawled at her feet.

'Shall I get you a beer?' she asked.

He shook his head and feigned a yawn. 'Nah, thanks. Think I'm gunna call it a night. Ned took ages to fall asleep and I've got an early start in the morning.'

She could have pointed out that he was a dairy farmer and had an early start *every* morning, but instead she nodded and smiled knowingly. He suspected she knew what he was up to but she didn't say anything.

He went back into the house, then into the bathroom, showered the day's grime off in record time, brushed his teeth and retreated into his bedroom, where he fell into bed with his phone in his hand. His feet had barely touched the mattress before his fingers dialled Meg's number.

She answered after only two rings. 'Hi, Lawson.'

'Hey, Meg.' He loved the sound of his name when she spoke it. 'Hope it's not too late to call. Ned took a while settling tonight.'

'Of course not. Is he okay?'

'Yes, just not tired enough after a week of no school.' He leaned back against his pillows, getting comfortable. 'Anyway, how are you? How was your day?'

'It was great. You'll never believe what I found.' She paused for obvious dramatics.

He grinned at the excitement in her voice. 'Well, don't keep me waiting. What was it?'

'I was just about to give up for the day … to be honest, I was thinking of giving up entirely. While I'm sitting there rifling through old records in the historical society, the renovations aren't doing themselves. But then I found this photo. It was of the general store, and out the front was a chalkboard sign advertising … *Eliza's Tea Room*.'

He got honest-to-God goose bumps and sat up straight in his bed. 'What?'

'I know, right.' She elaborated a little, giving him the exact details of the photo. 'If there is a ghost, and if she is Eliza, the woman who fell, then it looks like she had the same ideas as me for the building.'

'That's amazing.'

'It makes me feel like I came to the right place, like I'm here for a reason and maybe that reason is to help fulfil Eliza's dreams so she can rest in peace. Does that sound too whacky?'

He chuckled. 'No more than the idea of a ghost to begin with. You said you weren't really sure what drew you to Rose Hill. Maybe this was it?'

And just maybe it was also because they were meant to find each other. He'd never been a big believer in fate and stuff like that before, but then again, until Meg had opened his mind to the possibility, he'd never believed in ghosts either. Whatever the reason, he was glad she'd come.

'But do you really think this is why she's still lingering in our world? Because she wants her dreams realised?'

He frowned, but before he could contemplate her question, she continued. 'You know, something about all of this still doesn't sit right with me. It just doesn't make sense. I thought spirits only stayed in this world when there was unfinished business … and while I can understand the tea room might have been important to Eliza, it just doesn't seem a big enough reason to stop someone resting in peace. I can't help but feel her death wasn't suicide or an accident.'

'Perhaps you're right,' he said, but his mind had gone to Leah. If ghosts were a thing, why had he never felt her presence?

'I don't know why it matters to me. Whatever happened, it was so long ago that even if I found out the truth, I wouldn't be able to do anything with it.' Meg sighed—she sounded so utterly deflated, and he wanted to cheer her up, to give her hope.

Even though Lawson agreed there wasn't much she could do all these years later if she discovered something about Eliza's death, he admired how she wanted to fight for the underdog, or in this case, the under-ghost.

'It might make you feel better,' he said. 'And surely after all this time it also can't do any harm. If you're right and she didn't commit suicide, then maybe she just needs someone to believe that. To believe in her. And I guess, in opening your own tea room and maybe somehow honouring her while doing so, you might give her exactly what she needs.'

'You know, that makes a lot of sense. Thank you for not thinking I'm absolutely crazy about all this.'

Crazy was the last thing he thought of her.

'How was your day anyway?'

'You know, the usual,' he said, 'wrangling cows, wrangling Ned—it's all in a day's work. Tonight he wanted to know what vegetable I would be if I were indeed a vegetable.'

She laughed. 'Sounds like there's never a dull moment with Ned around.'

'Indeed,' he said, smiling. 'Are you all ready for the markets?'

'Yes. I've just come back from dinner with Archie and I'm going to finish one last tea-cosy before heading to bed.'

They talked for a little longer, until tiredness finally crept up on him. He couldn't stifle a yawn and she heard it.

'I should let you go,' she said. 'It's getting late. Thanks for the chat about Eliza.'

'You're welcome.'

'I'll see you on Sunday.'

'Yeah, Sunday,' he said, before disconnecting the call. He could hardly wait.

Chapter Nineteen

When Megan drove into Walsh early on Sunday morning—car loaded with crocheted goods, Cane leaping about dangerously and excitedly on the front seat—her hands were shaking on the steering wheel. Despite her conversation with Archie on Friday night about chasing dreams and living for the future, she felt sick in the stomach at possible discovery. The more people she met, the more likely it was that the truth about her past could emerge. Perhaps she should tell Lawson and Tabitha before they found out some other way.

With this thought sitting heavy in her gut, she almost turned her car around, yet excitement at seeing them again gave her the courage to find a parking space and start unloading. She wound the passenger window down slightly and left Cane in the car while she went to find out where she needed to set up. Her heart beat a heavy tattoo as she passed unfamiliar faces, but then she heard someone calling, 'Meg, Meg,' and recognised the voice as Ned's. She turned to see him and Tabitha waving from a stall about ten metres away, twin warm and welcoming smiles on their faces, and a little of her anxiety eased.

As she started towards them, Ned ran to meet her and gave her one of his big hugs; this time she hugged him back.

'I missed you, Meg,' he exclaimed.

'I missed you too,' she said, a lump forming in her throat because it was the absolute truth. It felt ages since they'd all hung out together the previous Saturday.

Ned grabbed her hand and led her towards Tabitha's stall. 'Aunty Tab and I have already set up your table; you're right next to us.'

'Thank you,' she said as they arrived in front of Tabitha's ice-cream stand, which looked way more professional than Megan thought her own stall would look when she'd set it all up. She smiled at the other woman. 'Hi there.'

'Hi yourself,' Tabitha replied as she came around the front of her ice-cream display cabinet and enveloped Megan in a hug that would give onlookers the impression they were old friends. Megan tried not to stiffen—the hug was lovely and very welcome but also felt incredibly weird. She simply wasn't used to people being kind to her. It had been too long since she'd taken comfort from touch.

'Do you want some help carrying all your stuff over?' Tabitha asked.

'Are you sure?' Megan nodded towards the other woman's stall. 'Are you all finished?'

Tabitha smiled widely and nodded. 'The perks of growing up on a dairy farm is I'm an early riser. I get out of working on the farm on market mornings—Lawson's friend helps out—but although I don't need to be here as early as I need to be with the calves, well, it's a habit.' She shrugged and gestured to the stall next to her where an empty table looked all lonesome. 'That's your spot right here.'

'Thanks for organising me a table,' Megan said and then they all walked together over to her car. On the way, Tabitha introduced her to a number of other stallholders, all whom were also warm and welcoming, offering 'nice to meet yous' and wishing her many sales. Tabitha seemed to be on first-name-basis with everyone and Megan guessed that's what being part of a small-town community was all about. If she were a different person, perhaps she'd enjoy living in a close-knit community like Walsh; instead she'd chosen Rose Hill where she thought she'd be able to lie low for a few years. To grieve and heal and work out how to live again.

'Oh, there's my gorgeous boy,' Tabitha cooed as Megan opened her car and Cane jumped out and leaped up at them. Ned squealed excitedly and she grabbed hold of the pup's leash, not trusting him not to do a runner.

'Don't be deceived by his cute face,' Megan said. 'He's very, very naughty. I almost left him with my neighbour today but I've been using his dog-sitting skills a fair bit lately while I've been working in the historical society and I didn't want to push the friendship. Besides, I thought it would be good for Cane to learn to behave in public.'

Now as he tugged at the lead and jumped between the three of them, Megan was second-guessing this decision. How was she supposed to look after him *and* her stall?

'I'm glad you brought him,' Tabitha said. 'And between me, Ned and Lawson you'll have plenty of keen dog sitters.'

Megan's stomach did a tumble-turn at the mention of Lawson and she bit down on the impulse to ask when he'd be arriving. She knew he'd still be busy with the cows but she had no idea how long each milking session took. Why was that something she'd never asked during one of their long conversations?

'Cane will be in his element,' she said instead.

With Ned looking after him on his leash, she and Tabitha began unloading her car and setting up her stall.

Tabitha exclaimed over every item as they laid it out on the table, which Megan had covered with a purple tablecloth. Megan smiled, encouraged by her enthusiasm. Maybe she might actually sell a few of her tea-cosies after all. Displayed on the old teapots Tabitha had conjured up from friends and the local op shop, they did look kinda funky and she wished her Granny Rose were there to see. She'd have been in her element at this country market.

'Thank you so much for suggesting I do this,' Megan said as they stood back to wait for the punters to start arriving. 'If I hadn't done something with these soon, I'd have been in danger of drowning in them.'

Tabitha winked. 'Death by tea-cosies. We couldn't have that.'

Not long after they'd finished setting up, a local teen band began to play—they were surprisingly good—and the first customers started to arrive. Smells from a sausage sizzle wafted over to Megan but she was too nervous to think about eating. What if no one bought any of her things? Or worse, what if someone recognised her?

It soon became obvious that Tabitha's ice-cream had a good reputation; despite the early hour of the morning people flocked to her. They bought their ice-creams and then, to Megan's utter relief, many of them turned to her table. Everyone was friendly and enthusiastic and within the first ten minutes she'd sold two tea-cosies to an elderly woman who looked like she'd be far better at crochet than Megan could ever hope to be.

More customers and sales followed. The tea-cosies were being snapped up fast and the other fun things she'd made—including some little crocheted animals—proved popular with the kids. Cane was a hit as well and far better behaved than she'd given him credit for. Perhaps hers and Archie's training attempts were starting to pay off.

'You're doing well,' Tabitha said, while scooping bright pink ice-cream into a cone for a little blonde girl.

Megan smiled back. 'I can't believe how many I've sold.' She was already thinking about the next market day and what other things she could add to her inventory when Cane started tugging on the leash she'd hooked around one of the table legs. She looked up to see Adeline's shadow falling upon her table and her good mood took a nose dive.

'Hi, Adeline,' she said, pasting a saccharine smile on her face before the other woman could speak.

Adeline replied with an almost identical twist of her lips. 'Hello. I didn't expect to see you here.' She glanced disdainfully down at the tea-cosies, then looked to Cane, who was struggling to get to her. 'How's my dog going?'

Megan gritted her teeth as she let Cane go over and shower the dog breeder in obvious love. She felt ridiculous jealousy tugging at her heart. '*My* dog is doing well, thank you.'

Adeline straightened and raised both her eyebrows at Megan. 'I take it he's had his next round of vaccinations?'

She nodded. 'Last Saturday.'

Adeline frowned. 'That's funny, I'm good friends with the vet and she didn't mention seeing one of my dogs.'

'That's because I took *my* dog to Bunbury.'

Adeline opened her mouth, no doubt about to tell Megan exactly what she thought of taking business out of the district, but thankfully at that moment, a middle-aged couple approached the table and began to gush over the tea-cosies. 'Oh, Richard,' said the woman, 'look at these. These are too adorable for words. I just have to have one, but how will I ever choose?'

Happily, Megan pulled Cane back towards her and turned her attentions on the couple, trying to focus on smiling and chatting with them, rather than on the uneasy feeling Adeline's presence had left in her gut. Even in prison, she couldn't recall ever getting *such* a bad feeling about another person.

The woman picked up a red-and-white checked tea-cosy. 'Did you crochet all these yourself?' she asked.

Rachael Johns

Megan nodded.

'And you live in the area?'

'I've just moved into Rose Hill,' she said, unsure whether she should have admitted this or not.

'Oh!' The woman's face exploded in recognition and her smile grew. 'I've heard about you. You're the talk of the town.'

'Really?' Megan swallowed as her extremities went cold. That did *not* bode well. The urge to turn and run came over her, but she managed to ignore the flight instinct. If she acted guilty, people would wonder what she was guilty of. If she acted as though she had something to hide, they might be more likely to start digging to try and uncover what.

'Well, it's not every day someone new moves into Rose Hill, is it, Richard?'

He shook his head and his cheeks wobbled a little as he grinned. Megan couldn't help but like them both.

'What do you plan on doing there?' The woman sounded genuinely interested.

Megan told her about her plans for the tea room—thoughts of Eliza once again spurring her on.

'That is a splendid idea.' The woman held out her hand. 'Excuse my manners; I'm Chloe Wellington and it's lovely to meet you.'

Megan smiled as she accepted the handshake and tried to sound confident as she introduced herself, using her mother's maiden name. 'I'm Meg Donald, and it's wonderful to meet you as well.'

Chloe dug her purse out of her handbag. 'I'm going to take that purple dotty one and the red and white too. How much are they?'

Once they'd exchanged cash for goods and Megan had wrapped the tea-cosies in tissue paper, Chloe said, 'I wonder, do you knit as well as crochet?'

Megan nodded.

'In that case, would you be interested in joining our knitting club? We meet fortnightly and soon we'll be starting our charity knit, making jumpers and blankets for the homeless. We can always do with an extra pair of hands.'

Although the idea sounded both fun and useful—and Megan would really like to do something good and helpful—her instinct was to say *no*. Sitting around with a bunch of women knitting sounded like a recipe for disaster. She'd be the newbie and they'd all be keen to *get to know her*. As she opened her mouth to politely decline Chloe's invitation, she looked up to see Adeline scowling.

'Thank you. I'd love to. That sounds great,' she said, beaming at Chloe. Her stomach and heart both spasmed at such a decision, but as Adeline turned and stalked away, Megan relaxed a little. She'd grown skilled over the last two weeks at making conversation without giving away too much detail about herself and that's what she'd do again at the knitting meeting.

'Splendid.' Chloe smiled. 'We meet every second Wednesday in the town hall. I'll look forward to seeing you again next week. Bye for now.'

When she and Richard linked arms and wandered off to the next stall, Megan turned to see Tabitha's ice-cream stall quiet for once.

'I'm so glad you said yes to knitting club,' Tabitha said. 'Adeline and I are the youngest members by about twenty years. It'll be good to have someone I actually *want* to talk to. Now, you've been working hard, so I think you deserve an ice-cream break. What flavour can I get you?'

'Try the Lolly Mayhem,' Ned piped up from where he was now sitting on the ground with Cane, leaning back against the puppy as if he were a pillow.

'Lolly what?' Megan asked.

Ned gave her an elaborate explanation and a few moments later she was sitting back in one of the fold-up chairs Tabitha had bought, licking her ice-cream treat and surveying the scene before them.

'I can see why people come from far and wide for your ice-cream. This is delicious.' Megan blinked as popping candy exploded in her mouth. 'And … surprising.'

Ned and Tabitha laughed as she went in for another lick, then he lifted his finger and pointed. 'Hey look. Dad's here!'

Megan and Tabitha looked up, their eyes following Ned's finger and coming to rest on Lawson striding towards them. Megan's stomach did that little jump thing that it only ever did when he was in her thoughts or vision. She licked her lips, hoping she didn't have ice-cream on her chin, and sat up a little straighter. Although they'd spoken on the phone almost daily the last few days, it felt so long since she'd seen him in the actual flesh.

'He's a lot earlier than he usually is,' Tabitha said, offering a knowing look and then rubbing her lips together as if stifling a smile. 'He must have worked hard to clear the cows so quickly. I *wonder* why?'

Her tone of voice indicated she didn't wonder at all and Megan sank her teeth into her ice-cream, needing the cold shot it brought to her brain. The thought that maybe Lawson had hurried because he wanted to see her pleased her far more than it probably should have. She didn't know how to respond to Tabitha, but in the end she didn't have to, as another customer came for ice-cream.

Lawson was only about ten metres away when Adeline intercepted him.

It was like a slow-motion movie—she landed in his way, blocking his path, then leaned forwards and pressed her lips against his cheek, her hand resting on his upper arm as her mouth lingered far longer than was customary. Megan's fingers twitched as she imagined the hard muscle that hid beneath his T-shirt and thought about how good his cheek might taste.

Even better than this ice-cream, she'd bet.

Adeline pulled what looked like an envelope out of her designer handbag and a massive grin exploded on her face as she waved it right under his nose. He looked surprised but then smiled. She couldn't help wondering what Adeline had given him that had him so excited and felt an undeniable jolt of jealousy.

Even though Lawson had made it clear he wasn't interested in Adeline, even though *she* shouldn't be getting ideas about him either, she couldn't help feeling as if this woman was dangerous. Adeline made the ice-cream that had previously tasted so delicious churn in Megan's gut.

Chapter Twenty

'I won?' Lawson stared down at the envelope in his hand and then looked back to Adeline, who was standing far too close for comfort. Hadn't she heard of personal space?

'You sure did. Congratulations,' she said, as if he'd won the thirty million dollar Powerball rather than a weekend away in Margaret River at some spa retreat. To be honest, he wasn't even sure what a spa retreat entailed.

He tried to summon the smile Adeline was clearly expecting, but he just wanted to get over to see Meg. The last few days, being unable to go visit her, had made him feel like he were in some kind of prison, and then knowing she was there at the markets had made his morning work drag on like it never had before. He'd wanted to leave Ethan and Funky to it, but that wouldn't have been fair. So, now that he was finally there, the last thing he wanted was to waste time talking to Adeline, but he gritted his teeth and tried to be polite. 'Geez, thanks. I can't remember ever winning anything in my life.'

She grinned. 'Well, maybe your luck is changing. Who do you think you might take with you?'

'I don't have time to go away for a weekend,' he said, folding his prize and shoving it in his back pocket. 'I'll probably give it to Dad and Sandra or maybe to Tabitha.'

Adeline cocked her head to one side and frowned at him. 'You really shouldn't rush to give it away. You won fair and square and you deserve a little time out. You work so hard.'

'Thanks. I'll give it some thought.' He forced a smile, patted his back pocket and started to walk away. As he did so, he glanced in the direction of the stalls and his gaze met Meg's. Warmth rushed through his body and he lifted his hand to wave as she met his grin with a beautiful smile of her own.

He'd pretty much forgotten Adeline's presence when she called out to him and halted his stride. 'Lawson!'

Reluctantly, he turned back. 'Yes?'

She pursed her lips together and then nodded her head in the direction he'd been headed. 'I've heard Ned's been having a bit of trouble at school.'

Lawson's chest squeezed. He knew Adeline meant well but something irritated him about the way she said these words. She almost sounded victorious, but he figured he must be reading into that because of his impatience to get away.

'Nothing we can't handle. Just kids being kids,' he said.

'I'm sorry. I've heard that Tate and Levi aren't being very kind to him. I know it's no excuse but they're going through a tough time at home at the moment. I can have a word to them though if you like.'

'It's fine.' Lawson waved a fly away from in front of his face. 'As I said, they're just being kids. The principal's got it under control.' He wasn't sure this was the case but he didn't want to find himself in debt to Adeline.

'Kids are so sensitive, aren't they?' she continued, sighing and then glancing again towards the stalls. 'Looks like Ned is getting along with that Rose Hill woman though.'

It was a statement loaded with insinuation and Lawson tried not to feel annoyed by her tone or the way she called Meg *that Rose Hill woman*. She had no right to butt into his business or treat Meg with such disdain. He opened his mouth to say something along these lines, but she got in first.

'I'm saying this as a concerned friend of the family, Lawson, but be careful there. Did you *know* she doesn't drink tea?'

'What?' He shook his head, wondering what the hell Meg's drinking preferences had to do with anything.

'She doesn't drink *tea*,' Adeline repeated, as if this had some huge significance.

'So what?' Lawson shrugged. 'Last time I checked not drinking tea wasn't a crime.'

'You don't think it's weird?' she asked. 'The woman crochets tea-cosies but *doesn't drink tea*. I'm telling you, there's something not quite right about her. I don't trust her and I think you should be careful, especially because of Ned.'

Adeline's logic was so illogical it was laughable. She was clearly clutching at straws and he felt sorry for her but he was also fed up with this conversation. He had feelings for Meg, he wanted to see her and he wanted to explore them, but he didn't feel obliged to spell this out to Adeline.

'Look, thanks for your concern,' he said, 'but Meg's a good person and to be honest, I'm—'

'Are you sure about that, Lawson? How well do you really know her? Where did she come from? Why is she here? Am I the only one who thinks it strange for a young single woman to turn up out of the blue and buy a building that should have been demolished years ago?'

'Demolished?' He laughed out loud. 'I think you're being a little dramatic. And not just about the building.'

She sighed deeply. 'I hope so, because I care about you and Ned and I'd hate to see you both get hurt. I'd be careful exposing your son to someone you know nothing about.'

'Just because you don't know Meg, doesn't mean I don't,' he said, no longer able to contain his irritation. The truth was he didn't know a great deal about her past—despite their long phone conversations late into the night these last few days, he still felt as if she was holding back a little, but that didn't make him uncomfortable. His gut told him she was good people and that her reticence in talking about herself was because someone had hurt her badly. He believed in time he'd gain her trust and that she'd open up, but he didn't want to push her to do that before she was ready.

Adeline opened her mouth as if to respond, but this time he got in first. 'Thanks for the prize. I'll see you later.' Then he turned and stalked off towards his son, his sister and Meg, determined not to be interrupted by anyone else.

'Dad!' Ned shrieked running to greet him. As he scooped him up for a hug, Cane also tried to solicit attention, but Lawson looked to Meg and couldn't help grinning. Any doubts Adeline had tried to sow evaporated as she smiled back and then dipped her head to lick the ice-cream she was holding.

'Your sister makes good ice-cream,' she said, seemingly unaware of how erotic she looked sliding her tongue over the cool treat.

'She does,' he agreed, muscles all over his body tightening as his wayward thoughts imagined her tongue roving over him instead. He felt his cheeks heat ridiculously and he prayed neither Tabitha nor Meg could read his mind. He honestly didn't know how to deal with such carnal thoughts. For years after Leah died, he'd genuinely believed his libido had gone too, but the way his body reacted around Meg proved otherwise.

'What did Adeline want?' Tabitha asked as she wrapped servi-
ettes round waffle cones in between customers. 'Looked like you
two were having quite the conversation.'

Lawson slid Ned back to the ground and stooped to give Cane
the attention he craved. 'She was just telling me I won first prize
in the Progress Association's latest raffle,' he said, looking up at
his sister.

'Congratulations,' Meg said.

'What'd ya win, Dad?' Ned jumped a little on the spot.

Tabitha's eyes widened. 'You won the spa retreat? But you
never win anything.' She pretended to pout.

He laughed. 'I know. Anyway you can have the prize if you
want. Either that or I'll give it to Dad.'

'What's a spa retreat?' asked Ned. 'Can we eat it?'

'Your guess is as good as mine, little buddy.'

'I think you should keep it.' Her eyes darted about in their
sockets saying far more than her words. 'I've heard that resort is
very romantic, and Ethan, Ned and I can hold the fort if you ever
want to get away for a night or two.'

Again his cheeks burned, but at least his embarrassment killed
his inappropriate erection. 'I'll think about it,' he answered, then
stood and surveyed Meg's table. 'Have you had a good morning
so far?'

She nodded. 'Better than I expected. The tea-cosies have been
selling almost as well as Tabitha's ice-creams. How was your
morning? With the cows and all?'

'Great. They mostly behaved, which isn't always the case.'

Meg laughed. 'Tabitha's been telling me about some of the
calves. Sounds like they have their own little personalities.'

'Dad writes their personalities on their tags,' Ned said. 'Sometimes he uses naughty words.'

'I do not!'

'Yes, you do.' Ned nodded vigorously. 'You wrote *moody bitch* on one. I saw it.'

Lawson smirked at his son. 'Bitch is not a naughty word. It's a proper animal term.'

'For *dogs*.' Ned shook his head and exploded in laughter. Both Meg and Tabitha joined him, and Lawson couldn't help smiling either.

He held up his hands in surrender pose. 'Okay, okay, I confess. Sometimes I call them naughty names. Life was a lot easier when you couldn't read.'

'Can I go get a sausage sizzle?' Ned asked. 'I'm starving.'

Happy for the change of subject, Lawson went to dig his wallet out of his pocket but Tabitha halted him. 'We're having a barbecue for lunch. I think sausages twice in one day would be overkill, but I've got some fruit you can have if you're hungry.'

'Aw, but fruit is so boring,' Ned whined, folding his arms across his chest in protest.

'Aunty Tab's right,' Lawson said and he knew her reference to the barbecue wasn't simply for Ned's sake. It was a reminder to do what he'd promised her he would. What he'd promised himself he would. He cleared his throat and looked at Meg. 'Um ... if you're not busy this afternoon, I ... I mean *we*,' he gestured to Tab and Ned, 'were wondering if you'd like to come over for lunch?'

'Please, Meg, *please* come,' begged Ned, sausage sizzle and fruit forgotten for now.

'It won't be anything fancy,' Lawson added, 'but Tab's made some salads and I'll barbecue some sausages and steaks.'

'Actually our worker Ethan will probably make his way over and he'll take charge of cooking the meat.' Tabitha smiled and shook her head. 'He doesn't like the way Lawson does it.'

'But he's wrong,' Lawson said, feeling the need to protect his masculinity, 'I'm awesome on the barbecue.'

Meg smiled. 'I guess *I'll* be the judge of that.'

'So you'll come?' Ned asked.

When she nodded, Lawson could have punched the air. While he didn't really want to share Meg with Tab and Ned *and* Ethan, it was better than the alternative of not getting to spend time with her at all.

'I'm curious about Ethan,' she said. 'From what Lawson tells me, he sounds like quite a character. What can I bring?'

'Just yourself,' he replied. *She* was more than enough.

At the same time, Tabitha said, 'Oh, you don't need to bring anything. You can follow us home straight from here. It'll be very casual but we've got plenty of food to go around and I'm sure Cane will love running all over the farm with Bonnie and Clyde.'

'In that case,' Meg said, 'thank you. We'd love to come.'

'It's a date!' Tabitha sounded victorious but Lawson couldn't help cringing at her use of the word 'date'. Could she be any more obvious?

At that moment a couple of women stopped in front of Meg's stall. Lawson stepped aside, dragging Ned and Cane with him to give her a chance to wow the potential customers. Not that the women needed much encouraging. They oohed and aahed over Meg's creative tea-cosies and Lawson watched, delighted by the way she blushed whenever one of them complimented her on her obvious skills. She sold five and took great care wrapping each and every one of them in tissue paper and then tying them up with a bow. The women were ecstatic and he felt proud and happy.

There was a rush on ice-creams *and* tea-cosies after that. Lawson was in charge of Cane, taking him for a little walk, while the others handled the sales. He wandered over to the sausage sizzle stall and bought a can of Coke from Funky.

'Don't tell me you caved and bought one of Adeline's puppies?' asked his mate with a disappointed shake of his head as he handed over the icy can.

'Nope. I'm looking after this little guy for a friend.'

Funky raised an eyebrow. 'What friend? I thought I was your only friend. Are you holding out on me, buddy?'

Lawson rolled his eyes and told him the basics about Meg—where she lived, how they'd met, her plans for the old general store. He left out the bit about how she made him want things he hadn't wanted in a very long time.

'She sounds intriguing,' Funky said, glancing across the car park to where Meg was still talking to customers. 'Is that her next to Tab's ice-cream stall?'

Lawson nodded and Funky let out a low wolf-whistle.

'You failed to mention how hot she was,' he said, fanning his face theatrically. 'I like me a good redhead. And you said she's living alone? Maybe I should go over and introduce myself.'

Lawson wasn't surprised at Funky's response. Meg was undeniably a looker and Funky's default instinct was to flirt with anyone in possession of an XX chromosome. Usually his mate's antics amused him, but today he fought the urge to tell Funky to back the hell off.

'If by introduce yourself you mean try and make her another one of your conquests, then forget it. She's a friend and I don't want you to mess with her.'

Funky blinked, frowned and then cracked a smile. 'Holy shit. Why didn't you just say so? You want to make her *your* conquest!'

'Keep your voice down,' Lawson hissed, annoyed at the way Funky was speaking about Meg like she were a piece of meat. 'Not everything is about sex, you know.' But inside his head a little voice called him out as a liar—he *did* want to sleep with her. But did she want to sleep with him as well? And, if she did, would he remember how to do it? It had been so long since he'd even kissed a woman, never mind anything more.

Funky reached out and squeezed his shoulder. 'Yeah, you keep telling yourself that, mate.' Then he chuckled. 'Welcome back to the land of the living. We've missed you.'

Lawson shrugged him off and glanced back to Meg, who looked to be deep in conversation with another customer.

'I'm sorry,' Funky said, sounding uncharacteristically serious. 'I think it's great you're getting to know someone new. Lord knows I adored Leah but she's gone, man, and you deserve to be happy again with someone else. If you like this Meg chick, then go for it, I say.'

With Funky's blessing—not that he needed it—Lawson wandered off with Cane back in the direction of Meg's stall. He stopped and half-heartedly chatted to locals as he went. There was fear in the air about the current dairy crisis—once again supermarkets were drastically cutting the shelf-price of their home brands and as usual the ramifications were most detrimental to the farmers—and as a dairy farmer himself he should have been more invested in these important conversations, but his head was full of Meg. Full of sex with Meg, if he were honest.

Finally, the crowds started to thin and he made it back to the others to find Meg had only one tea-cosy left. He tried to focus on that rather than the thoughts Funky had planted in his head.

He nodded to the one lone item sitting in the middle of her purple tablecloth. 'You'll have to get busy if you want to hold another stall at the next markets.'

'I know.' She rubbed her lips together and picked up the last tea-cosy—a blue and yellow stripy one. 'I can't believe how well they sold. But I feel a little sorry for this one.'

'How much is it?' he asked.

'Oh no.' She shook her head. 'I wasn't fishing for you to buy it.'

His hand was already pulling his wallet out of his pocket. 'I know, but I want to. I'll give it to my step-mum for a gift.' That was a lie; he planned on keeping it for himself and he'd think of her whenever he looked at it. Yep, he was a lost cause, and the sooner he did something about it, the better.

'In that case, for you, since you've been looking after Cane and helped me so much with the house and my research ...' she held it out to him and smiled '... it's free.'

Again, he shook his head. 'No way. I want to pay for it fair and square.'

'Fine.' She named a price he felt sure was a lot less than she'd charged everyone else, but he decided to let her win on that one. She grinned victoriously as he handed over a five-dollar bill, then he watched as she carefully wrapped it and tied it with a big gold bow. When she stretched out to give it to him, his fingers closed around the delicate package and he brushed his thumb lingeringly against the soft skin of her hand. Their eyes met and the breath caught in his throat as muscles all over his body stood to attention, begging him to give them more.

If they weren't in a public place, with his sister and son standing less than a metre away, Lawson might finally have done something about this attraction. But somehow he summoned all the restraint he'd ever possessed and broke contact, drawing the wrapped tea-cosy against his chest.

'All sold out now,' he said. 'Guess that means it's time to pack up.'

Meg dropped her hand back to her side but she didn't break his gaze. 'Guess so.'

'Lunchtime,' Tabitha announced, jolting them from their little bubble.

Lawson straightened and then once again handed control of Cane over to Ned while he helped the women pack up their stalls, fold the tables and load everything into the cars.

'Can I ride with Meg?' Ned shouted—why could eight-year-olds never speak at a bearable number of decibels? 'That way if she gets lost I can show her where to go.'

Lawson looked from his son to her. 'That's up to Meg, I guess.'

She smiled down at Ned. 'Fine by me. That's if you don't mind Cane sitting on your lap and slobbering all over your face.'

Ned giggled, clearly delighted by this concept.

'Guess that's all sorted then,' Lawson said, telling himself he would *not* feel jealous of his eight-year-old son getting to spend time alone with Meg.

Chapter Twenty-one

The long glances, the accidental brushes that made her tummy turn itself inside out—Megan told herself these were all meaningless. Her grandfather (on her dad's side) had always berated her for her overactive imagination, and right now her imagination was running rampant with thoughts of Lawson and the fantasy that maybe he felt a little bit of something for her. But that was ridiculous. Wasn't it? If he didn't want Adeline with her Barbie-doll legs, perfect gold locks and peach-like complexion, why on earth would he look twice at her? He and Tabitha were simply being friendly to the new kid in town.

It was with this reasoning that she allowed herself to follow his dirty old ute, bumping along gravel roads while Ned sat in the passenger seat beside her, chattering away. The thought of enjoying such a normal thing as a barbecue with such lovely people was simply too delicious to resist. She couldn't even remember the last time she'd been to a barbecue—the closest thing would have to be dinner with Archie on Friday night and that had been wonderful. She'd forgotten how satisfying the combination of good food and good conversation could be.

After about ten minutes—in which she and Ned spoke about Pokemon, something called Skylanders and another thing called Minecraft, which he promised to show her that afternoon— Lawson's ute slowed ahead of her and his right indicator flashed on. Meg put her foot on the brake as Ned shouted, 'We're home,' and pointed out the window at a large wooden sign in the shape of a cow off to the side. The words *Cooper-Jones Dairy* were scrawled across the front and the cuteness of the sign made Megan smile. She reckoned Lawson's mum might have been responsible for it.

As she turned her car into the driveway, Ned began a commentary of the things they passed—pointing out cattle yards, sheds, paddocks, a cottage where he said Ethan lived and some cows he called springers, which he took great care in explaining were the ones close to giving birth. She cringed when she saw the poor cows with massive bellies standing out in the sun, swishing away pesky flies with their tails, but there was plenty of gum tree shade they could have stood in if they'd wanted to.

Finally they slowed in front of a large house that looked like something out of *McLeod's Daughters*, a show her mother had watched religiously when Megan was a kid.

'And this is where we live,' Ned said proudly, his hand already poised to open the door.

'Wait till I stop,' she told him, not wanting him to jump out of her moving vehicle. That would be a great start to the afternoon.

Lawson and Tabitha parked in a carport off to the side of the house, and Megan found a spot under the shade of an old eucalypt tree not far away. By the time she undid her seatbelt, Ned and Cane had already leaped out and all but disappeared. She looked up to see Lawson walking towards her, a confident swagger in his gait and her mouth went dry.

'Will Cane be okay?' she asked.

'Yeah, Ned'll look after him. No doubt he'll be introducing him to our dogs. Clyde will love him, but Bonnie's getting a little crotchety in her old age.'

Megan laughed and Lawson gestured towards the house. 'Anyway, welcome. Let's go get a drink.'

A drink sounded like a good idea because it would hopefully be cold and help to lower her temperature, which was rapidly rising at being so close to Lawson again. 'This place is beautiful,' she said, gesturing to the trees surrounding them as they walked alongside each other. As it was summer, everything was a little brown but she could imagine how much prettier it would look in mid-winter glory.

'Thanks.' She heard the pride in Lawson's voice. 'We like it.' They walked a few more steps in comfortable silence and then he added, 'I'm glad you came. I've missed you these last couple of days.'

Oh dear. Her stomach squeezed with absolute glee at his words. Something about the way he said them didn't sound like the kind of thing you said to a just-friend.

Perhaps her imagination wasn't so overactive after all.

'I missed you too,' she confessed, all the while a little voice inside her head screamed that she was playing with fire. Screamed that she should turn around, run back to her car and speed on out of his life, never to return. She didn't deserve the attention of someone like him. Someone so *good* as well as so sexy.

But then she felt his hand brush ever so slightly against hers. It lingered just long enough to let her know it wasn't an accident, and that tiny touch sparked such a yearning inside her that she was helpless but to continue up the garden path with him towards the house.

'Hey!' Tabitha called as they took the few steps up onto the verandah.

'Hey yourself,' Megan managed, in spite of the fact her heart was still hammering in her chest like a one-man band. 'I was just telling Lawson how lovely it is out here.' She glanced back and forth along the verandah—two big wicker rocking chairs sat at one end, with pot plants displayed sporadically and balls and toy trucks littering the wooden decking. Boots of various sizes stood next to a front-door mat that read *Welcome*. The word *home* came to Megan's mind, and her eyes watered with emotion. It had been so long since she'd been anywhere that radiated such warmth and love.

Tabitha snorted. 'Sorry about the mess. Ned and Lawson are impossible to house-train.'

'Hey!' Lawson objected.

Megan laughed. 'What mess?'

'Lawson, get Meg a drink,' Tabitha ordered, then looked back to her. 'What do you fancy? Soft drink? Orange juice? Wine? I know it's early, but what the hell, it's the weekend. And we should celebrate your great sales today.'

'Thanks, but orange juice sounds wonderful. Is there anything I can do to help?'

Tabitha nodded. 'You can help me chop the veggies for the garden salad if you like, while Lawson gets the barbecue going.'

'Sounds good. Show me the way.'

The three of them ventured inside and Megan looked around as she was led down a long hallway to the massive old-fashioned kitchen at the other end of the house. All the ceilings were high, helping to keep the temperature down, and family photos with smiling faces hung on all the walls. For all Tabitha had said about mess, the interior looked like something out of *Country Style* magazine and Megan guessed that was down to her, not Lawson.

The moment she stepped into the kitchen, she was hit with the aroma of freshly baked bread. 'Which one of you had time to make bread this morning?' she asked.

'While I'd love to take the credit,' Lawson said, going over to the sink to wash his hands, 'that would be Tabitha. I'm a bit of lost cause in the kitchen and she's a bit of a superwoman.'

'Hardly.' Tabitha snorted as she went to open the fridge. 'I set the bread maker up last night so it was ready when I woke up. Now, it was orange juice, wasn't it? Sure I can't tempt you with wine?'

'No, thanks. Orange juice will be perfect.'

'Where's Ned?' Tabitha asked as she poured three glasses of juice.

'He ran off with Cane almost before I'd stopped the car,' Megan said. She bit her lip, thinking of all the news stories you heard about kids having accidents on farms. 'I hope they're both okay.'

Lawson picked up his glass. 'They'll be fine. Ned's got a good head on him and he knows where he's allowed to go on his own and what areas are out of bounds. Besides, Bonnie will keep them all in line.'

Megan forced a smile—telling herself that if Lawson wasn't worried about Ned, then she shouldn't be either. He was clearly a doting and sensible dad and Lord knew she had enough to worry about. Like not having a nervous breakdown while trying to make normal conversation with these people. 'Bonnie sounds like a character. I can't wait to meet her,' she said and then picked up her own glass and took a much-needed sip.

Lawson went out to start the barbecue after that and Tabitha smiled at Megan. 'I'm so glad you could come,' she said before turning to the fridge again to retrieve the vegetables. 'I don't mean to jump any friendship guns here, but I feel like we are kindred spirits.'

'Me too.' Megan swallowed, glad Lawson's sister couldn't see her face, which no doubt gave away her discomfort. She felt an affinity with Tabitha too, but couldn't ignore the heaviness in her stomach at the feeling she didn't deserve her kindness. She felt like an imposter, as if she were pretending to be someone she was not. Seeing Tabitha struggling to use her stumped arm to make a bag with her T-shirt and then pile the vegetables in with her good arm snapped Megan out of her bubble of self-pity and she rushed over to offer help.

'What can I carry?'

Tabitha looked up and laughed. 'I guess this must look like quite a feat but I promise you, I'm used to it.' She straightened and carried the vegetables in her T-shirt over to the bench and dumped them down. 'Now, do you want to peel the carrots? Oh and we should wash them first cos they're fresh from the garden.'

'Yes. Definitely.' Megan nodded, thinking she should plant a veggie garden at her place.

'Thanks.' Tabitha grabbed a chopping board, then a peeler and dumped them alongside the carrots. 'You can use Lawson's chopping board.'

Not thinking anything of this comment, she went to the sink, washed her hands and then set to work. It was only when Tabitha started chopping tomatoes beside her that she realised what she'd meant. Again, she found herself staring, almost mesmerised, as Tabitha sliced the tomatoes with one hand with the skill of a Michelin chef, her only aids a non-slip mat under her chopping board and a nail attached to it on which she stabbed the tomato so it didn't move around while she cut it. Megan couldn't chop vegetables that perfectly with two hands and here Tabitha was doing it with only one, like some kind of magician performing a trick.

Seemingly oblivious to Megan's awe, Tabitha said, 'How was your catch up with your friend last weekend?'

It took a second for her to work out what Tabitha meant and then she remembered her white lie to get out of the earlier barbecue invitation. 'Oh, it was fabulous,' she said, hoping she managed to keep her voice from wavering.

'Did she, or he, come to Rose Hill?'

Megan swallowed. 'No. *She* was in Bunbury for work and I met her there.' At least there was an element of truth in that—there might not have been a friend but she herself had gone to Bunbury. Feeling the conversation heading towards dangerous territory, she tried to change the subject. 'How long have your family been on this farm?' She hoped Lawson couldn't hear their conversation, because it was one he and she had already had.

'Four generations,' Tabitha said, sliding the first lot of chopped tomato into a bowl. 'We arrived when the area was part of the Group Settlement Scheme in the 1920s. My great-grandfather emigrated from Scotland with his young bride and bought this land, and by all accounts they worked their arses off to establish the dairy farm. I can't even imagine clearing the place without tractors and bulldozers, but that's what they did.'

'Wow.' Megan agreed it sounded horrendous, but watching Tabitha chop veggies and make salad while she spoke, she could imagine her ancestors were also very capable people.

'Of course we were a lot smaller back then,' Tabitha continued. 'The herd was only a dozen or so and they were milked by hand for starters—but dairy farming is in my father's family blood. Think it might have skipped a generation with Dad—he never seemed that keen or maybe he was before Mum died and I just can't remember. Things haven't been easy this last decade or so with the deregulation of the milk industry, but Lawson and I are different from Dad. We love it even during the stressful times.'

As if talking about him conjured him, Lawson waltzed into the kitchen. 'What stories is she telling you about me?' he asked, grinning. 'Don't believe a word.'

Megan tried to laugh, loving the playful banter between the siblings, but it didn't quite eventuate because she also felt a stab of longing for her own brother. Although she had better ways than drugs to deal with her sadness now, she lived in constant terror of returning to addiction if she dwelled on her grief.

But occasionally, at moments like this, her loss hit her hard.

'Are you okay?' Lawson's face fell and he stepped up close and put his hand on her arm.

'Sorry.' She sniffed and blinked, hoping the emotion didn't get the better of her. The last thing she wanted was to start blubbering in front of these two. 'Just watching you guys together made me think of my brother.'

'I'm so sorry,' Tabitha said, stopping what she was doing and turning to focus on her. 'Lawson told me what happened to your family. That's just terrible.'

Megan tried to swallow the lump in her throat. 'Thank you,' she managed just as the black fly-screen door clanged. Hurried footsteps in the hallway followed and moments later Ned exploded into the kitchen, Cane following closely behind and slamming into Ned's legs as he stopped. Ned laughed.

'Oi.' Tabitha pointed her finger at them. 'No running inside.'

'But I'm thirsty,' Ned panted, not showing the slightest bit of remorse.

Startled into action, Megan leaned over to grab hold of Cane's collar. 'I'm so sorry,' she said, looking at the sand they'd scattered all over the kitchen floor. 'I'll take him outside and then I'll clean up this mess.'

'Don't be silly,' Tabitha said with a nonchalant wave of her hand as she grabbed a cup, nudged the tap on with her stump and filled the cup with water. 'This house is used to dogs and kids.'

She handed the glass to Ned and he gulped the water down.

Less than a few seconds later the back door sounded again. 'Arvo, folks. How was the markets?' A clearly Irish voice travelled down the hallway.

'Good,' Tabitha replied as a tall, dark-haired bloke appeared in the doorway. He looked like a young Colin Farrell, or maybe it was his accent that had sent Megan's mind in that direction.

'Well, hello there,' he said. His lips twisted into a cheeky smile as he offered Megan his hand. 'Are you the mystery woman from Rose Hill? I don't think we've had the pleasure yet.'

She slipped her fingers into his for a polite shake and nodded. 'Guilty as charged. And you must be Ethan?'

'Aye, that I am. Come to save you from Lawson's shocking barbecue skills, or rather lack thereof.' He tapped the side of his nose. 'I have an impeccable sense of smell and knew the moment he flicked on the gas that my talents were required.'

Megan smiled. 'I love your accent.'

He shrugged one shoulder. 'It's gorgeous, isn't it? I'm perplexed that our dear Tabitha hasn't yet fallen for my charms and good looks.'

Lawson cleared his throat as he grabbed a tray of meat from the fridge. 'If you're quite finished, do you want to make yourself useful?'

The five of them and Cane headed onto the back verandah, carrying the salads and fresh bread between them. Megan and Tabitha laid the table and went back inside for the drinks while Ethan and Lawson argued over the best way to cook the meat. They were still arguing when Tabitha told Meg to take a seat. As she did so, she couldn't help laughing at the two men's antics.

'They're showing off because you're here,' Tabitha said, leaning close.

'Can I go for a swim?' asked Ned. He'd left the dogs to scrabble under a tree in the yard.

'After lunch,' replied Tabitha and Lawson in unison, making Megan realise that although Lawson seemed focused on the barbecue, his son was always on his radar.

'We should have told you to bring your bathers,' Tabitha said, 'but if you want to swim, you can borrow some of mine.'

Megan was about to politely decline—no way she wanted her pale body on display—when Ned said, 'Oh *please*, Meg. Come swimming with me. I'll let you play with my pink flamingo.'

It was impossible to say no to that cute face, so somehow she found herself agreeing to a post-lunch dip in the pool.

Ned raced inside to get changed, ready for later.

'Tell them about what you found out about the tea room,' Lawson said as he joined them at the table, finally giving in and letting Ethan take charge of cooking the meat.

Because talking about her house and the history of one of its past inhabitants was easy, conversation flowed. Megan relayed to Tabitha and Ethan what she'd discovered and they listened enthusiastically, both enthralled and intrigued. When the meat was ready, Lawson called Ned back and everyone sat down to eat.

Ned insisted on sitting next to Megan, which made her feel very special. When Lawson sat in the seat opposite, he stretched out his legs and his feet touched hers. She wasn't sure if it was accidental or not, but at the connection warmth that had absolutely nothing to do with the summer heat flooded her body.

'Now that's how you cook a steak,' Ethan said, prodding a piece he'd just cut off with a fork and holding it out to show them all.

Megan tried to focus her attention on the meat.

'What do you think, Meg?' Lawson asked. 'Is that perfect or a little underdone for your liking?'

She cut off a piece of steak, popped it into her mouth and chewed, then took her time carefully considering. 'It's not bad,' she said, once she'd swallowed the mouthful, 'but I have to say I prefer my beef a little more dead.'

'Yes!' Lawson punched the air like a little boy, smirked at Ethan and then turned his head back to her and winked. Her stomach tumbled and wasn't sure she'd be able to eat another bite.

'Now, now, boys,' Tabitha said, 'can we please have at least one meal where you guys aren't in competition?'

Ethan sighed. 'Fine.' And stabbed his fork into another piece of steak.

'Whatever,' Lawson added, still grinning.

Megan laughed. Ethan fit in so well with this family, as if he were the younger brother they'd never had, and she found herself enjoying the lunch and their company immensely. She couldn't help imagining what it would be like to be a permanent fixture at this table.

Conversation was diverse—everything from Ned talking about some new Xbox game he wanted to get, to discussions about the latest dairy crisis. The tone went from light-hearted to sombre as they talked about a neighbouring farmer who'd had his dairy contract cut. The latest in a number of surprising terminations.

Megan didn't really know what to say or how to add to this conversation, but she listened intently, silently hoping and praying that Lawson and Tabitha's livelihood would be okay. What with losing their mother, Tabitha's cancer, their father's heart attack and Leah's death, it sounded as if they'd been through hardships enough for one lifetime.

'Sorry,' Tabitha said, looking to Megan, 'we're probably boring you senseless with all this farming talk.'

She shook her head. 'Not at all. I hope you guys are okay, but have you considered expanding your ice-cream business as a safety net?'

'What do you mean?' Tabitha asked. 'Like making a larger quantity and trying to sell into shops?'

Megan nodded. 'Yes, that's one idea, but you could also become a tourist attraction and open up an ice-creamery here. You could even do tours of the dairy, have a few calves for kids to pat and show them how a cow is milked.' She realised she was getting carried away and perhaps sticking her nose in where it wasn't wanted. 'Or maybe I have no idea what I'm talking about.'

'I think it's a great idea,' Ethan said, clapping his hands together as if it were a done deal. 'There are lots of boutique breweries popping up all over the place, so why not boutique ice-creameries?'

Megan was more curious about Lawson's opinion so she chanced a glance up and her heart swelled when she found him smiling at her. 'I love it,' he said.

'There are lots of small ice-creameries dotting the south west already,' Tabitha said, 'but I guess there might be room for one more. It's definitely something to think about. Also, Meg, I was wondering, when your tea room's up and running, how would you feel about selling my ice-cream there as well? We'd work out some commission of course, either that or you could have as much free ice-cream as you can eat.'

She took a moment to speak past the lump that had formed in her throat. When the idea of the tea room had first popped into her head, it had been a relief to have something to tell Lawson, but she'd never seriously considered it a possibility until she'd found out about Eliza's Tea Room. Now, not only did she want to do it for Eliza—she wanted to do it for Tabitha as well.

'Of course,' she finally managed. 'I don't know how long it'll take to get the building into shape, never mind everything else that will need to be done before I can actually open, but your ice-cream will definitely be on the menu.'

'We can help you with the building,' Lawson said, and Tabitha and Ethan nodded. 'Ever heard of a slab party? I reckon if you promised to feed everyone those wonderful bickies and cakes you make, we might be able to get a group together to come over and get some of the big tasks out of the way.'

The lump in Megan's throat grew and her eyes were in sudden danger of sprouting tears. The thought that people might do such a thing for her threatened to unravel her.

Thankfully, Ned—bored of shop talk—interrupted the conversation. 'Can I swim yet? My teacher said it's an old wives' tale that you have to wait half an hour after eating.'

Lawson glanced at his watch. 'All right. But help us clear the table first and then wait until we're by the pool with you.'

'But Dad, I'm a good swimmer,' he moaned.

Lawson raised an eyebrow. 'That's the deal. Take it or leave it.'

He took it, and the five of them cleared the table and cleaned up the kitchen, before Lawson went to get his board shorts on and Tabitha took Megan to borrow some bathers. Luckily the two of them were almost exactly the same size and shape. Wearing a swimming costume was another thing she hadn't done in a very long time and she couldn't help being a little self-conscious as she headed back onto the verandah with a towel wrapped around her. The boys were already outside again, Lawson slapping sunscreen on the bits of Ned's skin that weren't covered by his knee-length board shorts and long-sleeved swim shirt. Ethan and Tabitha appeared to have vanished.

'Can I borrow some of that?' Megan asked, holding the towel tightly around her and trying not to gape at the sight of Lawson in nothing but a pair of low-on-the-hip board shorts.

'Sure.' He handed her the tube and then turned back to finish lathering Ned.

She squeezed a dollop of cream out onto her palm and then rubbed it over herself, starting with her legs. Only when Ned squealed, 'Ouch, you got it in my eyes,' did she glance up and catch Lawson looking at her. She didn't think she was imagining his appreciative gaze and it sent shivers through her already hot and bothered body.

'Sorry, mate.' Lawson barely glanced at his son as he said this. 'Do you want me to do your back?' he asked her.

She swallowed, and then handed the tube across to him. 'Thanks.'

He smiled as their fingers brushed against each other in the exchange and she almost forgot Ned was with them as she felt Lawson's strong, warm fingers land on her back. It felt good, better than good, as he rubbed the cream in, and she felt her body temperature rising to boiling point, but at least she'd be safe from the sun.

'There. All done,' he said, picking up the tube and recapping it.

'Finally,' Ned exclaimed as if he'd been waiting weeks to go in the pool. 'Come on then.'

With barely a glance at Lawson, Megan repositioned her towel and hurried after the kid. She felt Lawson only a few steps behind. Ned stepped onto the bottom of the pool gate so he could stretch up and un-do the latch, then he pushed it open and held it for them.

The moment the gate slammed shut behind herself and Lawson, Ned kicked off his thongs and plunged into the pool. Water splashed up, wetting them both and they laughed as they met each other's gaze.

'Ladies first,' Lawson said, gesturing to the sparkling water in front of them.

Megan didn't need to be asked twice. She dived right in, relishing the cool reprieve of the water. When she emerged, Lawson was right beside her, his hair wet and his tanned broad shoulders glistening like some kind of Greek water God.

'Thanks for offering those thoughts about expanding Tabitha's ice-cream venture,' he said, reaching up and running his hands through his hair. 'You've got quite a head for business. Have you run one before?'

She shook her head. 'No, I'm just interested.' The closest she'd ever got to small business was reading the brochure for the course offered in prison. She'd had no ideas for business back then so had chosen the more hands–on practical courses instead. 'I actually always wanted to be a teacher,' she found herself telling him. 'Both of my parents were teachers and so passionate about their jobs, but things kind of derailed for me after they died. I lost my way for quite a few years.'

This was an understatement but even if she felt ready to risk telling Lawson the truth about her past, her story wasn't the kind you told around young ears. Before he could say anything to this, she looked to Ned, who was now perched atop a massive blow-up toy. 'I thought you said *I* could use your pink flamingo!'

Chapter Twenty-two

As Meg struggled onto the pink flamingo he and Ned had given Tabitha as a joke for Christmas, Lawson considered this little nugget of information she'd just told him. She'd wanted to be a teacher, her parents were teachers—he didn't know them but now that she'd said this he could visualise her in this profession. Right from the start she'd been gentle and caring towards Ned, treating him like a little person. And Ned thrived on this. In a short time, he'd grown to adore Meg.

As much as this pleased Lawson, as much as he enjoyed watching Meg and Ned interact, he couldn't suppress a tiny bit of irritation that he didn't have her all to himself. As they splashed about, laughing over the blow-up flamingo, Lawson found himself reliving the feeling of sliding his hands over Meg's smooth neck and shoulders as he'd helped her with the sun-cream. Doing so had been both pleasure and torture and he'd had to summon all the unsexy images he could think of to stop himself developing another inappropriate erection. It was the middle of the day and they were with his son, for crying out loud, but he'd had more erections in the last couple of weeks, while thinking of Meg, than he'd had in the previous four years.

Thankfully the water in the pool now covered his annoying problem and he swam over to join them, telling himself to stop sulking and just try and enjoy the day.

'When do I get to go on the flamingo?' he asked, coming to stand beside Ned who was treading water alongside Meg.

'Never. You're too big, Dad. Remember the last time you tried to get on, you almost broke it.'

'We couldn't have that,' Meg said, sharing a secret smile with him as she wrapped her arms around the flamingo's long neck. He imagined himself in the position of the flamingo, her arms wrapped around his neck as he stooped his head to kiss her. Dammit, now he was jealous of a stupid blow-up bird.

'I might swim some laps,' he said, and then churned off through the water, hoping the exertion would ease some of the tension charging through his body.

As he swam back and forth, he shut his eyes whenever he passed Meg, not needing the glimpse of her long bare legs hanging off the flamingo. Finally, when he thought he'd got his embarrassing appendage under control, he emerged at the end of the pool.

'Can we have a horsey race?' Ned shouted.

Meg frowned. 'I don't see any horses.'

'He means a noodle race,' Lawson said, gesturing behind him to the fence where a number of pool noodles were threaded between the poles. Ned was already scrambling out of the pool to get them.

Meg raised an eyebrow. 'What am I getting myself in for?'

'Not scared of a little competition, are ya?' He chuckled, remembering just how competitive she'd been when they played Uno.

'Hell no.' She gestured to Ned. 'Can I have the yellow one please?'

Yellow was Ned's favourite colour and he always had that one, but it was a testament to how much he adored Meg that he didn't even bat an eyelid. He tossed her the yellow noodle, threw Lawson a red one and then jumped into the pool with the green one already positioned between his legs. Ned explained the rules of pool horse racing to Meg and she listened intently.

'On your marks, set, go!' Ned cried seconds after he'd finished explaining.

'He didn't give us a warning,' Meg objected as Ned paddled his arms and legs like his life depended on it.

Lawson winked. 'All's fair in love and horse racing.' Then before Meg could say another word, he too kicked off the side.

'I won, I won.' Ned was bouncing up and down in the shallow end when Meg finally made it.

'You cheated,' she said, a massive grin on her face. Lawson loved the way she didn't pander to Ned. 'I demand a re-race.'

They raced and raced until Meg exclaimed that she couldn't take another moment. 'My legs feel like they're going to drop off,' she said. 'You guys play hard.'

Ned grinned at this huge compliment.

'We've probably been out in the sun long enough anyway,' Lawson said, his muscles also feeling the exertion.

'Aw, just five more minutes,' Ned begged.

Lawson shook his head. 'How about we get out and go show Meg the baby calves?' Then he looked to her. 'That's if you can stay a little longer?'

She nodded. 'I can. And I'd love to see the calves.'

This suggestion appeased Ned, so they all climbed out. Lawson tried not to stare at Meg's nearly naked body as she wrapped the towel around herself.

'Would you like to have a shower?' he asked, trying not to trip on the word shower as the image of her *in* the shower landed in his head. *Good Lord*, he had a problem.

'Nah. I'll just get dry and throw my clothes back on.'

Back at the house, they found Tabitha sitting on the back verandah reading one of her Aussie romance novels. She and Meg chatted briefly about the book—Meg said the author was one of her favourites, Tab that it was a pity none of the guys round there were like the guys in her books—and then they went inside to get changed. Lawson showed Meg to the bathroom and then he and Ned went to their respective rooms to put on dry clothes.

Barely ten minutes later, they were standing in the sheds, Meg going crazy over the cuteness of the young calves. They'd left Cane in the backyard with Bonnie babysitting, much to her disgust.

'Oh my goodness. You must have the best job in the world,' Meg said to Tab as she rubbed her hand up and down the back of a one-day-old. 'I'd be out here with them all the time. I'd never want to be anywhere else.'

Tab laughed. 'You become immune to the cuteness. But you're welcome to come and hang with them any time you like.'

'You might never get rid of me,' Meg joked.

Lawson couldn't see a problem with this.

Ned, clearly wanting to sound grown up and knowledgeable in front of Meg, explained how he and Tabitha attended the calves twice a day during calving season. 'We feed the babies on the sick mob milk,' he said.

'The sick mob?' Meg asked, looking appalled.

'Yep, Dad separates the sick cows from the good ones, but they're not really sick. It's just something's a bit wrong with their milk—they've either just had a baby or they've got infection in their udders so we can't put their milk into the tanker that the milk company collects.'

'I see.' Meg nodded, her head cocked to the side a little as she listened intently to Ned describing in intricate detail their daily routine. He pointed out the milk trailer, explaining that he and Tabitha filled it by hand and then used buckets to pour the milk into the feeder trays, which had plastic teats from which the calves drank.

'The older calves also get grain and hay,' Ned explained. 'Oh and we put salt and pepper in the milk and if the cows are sick we give them sugar.'

'Sounds like a restaurant,' Meg said.

Lawson and Tabitha laughed.

'Salt and pepper is dairy code for special minerals we give the calves,' Tabitha said.

'And sugar,' Lawson added, 'is really electrolytes.'

'Right. I see.' Meg chuckled. 'And how old are the cows when they become milkers?'

Lawson shrugged. 'Between two and two and a half years. In that time we feed them up good with sorghum and corn silage.'

'And do you grow that here?' Meg asked. She seemed genuinely fascinated to learn more about dairy farming.

'We sure do.'

She asked a few more questions about what happened to the male babies and he explained they sold them off for beef, then Tabitha said, 'Hey, it's a little earlier than usual but we could feed one of the runts if you'd like to have a go?'

'Really? Are you sure?' Meg's beautiful eyes widened.

Tabitha nodded. 'Of course.'

They trekked over to the dairy, where Tab filled a bottle with some milk from a tank, and then they all headed back to the nursery shed. Lawson had plenty of jobs he could and probably should have been doing and he'd bottle-fed a hundred calves in his life, yet there wasn't any place he'd rather be, so he watched carefully as Meg held the bottle while their smallest, newest calf suckled hard.

'That was amazing. Thank you,' she said, handing the bottle back to Tabitha when she was finished.

'We'll make a dairy farmer of you yet,' Tab said and Meg blushed and laughed nervously.

'Shall we go and have some afternoon tea?' Lawson asked.

Meg glanced down at her watch. 'Geez, I didn't realise the time. I should probably get going soon.'

'Aw,' Ned whined, 'but I wanted to play Mario Kart with you.'

Lawson didn't want her to go yet either. 'If you stay a little longer, I could show you the milking later.' He hoped he didn't sound too desperate, but he really didn't want her to go.

'That sounds great.' She bit her lip, then added, 'but I don't want to outstay my welcome.'

'You're not,' said Lawson, Ned and Tabitha in unison.

Meg smiled. 'In that case ...'

They left the sheds and headed back to the house. In the kitchen, Tabitha conjured a packet of store-bought biscuits and apologised that they weren't homemade.

'These are my favourite,' Meg said as she sank her teeth into a Monte Carlo.

She'd barely finished the biscuit before Ned dragged her into the front room, leaving Lawson alone with Tabitha in the kitchen.

'I really like her,' Tab said, leaning back against the bench. 'And I can tell you do too.'

There was no point denying it. He was going crazy with like. 'But how do I know if she feels the same way about me?'

Tab raised an eyebrow. 'It's pretty clear from where I'm standing that she's interested. I could light a fire from the sparks flying between you two.'

'Really?' He couldn't help grinning.

'Yes.' She grinned right back.

He sighed as Adeline's words from that morning popped into his head. They'd been niggling at him since, despite the fact he thought them ridiculous. 'But we barely know each other. She occasionally lets something slip about her family and I've asked questions, but getting her to talk about the past is like trying to draw blood from a stone.'

'Lawson, she lost practically her whole family in one go,' Tab said, her voice low so Meg couldn't hear them. 'That's painful even thinking about. And then the only grandparents she was close to. Be patient. Give her time. She'll open up to you when she's ready.'

He nodded. 'You're right, I know. Thanks for the pep talk, little sis.'

'You're welcome.' She pointed towards the open door, then hissed, 'Now go and be with her. Don't waste your time chatting with me.'

Lawson found Ned and Meg in the lounge room sitting alongside each other on the couch, already ensconced in a game of Mario Kart. Neither of them looked up as he came in but he perched himself on the other end of the couch so Ned sat between them. It transpired that Meg was as competitive on the Xbox as she had been playing Uno and racing in the pool. At one stage she looked up briefly and mentioned that years ago she'd played video games with her brother. Another tiny seed of information that gave Lawson the confidence that she was starting to share more of herself with them.

He and Meg alternated playing against Ned and then finally they took on each other. It was the most fun he'd ever had with the Xbox and also helped release a little of the tension that had been building up in his body throughout the day. Finally the time came when he had to stop and start bringing in the cows.

Reluctantly, he heaved himself up off the couch and stretched. 'I'm heading out to do the milking. You still want to come and see what it's all about, Meg?'

'Do I ever!'

Usually Ned whined and argued at the end of screen time, but this time when Meg put down her game controller, he did the same. Lawson considered telling his son he could keep playing indefinitely, simply so he could have Meg to himself for a while, but parent-guilt got the better of him. How did anyone date with a kid? Not that he and Meg were dating—yet—but between the farm and Ned he felt like the world was conspiring against his desire to rejoin the 'land of the living', as Funky had put it.

Then, Tabitha—who had no doubt been eavesdropping—appeared in the doorway and even before she spoke, he knew she'd come to save him. 'Ready to help me with the calves, Ned?'

'But I want to help Dad with the milking,' he said, a pout already forming on his face.

Tabitha twisted her lips in feigned disappointment. 'Dad's going to have Meg's help, so I'd really appreciate it if you helped me.'

Ned looked as if he were about to object, but then he glanced at Meg and seemed to reconsider causing a scene. 'Okay, Aunty Tab, I'll just go get my boots on.'

As he marched out of the room, Tab met Lawson's gaze. Neither of them said anything but he made sure she knew how much he appreciated her intervention. Now it was up to him to make the most of the next hour or so.

He turned to Meg. 'Are you ready to get dirty?'

'What am I letting myself in for?' She grimaced then nodded. 'Yep. Let's do this.'

On the front verandah, Lawson pulled on his boots and Meg bent down to slide on her sandals. They were cute little white ones that would never be the same if he let her wear them into the dairy.

'Here,' he said, grabbing a pair of Tab's old gumboots. 'I know it seems hot for these, but you'll thank me later. I'll go get you some socks.'

He trekked into the house, dug a pair of Tab's socks out of the clean washing basket and then took them back outside. A minute later Meg stood in front of him in her denim shorts, a floaty pink top and Tab's ancient boots.

'How do I look?' she asked as she straightened.

'Ridiculous,' he said, while silently thinking *sexy-as-all-hell*.

She poked her tongue out at him. Smiling, he went to get Clyde, but left Cane fenced in with a still–unimpressed Bonnie in the backyard.

With Clyde racing ahead, Meg and Lawson started towards the shed. He almost took hold of her hand, but they were in plain sight of the house and he didn't want Ned to see. They met Ethan at the dairy shed and he looked like he'd just awoken from a long nap.

'You helping us this arvo, Meg?' he asked, turning on his flirty smile again.

'She's helping *me*,' Lawson corrected. 'We'll bring the cows in.' That would be more fun for Meg than getting everything ready inside.

'Aye aye, Captain.' Ethan saluted him and then turned to head inside.

Lawson indicated the motorbikes they used to help encourage the cattle into the pens prior to milking. 'Ever ridden one of these before?'

She shook her head.

'They're pretty easy,' he said, 'but if you prefer you can ride with me.'

'Are you *trustworthy*?' she asked.

He laughed as he swung his leg over and climbed onto the bike. 'I've been riding these things since I was younger than Ned. Come on, live a little,' he said, patting the spot behind him.

'Okay then. I'll trust you.' Meg climbed on behind him and he sucked in a breath as her thighs connected with his arse.

He swallowed—he might have been riding since Adam was a boy, but it was a long time since he'd ridden with a woman pressed against him and he hoped he'd been right when he'd told her she could trust him.

'Do we need to wear helmets?' she asked.

He shook his head as he turned around to reply. Their faces were so close he could feel her breath against his lips and he thought about leaning in a little and pressing his mouth against hers. But was this really the place for a first kiss? 'Just hold on. I won't go fast,' he said, sounding a little gruff as he turned back around and started the bike.

Her hands slid around his body and she held on tight as he rode off towards the paddock. He tried to focus on the task at hand, rather than the feel of Meg pressed against him, but it was damn tricky. Thankfully the cows were creatures of habit and made the trek towards the shed at this time of the day anyway, so he and Clyde didn't have to do much except hurry them on and usher them into the pens.

Once the first lot were waiting their turn to go on the rotary milking machine, Lawson took Meg to where Ethan was starting to encourage the first cows onto the rotary platform. On the ground, Lawson began to hook them onto the suction cups.

'It looks a bit like a merry-go-round,' Meg said.

Ethan laughed and Lawson nodded. 'Probably the slowest ride in history but yeah, sometimes we call it the horizontal Ferris wheel.'

Meg asked a few question about the big round platform, which took up most of the shed. He explained that the platform moved around while the rotary milked the animals, so that most of them were finished by the time they got to the exit point.

'How many cows fit on the platform at a time?'

'This one holds fifty and one rotation takes ten minutes.' He pointed to a tag on one of the animals. 'We've got an electronic tag-on system, to ensure all our herd have been milked. Technology has definitely made the process easier and faster,' he added with a chuckle.

'That one is trying to push the other one out of the way,' Meg said, sounding concerned as she pointed towards the cows hustling in the pen.

Lawson shrugged. 'The bossy ones always push in; it's almost like they have their own order that we're not privy too, hey Ethan?'

The worker nodded. 'Yep. And who are we to mess with the girls?'

Meg smiled. 'Is that water you're spraying them with?'

Ethan opened his mouth to answer but Lawson got in first. 'Yep, mixed with a little sanitiser. We clean the udders as they're getting on and again as they're getting off. It's not just milking that happens on the rotary. We can also do injections, give medication and inseminate.'

Meg kept firing questions and he found himself, like Ned, wanting to impress her with his knowledge. Even though he realised how stupid it was, he couldn't help himself and explained every damn thing in so much detail that he was probably in danger of boring her to death.

When the rotary was almost full, they left Ethan and headed round to the other side to start getting the cows off. Meg watched as he unhooked the suction cups, sprayed their udders and then sent them on their way.

For a while they stood in comfortable silence and then she asked, 'How come a few of the cows have chains across?'

'They're the ones we've identified as having more milk, so they go round twice.'

She nodded and rubbed her lips together in the most infuriatingly sensual manner. He didn't think she did it on purpose, but it drew his attention once again to her lips.

'Do you want to have a go spraying?' he asked, trying to distract himself.

'Do you trust me?'

'It's not rocket science,' he said, as he reached out to hand her the hose. She took it and again their hands touched in the interaction.

He had to step back to unhook a cow that had just finished its second time round, but then he turned back to watch her working. No one had ever looked so adorable in dirty gumboots, but the way he felt right now, she could be wearing a hessian sack and he'd still think her the sexiest woman on the planet. It might not be the most romantic place for a first kiss—what with the noise of the animals, the smell he no longer noticed and Ethan only metres away wrangling the cows into position—but Lawson couldn't wait a moment longer to show Meg how he felt.

There might never *be* the perfect place, the perfect time. He wasn't going to let another week pass by—another day, another hour, another minute—without knowing what her lips felt like against his.

He took a step closer to her and swallowed as he reached out and touched her arm. She turned to face him and he saw her eyes widen as the noise of the cattle and the machinery ceased to exist. The rest of the world ceased to exist. Their gazes locked, his breath halting as he reached out, took the hose and then tossed it onto the floor.

Then he lifted his hand, palmed it against the back of her neck and drew her face towards his.

For one split-second he panicked that maybe he'd read her wrong—that maybe she didn't feel the same pull of attraction that he did—but it was too late to chicken out. He lowered his mouth and pressed it against hers. Her lips were warm and soft, her mouth pliant. He felt Meg's hands land on his back, then slide upwards over his T-shirt. She wrapped her arms around his neck as she opened her mouth and welcomed his tongue inside. A little murmur of pleasure escaped her mouth into his, only increasing his desire.

She tasted amazing—better than all his favourite foods put together. He never wanted to stop doing this. The nerves that had stopped him from kissing her so many times before faded to nothing as a feeling of rightness descended.

Why the hell had he left this so long? They could have been doing it for days.

'Oi, what's going on over there?' came a shout from Ethan, which intruded into this most perfect kiss. 'I'm sure this one's been round three times already!' He chuckled loudly.

Lawson cursed silently and reluctantly tore his lips from Meg's. 'I've been wanting to do that for a long time,' he whispered as he let his hand fall away from her neck.

In reply, she simply smiled at him, and he could tell they were on the same page.

He waited for guilt about Leah to land, but it didn't. All he felt was utter joy and the desperate desire to kiss Meg again.

Who was he kidding? He wanted to do a lot more than kiss her.

Chapter Twenty-three

Megan had never been kissed like that before. She stood in front of Lawson now, her heart racing, her cheeks flushed, her lips tingling and her limbs shaking as her mind caught up with her body. Move over Romeo and Juliet, step aside Scarlett and Rhett: their passions had nothing on the sensations currently racing through her body.

As Lawson gazed down at her and admitted he'd been thinking about kissing her for a long time, she was helpless to do anything but smile. She felt exactly the same way but it appeared she'd forgotten how to speak in the aftermath of what had just happened between them. It couldn't have lasted longer than thirty seconds but it felt bigger than a simple kiss. It was like they'd kissed a hundred times before, yet at the same time it held the magic that only a first time could. A magic that none of her other first times *ever* had. From the moment his lips touched down on hers, she knew she'd been fooling herself that he wasn't interested in her as anything more than a friend.

After that lip-lock she could no longer live in denial.

You didn't kiss someone like that unless you were hoping to someday take things even further. Again her body shivered in delicious anticipation at that thought.

A tiny voice inside her head told her she needed to set things straight with Lawson right this second by telling him the secret she'd been harbouring since the day they met, but after a few moments' deliberation, she told that pesky voice to take a hike. You couldn't fight chemistry like the kind arcing between the two of them. And why should she? It wasn't like *she'd* killed anyone! Like Archie said she wasn't a bad person, she'd just been involved in a bad thing, and she didn't want to let that thing sour this most magical moment. Kisses like that didn't come along every day. She deserved to glow in the aftermath. So did Lawson. Even without this development, today had been near-perfect and she didn't want to ruin it.

She *would* tell him, but not just yet.

Decision made, she continued to smile and listened intently as he talked her through the motions of finishing the milking and cleaning down the rotary platform. Her fascination with the process surprised her and she wondered if it was simply because it was Lawson doing the talking. The way he spoke to and worked with the cows not only made her smile, but also made her toes curl in these ridiculous boots. Even as he ushered the cows out of the pens and back into the paddocks, he treated them like individuals, with love and care. It was clear to see dairy farming wasn't simply a profession to Lawson: it was a calling, and something he loved with every last bone in his beautiful body.

Finally, when they were done, they said goodbye to Ethan and headed back to the house. Lawson took her hand as they walked and they smiled goofily at each other without saying a word. When they got to the house, he let go to open the door and Ned came running down the hallway.

'I missed you. We fed Cane dinner with Bonnie and Clyde, hope you don't mind.' Clyde had taken himself back to the house once the cows had headed out to pasture for the evening.

Megan shook her head. 'Of course not, thank you.'

'Are you staying for dinner?' Ned asked, taking hold of the hand Lawson had been holding only moments before.

'Oh, um. It's getting late, and I should probably be heading home.' She'd meant it earlier about not wanting to outstay her welcome, but neither was she ready to say goodbye to Lawson just yet.

'Why don't you stay to eat?' he said. 'We'll only be having leftovers, but you're more than welcome.'

'Can we watch *Oddball* while we eat?' Ned asked, jumping up and down in anticipation.

Lawson laughed. 'Give Meg a chance to answer.' He smiled at her. 'Sunday night we have a bit of a habit of eating on the couch while watching a movie.'

'Sounds like a wonderful habit. If you're sure you don't mind me joining you, then I'd love to.'

'We don't mind at all,' he said, his voice low and his gaze meeting hers in much the same way as it had just before he'd kissed her. Shivers flooded her body. She didn't know whether she had an appetite for food, but she was definitely hungry for something.

Ned raced off to get the movie ready and Megan followed Lawson into the kitchen to find Tab getting the leftovers out of the fridge.

'Since it's still hot, I thought we could just eat the meat cold,' she said. 'Are you staying to join us, Meg?'

'If that's okay with you.'

'More than okay. Having female company around here is such a treat.'

Megan half-laughed as an annoying thought popped into her head about how for the last few years she'd been living in confinement with nothing *but* female company. She pushed it aside, determined not to let such thoughts ruin her day. 'Thanks. Anything I can do to help?'

'Nah.' Tabitha shook her head. 'I'll just put it all onto the table and we can serve ourselves.'

Lawson went over to the sink and scrubbed his post-dairy hands. Megan followed suit and then they piled their plates with leftover sausages, salad and bread. He put together a plate for Ned before he made his own and then they took everything into the lounge room.

Tabitha immediately claimed the armchair and Ned was already perched on one end of the couch, his skinny little legs curled up beside him, leaving Megan to sit with Lawson at the other end. She lowered herself onto the couch next to Ned and then Lawson landed beside her. His thighs were pressed right up against hers and their bare skin touched below the hems of their shorts, send-ing delicious messages right to her core.

She swallowed and dared not look at him—it was wrong to be having such wanton thoughts while sitting next to his son.

Ned aimed the remote at the TV and pressed play. As the music of the opening scene began, he said, 'You're gonna like *love* this movie, Meg. Oddball is *so* much like Cane.' Then he looked past her, to Lawson. 'Dad, can we let the dogs inside so Cane can watch himself on the TV?'

Lawson shook his head. 'I think the dogs are just fine outside. Now, eat some dinner.'

Ned sighed, flopped back onto the couch and started pick-ing at his food. Megan took his lead, cut a slice of sausage and then popped it into her mouth. She wasn't a fan of cold leftovers, but she wouldn't have cared what the food tasted like. It was the people and the situation that filled her with a kind of satisfaction she hadn't felt since her family died. This was what normal felt like—eating leftovers on the couch while watching a movie with people you cared about. Because she *did* care about the Cooper-Joneses; whether she should have let it happen or not, they'd got under her skin.

Today had undoubtedly been the best day she'd had since before the fire—maybe even the best day of her life.

Halfway through the movie, when it had finally gotten dark outside and nobody had bothered to get up to turn the lights on, Lawson lifted his arm and stretched it up across her shoulder. She leaned into him and rested her head on his shoulder. It wasn't soft but she felt more comfortable than if she'd laid her head down on a fine goose-down pillow.

He was careful to remove it as the credits rolled up the screen and Ned turned to them.

'Well, Meg? What was your verdict?'

She laughed at his seemingly grown-up phrasing, but the truth was she couldn't tell anyone the plot of the movie if her life depended on it. 'It was very funny,' she said, hedging her bets.

'I still think we should have let Cane watch it,' he said, shooting daggers at his dad.

Lawson pushed to a stand. 'Maybe another time. It's time you went to bed.'

'Aw!' Ned whined.

'Ned,' Lawson warned. 'It's late enough already.'

'Can Meg put me to bed?'

Meg blinked, so surprised by this question.

'That's up to Meg,' Lawson said, giving her an apologetic look.

'*Please*, Meg?'

She found herself nodding. How hard could it be to put an eight-year-old to bed?

As if Lawson could see her hesitation, he said, 'Ned will go brush his teeth and get changed, then you can pop in and say good night to him in bed.'

'Okay.' She nodded. That didn't sound too difficult.

Lawson went with Ned to get him ready and Megan helped Tabitha scrape the plates clean and then load them into the dishwasher. They spoke more about the ice-cream business possibility until Ned returned, telling Meg he was ready. Holding her hand, he led her down the corridor with Lawson following closely. Once again she noticed the photos on the wall and once again, she wished she could stop and look at them properly. She saw a glimpse of a beautiful blonde with a baby who could have been Ned and guessed this must be Leah.

'This is my room,' Ned said, his voice full of pride as he pushed open the door and turned on the light. It was your typical eight-year-old boy's bedroom. The floor was a sea of Lego and Matchbox cars they'd have to navigate to get over to his bright-red, car-shaped bed.

'It's really cool,' she said.

'Watch your step.' There was an amused edge to Lawson's voice. 'We usually have a tidy-up on Sundays but we had better things to do today.'

She couldn't help but smile at that comment. Then she tippy-toed through the mess and pulled back the sheet on Ned's bed. Although no one had tucked her into bed for a very long time, she remembered all too clearly the way her mother had done so years earlier, and how loved and secure it always made her feel. She smiled down at him as he climbed into bed, and then she pulled the thin sheet over the top of him.

'Sweet dreams, Ned,' she said.

He reached his arms up for a hug and she willingly gave him one. 'See you soon, Meg,' he said, when she eventually pulled away.

'Good night.'

She stepped back to allow Lawson his turn. He stooped down, kissed Ned, then switched on the bedside light. 'See you in the morning, little man.'

As they left the room, Lawson switched off the main light.

'He's such a great little boy,' she said as they walked away.

'Thanks. He has his moments, but most of the time I can't believe my luck that I got such a cool kid.

Megan smiled. 'I really must be getting home now,' she said, knowing that despite the fact she never wanted this day to end, Lawson had to get up early in the morning.

'I'll miss you,' he said, slipping his hand into hers as he led her out onto the verandah.

'Me too,' she admitted, although a heavy weight filled her heart at this truth.

Out the back, he whistled for Cane, who came running out of the yard with Clyde. Bonnie was resting beside the back door; she looked up at them and then flopped her head back down onto her paws. Lawson scooped Cane up and carried him back through the house. Megan paused to say good night to Tabitha, who was still sitting in the lounge room, now knitting.

'Good night,' Tabitha said. 'See you on Wednesday.'

Lawson walked them to her car, opened the back door and deposited Cane inside.

'Thanks for a wonderful day,' she said, her hand on the driver's door.

In reply, he closed the gap between them and kissed her again. *Oh Lord!* Her body melted. She'd thought it had been magical the first time because it *was* the first time but this time hit it out of the ballpark. She could only lean into his kiss, into his body, and give herself wholeheartedly. He pressed her up against the car, again holding her face between his two hands as if he couldn't get enough. She slid her hands up into his hair, loving the feel of his curls, and wished this moment could last forever.

They finally had to pull apart to breathe and when they did, they simply stood there a few moments staring at each other. The only light was from the moon above and they were so close she could see the stubble on his jawline glinting. She recalled the feel of his five o'clock shadow brushing against her skin only seconds earlier and shivered again.

'Sorry, I couldn't help myself.' Lawson smiled sheepishly at her and shoved his hands in his pockets as if he didn't trust himself with them. He didn't look sorry in the slightest.

'Sure you are,' she said, licking her lower lip and tasting him on it.

His gaze lingered on her mouth. 'Don't do that or I'll do it again.'

'And that would be a problem because …?'

He groaned and rested his forehead against hers—it felt, weirdly, even more intimate than when his tongue had been half-way down her throat.

'Okay, I'm going now,' she said reluctantly after a few long moments.

He nodded. Sadly, he didn't kiss her again, although the expression on his face told her he wanted to. Instead, he grabbed her hand, gently pulled her away from the door and then held it open as she climbed inside.

'Drive safely. Text me when you get there,' he said and as she nodded, he shut the door. The *thunk* echoed through the car but Cane, who was already slumbering in the back, didn't even flinch. She smiled as she turned the key in the ignition—if only he could hang out with Bonnie, Clyde and Ned every day maybe it would put a dent in his endless energy.

Megan lifted a hand in a final wave to Lawson and then drove off into the darkness, her high-beam headlights lighting the cattle in paddocks on either side of the long gravel driveway. At the road, she turned right in the direction of Rose Hill but had gone less than a kilometre when her euphoria faded; panic filled every little space where it had been.

Her hands trembled on the steering wheel. What had she been thinking letting Lawson kiss her like that? When she was with him and Ned her past faded into insignificance. She genuinely felt like a different person. A better person. But who was she kidding? She had to tell him the truth about herself. She'd be delusional if she contemplated any other scenario. Putting off that conversation had been the worst thing she could have done.

If only she'd told him right from that very first day.

When he introduced himself, she should have said, 'Hi, my name's Megan and I'm an ex-con.' He'd probably have run for the hills, but at least he'd have known. But then he'd also probably never have allowed things to develop as they had between them and, despite the nausea now rising in her gut at the thought of facing him, she couldn't entirely regret keeping the truth close to her chest. Because that would mean regretting his kisses, regretting getting to know him, Ned and Tabitha, and regretting spending the day with them as if she truly belonged.

He might reassess his desire to be with her when he found out, but they'd always have this day. She'd always be able to hold it close to her heart.

As hard as it would be, it was no longer a question of whether or not she *should* tell him, but rather when, where and how. It didn't feel like the kind of conversation you should have with someone over the phone or via text message. Sure, that would be easier, but this was too important for her to be gutless about it. She needed to see his face. She needed him to see hers and to know just how much remorse and guilt she carried inside her.

The next time he came out to visit, she would tell him.

Having made this decision didn't make living with it easy. By the time Megan arrived back in Rose Hill, she couldn't be bothered parking her car round the back out of sight. Now that she was known in Walsh, it seemed pointless to try and hide out here.

Cane woke up the moment she stopped the car, suddenly full of energy again, but all she wanted to do was crawl into bed and try and forget reality. She wanted to dream of Lawson, to re-live his lips on hers all through the night. Instead she lay awake until the early hours of the morning, listening for sounds of Eliza, simply wanting to hear the comforting presence of another soul.

Chapter Twenty-four

Feeling as if he were floating on air, Lawson watched until Meg's car lights faded into nothing and then headed back inside to check on Ned. Hopefully he was already asleep so that Lawson himself could head to bed and bask in the glow of a glorious day. Bask in the glow of Meg. He hadn't experienced such an intense attraction towards anyone since he was a hormone-filled teenager lusting after Leah.

'Great day, hey?' Tabitha's voice floated from the lounge room as he entered the house.

'The best,' he replied, unable to stifle the massive grin on his face.

'Do I need to give you the safe sex talk, big brother?'

He stuck his head round the door and poked his tongue out at her, before continuing down the hallway. He heard her laughing as he paused in Ned's doorway to listen for the telltale sound of his deep-sleep breathing. Lately Ned had been needing the bedside light to settle, but once he was asleep Lawson always turned it off.

'Dad?' Ned sat up straight and smiled his big cheeky grin. He didn't look the least bit tired, but for once Lawson didn't care. Nothing could dampen his good mood right now.

Still, he remembered his parental responsibilities. 'It's getting late, Ned. You need to get some sleep.'

'I will, Dad, but,' he shuffled over, 'can you lie with me a bit?'

'Okay, but no talking,' Lawson said, careful not to step on Lego as he walked over to the bed. 'We both need to rest.'

'Promise. Cross my heart.'

Lawson shucked off his boots before he climbed in beside him. 'Don't tell Aunty Tab I forgot to leave my shoes outside,' he whispered.

Ned giggled. 'Your secret's safe with me.'

He switched off the light and then snuggled down next to Ned, who was quiet for all of about ten seconds before his little voice broke the silence.

'Do you like Meg?'

'Of course I like Meg,' Lawson replied.

'No, dad, I mean *really* like her. Do you want to kiss her and do romance and stuff?'

Romance? Stuff? Lawson's eyes widened and his cheeks burned—thank God he'd turned off the light. 'Um …'

'It's okay if you do. I want you to know if you wanted to get married and make babies with her, I'd be okay with that because I really like her as well.'

Make babies? Lawson knew that one day he'd have to have the birds and the bees talk with his son but he hadn't imagined it would happen like this. It felt like Ned was the grown-up and he the embarrassed teen. Somehow he managed to compose himself.

'Thanks, little man. I appreciate that. And I'll be honest, I really do like Meg a lot, but it's early days. We're just getting to know each other, so I don't want you to get your hopes up about brothers and sisters just yet, okay?'

'I'm not stupid, Dad. I know they take nine months to make.'

Lawson snorted; he couldn't help it. 'Geez, is there anything you don't know?'

Ned thought a moment. 'Well, I'm not exactly sure how the babies get in the mum's tummy? Do *you* know? Is it the same way we insem'nate the cows?'

Lawson's cheeks grew even hotter. He cleared his throat. 'It's … a *bit* different. Look we'll discuss this later, okay. Time for sleep.'

'Okay.' Ned let out a massive sigh. 'But you'll kiss Meg soon, won't you?'

Lawson smiled. 'Shall I let you in on another little secret?'

'Yeah! What is it?'

'I've already kissed her.'

'Really? Onya, Dad!' Ned wrapped his arms around Lawson and squeezed him tightly.

Lawson laughed and then kissed his forehead. 'Good night, Ned.'

'Good night, Dad. Love you.'

'Love you, too.'

Within two minutes Ned was asleep and Lawson slid out of bed, tickled pink at the thought that his son had just given him his blessing. Ned liked Meg, Tabby liked Meg, there was just one more person he needed to talk to and one more thing he needed to do before he could truly throw himself into this new relationship. He went into the bathroom, brushed his teeth, washed his face, ran his fingers through his hair, called out 'good night' to Tabitha and then retreated into his bedroom.

He went across to his tall boy, where a framed photo of Leah sat in pride of place on top. It had been taken on their wedding day. Her skin was glowing and all her blonde hair curled and piled up on her head—she looked radiant. He'd always loved it because she wasn't looking directly at the camera; she'd been looking at him, and he vividly remembered the feeling her smile had given him. He'd loved her so much. He still did, but she was gone and, for the first time since her death, he finally felt alive again.

'I've met someone,' he told her. 'She's great with Ned and I think things could get serious between us. I hope that's okay with you.'

And then, he picked up the frame, lifted it to his lips and kissed his wife one final time. A lone tear trickled down his cheek and he didn't wipe it away as he opened the bottom drawer, shoved his clothes aside and buried the photo. He swallowed the golf-ball-sized lump that had formed in his throat and gazed down at the gold wedding band still sitting on his finger. So many times over the last four years he'd thought about taking it off, but he'd never been able to bring himself to do it.

Tonight, with Meg's face clearer in his head than Leah's, he easily slipped it off. And it felt surprisingly good. He felt lighter, as if he'd not only removed the ring from his finger but also a heavy weight from his shoulders, a burden that had been keeping him down for years. He put the ring into the drawer next to Leah's photo, covered it over with clothes and then closed the drawer gently.

When he straightened, he looked into the mirror, almost not recognising the face that smiled back. It belonged to a man ready to live in the present, finally hopeful for the future, no longer chained to the past.

Chapter Twenty-five

Megan let Cane out for a pee just after dawn and then crawled back into bed. She felt like she'd been on an all-night bender and hoped that perhaps she'd finally be able to get some rest. But it was wishful thinking. After another few hours of tossing and turning, she admitted defeat and was just climbing out of bed again to go for a run when her phone beeped with a message.

Only the day before she'd have snatched up the phone with excitement at the thought of a message from Lawson, but today her stomach lurched as she reached over to pick it up.

He'd sent her a selfie—himself by the rotary platform with a load of cows' bums in the background. The words *It was more fun with you here* accompanied the photo.

'Oh!' The one word slipped from her lips on a sigh and she pressed the phone against her chest. Before she could reply another beep arrived. Slowly, she lifted the phone and looked at the screen.

You busy this morning? I want to see you again.

A war raged within her. While her heart and her hormones wanted to see him, her mind reminded her of the conversation that had to be had. Still there was no point putting off the inevitable.

She typed back, her fingers trembling. *No. I was planning on some more research.*

Can I keep you company for a bit? Once I've finished the milking.

Sounds great, she lied, knowing that what was about to happen would probably be anything but great.

She climbed out of bed, pulled on her running gear and traipsed downstairs with Cane under her arm. She let him outside to pee again while she threw on a load of washing, and then when they were both done, they set off. Today, however, running didn't calm her at all and so she returned home sooner than she usually would, collected the eggs Archie had left on the front door step and then jumped into the shower.

After that, she spent a ridiculous amount of time trying to make herself presentable. Heading downstairs again, she tried to stomach some dry toast, all the while rehearsing in her head over and over all the different ways she could tell Lawson the things that had to be said.

After eating a few bites, she gave up on breakfast, choosing instead to head on over to the historical society and try and distract herself with research. Not wanting to abuse Archie's dog-sitting generosity, she tied Cane to a post outside and tossed him a bone to chew. She was also scared that if she saw Archie this morning, he'd take one look at her and know something was wrong. She couldn't fall apart until after her conversation with Lawson. By then, nothing would matter any more anyway.

Inside the building, she flicked on the light but didn't open the blinds; she'd worked out that keeping them down helped to stop the heat from building up inside. Lawson's generator and fan had been such a blessing and, as she turned the fan on now, she wondered if he'd take them both back after today. Then she shook her head and got to work—that was the least of her worries.

Focusing on the far past and thinking about Eliza was a lot easier than worrying about Lawson, and Megan soon found herself lost in old photos and documents from the 1930s. There weren't a great deal of photos—back then people didn't take the thousands of snaps they did today—but the few she found were fascinating. She loved seeing Rose Hill back in its heyday and imagining what life would have been like here decades ago. This morning, one particular photo caught her interest—it was of a group of young people. They were all dressed as if they'd been out riding and were all men except for one woman. She recognised the woman immediately as Eliza. Every person in the photo was looking directly at the camera, except for Eliza and one of the young men, who were looking at each other instead. From the expression on their faces it was clear to see they had the hots for each other.

Megan turned the photo over, hoping to find names on the back indicating who the others in the picture were, but there was nothing but an old yellow stain. *Dammit.* It was frustrating to have all this history at her fingertips, yet not be able to find the answers she wanted. With another glance at the mystery man, she put the photo to one side and went back to some of the newspapers from around the same time. If she found a photo of this guy in the paper, there would likely be a name alongside it.

She flicked through a few editions and was feeling disheartened at not finding anything when Cane started barking, alerting her to the fact they had a visitor.

Her heart flipped. Lawson had arrived. While she'd been lost in Eliza's world, she'd managed to forget her own worries, but now … Both her stomach and her grip on the photo tightened as she shot to her feet. For some reason this felt like a conversation she wanted to have standing up.

She heard him stop to talk to Cane, giving her a second to collect herself. This was it. *Do not chicken out.* And then suddenly he was standing there in the open doorway, looking so sexy it should be illegal in a checked shirt pushed up to the elbows and knee length khaki shorts. Her mouth went dry.

'Hi there,' he said, his voice low, as his lips curled into a smile and he unashamedly looked his fill from the top of her head right down to the red-painted toenails that poked out of her sandals.

'Hi,' she managed, although that one word came out more like a puff of air.

He stepped into the room and came to stand right in front of her, so close she could see he hadn't bothered to shave that morning, and it only made him more sexy. 'I couldn't sleep last night,' he admitted.

'Oh?' Her fingers started to tremble around the photo.

He nodded, his eyes searching hers. 'And it was entirely your fault. You refused to get out of my head.'

His beautiful words were intoxicating and she tried desperately to keep her head. 'I couldn't sleep either,' she said, 'so I finally gave up and came in here.' She thrust the photo up between them, almost like a shield. 'Look what I found!'

His brow furrowed a little as he looked down at the photo.

'There's Eliza,' she explained, pointing first to the young woman and then to one of the men, 'and look at that man.'

He scrutinised the face she pointed at. 'What about him?'

'You don't recognise him by any chance, do you?'

He half-chuckled. 'Sorry, but I wasn't even a twinkle in my grandfather's eye back then. Why the interest in him?'

Megan's heart sank. Of course Lawson wouldn't know who the guy was any more than she did. Still, she pressed on. The truth was, she was stalling. Talking about anything but what she knew she *needed* to talk about. 'Look how he and Eliza are looking at each other? Not at the camera at all. I think they were lovers, or at least interested in each other.'

'Is that right?' He glanced up from the photo and refocused his gaze on her; she could tell he wasn't really listening.

'If I could just find out who he was—'

Lawson cut her off, taking the photo from her grasp and gently putting it down on the desk behind them. He smiled down at her in a way that sent her heart galloping. 'This is truly fascinating, but, to tell you the truth, right now, I'm more interested in the present.'

And then, before she had the chance to say anything in response, he pulled her into his arms and kissed her. Hard. Hungry. Like they hadn't seen each other for weeks.

Megan felt her body melting, along with her resolve, as he pushed her back against the desk. The back of her thighs slammed into the hard wood, but she barely flinched as desire burned within. Compared to that first kiss in the dairy and then the next against her car, this one was X-rated, and she kissed him back, unable to stop herself. Tongues duelled and hands wandered. His fingers drew tantalising patterns on her face and neck before trawling lower, igniting her skin wherever they went.

Megan moaned as his thumb found her nipple. The sensations were so strong, it felt as if the material of her bra and T-shirt wasn't even there. She arched up into him, her body acting of its own accord, ignoring the warning sirens blaring inside her head. When he cupped her whole breast, she gasped into his mouth with a pleasure stronger than anything she'd felt before.

He tore his mouth off hers and looked into her eyes. 'You all right?'

No, said a barely audible voice in the far depths of her mind. *You may be enjoying this, but it is* not *all right.*

'Yes, but …' She stumbled on her words, not wanting to say them. 'There's something I should tell you.'

He frowned. 'You're married?'

'No.' She would have laughed if she wasn't so strung-out.

'You're a lesbian?'

'No!' Couldn't he feel the way her body reacted to him?

'Then,' he pressed his forehead against hers and whispered, 'right now, what could possibly be more important than kissing me?'

Telling him the truth, declared that pesky voice in her head.

Nothing, said a much stronger one. It sounded a lot like hormones. Apparently, she said the latter aloud, because Lawson grinned and then put his mouth back on hers.

And the taste of his lips silenced her.

Within moments, his hands moved lower again, skimming down over her breasts and then skating under the bottom of her T-shirt. Megan sucked in a breath as he touched her bare skin. Her mind cleared itself of everything but him. Everything but how his hands and mouth made her feel. She wasn't sure whether it was him or her who whipped off her T-shirt, but suddenly it was on the floor between them.

Her heart raced. They looked into each other's eyes as he reached one hand up to undo her bra. She shrugged out of it and if fell to the ground too. Megan hadn't been this exposed to someone in years, but she didn't feel vulnerable or embarrassed as Lawson gazed down at her bare chest. She felt nothing but pure, unadulterated need. Nothing else mattered but the two of them.

'You're beautiful,' he said and then he dipped his head and took a nipple into his mouth. A gasp burst from her and then she moaned as his tongue flicked her bud, creating a flood of wetness below.

She thought she might actually come as she looked down at the top of his head moving seductively while his tongue laved her tight nipple. Then, as if his mouth weren't potent enough, he pressed his hand against her belly and slipped it down past the waistband of her shorts. Things were moving so fast but she didn't want them to stop.

'Lawson.' She breathed out his name as he moved his fingers in her slick wetness. Within seconds she was a writhing mess of need and satisfaction. As waves of pleasure rippled through her, she reached between them and palmed her hand against his shorts, loving what she felt and the knowledge that all that delicious hardness was because of her.

He groaned, which only turned her on more.

'I need you,' she whispered.

She didn't have to ask twice. He removed his hand from inside her knickers, whipped a small foil packet out of his pocket, then shoved his shorts down and sheathed himself. She couldn't get her own shorts and knickers off quick enough. Megan leaned back against the desk as he stepped between her legs. Their gazes met in an explosive heat as he pushed inside and filled her completely. It was embarrassing (and surprising) how quickly she came, considering he'd brought her to climax only moments before with his fingers, but he was right there beside her every second of the way.

He cried out, 'Oh, Meg,' as he thrust hard one final time and she knew from that moment onwards she never wanted to be called 'Megan' again.

Afterwards they held each other, barely moving an inch, as her heart rate attempted to return to normal. Judging by Lawson's erratic breathing, she guessed his might be trying to do the same.

'Oh my goodness,' she shrieked, when she finally glanced up and saw the wide-open door. 'The door!'

Lawson's eyes widened, but he chuckled as he extracted himself and walked over to kick the door shut. 'Let's hope Archie didn't decide to go for a walk or he might have got an eye-full.'

'*Oh Lord.*' Meg dropped her hands into her face unable to believe what they'd done with the door wide open. She'd totally lost her head, as well as her clothes.

Lawson came to stand in front of her again. He put his thumb on her chin and gently lifted her face up to look at him. She swallowed, fighting back tears as she looked into his warm eyes.

How could she ever tell him the truth? She couldn't bear for him to look at her differently.

'That was amazing,' he said, moving his thumb upwards to brush over her lips. 'But believe it or not, I didn't come here to seduce you—I just wanted to see you, maybe kiss you again—but you drive me crazy. I can't think about anything but you right now. I definitely didn't plan on consummating our relationship in the middle of a pile of old papers and photos.'

She forced a smile and he added, 'I promise you, next time, we'll take things slower ... maybe even do it in a bed.'

His words were so seductive, they rode right over the top of any doubts that were trying to creep through. 'I don't have any complaints,' she whispered, 'but I do have a question.'

He smiled. 'Yes?'

'If you *weren't* planning all that, then why did you bring a condom?'

He laughed and the sound rippled through her limbs, relaxing her. 'Caught. Okay, I'll admit I was hopeful, but I didn't envisage it exactly like this. I was hoping to wow you with my powers of seduction, make you scream in ecstasy and last a lot longer than an adolescent boy desperate to get his rocks off.'

Now *she* laughed. 'Well, two out of three ain't bad.'

'Speaking of which ...' Lawson indicated his nether regions. 'I better deal with this. Are there any tissues in here?'

She bit her lip and shook her head. 'Sorry.

'No worries.' He grinned sheepishly. 'This is going to be interesting then. Which of these old papers aren't really important do you think?'

She grimaced. 'How about you come back to my place to have a shower?'

He leaned in close. 'Will you be sharing the water with me?'

She swallowed, the image of water, soap and the two of them naked landing in her head and making her blush. 'Do you want me to?'

'Sweetheart, that is the most stupid question I've ever heard.'

* * *

'What was that thing you were trying to tell me?' Lawson asked, when they were finally sitting down at the kitchen table drinking coffee after the raunchiest shower of her whole life.

'What do you mean?' she asked, her mind void of pretty much everything except what they'd just done.

'Back at the historical society. You said you needed to tell me something, but then I persuaded you it could wait.' He leaned back now in the chair as if he was all ears and her heart clenched. The steadfast belief she'd had that morning that she needed to tell him about her past wavered.

Was this really a post-coital kind of conversation?

'You mean ... about Eliza?' she stumbled, her grip tightening on her mug.

He shook his head and she suddenly noticed he was no longer wearing his wedding ring. The floor felt as if it moved beneath her. When had he taken it off? She racked her brain, trying to remember if he'd been wearing it yesterday. If circumstances were different, she'd be overjoyed by this development, but it only made her heart sink further.

'No, I don't think so,' he said. 'I got the feeling there was something else on your mind and I want you to know, I care about you a lot, and if there's anything you want to talk about, I'm here for you.'

Oh Lord! Guilt flooded her at his kind words and tears burst from her eyes. She retrieved her hand. 'I'm so sorry,' she said, trying to wipe them away. 'I shouldn't have slept with you.'

'What?' Lawson's head snapped back as if she'd slapped him. Then, he looked into her eyes and his face fell. 'Oh, shit.' He skidded his seat closer to hers and pulled her into his arms. 'What is it, Meg? Did someone hurt you? I'm so sorry if I rushed you into anything. The last thing I wanted to do was make you cry.'

'No!' She shook her head and pulled away from him, not wanting Lawson to feel bad. She was the villain, not him. 'No, it's nothing like that.' She sniffed. 'You've been nothing but wonderful. It's just that … I don't … deserve you.'

'Now, that's *bullshit*,' he said, his voice more forceful than she'd ever heard. 'What could possibly make you think such utter nonsense?'

His absolute faith in her only made her feel worse. 'You know how I told you I lost the plot a little after my parents died?'

He nodded. 'Totally understandable.'

'Well, the thing is, I turned to the wrong people and the wrong things to try and block out what had happened. I got messed up in drugs for a bit—getting high was the only thing that would allow me to forget. At least for a little while.'

He nodded slowly and then rubbed his lips together. It pained her to imagine the thoughts that must be spinning through his head. She already felt him slipping away and couldn't bring herself to say another word. She was definitely *not* going to get through the whole story in one go.

'What kind of drugs?'

She swallowed. 'To start with, just a little weed. But later, pretty much anything I could get my hands on. Then I got hooked on crystal meth.'

Lawson frowned. 'Ice?'

She nodded, a lump forming in her throat.

He was quiet a few long moments and her heart beat heavily, anticipating doom. Then he finally asked, 'Do you take anything now?'

'No!' She shook her head vigorously. Kicking her addiction hadn't been easy but she'd been determined. 'I'm completely clean. I have been for over four years.'

'That must have been tough,' he said, 'breaking that habit. Did you get help? Like counselling? Treatment?'

'Yes.' Being thrown into prison had actually been a good thing—it wasn't easy to access drugs unless you knew the right people, and she'd kept to herself, not wanting to make waves. Following the hell of withdrawal, she'd been a model inmate—working hard when required, using the courses and workshops as a way to distract herself from the urges, and attending counselling. 'Eventually I did. On the surface the counselling was to help deal with my addiction, but I also finally had an outlet to talk through and deal with my grief. Until then, although my grandparents tried to get me to open up, I shut myself off—I think I was scared to feel too close to them in case I lost them as well. But I finally realised that my drug problem wasn't just hurting me.'

He still didn't say anything so she kept on talking. 'I thought of how ashamed and heartbroken my parents would have been if they saw me travelling down such a destructive path, and realised that if I didn't change, I may as well have died with them.'

At the mention of her parents, more tears prickled the corners of her eyes, but she blinked, not wanting to cry again, not wanting him to think she was trying to manipulate him into feeling sorry for her.

'I'm glad you didn't die,' he said, reaching out and taking her hands again. When he brought them up to his lips and kissed her knuckles, her stomach turned over.

'Really?' she whispered.

Lawson nodded. 'I won't pretend I'm not shocked by this but I'm in awe of you, Meg. You've been through so much and it's hardly surprising you needed something to get you through all that tragedy. If I hadn't had Leah and Tabitha to get me through

Mum's death, and then Ned to keep going for after Leah died, I might have done something similar. Lord knows there were many times I just wanted to be able to stop feeling anything.'

He squeezed her hands and continued. 'But despite all you've been through, you've come out the other side, stronger. I wish I could erase all that pain you went through, but all that's in the past now. I want to explore this thing between us, I want a future with you.'

Meg blinked. She couldn't believe her ears. How could she *not* want a future with this wonderful guy? She'd never wanted anything more. But she hadn't told him everything yet. Her heart trembled in her chest at the thought. He'd been so understanding about the drugs, but that was only a fraction of her story.

Lawson raised an eyebrow and his lips quirked up at the edges. 'Although maybe I'm being a little presumptuous? Maybe you just want me for hot sex?'

At his attempt to lighten what was the darkest conversation they'd ever had, a nervous laugh escaped her mouth. A place low in her belly quivered at the mention of hot sex, but she most definitely wanted more than just that. Until that moment she hadn't known the power the word 'future' held over her. But being in Lawson's arms, feeling so cherished by him, filled a hole that had been gaping inside her for far too long.

What he was offering was too damn tempting and maybe she was simply chicken, but she couldn't bring herself to strike a match and throw it on it all. Not just yet.

'Thank you,' she whispered. 'I do want more than just hot sex. I want it all.'

As Lawson leaned forwards and kissed her, as his tongue teased open her mouth to close the deal, Meg promised herself that she *would* have the rest of this conversation. But it could end up being the most important conversation of her life, so she needed to choose the most perfect moment to have it and to spend a little more time working out the perfect words to say.

Chapter Twenty-six

Lawson's head spun from Meg's confession. For a few moments following, he'd sat in disbelief. Would it have changed things if she'd told him before now? Would he have kept his distance? Stopped her from getting close to Ned?

She'd tried to tell him earlier when they'd been in the throes of pre-sex passion but he'd been too drunk with lust to listen. Still, surely there'd been opportunities before today? All those times they'd sat together pouring over the newspapers at the historical society, the day they'd driven to the tip, yesterday when they were alone together in the dairy. This was a *huge* revelation.

He'd met her gaze, not sure what he wanted to say. But one look at her vulnerable, tear-soaked eyes and it had hit him. Who was he to judge? They hadn't known each other long, and he hadn't walked in her shoes.

This wasn't about him—this was about Meg. As hard as it had been to hear about her addiction to drugs, he knew it had to have been even more difficult for her. Not only to experience all that— to fall so low and then all the motivation and determination it must have taken to recover—but also to open up to him, to admit what she'd once been. And he found himself glad she'd trusted him enough to come clean.

If he had any suspicion that she still dabbled in drugs, he'd have been out of there faster than a bull at a gate—he couldn't risk Ned being close to anything like that—but he believed her. He'd always suspected she'd come to Rose Hill to escape something and now he knew what it was, her desire to open the tea room and make a new life for herself only impressed him more. He'd been honest when he told her that he was in awe of her.

But now time was marching on. Lawson needed to head back to the dairy soon but he hated the thought of leaving Meg alone after the conversation they'd just had.

His face still only inches from hers, he tried to take her mind off all that, to let her know they were okay. 'Want to hear something funny?' he asked.

'Desperately,' she admitted on a half-laugh.

'Last night after you left, I went to check on Ned and he was still awake. We ended up having a heart-to-heart. He told me how much he likes you and he gave us his blessing.'

'He what?' A full smile finally blossomed on her face and he knew he'd made the right decision not to dwell on her past.

'I know, right?' Lawson grinned. 'It was hilarious. He was so earnest. I think he likes you almost as much as I do.'

'The feeling is entirely mutual. On both accounts.' She pulled back a little. 'Do you have time for another coffee?'

'Unfortunately, no.' He pushed back his seat and stood, feeling as if they'd been sitting there for a lot longer than they actually had.

She nodded. 'The cows wait for no man?'

'Something like that.' He pulled her to her feet and then into his arms. Although his body immediately reacted to the feel of her against him, this embrace wasn't sexual. 'Thank you for talking to me,' he whispered into her hair.

She nodded as they broke apart and, then holding hands, headed out of the kitchen and down the hallway towards the front door. On the side table near the stairs, he noticed the photo she'd tried to show him when he'd first arrived at the historical society. He vaguely remembered her carrying it back and she must have tossed it there right before he'd pulled her into his arms and ravished her again.

'Hey,' he said, picking it up and looking down. 'What was it you were saying about these people?'

'Oh.' Meg leaned close and pointed to a woman. 'That's Eliza.' Then she slid her finger across the image and landed on a young man. 'And check out the way that guy is looking at her.'

'He's looking at her the way I look at you.'

She blushed, then whispered, 'I know. I'd really like to find out who he is. It looks like he and Eliza had something between them and so I'm wondering if maybe he's a key to the mystery of what happened to her.'

'You think he killed her?'

She shrugged one shoulder. 'I don't know what to think. But I'd like to know who he is and what happened to him.'

Lawson took another look at the photo; something about the man in question felt a little familiar. He frowned.

'What is it?' Meg asked.

'He's the spitting image of one of Adeline's brothers.'

'You think maybe he's one of her ancestors?' Meg sounded excited at the prospect at a possible discovery.

He shrugged. 'I'm probably wrong, but if he is, then I doubt he had a thing with Eliza. The Walshes and Elverds founded this region and they're, well, they're what people call blue bloods. None of them would have ever looked twice at a townie like Eliza.'

'Eliza was very beautiful,' Meg said, pouting.

He smiled. That he had to concede. 'Maybe she committed suicide because they *did* have a fling, but he wouldn't acknowledge it. Or maybe …'

Before he could offer another speculation, a door on the second storey by the stairs slammed shut, making them both jump. He dropped the photo and it floated back down onto the side table. They glanced upwards.

'You've got a window open upstairs, right?' he asked.

She shook her head. 'Nope. I don't think someone likes what you said about her.'

He shuddered. 'I was just speculating.'

'Apologise to her.' Meg held her chin high.

'What?' He scoffed.

'Apologise,' she said again, her lips twitching and her eyes sparkling.

'Fine.' He smiled as well and then looked upstairs again. 'I'm sorry, Eliza. I had no right to make such assumptions.'

Immediately, the door that had slammed opened again and seconds later he felt a cool air waft past him. He looked back to Meg and knew from the expression on her face she'd felt it too. He was now a fully-fledged believer.

'If only she could talk,' he said, with a sad shake of his head.

'Sometimes I feel as if she does.' She paused a moment, then, 'You know how I want to start the tea room?'

He nodded.

'Well, that idea just popped into my head, seconds before I told you about it. It was almost as if someone else had thought it, and then …'

'And then you found out about Eliza's tea room.'

'Yes.'

'Wow.' He let out a long whoosh of air. Today was making his head spin.

'I know,' she whispered. 'I know.'

Cane came barrelling out of the kitchen where they'd left him lying under the table as if he were dead. He must have been jolted from his slumber by the door slamming. He halted by the stairs, skidding on the newly polished floorboards and whined as he looked longingly over at them.

Lawson chuckled, handed Meg the photo, then went over and picked up the pup. 'You decided to say goodbye after all, did ya? You big scaredy-cat.'

Cane barked once as if disgusted with this tag. Meg laughed and walked with him as he carried the pup over to the front door. She opened it and he put Cane down. He was fairly well trained now—he didn't bolt whenever he had the chance and he always came back when they called him.

As Cane sniffed the ground near by, Lawson turned to face Meg and placed his hand on her arm. 'You okay?'

She shrugged one shoulder. 'I'm not scared of Eliza.'

He chuckled, knowing she knew he didn't mean that but not wanting to push the issue. She'd finally opened up to him and that was enough for now.

'Hey, do you mind if I take a photo of that photo to show my gran? Her body might be failing her but her mind's as sharp as a tack; she might be able to tell us who some of these people are.'

Meg's eyes lit up. 'That would be great. If it's not too much trouble.'

'To be honest, I'm almost as curious as you about Eliza.' He got out his mobile, took a quick snap and then leaned forwards and kissed her on the lips, resisting the urge to prolong this goodbye. 'I'll call you tonight, okay? And visit Gran tomorrow and let you know if I get any intel.'

She laughed. 'That'd be great. Thanks.'

'No worries.' He almost asked if she wanted to come meet Gran, but when two of the most important women in his life met he wanted it to be special. Maybe he'd bring them both out to the farm for lunch some time soon.

They kissed one final time before he pulled himself away, walked over to his ute and climbed inside. The radio came alive with talkback radio as he turned the key in the ignition, but he barely noticed as he looked back to the house and saw Meg waving. He lifted his hand in return and then finally drove off, his mind full of her and everything she'd told him.

Adeline had been right: Meg had been hiding something. But she'd chosen to tell him and, despite the news of her drug addiction shocking him, he felt like they'd knocked down a wall that had been lingering between them. In some ways, the fact Meg wasn't perfect made him feel even more affection for her. Leah had always had her shit together. Nothing ever fazed her. Yes, she'd loved him but she'd also been so competent and independent that occasionally he hadn't felt very needed or necessary.

With Meg, it felt different—he felt as if he could help her heal her past just as much as she was helping him heal his. And that felt bloody good.

He found himself grinning and reached over to switch radio stations—he was in the mood for music, not dry chatter—but as his finger landed on the button, the words 'dairy crisis' registered in his head. His smile faded and his hand fell back.

The news wasn't good—WA Country Milk had just gone public with the announcement that their company was in dire straits and that this week they'd be 'in discussions' with some of their farmers.

Lawson's mood plummeted. What the hell did 'in discussions' mean?

Chapter Twenty-seven

The ancient ceiling fans in the Walsh town hall made a dull buzzing noise as they whirred overhead, but did nothing to allay the late February heat. Sweat pooled in Megan's cleavage. She put her knitting down for a moment and wiped a hand across her brow.

Still, in spite of the less than pleasant temperature, she was truly enjoying the camaraderie of sitting in a circle on plastic chairs, listening to the various conversations as she and the other women knitted. She wasn't as quick at knitting as she was at crocheting, but no one seemed to care how fast things got done. As well as doing their bit for charity, it was clear this was also a worthy excuse to get together and have a good chat. Tabitha sat beside Megan, knitting almost as quickly with one arm as everyone else was with two and punctuating the chatter with funny remarks that made everyone laugh.

Everyone except for Adeline, who'd barely said a word to Megan when she'd arrived and had sat glowering at her from the other side of the circle ever since.

'You okay?' Tabitha said, nudging Megan with her good arm as if she sensed her discomfort.

Megan smiled at her, wondering if Lawson had told her any of what she'd shared on Monday. Tabitha hadn't acted any differently towards her but then again she didn't seem the type of person to judge. 'Yes, I'm really enjoying myself.'

'Good.' Tabitha grinned back, then whispered, 'my brother's been in a *very* good mood this week.'

Megan's cheeks flamed as if they'd been licked with fire.

Tabitha chuckled softly. 'It's all right, I don't want to hear any sordid details, but I just wanted you to know I'm pleased as punch for the pair of you. It's been a long time since Lawson has smiled like he just won the lottery.'

'Who won the lottery?' asked Chloe Wellington, the woman from the markets.

'No one,' said the elderly lady sitting next to Tabitha. Beth (if Megan remembered her name correctly) had a blue-rinse bob and spoke with an accent not unlike the queen's—she'd informed Megan earlier that she'd moved to the country after meeting her second husband (a farmer) online. 'Tabitha was just saying that Lawson feels like he's won the lottery now he's found Meg.'

'Ooh,' said Chloe. 'Are you and Lawson an item?'

Megan swallowed. 'Well … we … yes, I suppose we are.'

There was a collective sigh all around the circle. All except one of the group appeared overjoyed by this news. So much for Tabitha whispering!

The questions came fast and furious after that. *How exactly did you meet? How long has it been going on? Do you get along well with Ned?* And grew more and more personal with each one. *Where did you come from?* Megan shifted in her seat, hoping they didn't notice her discomfort. *Do you have any family near by? Where did you first kiss?*

'Do you think it's time we break for lunch?' Tabitha asked, saving Megan from answering this last one. Megan could have kissed *her*.

'Good idea.' Adeline shot to her feet and stalked off into the kitchen.

One by one, the other women put down their knitting needles, stood, stretched their backs and followed. Megan opened the container she'd brought and laid her slice pieces out on a plate as the other women were doing with the food they'd brought. The various dishes were put out onto a couple of trestle tables in the hall and then everyone grabbed a plate and served themselves. There was enough food—sweet and savoury—to feed the whole town and all of it was home-cooked fare.

'We each take home a plate of leftovers for our families,' said Beth, who stood next to Megan as she surveyed the offerings. 'My husband loves our knitting sessions.'

'I can imagine there's usually plenty left over,' Megan replied, as she picked up a curried egg sandwich.

'You'd be surprised,' said one of the others. 'We country ladies know how to eat well.'

They all laughed and then continued piling up their plates.

Chloe came up beside Megan. 'I wanted to say how happy I am for you and Lawson. My boy Sam and he have been best friends since they were toddlers and he's like another son to me. It was so tragic what happened to Leah, but Lawson deserves a second chance at happiness.'

Megan just smiled. What *had* happened to Leah?

Another knitter—Megan thought she'd introduced herself earlier as Kathy—said, 'He certainly does. After all he's been through. Leah's death was such a shock, not just for the family but for our whole town. Walsh had always seemed such a safe place until then.'

There were murmurs of agreement from around the table as the happy chatter of seconds before faded. Megan had no idea what to say to any of these women. She desperately wanted to ask them how

Leah had died, but they obviously assumed Lawson had already told her. They had spoken about his wife but she realised he'd never mentioned exactly what had happened to her. Megan had assumed something like cancer or a car accident, but the way these women spoke had her wondering if she'd been barking up the wrong tree.

Now the fact she'd slept with the man but didn't know how his wife had died seemed embarrassing and somehow wrong.

'Hmm …' She nodded and reached for a mini-quiche, noticing her hand was shaking slightly.

Once everyone was seated back in the circle with their plates on their laps, Adeline walked around with a tray of glasses and a jug of iced tea, which was, apparently, her speciality. She served the women sitting either side of Megan but ignored her.

'You forgot Meg,' said Beth, who seemed to have taken quite a shine to her.

'Oh, didn't you know?' Adeline smiled nauseatingly. 'Meg doesn't drink tea. That's *right*,' she continued before any one else had a chance to say a thing, 'she makes *tea-cosies,* but she *doesn't drink tea.*' She glared at Megan and said these last three words with such force and emphasis that Megan jumped a little and almost knocked her plate off her lap.

'Fair enough,' said one of the women across the circle. 'I don't drink tea either. Or coffee, though I love tiramisu.'

Adeline tsked and continued on serving the others.

'Don't take her personally,' Tabitha leaned close to Megan and whispered, 'she's just jealous because she's had her eye on Lawson since high school. She thought she finally had a chance when Leah was killed and now you've come along and blown it.'

Killed? Megan's scalp prickled. She forced a smile and took a bite of her sandwich.

'So, Meg,' Kathy said from across the room. 'What do you plan on doing with that old building in Rose Hill?'

All gazes returned to her, everyone obviously curious.

Tabitha nudged her again and smiled in encouragement. 'Tell them about the tea room.'

So Megan swallowed her mouthful and told everyone about her plans to start a business. 'It'll be a café slash art and craft shop type thing. Showcasing local stuff, I'm hoping.'

'She's going to sell my ice-cream,' Tabitha announced.

Megan nodded, nerves making her talk fast. 'I'm still thinking through the details and I have a lot of work to do on the building before it'll be even close to being possible. But I like a challenge.'

'Oh.' Kathy waved a hand in front of her face. 'It won't take as long as you imagine. Not if we all get involved and help.'

'Lawson suggested a slab party,' Tabitha said and everyone there (all except one again) nodded their enthusiasm.

More questions followed about the structural things that needed to be fixed and Meg's vision for the tea room's appearance. Consumed with Lawson and Eliza-research, she hadn't had a chance yet to think about this in great detail, but she found herself making it up as she went along.

'I want it to be quite old-fashioned—with framed black and white photos on the walls. I've been doing some research at the historical society and I'd love to use some of the old photos of Rose Hill. Maybe even frame some of the newspaper's front pages.'

'Who is going to come to a café so far off the main road?' Adeline asked, but nobody bothered replying. If Adeline had been nicer, Megan may have felt sorry for her but as things stood she couldn't summon one iota of sympathy.

'I think that's a splendid idea,' said a woman knitting a hot pink jumper. 'You could have antique-look furniture as well.'

'Ooh yes, and fine china teapots dressed up in your gorgeous crocheted tea-cosies,' said another. 'You could sell them too and other gift items.'

Megan couldn't help smiling at their enthusiasm and her thoughts of Lawson's wife faded as she made a mental catalogue of all the ideas. The suggestions kept coming as they finished their lunches, carried the plates back into the kitchen and washed up as if they were a well-oiled machine. When the leftover food was boxed up for the spouses and the kitchen looking as if it had never been used, the women went back to the chair circle to keep knitting.

'Have you thought of what you're going to call your business?' asked Beth as she plonked herself back down in her plastic chair.

'Well,' Megan began, wondering if she were crazy to tell them about Eliza, 'you know the rumours about Rose Hill being haunted?'

'Yes,' said everyone at same time, all leaning forwards in their seats.

'I've felt a presence in the building with me.' Goose flesh rose on her arms as she told them about the coolness near the stairs, the noises and the way the tea room idea had landed in her head as if not quite her own. 'Lawson suggested I do some research on the building, you know, see if anyone had died there, and I discovered that a woman named Eliza Jane Abbott died, fell over the stair railing to her death. Or rather, the story goes that she *jumped* over the stair railing.'

Chloe gasped. 'She committed suicide?'

Megan hadn't meant to go into all this detail, but she shook her head. 'That's what the newspaper said happened but I get the feeling there's more to it. You see, the day before she died, she opened a tea room at the front of the general store and there was definitely excitement in the town about the ladies having somewhere to go and drink tea while the men were at the pub. So why would she kill herself?'

'Love!' exclaimed Beth. 'It's always down to love.'

'I can't believe you guys are talking about this,' Adeline piped up. 'What are you all? Fifteen? I thought ghost stories were for high school slumber parties.'

Once again, her objection went unnoticed.

'So what do you think happened to her?' asked another woman, her knitting needles poised in mid-air.

Megan shrugged and then looked to Adeline, wondering if it would alienate her more if she told them what else she'd found. Then again, she owed the other woman no favours.

'I think it's something to do with love like you said, Beth. You see I found a photo of her and a man and it's clear they had something going on.'

'Do you know who he is?'

She shook her head. 'Lawson was going to ask his grandmother.'

'But she was unwell yesterday,' Tabitha finished. 'Hey, let's get him to text the photo to us and see if anyone here recognises the man in question.'

'Ooh, yes, do,' encouraged the others.

Before Megan could say anything, Tab had whipped out her mobile and was shooting off a text.

'Aren't we supposed to be here knitting?' Adeline's protests went unnoticed as the women continued speculating about the mystery of Eliza.

After less than a minute, Tabitha's phone beeped. 'Bingo,' she said, glancing down at the screen.

The women passed the phone around the circle, each of them shaking their head and sighing in disappointment when they couldn't recognise the man. When the phone got to Adeline, Megan expected her to refuse to look, but instead she glanced down and her face went pale.

'That man was my great-grandfather!' she exclaimed.

'Henry or Edwin,' asked Chloe, who was clearly familiar with both sides of Adeline's family tree.

'Henry,' she replied through gritted teeth, narrowing her eyes at Megan. 'So you must have it wrong. There's no way he and your stupid ghost were together. Henry and my great-grandmother, Penelope, were childhood sweethearts. He only ever had eyes for her.'

'Funny,' mumbled a woman about Beth's age, 'that's not what my late sister-in-law used to say. She was Henry and Penelope's niece, and she said they fought worse than cats and dogs.'

Adeline glowered at Megan but everyone was too busy snickering and hypothesising about Eliza to notice.

'Perhaps Eliza was Henry's true love and they were having a passionate, secret affair,' Beth said, clearly a lover of romance and drama.

Meg couldn't help but smile.

'Or maybe,' added Tabitha, her eyes gleaming as she darted them towards Adeline, 'he got her pregnant and killed her to avoid a scandal!'

'Tabitha Cooper-Jones!' Adeline exclaimed. 'That is simply ludicrous. And I won't have you all badmouthing my family like this.'

Some of the other women raised their knitting up a little to try and hide their chuckles.

'Aw, Adeline dear.' Chloe, who was sitting next to her, reached across and patted her hand. 'No one means any harm. Whatever happened it was almost a century ago.'

But Tabitha had got Megan's mind ticking. *Could* that have been what happened? It wasn't actually a stretch of the imagination to consider someone related to Adeline capable of murder. Perhaps she should turn her research efforts on him and see what she could dig up.

'Well, whatever happened to her,' she said, feeling a chill down her spine, 'I've decided to name the business Eliza's Tea Room in her honour.'

All (except one) agreed this was a fantastic idea. The conversation continued in the same vein until someone mentioned the dairy crisis and then the mood in the room changed from frivolous to funereal. Not knowing enough to participate, Megan didn't say anything but focused on her knitting and listened. Apparently one of the big milking companies was in a bad way and of course the farmers that supplied them would suffer as a consequence. The women spoke about a local family—the Baxters—who'd recently lost their contract with their milk processing company.

'I really feel for them,' said Chloe. 'With three young mouths to feed, it's an awful situation to be in.'

'And the thing is,' said another woman, 'if it can happen to them, then it can happen to any of us.'

There were murmurs of agreement as they contemplated the worst case scenarios and discussed possible solutions. Megan started to worry about Lawson and Tabitha, who had already gone through so much in their lives, but the more the women talked, the less she understood, and her thoughts drifted elsewhere. Talk of the dairy crisis faded into background noise and she again began to hypothesise about what might have happened to Leah Cooper-Jones.

Why *had* she never asked Lawson how his wife had died?

The truth was she hadn't asked him too many questions about anything because she didn't want to have to answer any of his, and also, she hadn't wanted to know too much about his wife. But now she did. Now she itched to know so that she didn't feel like a fool when people started talking about Leah's *tragic* death.

Maybe she'd drowned? Committed suicide? Nah, that didn't fit—and surely Lawson would have said something when they'd been discussing Eliza possibly killing herself. Could she have died in some sort of awful farming accident? Been trampled by a cow? Then again, what was it Kathy had said about the town feeling safe until then? The skin on the back of Megan's neck crawled and she just wanted this day over so she could call Lawson and ask him.

Finally, just before three o'clock, Chloe remembered that the after school drama club used the hall on Wednesday afternoons. There was a mad rush to pack up all their stuff and then Megan found herself enveloped in hugs as the other women gushed about how happy they were that she'd joined them.

Outside in the car park, she was garnering the courage to ask Tabitha about Leah, when the other woman leaned in and kissed her on the cheek.

'Really sorry, but I've gotta rush to do my calves. Got a CWA meeting tonight, which unfortunately means Lawson won't be able to sneak out to see you until later.' She winked. 'Chat soon.'

Her heart sinking, Megan nodded. 'Thanks for looking out for me today.'

Tabitha grinned. 'I didn't have to do anything. Everyone loves you.'

As her new friend turned towards her car, Megan retreated to her own, slumped into the seat and then dug her mobile out of her handbag. She brought up Lawson's number and hit *call*. The phone pressed against her ear, she counted the rings, willing him to pick up, but the call finally went to message bank.

'Hi, you've reached Lawson, sorry I missed you. If ya leave a message after the beep, I'll get back to you ASAP.' And then came the promised beep.

Megan sighed, pasted a smile on her face and left a chirpy-sounding message. 'Hey, it's … Meg … Just wanted to say hi and tell you about my knitting club shenanigans, but we'll chat later. Bye.'

She'd almost said 'love you' before she disconnected but she swallowed the words just in time. They would have surprised her as much as they did him. They'd barely known each other a month, but it felt like a natural thing to say and she realised suddenly that was because she *did* love him.

Oh Lord, how she loved him.

No one had ever made her feel like Lawson did. He was her every thought, her every breath. When they were together, she felt like the luckiest girl alive and when they were apart, she could think of nothing but him.

Frustrated, she dumped her phone on the passenger seat, but just as she shoved the car keys into the ignition, she remembered Google.

Why on earth hadn't she thought of it before? Any *normal* person would have googled the hell out of a new love interest! Yet, quite aside from the fact she'd become accustomed to life without the internet, Lawson had seemed so straightforward that an online search had never crossed her mind.

She snatched her mobile back up and found the internet search icon. It felt a little stalkerish searching her boyfriend's dead wife and she knew from experience you couldn't trust everything written in print, but she was rapidly running out of ideas. Without thinking too much more about what she was doing, she typed *Leah Cooper-Jones* onto the screen and pressed Go.

Three seconds later she had a list of websites—the first few were Facebook and Twitter accounts belonging to various Leah Coopers, then there was an American actor, and finally …

'Oh my God!' Megan gasped as she looked down at the screen. *No. No!* She wished she could turn back time and un-see this. It was worse than she could ever have imagined. Her whole body began to tremble, but she tried to steady her hand so she could keep the screen still long enough to read past the headline.

An 18-year-old man will face court charged over the death of a pregnant woman who was working at a petrol station in the southwest town of Walsh. The woman, 24-year-old Leah Cooper-Jones, died after being shot in the chest during an armed robbery. Local volunteer ambulance officers—who knew Mrs Cooper-Jones well—tried to revive her, but she and her unborn baby died at the scene. Mrs Cooper-Jones has a four-year-old son with her husband, a local dairy farmer. The devastating incident has left this close-knit rural community in shock.

Before she'd even finished reading the last sentence, Megan wrenched open her car door, leaned out and threw up everything she'd eaten at lunch onto the hot black bitumen of the car park.

She felt as if *she'd* been the one to put the bullet in Leah's chest.

Once she thought she'd finished vomiting, she swigged from her water bottle, wiped her mouth and then closed her eyes as she tried to regulate her breathing. But it was no good. The moment her eyes were shut, images flashed up in front of her eyelids—images she'd spent the last *four and a half* years trying to forget. It was so real—the click of the trigger, the sharp piercing sound of the gunshot and then blood. So much blood. Everywhere.

'Oh my goodness, Meg, dear. Are you okay?'

So lost in her own horror, she hadn't heard the footsteps of Beth, but she recognised her prim and proper voice without even opening her eyes. The sound of the older woman's concern only made her want to throw up more, but somehow she swallowed it, opened her eyes and glanced up. Better Beth than Adeline.

Megan grimaced and placed a hand on her stomach. 'I think I must have eaten something that disagreed with me.'

'You poor love, I hope it wasn't my egg sandwiches.'

She shook her head. 'I don't think so; those were delicious.' Although her stomach rolled at the thought.

Beth frowned. 'Is there anything I can do for you?'

'No thanks.' She tried to swallow the lump in her throat, desperate not to cry in front of this woman. 'I think I just need to go home and lie down.'

'You'll be right to drive?'

'Yes. I think I'll manage.' That really was the least of her problems.

'Well, then, I'd better be getting home to Howard.' Beth heaved her handbag up on her shoulder. 'But you look after yourself, love.'

'I will, thanks.' Her heart racing, she forced a smile and waved the elderly woman off. Then, she swung her legs back into her car and closed her door with a thud. She felt as if it wasn't just the car door slamming, but also other doors that had recently opened for her. She'd been so stupid, so *damn* naïve, to even think she might actually get to have a happy ever after.

With this heavy thought in her heart, Megan turned the key in her ignition, briefly looked into her rear-view mirror and then reversed. Part of her believed she should drive out to Lawson's farm now—to hell with the fact that Ned would also be home—but she couldn't bring herself to do so in her current state. She couldn't face him. Not yet.

Instead, she detoured via the pub's drive-through bottle shop, and, with barely a thought to what she was doing, bought herself a bottle of wine and then headed out of Walsh towards Rose Hill. Archie had been dog-sitting Cane all day and, while she craved the comfort of her dog, the last thing she felt like doing was making conversation.

Come on, she cajoled herself as she parked her car at the service station and climbed out. *This is nothing compared to what you will have to face soon.*

Unless she just left. Running would certainly be easier than telling Lawson the truth now she knew exactly how Leah had died, but where would she run to?

Argh. Her head ached as she put her hand on the latch to open the side gate. On the other side, Cane leaped up and barked with excitement. His love and affection were so uncomplicated—even if he knew exactly what she'd done in the past, it wouldn't change the fact he adored her in the present. Today, that thought made her eyes sting as she fought back tears and pushed open the gate.

'Hello, hello,' Archie said, coming out of his house as Cane jumped up at her. He had paint splattered all over his clothes as if he'd been deep in his art. Usually she'd ask to see what he'd been painting but she just wanted to get home and crawl into bed with her bottle of cheap wine.

She managed a weak smile. 'Hi.'

Archie's grin faded and his brow furrowed. 'You all right, missy? You don't look so great. Were the old biddies at the knitting thing not that welcoming? Small towns do tend to have their cliques and—'

Megan shook her head interrupting him. 'No. They were all lovely. Very friendly.' She placed a hand against her stomach and made a face. 'I'm just not feeling very well all of a sudden.'

'Ah.' Archie held out his hands and chuckled. 'Don't come near me then. I haven't been sick in decades and I don't plan on starting now. You go home to bed and rest up. Do you want me to keep Cane a little longer?'

'Thanks, but I …' Her voice drifted off as she struggled not to fall apart. 'I want him with me.'

Archie nodded. And then she left. Cane bounded to the car and when she opened the passenger door, he leaped up into the front seat as if jumping into cars were an Olympic event. His boundless energy seemed somehow wrong considering her current mood. She should take him for a run—it would no doubt be good for both of them—but what she *should* do and what she *wanted* to do were two different things.

So instead Megan drove the short distance up the road, parked her car, grabbed her bag and the wine bottle and then followed Cane up to the house. She slipped her key into the lock and pushed the door open. He ran inside, taking a wide berth around the stairs as he ran towards the back door. He loved being out in the yard—sniffing around the weeds and digging up the dirt—and no doubt wanted her to open the door and let him out. But even that seemed like an effort.

Unable to even summon the energy to climb the stairs to bed, she took her bottle of wine into the front room and fell onto the old weathered sofa. Then, she unscrewed the cap—thank God not all bottles had corks these days—and took an undignified swig. Who needed glasses when your world was falling apart?

She drew her knees up to her chest and let out a gut-wrenching sob. Cane came barrelling into the room, took one look at her and then climbed up onto the sofa beside her. She wrapped the arm that wasn't holding the wine bottle around him and buried her head in his soft, white fluffiness. The tears fell fast and furious down her cheeks as she sculled the wine from the bottle, willing the alcohol to knock her out so she could erase today's discovery from her mind.

'I should have bought two bottles,' she muttered as she raised the bottle and saw it was already half gone.

Cane looked up and cocked his head to one side as if trying to work out what she was saying.

'Why can't life just cut me a break?' she asked him. 'I wish I'd never come here. I wish I'd never met Lawson. Whoever said it was better to have loved and lost than never to have loved at all was full of shit.'

Don't give up on him. True love is worth fighting for.

Megan snapped her head up and glanced towards the door. The unknown voice in her head sounded so much louder than usual that she fully expected to see someone standing there, but of course there was no one. She'd probably imagined the words—wishing someone would make her believe them to be true.

Yet, when Cane also whimpered as if he'd heard it, Megan's heart beat faster. She stroked his head, wanting, *needing* the comfort of both him and Eliza.

'Eliza?' she whispered staring at the open doorway and out towards the stairs. 'Did you love Henry Walsh?'

She held her breath a moment and although there was no direct answer back, Cane whimpered again. Perhaps she should get her hands on a Ouija board and try and contact Eliza through that. But almost the moment she had this thought, she rejected it. For some reason the idea didn't sit right and anyway, she felt certain she knew the answer to her question. Henry had loved Eliza. A picture spoke a thousand words and the look between Eliza and Henry in the photo was one of true love.

In her heart, she simply couldn't believe that Henry had murdered her.

But if Eliza didn't kill herself and Henry didn't do it either, then who did?

Before she could contemplate this question, her mobile phone started ringing. Cane leaped off the couch and started barking at the doorway. She wasn't sure if he was barking at Eliza or at her phone, which was buried in her bag by the front door, but the horror of not answering and Lawson worrying about her, and dragging himself and Ned out here to check if she was okay, forced her legs into action. She couldn't let them see her like this.

As Megan stumbled across the room, she knocked her knee on the corner of her makeshift coffee table but barely registered the pain; it had nothing on the ache in her heart. She thrust her hand into her bag, yanked out the phone and slid her finger across to answer the call before she could chicken out.

'Hel-lo.'

'Hey, Meg.' Lawson sounded his usual cheerful self and her heart squeezed. 'Tabitha just told me all about knitting club. I can't believe that dude was Henry Walsh.'

'I know,' Megan whispered, 'I …' She didn't know what to say.

'Meg? Are you okay?' Lawson's voice swam with care and concern. 'You sound weird.'

'I'm … I'm …' *Having a panic attack. Drunk and desolate. About to break your heart.* 'Not feeling well. Stomach thing,' she spat out. A little voice in her head said she should stop prolonging the agony and just tell him the damn truth but she couldn't bring herself to do so.

'Oh no, did it come on quick? Tabitha didn't mention you weren't well. Was it something you ate? '

If only that *were* the problem. If only she'd never read that article online. If only she'd made better choices after her family had died. If only her house had never burned down. *If only …* was the most pointless game on the planet. All those things *had* happened and she couldn't change them.

'Maybe,' she finally whispered, her fingers clutching the phone.

'Geez, you sound terrible,' he said, his tone no longer amused. 'I've got to finish the milking but Ned and I will come over straight after that. Can I bring you anything? Lemonade? Something from the chemist?'

'No!' She swallowed and tried not to sound so appalled by the idea. She desperately wanted to see him but at the same time she never wanted to see him again. 'Isn't Tabitha out tonight? I don't want you to bring Ned over and risk you two getting sick if it isn't food poisoning. Please, I'll be fine. I'm just gunna put myself to bed and hopefully sleep it off.'

'Are you sure?'

'Yes.'

'Well, okay then.' A deep sigh came down the line. 'But I'm gunna miss you tonight.'

Her heart clenched and more tears threatened at his words. She thought she'd cried it all out. 'Me too,' she whispered back. But she wasn't just talking about tonight.

'And it doesn't feel right knowing you're not well and all by yourself over there.'

'I'm not by myself. I've got Cane. And Eliza.' If things were different she would tell him about just how close Eliza felt right now, but she just wanted to get him off the phone.

'They better look after you,' he said. 'I'll let you go and I won't call or text because I don't want to disturb you if you're sleeping, but if you need anything or you get worse, call me and I'm there. All right?'

Megan pressed her lips together, trying to fight back the tears. 'All right,' she finally managed.

'Bye, Meg.'

'Bye, Lawson.' She went back into the lounge room, where she lifted the wine bottle again and took another huge gulp. For so many years no one had given a damn if she got sick. And now there was Lawson and he cared, but would he still feel the same when she told him the rest of her story?

Chapter Twenty-eight

Lawson woke even earlier than usual on Thursday morning and his first thought was Meg. He rolled over and snatched his phone off his bedside table, worried he might have slept through an SOS call. He breathed a sigh of relief when he saw he hadn't and immediately started tapping out a message.

Hope you're feeling better this morning.

His hand hovered over the screen a moment and then he added *love Lawson*. He might only have known Meg for a few weeks but she'd made more of an impact on him and his life than anyone had in the last four years.

He hoped she had her phone switched off or on silent because he didn't want to disturb her, but he wanted her to know the moment she woke up that he'd been thinking of her. She'd sounded awful and it had killed him not to be able to go to her.

The two previous nights he'd got Ned to bed and then snuck over to visit Meg, where he'd snuggled in her bed until he snuck out again in the early hours of the morning to go bring in the cows. It wasn't ideal leaving his son with Tabitha but she'd assured him she didn't mind and the feeling of Meg's hands in his hair as they kissed and her skin sliding against his was worth the little bit of parent guilt.

Last night his bed had felt lonesome and uncomfortable and he'd tossed and turned for hours. It was amazing how quickly he'd got used to sleeping with someone again and he'd missed Meg's body spooned against his. At one am he'd almost given up and driven to Rose Hill, but common sense had halted him as he'd been yanking on a pair of shorts.

Meg was sick and she needed to rest more than she needed to see him.

Somehow he'd eventually fallen asleep, but now that he was awake his desperation to see her again felt even stronger.

With that thought he rolled out of bed and started to get dressed, determined to get through the milking in record time. Those girls better not misbehave or dilly-dally this morning. *Or else.* Lawson headed out of his room and into the kitchen, popping his head into Ned's room on his way past. He smiled at his son sleeping soundly, his little hands pressed under his cheek and the early morning dawn creeping in the through the gaps in the curtains and falling across his face. His heart swelled with warmth and pride and a happiness he hadn't felt in years.

Life finally felt as if it were getting back on track.

He scoffed a couple of slices of Vegemite on toast and three Weetbix and was just putting his bowl in the dishwasher when Tabitha strolled into the kitchen with a yawn.

She blinked. 'Well, good morning. Didn't you sneak out to Meg's place last night?'

'No. She's got some gastro bug, so thought it would be better if I stayed away. I'm going to go check on her once I'm done with the milking.'

Tab frowned as she went to switch on the kettle. 'She seemed fine yesterday.'

He nodded. 'Apparently it came on quick. She sounded awful.'

'Poor thing. Shall I make Ned some French toast for breakfast?'

'Thanks, sis, that'd be great.' Lawson smiled, then leaned forwards and kissed her on the cheek. If it were left up to him, the two of them would probably live on Weetbix. 'Tell him to come say good-morning to me when you guys are feeding the calves.'

Tab nodded and offered him a sleepy wave as he strode out of the kitchen, out of the house, yanked on his boots and whistled to Clyde that it was time to start work.

Chapter Twenty-nine

Megan walked out of her bedroom to find Adeline standing on the landing at the top of the stairs. Immediately her hackles rose.

'What the hell are you doing here?' she asked. *And how the hell did you get inside?* She felt certain she'd locked the door when she'd come home that afternoon, but then again she had been in quite a state.

Adeline narrowed her eyes at Megan as if she were in fact the intruder and had no right to ask such a question. 'I'm here to set things right,' she said, taking a step towards Megan.

'What do you mean?' Megan scoffed, then glanced around for Cane but he was nowhere to be seen.

'You've set your sights above your status and I can't let things go on the way they are. The man is mine. He's always been mine and I won't let you come between us.'

There were so many things Megan could say or wanted to say in response to that but even more so she wanted Adeline out of her space. She didn't trust her and the fact she'd entered the house without an invitation only proved that perhaps she was unhinged as well as nasty. Not a good combination in Megan's experience.

'I think it's time you leave,' she said, indicating the stairs.

Adeline shook her head. 'Oh, no, no, no. I'm not going anywhere until I've done what I came to do.'

And then, before Megan had time to open her mouth and ask in a less-polite manner, Adeline launched herself towards her. Closing the distance between them, she reached out and grabbed hold of Megan's hair.

'Ouch!' Megan squealed. For two seconds she was too stunned to react or defend herself, but when Adeline started yanking her towards the stair railing, her instincts kicked in. She tried to push the other woman away but Adeline was surprisingly strong for someone with the physical width of a beanpole.

'Let me go,' Megan demanded, lifting her hands to Adeline's and gripping them hard as she tried to remove them from her hair.

A struggle ensued. They almost danced as Adeline tugged harder and Megan tried to extricate herself. *Where the hell is Cane?* Surely he wouldn't stand by and let his master be abused like this?

'You're insane,' Megan shouted, wondering if she might have to bite Adeline on the wrist to get her to loosen her grip.

'I'm just protecting what is rightly mine,' Adeline spat, spittle actually landing in Megan's face.

Eugh. 'Let me go!' she tried again, giving the other woman one final chance before she upped the ante and did whatever it would take to get her out of her personal space.

'With pleasure!'

Before Megan could realise exactly what her nemesis meant, Adeline's hands left her hair and landed on her chest. She pushed hard and Megan slammed back against the wooden stair railing. Her back screamed with pain, distracting her a moment. Whatever happened next happened so fast Megan didn't realise she'd gone over the rail until she felt a falling sensation like she'd never felt before. Seconds later she heard a loud crack as her head slammed down hard onto the floor below.

Ouch!

Everything went black.

She woke a few moments later to find Cane sitting on top of her licking her face and the worst headache she'd had in years. Despite the throbbing at her forehead and the racing of her pulse, she pushed Cane aside and then sat up fast, her head snapping from side to side as she looked around for Adeline. But Megan realised she wasn't on the cold floor by the stairs having survived attempted murder: she was lying on the old sofa, a pain in her neck as if she'd fallen asleep at an unnatural angle.

'Thank the Lord,' she whispered, reaching out to Cane to draw him back in for a comforting cuddle. She laughed nervously, relieved she'd only dreamed of Adeline. Stress had combined with the news of the previous afternoon and a full bottle of wine on an empty stomach to give her terrifying nightmares. After the way Adeline had acted at the town hall yesterday, it was surprising she hadn't dreamed of death by knitting needles, but she guessed her obsession with Eliza's death had followed her into her dreams.

Cane whined and leaped to the floor, fully bringing her back to the present. Light crept in through the threadbare curtains and she realised she hadn't moved from the couch since last night.

'Oh you poor baby. I'm so sorry,' she said, tearing back the light throw rug that was on top of her. As she got to her feet, she tried to remember covering herself up but everything after her phone chat with Lawson was a horrifying blur. She noticed the empty bottle of wine on its side on the floor and all thoughts of the dream evaporated as she remembered exactly why she'd drunk a whole bottle of wine in the first place.

Chapter Thirty

When the milking was over and the last cow sent back out to pasture, Lawson did something he never did. He told Ethan about Meg being sick and asked if he'd mind doing the wash-down on his own.

'Not at all, boss.' Ethan made shooing movements with his hands, indicating he should be on his way. 'You go look after your girl. There's something special about her, I reckon, and if you don't treat her right, I might just have to step in and—'

Lawson didn't hear the rest of Ethan's idle threat as he was already jogging out of the dairy and back towards the house. He discarded his boots on the verandah and then pulled open the screen door to find Tab reading the mail. She usually picked up any post from the day before in their road mailbox each morning when she saw Ned to the bus.

'Hey.' He nodded at his sister, his hands already on the hem of his shirt, about to yank it off. Although desperate to see Meg, a shower was a necessity after a morning with the cows. 'I'm gunna clean myself up, then I'm off to check on Meg. Do you need me to pick up anything in town on my way home?'

'You might want to read this first.' She held a piece of paper out to him. Tucked under her stumped arm was an envelope.

The tone of her voice made his heart drop to his stomach. 'What is it?' But even as he asked this question, he knew.

'It could be worse,' she said as he reached out to take the piece of paper.

His gaze fell on the logo of WA Country Milk on the top of his page, confirming his worst fears. Lawson skimmed the letter, his pulse quickening and his jaw locking as he registered the news.

'Fuck,' he breathed. Maybe it could be worse but this was pretty damn terrible. With the contractual requirement of six months' notice, WA Country Milk had informed them that come July they would no longer be able to take as much milk from them as they had been. His fists curled around the piece of paper. 'I can't believe it.'

'I know,' Tab whispered and he could hear something in her voice that he very rarely heard. Sadness. Fear. Anxiety.

And then he noticed something else he rarely saw where Tabitha was concerned. Her big brown eyes glistened with tears.

'Hey,' he said, discarding the letter on the side table and pulling her into his arms. 'It'll be okay. We've been through tough times before and we've survived. This farm has been operating for almost a hundred years and weathered many a dairy crisis. We're not gunna let this break us. As you said, it could be worse. Some farmers have been told the processors have overpaid them and they are being forced to pay them back out of future earnings and others still have had their contracts cancelled altogether.'

She sniffed and wiped her nose with the back of her hand. 'What are we going to do with all the rest of our milk?'

Tab's defeated tone hurt him almost as much as the actual letter.

'There are other milk companies,' he said, trying to sound more positive than he felt. 'We'll approach them.'

She pulled back and raised her eyebrows at him. 'Country Milk are the biggest and you know as well as I do that the others are struggling as well. There's just too much milk right now and not enough demand.'

'Then we'll make more ice-cream,' he said, trying to keep his voice chipper. 'Well, you will and I'll help you work out how to market it. We've got a little bit of savings and so maybe we can look more seriously into Meg's idea for making the dairy a bit of a tourist attraction.'

'Maybe,' she said with a defeated sigh.

Lawson knew Tab was thinking of the other options they might have to contemplate. Like other farmers who had been in this situation recently, they'd have to consider selling off some of their stock. Cattle they'd hand-raised to be prime milkers would now be destined for the abattoir. The thought made his gut ache.

A knock on the front door interrupted his thoughts and he turned to see Meg standing on the other side of the fly screen. So consumed in the drama of the letter, neither of them had heard her car coming up the gravel drive but to him she was a welcome interruption.

It was hard to be too disheartened when his gaze fell upon her face and all he could think about was kissing her. He smiled. 'Hey there. You feeling better?'

At the same time, Tab said, 'Hi Meg.'

'I'm sorry to just arrive unannounced like this. Am I ... interrupting something?'

'No, come on in.' Tab shook her head furiously—he knew she didn't like to show any kind of weakness—and then smiled, but for once it didn't reach her eyes. 'I'll go put the kettle on.'

As she turned and fled in the direction of the kitchen, Lawson opened the door and wrapped his arms around Meg. She felt so damn good and he never wanted to let her go. 'Boy, am I glad to see you.'

'Oh?' Her voice almost sounded like a squeak.

'Yes.' He pulled his head back and looked down at her. 'We just got some bad news and I could do with a hug.'

'Oh?' she said again.

'WA Country Milk has informed us they will be reducing the amount of milk they buy from us from July onwards.'

Meg's eyes widened. 'Oh my God. Can they *do* that to you? Isn't that breaking a contract?'

'Yes, but if we fight them on this, then we risk them not renewing our contract at all next year. To be honest, I'm still a little shell-shocked; there's lots to think about, lots to consider. I'll need to talk to someone at the company and find out exactly what the situation is and then look for possible alternatives for our milk. We literally just found out.'

'I … I see.'

'You still look a little pale.' Lawson took a moment to look at Meg properly. 'Gorgeous, but pale. Are you feeling any better?'

A glimmer of colour flashed on her cheeks as she rubbed her lips together. 'Physically … a lot better than last night. I must have just eaten something that didn't agree with me.'

'Good. I was worried about you.' He smiled, then dipped his head and stole the kiss he'd been dreaming about since the last time they were together. 'You're a much-wanted distraction from this Country Milk crap. Looking down at your gorgeous face, nothing seems as bad as it could be.'

Meg opened her mouth but before any words came out, Tabitha came back into the hallway.

'I'm going out to see Ethan,' she announced, giving them a little wave of her fingers. 'The kettle's on if you want it but I need some fresh air. Hope you don't mind, Meg.'

'No, of course not,' she said, smiling sympathetically at Tab. 'Lawson told me the bad news. I'm really sorry.'

Tabitha shrugged. 'Thanks. I guess with the industry the way it is at the moment, we shouldn't be surprised, but it's still a big blow. I'll see ya later.'

As the door thudded shut behind her, Lawson turned back to Meg. The house sounded silent with just the two of them. *Finally.* His head *should* be full of the devastating news he'd just received, but instead all he could think about was Meg. Specifically about getting her naked. Now that he'd broken his sex-drought, he was like a horny teenaged boy.

'Are you really feeling better?' he asked, putting his hands back on her waist and drawing her against him again. She felt so good, so soft. His body reacted immediately.

Meg licked her lips and her voice came out breathy. 'Why? What do you have in mind?'

The heat in her eyes told him she knew exactly what he had in mind—his cock wasn't exactly being shy about it. But instead of verbalising his reply, he dipped his head and kissed the side of her neck. Her head fell back a little and she moaned as he worked his way upwards across her jaw until his lips landed on hers.

Within seconds of their mouths meeting, her hands were sliding under his shirt and Lawson knew he couldn't get her to his bedroom fast enough. Their lips still locked, he cupped her bum and lifted her up so he could carry her down the hallway. Nothing had ever felt so good as her legs wrapped around him, her hands in his hair as they kissed like a couple of maniacs. He stumbled towards his bedroom, barely noticing when he bumped into furniture. He kicked the door shut behind him and then they collapsed as one onto his bed.

Although it hadn't even been two days since he'd seen her, there wasn't time for small talk. She was wearing a short denim skirt, which left little to the imagination. His erection pressed against his shorts, desperate to escape and breach the thin black scrap of her knickers.

Trying to slow things down so this wasn't over in a matter of seconds, he lowered his head and kissed her again, drinking in the tantalising taste of her.

But Meg didn't seem to care about taking things slowly. As his tongue slid into her mouth, her hand dived down between their bodies and slid inside the waistband of his shorts. He groaned as her hand closed around his hard throbbing length.

As delicious as her actions felt, there were far too many clothes in this scenario. He rolled them over so that she was straddling him and then he whipped her T-shirt up and over her head. She wore a black bra that contrasted against her pale skin, but he reached his hand around her back and undid it. As sexy as her lingerie was, it had nothing on her bare breasts. He gazed up at them, totally mesmerised—frozen as he deliberated whether to touch or taste or both.

Meg pushed up on her knees so she had room to pull down his shorts. Her beautiful long hair fell over his hips as she bent her head and took him into her mouth. He slid his hands up into her hair, loving its silky feel as her mouth drove him to the edge. Just when he was about to explode, she pulled back, locked eyes with him and mouthed one word: 'Condom?'

Somehow despite the sensations flooding his body, he managed to reach over and retrieve a small foil packet from his bedside table. Meanwhile she shimmied out of her knickers and pushed her skirt up higher. Then, as if just as desperate as he was, she snatched the packet out of his hand and ripped it open with her teeth. Nothing had ever seemed so erotic. She slipped the condom on and then sank down onto his cock. As she whispered his name, he reached around and cupped her buttocks, driving himself even deeper inside her. They moved as one, so in tune with each other that he heard her breathing quicken at the exact moment he felt himself losing control. They came together, each crying the other's name as they flew over the edge.

Afterwards, he pulled her down on top of him so her breasts pressed into his chest and her head rested on his shoulder. He ran his hands through her hair, loving its silky feel, loving absolutely every tiny thing about her.

'Back in a second,' he said a few minutes later, extricating himself and then climbing out of bed to deal with the condom. Even the brief time he left her alone in his bed, he missed her. It was hard to believe how much a part of his life she'd become in such a short time, but he honestly couldn't imagine going forwards without her. Being with Meg felt so right—as if she were the missing secret ingredient in the recipe of his life. Now, he knew why he hadn't been able to look at any of the other women his friends had been trying to set him up with over the years. It wasn't just that it'd been too soon after Leah's death, but also that he'd unknowingly been waiting for Meg.

With this thought, he climbed back into bed, pulled her naked body back against his and wrapped his arms around her. Although he knew he couldn't stay here like this forever—there was so much work to be done around the dairy, especially with this latest unwelcome development—he wished they could spend the whole day together in his bed drinking each other in and making love.

'Meg?' he asked, an idea landing in his head.

'Yes?' she whispered.

'You know how I won that weekend away to a spa retreat in Margaret River?'

'Yes.'

'I was going to give it to Dad and Sandra, but how would you feel coming away with me instead? I can get Funky to help Tab and

Ethan with the cows and I'm sure Tab will be happy to look after Ned—she's always telling me I work too hard. I'd really love us to spend the weekend together, just you and me. What do you say?'

'What about your dairy contract problem?'

'Forget about that for a moment. I just want to know if you'd like to spend the weekend with me. We haven't even been on a proper date yet, and I want the chance to wine and dine you.' He was already imagining what it would be like—no rush to get up for the first time in as long as he could remember, no pressing engagements or jobs to be done: maybe they'd have breakfast in bed, followed by sex, then a shower and then whatever it is they do to you at day spas. Massages? Facials? Things he'd previously turned his nose up at sounded positively tempting when he thought about doing them with Meg.

'I'd love that,' she said finally, turning over to face him and pressing her mouth against his cheek. 'Thank you for asking.'

'Good.' He grinned. 'I'll call the resort and see when they can book us in.'

'Okay. Sounds good.'

That settled, and Lawson excited about the prospect of a naughty weekend away in Margaret River, they lay in bed a while longer, talking about the things they could do down south. There were oodles of wineries, gorgeous beaches to stroll along, caves to visit and even a chocolate factory. That's if they ever made it out of the bedroom.

After a while, he realised he was the one doing most of the talking.

'Are you sure you're okay?' he asked, hoping he hadn't pressured her into sex when she wasn't feeling so great.

'I'm fine,' she said, 'just tired.'

'Okay.' He pressed a kiss against her forehead. 'I better be getting back to work,' he said, reluctantly. 'As much as I'd rather come with you back to Rose Hill and continue our investigation into Eliza's death, I really do need to make some phone calls regarding our milk contract. But can I make you some lunch first?'

She shook her head. 'Thank you, but I'm fine. I left Cane inside at home so I better be heading back.'

Chapter Thirty-one

What the hell game are you playing at? Megan asked herself this question over and over again as she drove home. *So much for telling Lawson the truth!* Instead she'd continued to weave herself a complicated web of deceit. What was she thinking sleeping with him when she should have been spilling her guts. She was a bad, bad person.

A few hours ago she'd been determined to tell him every sordid little detail about her past. No more leaving out vital pieces of information to protect herself—she'd been ready to bare her soul and face the consequences. During the drive to the farm she'd rehearsed her speech and, although her legs had been shaking when she'd climbed out of her car and walked towards his house, she'd had every intention to follow through on her decision but once again life had thrown an obstacle in her path.

The moment Lawson had told her about their devastating dairy contract news, she knew it would be even harder to tell him. How could she when he'd told her how happy he'd been to see her and that with her in his life now nothing could ever be too bleak?

She blinked back tears as she recalled his words. However wrong it might be, she'd been unable to resist when he'd pulled her into his arms and carried her down the hallway to his bedroom. Letting him kiss her senseless—kiss her till she forgot she had anything to tell him anyway—had been the much easier, much more appealing option, and she'd appeased her remorse by telling herself she was doing it for him because she didn't want to make his day any worse.

But now as she approached Rose Hill, the guilt inside her grew and twisted like a gnarly weed. She knew she was digging herself deeper and deeper into a hole but she really had no clue how to climb out of it. If she told him everything, she was sure she'd lose him. But if she didn't tell him and somehow he eventually found out …

That thought was unbearable. So much that she'd even contemplated stopping at the bottle shop for more grog to help her obliterate it but somehow she'd resisted the temptation, a little voice inside her reminding her how easy it would be to come to rely on as she had other drugs to help her through her problems.

No matter what happened with Lawson, she didn't want to go back to that dark, dark place ever again. A place where she had no control over her own actions and lost perspective on what was happening around her.

When she arrived at the general store, she found Archie turning away from her front door, Buster looking solemn by his side. She surreptitiously wiped her eyes and pasted a smile on her face.

'Hello, missy,' he called, lifting his hand in a wave.

'Hi, Archie,' she replied as she walked on shaky legs towards him.

'I just came to check on ya. You didn't look so great yesterday arvo and I was worried. I wanted to make sure you're okay.' The smile on his face dimmed a little. '*Are* you okay?'

She opened her mouth to tell him that yes, she was fine—much better than yesterday, thanks for asking—but the words caught on a lump in her throat and she knew tears were imminent. 'Actually,' she said with a shake of her head, 'I'm a mess.'

'Oh, love.' Archie stepped forwards and drew her into his arms. It wasn't at all like being embraced by Lawson but it was exactly what she needed. 'It can't be that bad.'

'It is. It's worse,' she sobbed, no longer even trying to hold back her tears.

'Now, now,' he said, rubbing her back. 'Don't cry. I don't know how to handle women and tears.'

Yet, despite his declaration, he was wonderful. He dug her key out of her bag when her hands were shaking too much to do so herself, then he unlocked the door and ushered her inside. Cane jumped up all over them, unable to decide who to welcome first. Once the pup had calmed down, Archie put him and Buster outside while Megan went into the kitchen to make them cups of coffee.

He returned to find her holding the kettle under the tap, staring at it. As the water overflowed, Archie stepped in and switched off the tap. He took the kettle out of her hand, led her over to a chair and all but pushed her into it. Then he proceeded to make the drinks himself and even found a container of chocolate bickies that he put on the table between them when he finally sat down. She didn't feel like eating but she picked one up and broke it into little pieces.

'Now, tell Uncle Archie what the problem is,' he said, picking up his mug and peering over it down at the remains of the cookie.

Megan sighed and dusted off her fingers. She had no idea where to begin. Archie was patient and gave her a few moments before he prodded. 'Is it something to do with that man who's visited you a few times?'

His words surprised her—she hadn't known he'd ever seen Lawson in Rose Hill. As far as she knew he never ventured further than the service station. She pursed her lips together and nodded.

'If he's done anything to hurt you, I'll kill him,' Archie said, his expression dead serious.

'Lawson has been nothing but wonderful to me. No one has ever made me feel like he does.' She blushed a little then added, 'Do you know how his wife died?'

Archie shook his head. 'I didn't know he had a wife. Might have seen him once or twice but I didn't even know his name until you said it then. Why?'

Megan swallowed. 'Five years ago there was an armed robbery at the petrol station in Walsh. Lawson's wife was behind the counter and she was killed.'

She saw the moment realisation dawned in Archie's eyes—they widened slowly and then his whole face twisted as if he were in pain, but he didn't say anything.

'You were living here when she … when *it* happened. Didn't you hear *anything* about it?' Megan knew she sounded accusatory but she couldn't help it. If she'd known about this from the beginning she wouldn't have let herself get so close to Lawson.

'Maybe I vaguely remember something but I didn't put two and two together.' He frowned. 'So I take it you haven't told him what you got locked up for?'

'I haven't even told him I've been in prison,' she spat, nausea rising in her stomach again.

'Ah, girl, you've got yourself into a bit of a pickle, haven't you?'

She glared at Archie. 'You were the one that told me not to tell people in the first place.'

He raised his hands. 'That was when you said you were making friends with people, not sleeping with them.'

Her cheeks burned—she didn't want to talk about this with Archie; it was too much like talking about sex with her dad would have been. Plus, thinking about sex with Lawson only made her want to cry all over again.

'So,' Archie continued, 'when did he tell you about his wife?'

'He didn't. I found out from the internet.'

Archie raised his eyebrows. 'Sounds like you're not the only one keeping things close to your chest then.'

'I think it hurts him to talk about her. He's mentioned her a couple of times but actually how she died never came up. Obviously the whole town knows so perhaps he just forgot I didn't know or assumed I did. Now I wish I'd asked but I didn't want to upset him.'

'Hmm.' Archie took a long sip of his coffee.

'What's *hmm* supposed to mean? I need more than *hmm*.' When Archie still didn't offer a solution, Megan said, 'I went over to tell him today but when I got there I found out that he'd just been given bad news about his dairy contract. He and his sister were obviously distressed about it and it didn't seem the right time to drop my bombshell, but the longer I leave it the worse it's gunna be, right?'

'You know,' Archie said slowly, 'there is another option.'

Megan leaned forwards, all ears.

'You've told everyone your name's Meg Donald, but it's really Megan Mc-something, right?'

She nodded. 'McCormick. Donald was my mother's maiden name. I thought using it might help my efforts to move on, but I never dreamed of getting involved with someone, so I didn't think the swap would ever be an issue.'

'So why don't you officially change your name?'

Silence rang in the kitchen a few moments as she contemplated this suggestion. Could it be possible to totally reinvent herself? Was this the answer to finally leaving the past behind? Maybe no one would ever have to know who she'd once been. It wasn't like there was anyone from her past likely to show up and call her on it.

'Do they even let convicted felons do that?' she asked.

Before either of them could answer, her mobile beeped. Almost on autopilot, she pulled it out of her bag and glanced down at the message icon on the screen. 'It's him,' she said, her heart thudding into her chest cavity.

Archie nodded at the phone. 'Are you going to read it?'

Somehow she slid her finger across the screen to unlock the message.

Good news. I called the retreat place and they had a cancellation this weekend. Can you get Archie to look after Cane? If not, Tab says she's happy to have him here. Please say you can make it? xx

'Oh *God*.' She groaned as she reread the message.

'What is it?'

Megan swallowed. 'Lawson wants me to go away with him to Margaret River for the weekend. Like tomorrow.'

Archie frowned. 'I didn't think dairy farmers took holidays.'

'I know. That's why I feel so terrible. Taking time off is a big deal—it shows how much he's invested in our relationship and yet … he doesn't know who I really am.'

'Hey, don't beat yourself up too much,' Archie said, quite fiercely. 'For one, he does know you—he knows who you are now and who you want to be. And for two, he never told you about his wife either, so you're not the only one to blame here. Seems to me the two of you have a lot to talk about and that maybe a weekend away from other distractions will be the perfect opportunity to do so. And to work out if you really have a future together after all.'

'A second ago you were telling me to change my name and reinvent history.'

He chuckled, then shrugged. 'Still an option.'

Megan shook her head. She wanted a relationship with Lawson, she wanted a future and a family, and she knew deep down that if she had the chance she could be a good mother for Ned and a good partner for Lawson. But she'd never be able to give herself entirely to any of that if she continued living a lie.

'Can you look after Cane this weekend?' she asked Archie.

He nodded. 'You know it's always a pleasure. He exercises Buster for me, which means I don't have to drag my sorry arse out for a walk.'

'A walk would probably be good for you,' she said, 'but thanks.'

Then without another word she picked up her phone and, despite shaking fingers, managed to type out a reply: *Archie here now and said yes to looking after Cane. I can make it. xo*

His reply was almost instantaneous: *Awesome. Tell him I said thanks. I'll pick you up about midday tomorrow. I'll miss you tonight but since I'm leaving Ned with Tab all weekend I'd better stay home. xx*

Relief flooded Megan at this news.

Of course. I'll see you then. xo

'Do you want another coffee?' she asked Archie.

He shook his head and pushed to his feet. 'Nah, I want to be getting back to my painting, but just needed to check my girl was okay first. Are you?'

She smiled, warmth flooding her at the way he said *my girl*. Even if the worst happened tomorrow, she now had someone in her life and that was a lot more than she'd had when she first drove into Rose Hill. 'I'm not sure *okay* is the correct term, but I'm a lot better than I was before this chat. Thank you.' She gave him a massive hug. 'I'm going to head over to the historical society and concentrate on Eliza for a while. I'll see you out.'

They went out the back and collected Buster, who was panting hard after running around the garden with Cane. She clipped a leash onto her dog and then the four of them walked out the side gate and down the deserted street. She and Cane stopped at the historical society and Archie and Buster continued down the road.

Once inside Megan threw herself into her research. She made a concerted effort to try and not think about Lawson and the weekend ahead. The last few times she'd meant to tell him, she'd rehearsed long and hard beforehand about what to say, but those times something had always got in the way. This time would be different—she'd put it out of her mind until it was upon them and this time she would tell him everything: nothing would get in the way. Whatever happened, if there was an earthquake in Margaret River, if a tsunami swept the south coast, if aliens invaded Western Australia, she would still confess all.

With this decision made, she pulled out a wooden chair and sat down at the desk where she'd piled up all the 1930s copies of the local newspaper. The first time she'd gone through she'd been looking for information about a death in the general store and after that focusing on finding out whatever she could about Eliza, but today, she was going to change tack. It was time to focus her attentions on Henry Walsh.

Starting at the very first newspaper of 1930, Megan reread each one in dedicated detail—she didn't want to miss something important. Finally, as her stomach started to rumble and the sun began to descend in the sky outside, she found something in the announcements column of the newspaper.

Henry Walsh and Penelope Elverd regret to inform of the dissolution of their engagement.

What? But Henry *had* married Penelope.

Megan glanced upwards to the date at the top of the page and realised it was only a week or so before Eliza's supposed suicide. She put the newspaper into her important pile and started on the next one, this time flicking through faster and faster looking for one particular thing.

A year later she found it—the wedding pictures of Mr and Mrs Henry Walsh. And it was as if Adeline were smiling up at her from the black and white, now yellowed, photograph. The likeness between her and Penelope was uncanny. A chill scuttled down Megan's spine and spread right to her extremities as she recalled her dream of last night—it hadn't been Adeline she'd been dreaming of, but her grandmother.

Scrambling to her feet, she gathered the significant newspapers to her chest, roused Cane from where he'd been slumbering at her feet, locked up the historical society and hurried home.

Once there, she filled a bowl with dog food and deposited it on the back verandah, then shut the door behind him, not wanting Cane to be upset by what she was about to do. She walked down the hallway and paused when she felt the chill by the stairs.

'Eliza?' she whispered. 'Are you here?'

Megan's heart froze as she waited for some kind of a response. When the house remained deadly silent, she spoke again. 'Was it Penelope Elverd? Did she push you?'

Finally the hall light flickered on and off. Megan's skin swam with sudden goose bumps.

Oh God. Adeline's grandmother had robbed Eliza of not only her man and her happily ever after, but of her *life*. She shivered as a tear for what Eliza had lost snuck down her cheek. No wonder the ghost had taken an instant dislike to Adeline. She was the spitting image of her murderer.

The question was, what could Megan, without any proof, do to set things right?

Chapter Thirty-two

Totally buoyed for the weekend ahead, Lawson stooped down to lift his overnight bag off the floor by the front door.

'Have a fabulous weekend,' Tab said as she gave him a kiss on the cheek. 'And don't do anything I wouldn't do.'

He rolled his eyes and grinned at his sister. 'That means I can do pretty much anything.'

'Yep.' She smiled and nodded. 'Live recklessly. You deserve the break. And don't call home every five seconds, okay? Both Ned and I will be fine and we'll phone if there are any emergencies. Just enjoy yourself.'

'I promise I'll try,' he replied as Tab turned to open the front screen door for him. It felt a little reckless heading off on a naughty getaway with his girlfriend the day after they'd been given the devastating news about their dairy contract, but, as Tab had said, spending the weekend lamenting their problems likely wouldn't resolve them.

And the truth was, his arm hadn't needed much twisting.

The fact the retreat had a cancellation and thus could fit them in at such short notice made it feel as if it were meant to be.

'Well, hurry up then.' Tab gestured through the now open door. 'You don't want to leave her waiting.'

'All right, all right, I'm going.' Lawson chuckled as he stepped through the door and headed for his ute, once again finding himself whistling as he walked.

He was putting his bag in the back tray when he heard a vehicle coming up the drive. Not expecting anyone, he frowned and squinted a little, identifying it as Adeline's pristine white four-wheel drive. How did she keep it so clean? And what the hell was she doing there? He groaned. If he got stuck talking to Adeline, he could be waylaid for ages.

With this thought, he wrenched open the door of his ute, jumped inside, turned the key in the ignition and sped off down the drive. He offered Adeline a cheery wave as he passed but couldn't be sure she saw it due to the dust blowing up between the two vehicles.

Sorry, Tabitha, she's all yours.

He didn't slow down until he reached the end of the gravel driveway and turned right on the road that would take him to Rose Hill. Then, he let out the breath he'd been holding since he'd leaped into the ute, and smiled. With the car stereo blaring and the responsibilities of the farm getting further and further behind him, Lawson felt lighter than he had in years. Tapping his fingers on the steering wheel and singing along to his favourite country song, he let his imagination run away with him dreaming of what he and Meg would get up to in Margaret River. He'd booked them into a flash restaurant for the evening—he'd meant it when he said he planned on wining and dining her before keeping her up all night.

The sound of a horn blaring snapped him from his fantasy. He glanced up into the rear-view mirror and the smile fell from his face. 'What the ...?'

Adeline's four-wheel drive was so close to his back bumper that if he braked fast she'd slam into him. Her lights were flashing on and off and she hadn't taken her hand off the horn. He'd been so lost in fantasies of the weekend ahead he hadn't even noticed her following him.

Cursing loudly, he indicated to stop, giving her a chance to back off a little, and then he pulled over onto the gravel strip at the side of the road.

'This better be good, Adeline,' he called, slamming the driver-side door shut behind him and crunching across the gravel towards her.

She was already out of her four-wheel drive and heading towards him, clutching what looked like a bunch of papers to her chest. 'I'm afraid it's not good at all, it's terrible. But please, don't shoot the messenger.'

Lawson folded his arms across his chest, making his annoyance clear. 'Whatever game you're playing, I don't have time. I'm going away for the weekend, to use that spa retreat I won.'

Adeline's lower lip wobbled a little as she nodded. 'You're going with *her*, aren't you?'

He swallowed and tried to maintain his cool. 'If by her you mean Meg, then yes.'

'Then I'm glad I got to you in time. There's something you need to know about her.'

'If this is about Meg not drinking tea again, then I really don't want to—'

'*It's not.*' She held up the hand not holding the papers to silence him. 'This is serious, Lawson.' A brief pause and then she landed the blow. 'She killed someone.'

Chapter Thirty-three

Friday morning dragged longer than any other morning of Megan's life, even worse than the day she'd been in court waiting for the verdict of her case. First she'd gone for a long run with Cane to try and combat her nerves and then she'd spent hours in the kitchen, cooking meals to take to Archie for the weekend, but nothing had been able to distract her entirely. Lawson sent a few messages of excitement and she'd responded accordingly, while inside every bone in her body had been rattling.

Although Archie had encouraged her to wait until they were in Margaret River to tell Lawson every last awful detail about her past, she'd made the decision to tell him the moment he arrived. No way she'd be able to sit in his ute alongside him for the time it would take to get to the retreat and pretend everything was hunky dory. Then there was the horror of being left stranded there if he decided he no longer wanted anything to do with her.

Her nails were bitten down to the quick and she'd cooked far more than Archie could ever eat by the time midday finally rolled around. With less than half an hour until Lawson was due to pick her up, she clipped Cane's leash onto his collar, filled a large green recycled bag with the food she'd made for Archie and then started up the road to his place.

The first sign that something was wrong came when Buster didn't greet her at the gate with his usual grumpy bark.

'Archie!' she called to alert him to her arrival as she lifted the latch to open the gate.

Before it was fully open, she saw her old friend lying on the ground, half-on–half-off the patio and his face in full sun. Buster lay beside him, his head resting on his chest, his eyes drooping as he looked up at her. Letting the leash and the shopping bag fall to the ground, Megan rushed over to Archie and dropped to her knees beside him.

'Get out of the way,' she ordered Buster, pushing him off as she bent over him and looked into his pale face.

'Archie, wake up.' Panicking, she shook his shoulders but there was no response. She bent her face to check for his breath. *Nothing.*

Cane came up alongside her and tried to shove his nose between herself and Archie.

'Go away,' she yelled. He cowered as if she'd hit him but she didn't have time to feel bad.

Her heart thudding, she searched for Archie's pulse. *Weak but there. Just.*

Had he had a heart attack? Or fallen and knocked his head?

CPR. You need to start CPR. Don't ask questions; just act.

She rolled Archie onto his side—he wasn't a large man so it wasn't too difficult—and checked for obstructions in his throat. Satisfied there weren't any, she rolled him onto his back again and prayed she could remember what she'd learned during the first aid course she'd done in prison.

Three compressions in, she remembered the need to call an ambulance. Stupidly she glanced around, looking for someone to delegate the task to, but all she saw were two terrified dogs.

Dammit. Another few compressions, a couple of breaths into his mouth, and she dug her phone from where she'd shoved it in the pocket of her skirt. She punched triple zero into the keypad, then put it on speaker and rested it beside her as she continued pumping Archie's chest.

It rang once and then a voice came from the phone. 'Emergency services. Do you require police, fire or ambulance?'

'Ambulance!'

'Connecting you now.'

While she continued CPR, she spoke to someone, giving them the bare details—her friend was unconscious, no she wasn't sure how long he'd been like this—and Archie's address. The operator assured her an ambulance crew would be with her as soon as possible.

Megan couldn't say how long that was, but by the time the dogs barked alerting her to the arrival of a man and a woman dressed in green uniforms, her arms ached and tears streamed down her face. Archie's condition hadn't changed at all.

'We'll take over now,' ordered the man.

As the ambulance officers dropped to their knees on either side of Archie, Megan gratefully crawled back and tried to catch her own breath. Her legs were almost as shaky as her arms and she couldn't find the strength to stand just yet. She watched in horror as they assessed and then shocked Archie with a defibrillator and his lifeless body shuddered. Silently, she prayed—she prayed to a God she wasn't sure she believed in any longer, begging him to save this kind, lovely man who'd become a friend, an ally and almost a father-figure these last few weeks.

Finally, the officers looked at each other and let out audible breaths of what she hoped was relief. They quickly rolled him into the recovery position.

'Is he going to be okay?' Megan asked.

The woman glanced up as the man applied some kind of oxygen mask to Archie's face. 'We've got him stable but we need to get him to the hospital as soon as possible.'

All she could do was nod as they turned their attention back to Archie. She felt helpless and hoped she hadn't done anything to make his situation worse.

After a few more minutes, the male officer announced he was off to get the stretcher.

Megan leaped to her feet and ran to open the gate for him. 'Is there anything I can do to help?'

'Just keep the dogs back,' the officer said as he strode towards the ambulance, which was parked between the petrol bowsers.

She grabbed hold of Cane just as he made a dash to follow after the man. Thankfully, she hadn't unclipped his leash. Buster hadn't moved from his position a few feet from Archie. He hadn't growled or tried to interfere with the medical attention—almost as if he knew the officers were trying to help.

Five minutes later, they were wheeling Archie through the gate towards the waiting ambulance.

'Which hospital are you taking him to?' Megan planned to follow immediately behind.

'Walsh,' the officers said in unison, making her feel a little stupid, but she hadn't been sure whether they'd take him to a larger hospital in Bunbury or even Perth.

The mention of Walsh sent a shockwave through her body. In the chaos of Archie's medical emergency, she'd almost forgotten why she'd been over here in the first place.

Her chest squeezed as if *she* were having a heart attack. Shouldn't Lawson be here by now? She looked down at her phone, which she'd scooped off the ground only moments before, to check the time. Yes, it was definitely well past the time he'd agreed to collect her, but surely he'd have seen the ambulance zoom past him on his way into Rose Hill and would've guessed why she wasn't at the general store waiting. Frowning, she took a few steps forwards so she had a clear view down the road, but there was no ute parked in front of her place.

She thought he'd have called if he were going to be late, but the only action her phone had recently had was with Triple Zero.

As the doors of the ambulance slammed shut, the female officer said, 'You did well. If it weren't for you, Archie wouldn't have stood a chance.'

Megan blinked. 'Thank you,' she said, 'for all you've done. I'll make sure the dogs have water and then I'll be right behind you.'

Once again life had thrown an obstacle in the way of her coming clean to Lawson, but she couldn't very well send Archie off to hospital on his own. The thought of him waking up in a cold, clinical room all alone and wondering what had happened didn't bear thinking about.

The woman smiled for the first time and then trekked round to the driver's side of the ambulance and climbed up into the seat. She pulled the door shut behind her and seconds later they were gone.

Megan rubbed her hands up and down her arms, which felt cold, despite the warm weather. Should she take this as a sign? Maybe fate was trying to tell her something? The sound of Cane barking on the other side of the gate, jolted her from her thoughts and snapped her into action. She collected the food from the ground, put it away, filled the dogs' water bowls and then made sure they'd be secure in the yard until she got back.

'Be good,' she ordered Cane, who looked at her with his head cocked to one side as she snuck out the gate again.

Without Archie, Rose Hill seemed eerily quiet, which was ridiculous considering that when Megan had first arrived she'd welcomed the ghost-town feel. The fact there was still no sign of Lawson only added to her uneasiness.

As she jogged down the street to get her keys and purse, she tried to call him but the rings continued until his voicemail clicked in. Trying to ignore her worry that something else terrible had happened, she left a quick message telling Lawson about Archie and that he'd find her at the Walsh hospital.

Chapter Thirty-four

It took a second or two for Adeline's words to register. Lawson's face screwed up in confusion and then every last inch of him turned to ice. *She killed someone?* Even as his mind asked this question, he shook his head.

No, it can't be true.

If Meg had killed someone, she'd be in prison. And he'd seen the way she was with Ned, with Cane, the way she spoke about looking out for Archie—she wasn't a killer. 'What the hell are you talking about?'

Adeline didn't even flinch at his harsh tone. 'She's a drug addict and a murderer. I'm so sorry to be the one to drop this bombshell.' Then she lifted her hand and rested it on his upper arm—he was so shocked he barely registered it. 'But I care about you and Ned so much that I'd never have forgiven myself if I didn't tell you. I've not had a good feeling about Meg right from the start. I couldn't sleep easy until I checked her out.'

'What do you mean checked her out?'

'I consulted the real estate agent that sold her the building and found out her *real* name—oh, did I mention she's been lying about that too? Her real name is Megan McCormick. Once I knew her true identity, it didn't take long to find out the truth. It's all over the internet.' She thrust the papers towards him.

He glanced down and saw she'd printed off online newspaper articles. The headline *Deli Manager Killed—Armed Robbers Caught* flashed out at him making him feel physically ill.

'Was it even legal for the estate agent to give you her details?' he asked.

Her eyes widened. 'I'm not the one at fault here, Lawson. I only did what I did because I love you. I've always loved you.' She moved her hand further up his arm and took a step closer but he shook her hand off and stepped back out of her grasp.

He held up his hands, warning her not to come another step closer. How could she stand there and talk about loving him when she'd just detonated a bomb in his world?

Adeline blinked, rubbed her lips together and then said. 'I'm sorry, Lawson. *Please.* Talk to me. I want to be here for you.'

'I don't give a damn what you *want*!' Right now he didn't even want her in his sight.

He could actually feel the blood coursing through his body, his heart beating so fast he could hear it in his ears, yet strangely he struggled to catch his breath. Somehow he turned and stumbled back to the ute.

He couldn't remember climbing into the driver's seat, turning the key in the ignition or doing a U-turn on the road and heading back towards the farm, but less than five minutes later he arrived home. Leaving his overnight bag in the back, not even bothering to close the ute's door or discard his shoes on the porch as he usually did, Lawson stormed inside and made a beeline for the computer in their home office.

'Did you forget something?' Tab called from the kitchen.

He didn't answer. He sat down on the swivel chair and got into the search engine. His fingers shaking—the affect of shock and anger combined—he tapped *Megan McCormick* and pressed enter.

A second later he had all the information he never wanted to have. Meg had obviously darkened her hair colour since the photos in the image gallery, grown it out and chopped a fringe but unless she had a twin or a doppelganger, then every awful accusation Adeline had made was true. Almost exactly the time he'd lost Leah to a senseless attack, Meg (or rather *Megan*) and her boyfriend had been taking the life of someone else's loved one.

Had there ever been a bigger fool than him? She'd been lying to him by omission from that very first day and he'd fallen hook, line and sinker for her beauty and charms. Had she been laughing at him all along? Getting close to someone else, opening his heart to the possibility of a future with another woman had been a huge thing for him, not something he'd done lightly, and that only made this discovery worse.

Tab entered the room. 'What's going on? Why are you back?'

His stomach feeling as if it might expel his lunch at any moment, Lawson couldn't bring himself to utter what an idiot he'd been. Instead, he stood and thrust his finger at the computer screen. Giving him a confused look, Tab stepped forwards and stooped down to peer at the screen.

He heard her gasp—'Oh my God'—as he headed for the door and stormed out onto the back verandah. As he stood there wondering *What next?*, his phone started ringing. He knew it was Meg, but he dug it out of his pocket and glanced down at the screen to be sure. Then he lifted his arm and hurled the phone into the backyard. While Clyde leaped off the verandah and ran off in pursuit, Lawson turned around and punched his fist into a wooden railing.

He welcomed the pain that shot through him and the blood that wept from his knuckles. As he glanced down at his hand and noticed the absence of his wedding ring, nausea rose within him again at the thought of how quick he'd been to take it off once Meg had arrived on the scene.

Although he'd never been one to believe his wife was up above watching over them, he looked up to the bright blue afternoon sky now and shook his head. 'I'm so sorry, Leah.' How could he ever expect her to forgive him for getting close to a cold-blooded killer—for letting their son get close to her—when he would never forgive himself?

And what was he supposed to tell Ned about Meg? The poor kid was infatuated with her. She hadn't just deceived him—she'd deceived his son, let his son fall in love with her without really knowing who she was.

Before he could contemplate this question, the screen door opened and Tab came up behind him. 'Shit.'

He shook his head. 'That word isn't strong enough for this. They haven't yet invented a swear word that is.'

'Shit,' she said again, this time with much more force. 'What have you done to yourself?'

As she grabbed his wrist, he looked down and shrugged. 'Just letting off a little steam.'

'Come inside and let me clean you up. You don't want Ned to come home and see you like this.'

Tab's mention of Ned convinced him to follow her inside instead of punch the railing again. She led him to the laundry and thrust his bloody hand under the tap in the trough.

'Stay there,' she ordered, 'while I get a clean towel and some ice.'

He stared at the water cascading over his hand and went back in his head over all the times he'd been with Megan since they'd met. Had he at any moment ever suspected her of something like this? The quiet reserve he'd found so endearing in the beginning had been down to guilt, not because she was a victim as he'd initially suspected. Now as he looked back there were many clues—the way she'd been so nervous that first day, so reluctant to let them inside her house; the fact she said she didn't have a phone (if indeed that was the truth, who knew now?); the drug confession; the way she'd moved from Melbourne to a ghost town for fuck's sake!

But he'd made excuses for every little thing. He'd put it all down to her being hurt and trying to recover from her traumatic past. He'd given her the benefit of the doubt, time after time after time, proving himself over and over again to be a lovesick fool.

Shakespeare said love was blind; well, Lawson had sure proven that to be the case.

'How's that hand?' Tab asked as she returned to the bathroom and turned off the tap. She proceeded to wrap his hand in a clean towel and then pushed it up against his chest. 'Hold it there; keep the pressure for a few moments until the blood stops and then we'll apply the icepack.'

He nodded glumly.

'You do know,' she said after a few moments, 'Meg didn't actually kill the person.'

He was so numb it took a second or two for her words to register. 'What? But that's what Adeline said. And … the internet.' He'd been so blindsided when he'd seen validation of her words on his computer screen that he hadn't even read past the headlines. *TWO DRUG ADDICTS STEAL ATTENDANT'S LIFE.*

He took a breath, and silently berated himself for being so quick to judge without having all the facts.

Tab rolled her eyes. 'Of course Adeline would say that. She'll do and say anything to break you and Meg up. She's been planning her wedding to you since the day Leah was killed, if not before.

But, according to the news articles, Meg pleaded not guilty. Does she really seem the type of person to kill someone? She crochets tea-cosies—not really a bad-girl thing to do.'

'Just because she pleaded not guilty,' he said, wincing a little at the pain in his hand, 'doesn't mean she *didn't* do it. Most violent criminals will plead that way if they think they can get away with it, but people aren't convicted of murder for no reason.'

He shook his head, unable to believe they were even having a conversation about this. Less than an hour ago he'd been high as a kite on new love, now …

How quickly things could derail.

'She *wasn't* convicted of murder,' Tab continued. 'Did you not read any of the articles properly? She was convicted of armed robbery, even though her prints weren't on the gun. She said she had no idea her boyfriend was armed when they went into that deli. It was her word against his and he said it was her idea. She also got made an example of because her granddad was a supreme court judge and the courts couldn't be seen to be playing favourites.'

'Her grandfather was a supreme court judge?' It was a rhetorical question and Lawson didn't wait for Tab to respond before he said, 'Did the articles mention her drug addiction?'

'Yes.' Tab nodded, then frowned. 'I must admit that shocked me—she wouldn't even have a glass of wine when she was here. I know you can't believe everything you read in the papers, but a drug addiction would certainly account for the rest.'

'I knew about the drugs,' he said. 'She told me about that—but she failed to mention all the other stuff.' He hadn't told Tab: he didn't want anyone thinking badly of Meg.

'And the drug thing didn't bother you?' she asked, her tone sceptical.

He grimaced. 'I believed her when she said she'd recovered, but who knows what I believe now.'

She sighed and unwrapped the towel from around his hand. The bleeding had stopped, even though his fist still throbbed.

'Did she think I'd never find out?' he almost shouted.

That was the real kicker here. Not what she'd done or supposedly not done, but the fact she'd never trusted him enough to confide in him. When was she planning to tell him she'd been in prison? Even if he believed her innocent—and that was a big if—even if he could recover from her association with someone's brutal murder, how could he ever trust her completely?

And what was a relationship if it wasn't built on trust?

Tab pressed an icepack wrapped in a tea-towel against his knuckles. 'Hold that there for a bit. Let's go out into the kitchen to finish this discussion. I'll dish you up some ice-cream.'

He snorted. 'No offence, sister dear, but right now I feel like something a lot stronger than ice-cream. Even ice-cream as good as yours.'

'How about a beer then?'

Although he'd have loved the numbness an alcoholic drink could bring, he wasn't sure whether he'd be able to stop at just one and he didn't want to be drunk when Ned got home. A much better solution would be to head out to bring in the cows and throw himself into work to try and forget this absolute debacle. He guessed the news would be round town by now—Adeline wasn't one to be discreet—and he'd be the laughing stock over everyone's beers tonight, but he hoped in time he'd be able to move on and put this unfortunate liaison behind him.

It'd be back to focusing on the things that truly mattered— Ned, and making sure the dairy didn't go under.

'Nah,' he said, with a shake of his head. 'I'm gunna go do some work.'

Tab frowned. 'But Funky and Ethan are handling the milking this arvo, and surely anything else can wait for now.'

'I'll call Funky and tell him not to bother.'

Tab opened her mouth but he gave her a look to tell her not to push it.

'Fine. Go work. But what about Meg?'

He raised an eyebrow. 'What *about* her?'

'You were supposed to have picked her up almost an hour ago. She'll be wondering what's happened to you. Worrying. You should at least talk to her.'

He thought of his phone languishing somewhere in the back-yard. And then he did something he never did—he raised his voice at Tabitha. 'Don't tell me what I should and shouldn't do, okay?'

And he stormed back out of the house.

Chapter Thirty-five

It wasn't hard to find the Walsh hospital. Megan followed the signs off the main street and came to a red-brick building that looked unlike any hospital she'd ever visited. After parking in the small parking lot, she headed towards the entrance where automatic doors peeled back to let her into reception.

The woman behind the desk looked up and smiled. 'Can I help you?'

'Yes, thanks. I'm from Rose Hill and my neighbour, Archie ...' Her voice trailed off as realised she had no idea what his surname was. Would they let him see her or even tell her about him because they weren't related? 'He's been brought in in an ambulance and ...'

Even before she finished speaking, the receptionist's eyes narrowed. 'Oh my gosh: you're *Megan McCormick*!'

Her heart squeezed and she swallowed a flood of nausea as terror that someone had finally recognised her scuttled down her spine but she forced herself to speak calmly. 'I'm Meg, nice to meet you.'

The receptionist didn't accept the gesture or offer her own name and after a few awkward seconds, Megan withdrew her hand. 'Who can I talk to about my friend Archie?'

'The doctor's in A&E with him now. He won't be in a room for a while, but you can wait,' said the woman coolly, pointing to a line of grey plastic chairs off to one side of the tiny reception.

Megan retreated to the furthest chair. She dug her mobile phone out of her bag again and glanced at the screen. Lawson still hadn't called but she tried not to let that panic her further. There was only one ambulance outside and if he'd had some kind of accident—or Ned or Tabitha had—there'd be another. Wouldn't there? She pushed his name on her recent calls list and lifted the phone to her ear as she waited for it to start ringing.

Once again, it went straight to voicemail. *Dammit.* She squeezed her eyes to keep from crying. She was worried about Lawson but she also craved his big strong arms wrapped around her and his deep, soothing voice telling her Archie would be okay. Telling her that *everything* was going to be okay.

She was about to try Tabitha's number when the automatic doors peeled open again and she instinctively looked up. Her heart sank as Adeline walked in, her hair tied back in a perfect high ponytail and her face done up as if she'd just stepped off a Broadway stage. Their eyes met.

'Adeline,' Megan said, not even bothering to feign a smile.

The other woman pointed her index finger straight at Meg, reminding her of the dream she'd had only a few nights earlier. 'You've got a nerve showing your face in here. You've got a nerve showing your face anywhere in this town!'

Everything fell into place. The receptionist suddenly knowing her when no one had this whole time. Lawson not answering her calls. The breath whooshed from her lungs and she knew it was all over.

'Yes, I *know* who you are.' Adeline smiled smugly. 'I know what you did and Lawson does too. Everyone does. I made sure of that. Walsh is a nice town and we don't want a killer in our midst.'

She looked up at the receptionist. 'Do we, Jenny?'

The woman behind the desk shook her head and looked at Megan as if she wasn't sure whether she should be scared of her.

'If you think Lawson will have anything to do with you after knowing your involvement in a crime so like Leah's murder, you must be insane. I think you should leave.'

Adeline's words confirmed Megan's worst fears. Lawson wasn't running late. He hadn't been in an accident. The reason he hadn't arrived was because he'd found out what she should have told him the moment she realised they had feelings for each other.

Oh God. Her heart was shrivelling up, but she spoke through clenched teeth. 'I'm here for my neighbour and I'm not going anywhere!'

'What?' Adeline spat. 'What are you talking about? What neighbour?'

Jenny, the receptionist, piped up. 'Trish and Doug picked up that old bloke from Rose Hill in the ambulance.'

Adeline screwed up her nose, then shook her head as if she were flustered. 'Whatever. I'm off to see my great-grandmother. Don't come near me *ever* again.'

With pleasure, Megan thought as Adeline stalked off down the corridor to see her murderous relation. She had some nerve acting all high and mighty when she was the great-granddaughter of an actual killer. If only Megan could prove this, it would bring some kind of closure for Eliza *and* it would have the added bonus of wiping that smug smile of Adeline's pretty face.

But that was the least of her worries now. Realising she hadn't breathed since Adeline had opened her mouth, Megan forced herself to inhale and exhale deeply. Then she glanced down at the phone still silent in her hand. The thought of Lawson out there somewhere thinking terrible things about her made her want to run into the street and throw herself in front of a bus.

Only there was no public transport in Walsh. And what would happen to Cane, to Archie, if she took such an easy way out? Ending it all or even simply running away was the weak solution and she didn't want to be that person anymore. Not facing her problems head-on had been what had landed her in this mess in the first place.

If only Lawson would answer his phone, then she could tell him ...

What? What on earth could she tell him that would make this right? She didn't know: all she knew was that she needed to see him. But she couldn't leave Archie until she knew he was going to be okay.

Frustrated, and fighting tears she didn't want to cry in front of Jenny, whose eyes she could feel boring into her, Megan picked a magazine off a table between the seats and opened it. When she discovered it was *FISHING WA*, she didn't put it down. Going through the motions, she flicked through ancient magazine after ancient magazine, until finally someone approached her.

'Hello?'

She looked up hesitantly at the tall, dark-skinned man. Whoever he was he'd no doubt heard about her criminal past as well. 'Are you Meg?'

She nodded, ready for whatever he hit her with.

But instead of harsh words, he smiled warmly and thrust out his hand. 'I'm Dr Harpreet and I just wanted to let you know your first aid saved Mr Weaver's life.'

'You mean Archie?' she asked as she shook the man's hand. So that was his surname. Relief flooded her and she couldn't help grinning despite knowing her secret was out and the peaceful life she'd been hoping for was once again a dream. 'He's okay?'

When Dr Harpreet nodded, the tears Megan had been fighting sprang from her eyes.

'We've just settled him into a ward and he's very groggy, but he's asking for you. Would you like to come through?'

She nodded. 'Yes. Yes, please.' And jumped to her feet, shoving her mobile phone into her bag as she did so.

'Come on.' Dr Harpreet touched her arm gently as he led her down the corridor that Adeline had gone down who knows how long earlier. Megan's tummy quivered a little at the thought of another altercation, but she ignored it and focused on following the doctor.

After a short distance he paused in front of an open door. 'Here we are,' he said, gesturing for Megan to go inside. As she stepped into the room, she saw Archie lying on the bed, propped up ever so slightly with pillows. There was some sort of oxygen tank beside him and tubes going into him, but when he saw her, his old weathered face cracked a smile.

'Oh, Archie,' she rushed over to him and took his hand in both of hers, careful not to disturb the tubes, '*never* give me a fright like that again!'

'Don't cry,' he said, his voice weak. 'I told you I can't handle women and tears.'

His words only made her bawl more. Tears streamed down her face, but she didn't want to let go of him to wipe them. Her joy on seeing him conscious again was stronger than you'd think it should be after only knowing someone a month, but after the news Adeline had just given her, Megan suspected Archie might be the only friend she had left and she didn't want to lose another person she cared about.

'Sorry,' she whispered, smiling at him.

Neither of them said anything for a few long moments, then he broke the silence. 'Hey, aren't you supposed to be off on your dirty weekend with that cow-loving fella?'

If her heart didn't hurt so badly at the thought of Lawson, she'd have laughed. Part of her wanted to confide in Archie about the whole Adeline/Lawson thing but she resisted, not wanting to cause him any further stress. She summoned her best carefree smile. 'It's fine. There'll be other weekends. I'm just so happy you're okay.'

Archie opened his mouth as if to speak, but the doctor, who Megan had almost forgotten was standing there, got in first. 'I'd like to keep Mr Weaver in for a couple of days for observation and to run some further tests. Perhaps you could bring him in a change of clothes and some toiletries?'

'Of course.'

'I'm not staying here,' Archie objected, but his voice didn't hold quite the conviction she thought he meant it to.

'Yes, you are,' she told him firmly. 'You'll stay as long as the doctor says you need to and you'll not worry about anything back home. I'll look after Buster and the chickens and you tell me what you need and I'll bring it.'

Archie sighed begrudgingly and Megan saw Dr Harpreet smile before retreating.

'Tell me what the hell happened to get me in here?' Archie said. 'The doc reckons I had a heart attack but that can't be right; I'm fit as a fiddle.'

She squeezed his hand. 'Try to get some rest,' she said.

For a brief moment he looked as if he were about to object to this as well, but he closed his eyes and seconds later he was asleep. When a nurse came in to do Archie's obs, Megan retrieved her hand and whispered she'd be back later with his stuff.

As she left the room and turned into the corridor, she almost ran into Adeline pushing an old woman in a wheelchair. *Penelope*, she thought, her heart thudding.

This woman is the person who pushed Eliza over the stair railing.

So skinny that her bones were almost sticking out from her paper-thin skin, it was hard to imagine this frail old woman ever having the strength to do such a thing.

'What are you looking at?' Adeline snapped, yanking the wheelchair backwards so her grandmother almost tumbled onto the floor.

Megan looked the old woman in the eyes. 'Hello,' she said. 'I believe you knew Eliza Abbott from Rose Hill?'

'Step away from my grandmother!'

Ignoring Adeline again, Megan looked into the older woman's eyes and saw a flash of recognition. The spidery veins on her face reddened, and ... was that a tear glistening in her eye?

Megan looked up to tell Adeline what she suspected about Penelope, but changed her mind at the last moment. What good would it do? She couldn't rewrite history and who would believe her anyway? Even if they did, Penelope could never be tried and they wouldn't throw such a frail old woman in prison after all these years. Perhaps living here—confined to a wheelchair, unable to do anything for herself—was punishment enough for Eliza's murderer.

And right now Megan had more pressing concerns.

Chapter Thirty-six

'Dad!'

Halfway through the milking, Ned ran into the dairy and over to Lawson, who was at the tail end of the rotary spraying the cows' udders as he removed their suction cups.

'Hey, son.' Lawson looked down and summoned a smile when the last thing he felt like doing was smiling. With the news of Megan's real identity following close on the heels of their own personal dairy crisis, today was up there as one of the worst days of his life. 'How was school? You been helping Tab feed the calves?'

Ned nodded. 'Yep—we just finished and Aunty Tab told me to come check you were okay. Why wouldn't you be okay, Dad?'

'I'm fine,' he said through gritted teeth as he tightened his grip on the hose and lifted it to spray the next few cows.

Ned kicked at a bit of cow shit with his boots. 'I thought you were going away with Meg today?'

'Something came up. Plans changed,' Lawson told him. He'd have to have a conversation about Meg with Ned but he really didn't know what to say.

'Can we go see her tomorrow then?' Ned asked.

'No,' Lawson shouted, and immediately regretted it. This wasn't Ned's fault.

'Look,' he said, dropping to his knees in front of his son. 'I'm sorry for yelling. It's been a long day. Why don't you run back to the house and see if Aunty Tab needs help getting ready for dinner? I won't be long.'

As much as he loved Ned, he just wanted to be alone right now. Ethan had been visibly surprised when Lawson showed up for afternoon milking instead of Funky, but he'd been sensible enough not to ask questions and had refrained from trying to make conversation, for which Lawson was grateful.

'Okay, then.' Ned turned to go, his head and shoulders drooping as he walked, making Lawson feel like the biggest dick on the planet. He was about to call him back, when Ned shrieked.

'Meg! What are you doing here?'

Lawson glanced over to the door as Ned rushed forwards to greet their uninvited visitor. For a moment he forgot to breathe. Seeing her standing there—as gorgeous as ever—was like an actual punch to the gut. Water sprayed out of his hose, none going anywhere near the cows, and the rotary continued on without him getting any cattle off. Part of him wondered why it had taken her so long to come looking when he hadn't shown up and wasn't answering his phone.

'Hey, sweetheart,' he heard Megan say to Ned as they wrapped their arms around each other. The sight jolted Lawson from his frigid state.

'Ned!' He shouted. 'I thought I told you to go home!' Again he sounded harsh but he didn't want *her* anywhere near his precious son.

'Aw, *Dad*.' Ned didn't let go of Megan.

She patted his back and extracted herself from his arms. 'Listen to your dad.' Her voice sounded shaky, but Ned looked up at her and smiled.

'Okay. Will you come back and have dinner with us?'

No, you most certainly will not!

Megan's gaze met Lawson's and although he hadn't said these words out loud he could tell she understood. 'I can't tonight. Go along now.'

With one final pout in Lawson's direction, Ned headed out of the shed, scuffling his feet as he went. Lawson's hackles rose at the way she told his boy what do to—she had no bloody right—and he almost called Ned back, but then realised he was being irrational. Hadn't he just *shouted* at Ned to leave?

Things were about to get messy and he didn't want his son to witness it.

As Ned retreated, Megan took a few steps towards him and his insides tightened. They were supposed to be in Margaret River having the best weekend of their lives and instead he could hardly stand to look at her.

'Why?' he spat.

At the same time, she said, 'I'm so sorry.'

He scoffed, switched off the hose and chucked it to the floor. 'What for? For your drug history? For being involved in a man's death? For the fact you've spent the last few years in prison? For failing to tell me about all that? *Or*, are you sorry you got found out at all?' He shook his head at her, trying not to be affected by her bloodshot eyes and red, blotchy cheeks. He refused to feel sorry for her.

'I never intentionally set out to lie to you,' she rushed. 'In fact, I never meant to get involved with you at all.'

Another blow to the gut; he'd been falling in love but it sounded as though she'd never been as serious as he was.

'So it's all true then?' His shoulders slumped—he'd wanted her to tell him there'd been some big misunderstanding, that somehow Adeline and the newspapers had it all wrong. 'You went to prison!'

Megan squeezed her lips together and her silence spoke volumes.

'I think it's time you leave,' he said, lifting his arm to indicate the door.

'Please, Lawson,' she pleaded, wringing her hands in front of her, 'just let me explain.'

He closed his eyes. 'Make it quick.'

Megan took a deep breath. 'It is true that I went to prison for armed robbery, but not for killing anyone, because I didn't kill anyone. That's not who I am. I was in a terrible state; I was twenty, and an addict, and desperate. I trusted my boyfriend. He said he knew a store where we could easily get cash and no one would get hurt. He was tried for murder, but I was found not guilty of even being an accessory to that crime. My sentence was for the robbery only.

'I served my time: four and a half long years. The shock of it all made me get clean, but when I got out and tried to rebuild my life, I realised I never would in Melbourne. I moved to Rose Hill where nobody else lived to put the awful things in my past behind me and to become the person I wanted to be. So yes, when I first met you and Ned, I tried not to get involved, and even when we started to become friends, I was scared if you knew the truth, you'd stop coming around.

'I decided to tell you after that first kiss, but then you came to Rose Hill the next day and ... all my good intentions flew out the window. You can't know how amazing you made me feel. I tried a couple more times to tell you everything, but things kept getting in our way. Maybe I didn't try hard enough—I admit that—but do you know how terrifying the prospect of losing you was?'

It sounded like a rhetorical question but before he could contemplate an answer, Ethan stormed around from the other side of the rotary.

'Lawson, what on earth's going on—Oh!' He halted in his tracks, looked between the two of them and then backed away like a domestic animal retreating from a wild beast. A moment later the rotary stopped turning.

'I'll admit I was guilty of not telling you everything about my past,' Megan continued, 'but if I'd known how Leah died, I promise I would have tried harder to stay away. Or forced myself to tell you.'

That couldn't be true. They'd spoken about Leah—surely he'd mentioned her tragic death? But even as he thought this, he knew Megan was right. He didn't like talking about it.

'I never *lied* to you,' he said, still furious.

'I didn't lie to you either,' she whispered. 'And I'm not blaming you or asking you to forgive me. I'm done with feeling guilty. It's been almost eight years since I lost my parents and my brother, and since then I've lost everything else that ever mattered to me as well. I'm sorry for hurting you, Lawson, but perhaps neither of us was quite ready for whatever this almost was.'

Her words twisted his heart, thawing some of the anger he'd been feeling, but he couldn't afford to let down his guard. He had so many questions, but what would be the point in asking them? Talking would only prolong the agony. For both of them.

'You finished now?' he asked, picking the hose back off the ground. 'Because I've got work to do.'

Her face fell. It was clear she was close to tears and he felt like a jerk, but he wanted her gone so he could lick his wounds in peace. He wanted that beer. He wanted oblivion.

She nodded. 'Yes, I'm done, Lawson. Goodbye.'

And then she turned and hurried out of the dairy, out of his life. Less than a week earlier this was exactly the spot where they had shared their first kiss, but now it would always be the place where everything had ended.

Chapter Thirty-seven

Megan opened Archie's gate to find Buster and Cane waiting for her in the same spot since she left them hours earlier. Cane jumped up all over her but Buster looked past; the expression on his face reminded her of Eeyore.

'Aw.' She dropped to her knees beside the dogs and pulled Buster towards her, burying her tear-soaked face in his rough, old-dog fur. 'You're gunna have to come home with me tonight, buddy, but Archie will be back soon, I promise.'

Feeling a little like she was violating her friend's privacy, she went into the house and found the clean underwear and change of clothes she'd promised to take him. After a trip to the bathroom to collect toiletries, she searched for his keys and this time locked up when she left. Then she bundled the dogs into the car and drove back into Walsh. She could have dropped them at her place, but she wanted them with her. As it was after hours by the time she arrived back at the hospital, she had to press a button outside to get the attention of the nurses. The woman who came to the door made no secret of how annoyed she was to be interrupted.

'Visiting hours are over,' she said, even before she'd fully opened the door.

Megan lifted the recycling bag that held Archie's things. 'I don't need to stay.' In fact she would prefer not; Archie would take one look at her and know something was up. 'I'm just delivering these things for my neighbour, Archie Weaver.'

'Oh, you're …' The nurse all but snatched the bag and then stepped back as if Megan were something to be scared of.

She fought the urge to bare her teeth at the woman. So much for thinking Rose Hill would be a refuge! She could never escape her past, however much she'd changed and wanted to move on. To everyone else she'd always be the criminal junkie. In some ways, this realisation was freeing. She no longer had to walk around on eggshells, terrified everyone would discover her deepest darkest shame, because now they already knew.

Maybe finally everyone would leave her in Rose Hill in peace, which was what she'd wanted in the first place.

'I'm Megan McCormick, yes.' She held her chin high as if she were proud of this fact. 'And I'll be back tomorrow to visit my friend.'

It didn't matter what this random person thought of her. Not any more. No cruel words or harsh looks could hurt as bad as Lawson telling her to go. Nothing anyone else could ever do would ever hurt more than when he'd looked at her with such loathing.

She turned away before the nurse could shut the door, and stalked back to the car, where Cane licked her all over her face. 'At least you guys love me,' she said, rubbing his neck and then starting the ignition. She told herself that was enough and was still repeating this mantra in her head when she arrived in Rose Hill fifteen minutes later.

But the moment she opened her front door and let the dogs inside, the devastation of the day hit her and the quiet loneliness of her house felt almost claustrophobic.

'Eliza?' Megan whispered as the dogs ran ahead, giving the stairs the usual wide berth. Part of her felt stupid craving the company of a ghost, but beggars couldn't be choosers.

Coolness wafted past her and she let out a satisfied breath; a tear trickled down her cheek as she slid to the floor. She told Eliza everything that had happened that day—from the terror of finding Archie unconscious to the bone-aching heartbreak of confessing all to Lawson.

'I wonder, would things have been different if I'd got to him before Adeline?' The thought of that woman left a bitter taste in her mouth and she made sure Eliza knew Adeline's connection to her own nemesis, telling her also about the confrontation with Penelope.

'This thing with Adeline and Lawson feels like history repeating itself.' Adeline might not have physically hurt Megan, but, like her grandmother, she'd gone out of her way to ruin things.

Eliza made no sign of being annoyed by this comment but Megan realised two seconds after she said it that hers and the ghost's situations weren't exactly the same. Eliza hadn't only lost her love—she'd also lost her life; however bad Megan might feel, at least she still had that. She also had Archie and Cane. This might not seem that much right now when she was still so raw from the pain of losing Lawson but she remembered something her grandmother used to say—*there's always someone in the world worse off than you.*

After their conversation that evening, she couldn't see any hope of changing Lawson's mind about her, but at least she couldn't imagine him hooking up with Adeline either.

Part of her wished she'd bought herself a bottle of wine (or two) on the way home, but the other part of her thanked the heavens above that the thought hadn't crossed her mind until she was too far out of Walsh to make it worth going back. She didn't want to numb this pain; she wanted to use it as a reminder for the future. She'd tried to dip her toes into the realms of normal and a shark had almost bitten them off.

At least now she knew to keep out of the water.

Plan B had failed and it was back to Plan A—making a life for herself, and *only* herself, in Rose Hill. She'd avoid Walsh altogether and then she'd never have to see any of them. Archie had been happy enough there on his own for years; if it was good enough for him, it was good enough for her.

And at least she'd have him for company as well.

Chapter Thirty-eight

At the sound of Tabitha's footsteps coming down the hall, Lawson yanked open the desk drawer and shoved the blue and yellow tea-cosy he'd been holding inside. By the time his sister appeared in the doorway, he was sitting upright in his chair, staring at the computer screen, pretending to work.

'Have you been up all night again?' Tab asked, with a yawn.

'I can't sleep worrying about the dairy,' he lied without even turning around to look at her. The part about not being able to sleep was true—he'd given up sometime after midnight as he had the two nights preceding—but it wasn't farming issues keeping him awake. Still, he'd decided he might as well make the most of the time to make a crisis-action plan and, when his mind didn't keep drifting off to Meg, that's exactly what he'd been trying to do.

'I've written a list of other milk processors we can approach to sell our excess to and I've organised a meeting with all the farmers affected for Wednesday night. What do you think about starting a Facebook page alerting regular people to the cause?' Before she could answer, he continued, 'I've also written letters to the state and federal governments and to all our suppliers and service providers asking them to do the same, to explain the flow-on effects of losing dairy farmers. I'm feeling positive that we'll find an alternative processor for our milk by July, but if not, I see us as having two options.'

He turned around to finally look at her. 'We either talk to a stock agent about selling part of our herd, maybe even part of the land, and running beef on the rest *or*, and this is my preferred option, we talk to Funky about how much it would cost to build you a proper area for your ice-cream manufacturing and we go hard down that avenue.'

The fact Megan had suggested this idea soured it a little, but he wasn't going to let that stop him pursuing something that would protect his land, his animals and most of all his family. 'I've been looking into suppliers who might take our ice-cream and there are a number of gourmet stores in WA and the rest of Australia we could target.'

'Whoa—hold on a moment.' Tab placed her hand on her hip. 'You don't think I want to be involved in all of that? This is my farm, my heritage, my livelihood as well.'

He blinked—surprised by her angry tone. 'Of course I want you involved, I'm just … researching.'

'In the middle of the night when you should be sleeping?' She sighed and shook her head. 'This can't go on, Lawson. You look like shit.'

Why did he think she was no longer talking about the farm plans? 'Geez, thanks, and a very good morning to you too, sister dear.'

She sniffed him, then screwed up her nose. 'When was the last time you showered, never mind shaved?'

'Don't start,' he said. Who needed a wife when he had a sister who nagged like a pro? And what did he care what he looked like? He wasn't trying to impress anyone. 'Just get me a coffee, will ya?'

'I'll make you coffee *and* some eggs for breakfast before you head out to do the milking, but only if you come into the kitchen and eat it with me.'

He sighed, knowing that what she really meant was she'd cook for him if he *talked* to her. Why did women think talking was the bee-all-and-end-all? As far as he reckoned, talking did jack-shit but make you feel worse. But he was in dire need of caffeine and his stomach rumbled at the thought of Tab's scrambled eggs.

'Okay.' Lawson pushed back the swivel chair and stood, then stretched his hands above his head, needing to loosen up after hours in the one position.

Tab started out of the office and he followed her.

'Uh uh.' She halted and turned as she entered the kitchen. 'You're not coming in here looking like that. You shower and shave while I cook.'

He was about to object but got a whiff of himself and decided perhaps a shower would make him feel a little better. He drew the line at shaving, though. What was the point? He hadn't left the farm since Friday and didn't plan on doing so till the meeting on Wednesday night.

Five minutes later, with fresh clothes and wet hair, he entered the kitchen to a plate of eggs and toast on the table and a mug of steaming coffee beside it. 'Thanks, sis,' he said, smiling at Tab as he pulled back the seat and sat.

'No worries. And can I just say that you smell much better?' She carried an almost identical plate over to the table, where her coffee was already waiting, and sat opposite him.

He shovelled a forkful of eggs into his mouth but Tab didn't even pick up her cutlery. *Here goes*, he thought, mentally preparing himself for the onslaught of Tab's well-meaning advice.

'Do you think maybe you should talk to Meg?'

Just the mention of her name had the muscles in his neck and shoulders tensing. 'I told you. We talked on Friday night. There's nothing left to say.'

'Well maybe you need to talk to me then, tell me how you're feeling about all of this. I can see you're hurting—you can't just switch your feelings off for her.'

'I can and I have.'

'Aren't you worried about Meg?' Tab asked, her tone frustrated. 'The whole town now knows about her past, so people will no longer be so welcoming and friendly.'

'And that's *my* problem?' He pushed his plate away half-finished, no longer hungry.

'Fine. It's not your problem. Forget about her if that's what you really want to do, but you've gotta at least talk to Ned.'

'I have. I told him things between Meg and I had ended. He understands.' The boy hadn't talked to him since but Lawson knew he'd come round eventually. One day Ned would understand that he'd ended things to protect him as much as himself.

'Don't you think he deserves a little more explanation than that?' Tab said. 'He's a smart kid, he feels things deeply and you need to give him a little more credit for being able to understand.'

Lawson's jaw tightened. He didn't want to share Megan's shortcomings with his son. He didn't want Ned to know what an utter fool he'd been.

'Tabitha,' he said, as he pushed to a stand, 'I appreciate everything you've done for Ned and me, but please don't tell me how to be a parent. Every breath I take is for Ned; everything I do is for him. I'm the one who knows him best and I'm the one who knows what's best for him. Are we clear?'

Before she could answer, Ned appeared in the doorway of the kitchen, rubbing his eyes with his hands. 'What's going on? Why are you two shouting?'

God. Lawson ran a hand through his hair, hoping Ned hadn't actually heard what they were saying. 'We weren't shouting; we were just having a discussion about the farm,' he said as he crossed over to his son and went to pull him into his arms.

Ned jerked away, refusing to even look at him. 'Aunty Tab?' he said. 'I'm hungry, can you make me some eggs too, please?'

'Sure, sweetheart.'

Lawson silently cursed, thankful that no matter how much of a dick he'd been, Tab wouldn't take it out on Ned. He tossed her a smile which he hoped she understood meant *thanks* and *sorry* and then he left them alone and headed out to the cows.

Chapter Thirty-nine

Megan took the dogs for a walk first thing on Monday morning, then came home and showered. She was just deliberating about whether to leave Cane and Buster in the house or locked up in the yard while she went to see Archie in the hospital when a knock sounded on her front door.

She froze. She'd survived the last couple of days by focusing on the dogs, crocheting, cooking, visiting Archie and trying her damn best not to think about Lawson. But, as the knock sounded again, she couldn't help wondering if it was him. *Unlikely*, said a voice inside her head—their conversation on Friday afternoon had been fairly final and he'd made no attempt to make contact with her over the weekend. So who could it be? With Archie in hospital, she definitely wasn't expecting visitors.

Her heart lurched in her chest as another possibility dawned. *Adeline!* What if she'd come to take Cane back? Could she do that? Not wanting to take any chances, Megan gathered the dogs and shut them in the kitchen.

Another knock sounded, this time louder and even more persistent.

363

'Coming,' she called, not bothering to keep the irritation out of her voice. As she got closer to the door, she recognised the figure on the other side of the still grimy glass. Tabitha!

She didn't know whether to be scared or excited to see the other woman. Hand shaking, she lifted it to unlock and open the door.

'Hello,' she said, hearing the trepidation in her voice.

'Hi, Meg.' Tabitha smiled in the friendly way she always did and her voice held nothing but warmth and sympathy. 'Fancy a cuppa?'

'I … um …' There were so many things she wanted to say, but, so surprised to see her guest, she couldn't even put together a sentence.

Tabitha didn't wait for an invitation to step inside. She squeezed Meg's arm. 'How about I put the kettle on and make those drinks?'

Megan closed the door behind Tabitha and followed her down the hallway to the kitchen. When Tabitha lifted her hand to open the door, she suddenly remembered the dogs. She opened her mouth to warn Tabitha but she was too late.

Cane sprang out like a jack-in-the-box and leaped right up to try and lick Tabitha's nose.

'Sorry,' Megan called, rushing to restrain him.

Tabitha laughed and took his affections in the good-natured way she seemed to take everything. 'It's fine, honestly and … Oh, who is that?' She looked to Buster lying under the table.

'That's my neighbour's dog. Archie had a heart attack on Friday and is in Walsh hospital, so I'm looking after Buster.'

Tabitha looked from Buster back to Megan and raised an eyebrow. 'Sounds like you've had quite a drama-filled weekend. Is Archie going to be okay?'

'I think so,' Megan said, still standing in the doorway, leaning down and clutching Cane's collar. 'I'm hoping I'll be able to bring him home this afternoon.'

'Oh that's wonderful,' Tabitha said, as if it were just your average, everyday conversation. She stooped, ruffled Buster's fur and then walked across the room, picking up the kettle and taking it across to the tap to fill.

Megan loosened her grip and told Cane to behave, then she looked across to Tabitha. 'I must admit I'm surprised to see you.'

Tabitha smiled as she went about the business of locating mugs, coffee, etc. 'I must admit I was surprised at the revelations of Friday afternoon but I also know life's not black and white and I wanted to make sure you're okay.'

The fact she cared in spite of everything made Megan want to cry again, but thankfully she appeared to have used up all her tears. 'I'm surviving,' she said. 'Thank you.'

'I hope you're getting more sleep than Lawson is.'

Megan's heart squeezed at his name. 'I've not been getting much at all,' she admitted, remembering Tabitha was her guest and locating a container of cookies to go with the coffee.

Tabitha sighed. 'Do you love my brother?'

It was the last question Megan expected but she found herself answering honestly. 'I do. I didn't know it was possible to fall in love so fast, but losing him hurts worse than anything I've ever been through before.'

'Worse than losing your parents and your brother?'

She shook her head. 'I suppose not worse but different, because Lawson's still alive and I know how badly I've hurt him, and that no matter what I say, I can't change what I did in the past. I wish I hadn't come here and I wish I'd never met him, for his sake, and yours and Ned's. How is Ned?'

'Not good,' Tabitha said as she brought the first coffee to the table and then turned back for the second one. 'He misses you. He's confused.'

Her heart twisted at the thought of Ned hurting because of her. 'Does he know … know about …' She couldn't bring herself to say it.

Tabitha shook her head. 'No, Lawson simply told him that you and he are no longer seeing each other; he can't understand why.'

They both sat at the table and Megan wrapped her hands around her mug. It might be summer, but she craved the comfort that holding a warm mug offered. She wanted to say sorry but it didn't seem enough, so she took a sip of her drink instead.

'Why didn't you just tell us from the beginning?' Tabitha asked after a long, awkward silence.

Megan took a deep breath, put down her mug and went over the same stuff she'd told Lawson on Friday afternoon, but Tabitha reacted much differently. She made sympathetic noises and squeezed Megan's hand when she'd finally finished speaking.

'It might not feel like it now, but I think Lawson will come around eventually. He's hurting and he feels foolish, but I think he's more angry at the fact he heard your story from someone else than anything. He hasn't so much looked at another woman since Leah and then you came along and everything changed. *He* changed—you lit up his life again. Deep down, I think he knows, like I do, that you were a victim of awful circumstances and that you deserve a second chance as much as anyone else does.'

It was a nice theory but she didn't dare allow herself to hope. 'That's very kind of you to say,' Megan said, struggling against the emotion building in her throat, 'but I think you might be in the minority. You should see the looks that the medical staff, visitors and even the patients have been giving me at the hospital this weekend. It's like I have leprosy and they're scared I might infect them.'

Tabitha sighed. 'It'll take time. Maybe you need to do something to change people's minds about you?'

'Like what?'

'Have you ever thought about writing your experiences down like a memoir of sorts, and a cautionary tale? Show others how easily grief can lead you down a path of self-destruction? Or you could volunteer to speak at schools to teenagers about the dire consequences of taking drugs?'

English hadn't been her best subject at school, and neither had public speaking, but something inside Megan flickered at this possibility. If she could help even one person find better ways of dealing with grief and hardships by sharing her story it might give her life some tiny bit of meaning. 'I don't know if—'

She stopped mid sentence as her phone started ringing, and glanced across to where it sat on the kitchen bench. 'I'm sorry, that could be the hospital.'

Tabitha nodded. 'It's okay. Go ahead, answer it.' As Megan stood, Tabitha lifted her mug and took a sip.

'Hello?' Megan said into the phone.

'Hi Megan, it's Dr Harpreet here. I'm afraid Archie's had bit of a turn. He's not feeling very good and he's asking for you. Are you able to come in?'

Bit of a turn? 'What does "bit of a turn" mean?'

'It's probably better if I explain when you get here.'

'Okay, then. Thank you. I'll see you soon.' She hung up the phone and quickly relayed to Tabitha the information the doctor had given her.

'Do you want me to drive you there?' Tabitha asked.

'No. I'm fine to drive. But thank you. Thanks for visiting and for … for everything. I'll give your suggestions some thought.'

'You're welcome.' Tabitha wrapped her one arm around Megan. 'I may be Lawson's sister, but I'm also your friend, so if you need anything, even if you just want someone to talk to, please, ask me.'

'Thank you.' Worry for Archie, combined with Tabitha's unexpected visit and show of support threatened to unravel her, but she managed to grab her bag and see her guest out. Then she drove faster than she should have to the hospital, not wanting Archie to feel alone and praying his turn wasn't anything too serious.

She parked her car crookedly and ran into the building. Jenny looked up from behind the reception desk as Megan hurried through the double doors and ran down the corridor, not stopping until she turned into Archie's room.

The doctor was there, with two nurses, and Archie lay on the bed. He didn't look right but nobody seemed to be doing anything to try and fix him.

'What's wrong with him?' Megan shouted.

The staff turned to look at her and then Dr Harpreet took a step towards her, placing his hands on the side of her arms. 'I'm sorry, Meg, we did everything we could.'

'*No!*' She felt her face crumble and her whole body go cold. Her knees threatened to give way and the doctor must have anticipated this because he led her to a plastic chair by the door and lowered her into it.

'Can we get you a drink?' one of the nurses asked as she tucked a heavy blanket over her shoulders. Megan realised she was shaking.

'No.' She threw the blanket off. She didn't want a blanket. She didn't want a drink. She wanted them to stop fussing over her and put their efforts into making Archie well again. This could *not* be happening. He could *not* be dead. He'd been fine the day before.

Yesterday the nurses had been talking about sending him home. She glared up at Dr Harpreet. 'What the hell happened?'

His expression of sympathy didn't waver at her harsh question. He dropped to his knees beside her and took her hand in his. 'Archie had another heart attack just after we called you.'

Her lower lip trembling, she finally glanced up and took a proper look at Archie. She'd never seen a dead person before— her granny and pop had both died when she was in prison and the fire had left her parents' and brother's bodies unrecognisable. Not that anyone would have let her see them anyway. But now that she looked properly at Archie it was clear to see the life had left him. His eyes were open but they no longer held that cheeky spark.

Megan didn't care that these strangers would bear witness to her grief; she could no longer hold back the tears. Her heart ached as it never had before. She might not have known Archie very long, but his loss felt almost as great as the day she'd lost her family to fire. Back then she had still had two sets of grandparents who loved her; now she had absolutely no one.

'We'll give you a few moments alone with him,' Dr Harpreet said, before briefly squeezing her shoulder. He and the nurses retreated.

Megan stared at Archie a few long moments, then finally struggled to her feet and went across to stand beside him. She took his hand, which already felt painfully cold, in hers.

'Thanks for the friendship,' she whispered, tasting her own tears as they flooded into her mouth. 'You'll never know how much it meant to me. You gave me back my self-belief and listened when I needed a friend more than I knew. I'll miss you and I promise I'll look after Buster and the chickens.'

She bent and kissed him on his forehead, and then rested his hands on his chest. Sobbing, she lowered his eyelids, gently closing his eyes. 'Rest in peace, Archie.'

Less than five minutes later, the two nurses returned to the room. 'We need to sort things in here,' announced the taller of the two.

Sort things? The nurse's clinical tone and the way she gestured absentmindedly at Archie had Megan fuming. It irked her how quickly they wanted to get rid of him. Did they treat every corpse this way? Or was their near-on rude behaviour simply because

Archie was no one but a crazy old hermit and she even lower down in their opinion?

She opened her mouth to ask this when Dr Harpreet appeared. 'Meg, can I have a word?'

At least he sounded kind. She nodded and, with one final squeeze of Archie's hand, she followed him out of the room. She wiped her eyes as he led her into his office, sat her down and began to ask her questions she didn't know the answers to. Who was Archie's next of kin? Did she have contact details of any family that could be notified and thus deal with the funeral and the execution of his will?

Her head spun and she rubbed her forehead. 'I have no idea. He mentioned a son once but I don't know what his name was. They were estranged.'

Dr Harpreet smiled sympathetically. 'It's okay. We'll get the police to look into it and the shire might have some information also.'

A nurse knocked on the open door and the doctor nodded for her to enter.

'These are Mr Weaver's things,' she said, speaking it seemed to the doctor but dumping the green bag Megan had brought in on Friday night in her lap.

'Thank you,' she said, although her tone didn't match her words. She looked back to the doctor. 'Is that all you need from me?'

He nodded and stood. 'I'm really sorry, Meg. But Archie was lucky to have you in his life. I'll be in touch when we have some information about him.'

Lucky wasn't a word she'd use to describe either of them, but she forced a smile and pushed to her feet. She needed to get the hell out of that awful place as fast as possible and get home to the dogs.

Although she wanted to wrap her arms around Buster and never let him go, Megan went via Archie's place. She told herself it was to feed and water the chickens, but she felt the need to go inside. It was mid afternoon and the temperature outside was hot, but the second she stepped into the house, she shivered. She'd been hoping to feel him there, but as with his body, his presence had well and truly left. Rubbing her hands up and down her arms, she walked around looking at his paintings. Even the half-finished ones took her breath away. He'd had so much talent and it was a tragedy nobody had ever known.

What would become of all these beautiful art works? She couldn't bear the thought of them ending up at the tip but did she have the right to take them? Deciding that was a question for later when she'd recovered a little from the shock of losing him so suddenly, she spent some time searching in drawers and cupboards for anything that might lead her to his son. Even if they hadn't spoken in thirty years, the man should know his father had passed away. Perhaps he'd want the paintings.

In Archie's bedroom she found a framed photo of a family—a man, a woman, a boy and a girl. She took the old image out of the glass and turned it over. On the back were the words, *Archie, Katy, Gemma and Bradley.* It wasn't much to go on, but at least she had a possible name for his son, which she could pass onto the police.

Making a mental note of the name Bradley Weaver, she put the photo back into the frame, then she locked up again and went home.

Chapter Forty

Lawson looked up from where he was mending a fence, surprised to see Tab walking towards him. The day before he'd tried to apologise to her for his harsh words about her interfering with his parenting, but, like his son, she'd pretty much been giving him the cold shoulder ever since.

'I know you don't *care*,' she said by way of a greeting, 'but I thought you should know that Archie died yesterday.'

'Who?' Yet, even as the question left his mouth, the answer registered in his head. She had his full attention now. He dropped his pliers and stood. 'How? When? How did you find out?'

Tab crossed her arm over her stump—the closest she could get to folding her arms in a show of annoyance—and said, 'He had a heart attack. His second in a week, but you probably didn't know about that either because you've refused to talk properly to Meg and haven't left the farm. He died in Walsh hospital yesterday and the reason I know is because I was with Meg when they called her to tell her he wasn't doing so great, so I checked in just now to see how he was going and—'

'You went to see Meg?' he asked, unsure how he felt about that. His chest squeezed a little, almost as if he were jealous of Tabitha. Or was he simply annoyed that she'd gone behind his back to see her?

'Yes. You might be angry with her, Lawson, but I like her, and I didn't like the thought of her out there in Rose Hill so isolated. Breaking up with someone hurts and I wanted to check she was okay.'

'And?' he found himself asking.

'And,' Tabitha emphasised the word before continuing, 'she's heartbroken. She looks almost as bad as you do, just without the ridiculous beard. And that was before she lost her only friend. Now I'm even more worried about her. She's got nothing, no one but a couple of dogs to live for.'

He'd been feeling pretty damn lousy five minutes earlier, unable to get Megan out of his head no matter how hard he tried, and this news only made that worse.

He ran a dirty hand through his hair in frustration. His instincts told him to go to Megan, but his heart didn't know if he could take being so close. Then, he thought of how he'd felt after his mum died and how Leah had got him through, and he realised that no matter how angry he was with Meg, he didn't want her to be alone right now.

'Thanks for letting me know,' he told Tabitha.

'What are you going to do?'

He swallowed. 'I'm going to go see her and give her my sympathy.'

Tab smiled and unfolded her arms. 'You're a good man, Lawson Cooper-Jones. Let me give you some ice-cream to take with you.'

Chapter Forty-one

Megan slept—if you could call it that—with both Cane and Buster curled up at the bottom of her bed. She woke with scratchy eyes, a parched throat and a sore head—typical symptoms of a hangover, only she hadn't drunk a drop of alcohol last night. The moment she'd come home from Archie's, she'd taken one look at Buster looking up at her expectantly and had burst into tears again. Her body must have been working over-time to produce them because hours passed and still they wouldn't stop. She'd sat on the back verandah, Buster slumbering at her feet and Cane chasing insects in the garden, until the early hours of the morning, crying for Archie, crying for herself and wondering what next?

Rose Hill no longer felt like a safe haven and the idea of doing up the building and opening tea rooms was laughable. Now that everyone in Walsh knew the truth about her, they wouldn't want to patronise her business. Perhaps Eliza's Tea Rooms had been doomed right from the beginning. Leaving town seemed the obvious solution, but where would she go? And *how* could she? The measly inheritance she'd got from her grandparents was now tied up in this derelict old building. And while she could perhaps take Buster and Cane with her, what would she do about Archie's chickens?

Oh, why couldn't she have been the one to die instead of him? At least he had talent—he'd made a life of sorts for himself in Rose Hill and he'd seemed happy enough, and right now Megan didn't see how she could ever be happy again. She couldn't stop thinking how one day her own death would be as lonely and unnoticed as Archie's.

If it weren't for the dogs needing to go outside, who knew if she'd have been able to drag herself out of bed, but somehow she did. She carried a nearly-too-heavy Cane down the stairs and Buster trundled behind them—he'd got over the ghost where Cane looked like being permanently scared. As had become her routine, after Megan let the dogs out, she went into the kitchen, drank a coffee and made some toast, though today she barely nibbled at it. The day loomed ahead of her—depressingly long—and she couldn't even summon enthusiasm for the things that usually brought her joy, such as cooking and crocheting. What was the point? She had no one to feed and no one to buy her tea-cosies.

It was then that her gaze fell upon the notepad and pen on the table, the notepad she usually wrote her daily to-do list on. Making a list of things to achieve had given her a purpose, but suddenly a list of make-work tasks didn't seem enough. If she were to survive out here alone, she needed to do something that at least had the possibility of being worthwhile. She thought of Tabitha's suggestion that she write her story and, although she didn't think she'd ever be eloquent enough to do it properly, she stretched across and picked up the notepad and pen.

After tearing off the first page, which still had Friday's to-do list on it, she started to write.

Mum and Dad bickered a fair bit and a lot of the time my brother and I could barely stand to look at each other. For three months one year when

*the house was being renovated we had to share a room, and both of us
thought this was the worst thing ever. We put a line of masking tape down
the middle of the room and fought over who got the bed near the window.
We fought over everything back then, but when I really think about my
brother, it's not the fighting I remember. It's things like getting up in the
middle of the night on Christmas Eve, sneaking downstairs together and
unwrapping some of our presents and then wrapping them again. It's the
way he used to fall asleep on the journey to visit Granny and Pop in Bal-
larat and how his body would slump onto the seat and his head would rest
on my knee.*

*When I think about my parents, it's not their fights over who forgot
to put the bin out, it's the secret kisses in the kitchen when they thought
we weren't looking. It's mum's cooking and how every single thing she
made—whether it be a ham and cheese toastie or a full roast dinner—she
made with love. She used to make our clothes when we were little too—not
because they couldn't afford to buy new ones but because she loved doing
it. I wasn't a girly girl but the dresses Mum made for me, I wore with the
biggest grin on my face. They were gorgeous and unique—I never went to
a birthday party and found myself in the same pink dress from Target as
another girl. I remember the way Dad used to read us bedtime stories every
night, even when we were in high school. When they died, Dad was in the
middle of reading us* Twenty Thousand Leagues Under the Sea. *I
never have managed to finish that story.*

Having never been much of a writer before, it surprised Megan
the way the words poured from the pen onto the page. *Pages.* The
dogs came in from outside—Buster slumped at her feet under the
table and Cane nudged her with his nose, trying to get her attention, trying to get her to play—yet still she wrote. She wrote about
her childhood—the good parts and the not-so-great parts. She
wrote about her family—her mum's parents whom she couldn't
have been closer to and her dad's parents who never seemed to
approve of their son's choices. His decision to go into teaching

rather than follow the family profession of law, his choice of a wife, his slightly unruly children.

She was just sending herself off to school camp—excited about the contraband lollies she and her friends carried in their bags—when a knock on the front door startled her. The first time someone had knocked on her door in Rose Hill, she'd almost died, and although it had happened a number of times since, it still shocked her every single time. She glanced down at the scruffy T-shirt and shorts she'd slept in, then, reasoning it would either be Tabitha or the police, she heaved a sigh and went to answer it.

Standing on the other side of the door was the last person she expected to see. At least it looked like Lawson, though over the last few days he appeared to have grown a beard. She'd never thought facial hair attractive but on him it made her knees wobble. Her fingers itched to reach out and run themselves over his jawline, but somehow she resisted.

As he bent down to greet Cane, he glanced back up. 'Hi, Meg.' His voice was even deeper and sexier than she remembered.

This was where she was supposed to reply but all she could do was stand there gaping, her mouth wide open like the little boy from *Mary Poppins*.

Lawson cleared his throat and straightened again. 'Would you prefer I call you Megan, rather than Meg?'

She finally found her voice but it came out not much more than a whisper. 'I like Meg,' she said. *Especially when you say it*, but she managed swallow that last bit. She didn't know why he was there, but remembering his treatment of her on Friday night, something told her it wasn't to kiss and make up.

He nodded. They stood there awkwardly, staring at each other for a few long moments before they both spoke at the same time.

'I was sorry to hear about Archie.'

'Would you like to come in for a coffee?'

He smiled a little and she felt the effects in her core. 'Yes, please,' he said and then held out the small cooler bag he'd been holding. 'This is a little something from Tabitha. She sends her sympathies too.'

'Thank you.'

'She thinks ice-cream can fix everything,' he added with a clearly nervous laugh.

Megan returned an equally nervous smile, then stepped aside to let him into the house. Cane followed without being asked, no doubt hopeful that Lawson would be more fun than Meg had been the last few days. They walked down the hallway into the kitchen without a word spoken between them.

'Is that Archie's dog?' Lawson asked when he saw Buster still lying on the floor where he'd been when she'd gone to answer the door.

'Yes.' Megan unzipped the cooler bag and put the ice-cream into the freezer. She liked having something to do and immediately set to making drinks. 'The poor thing is broken-hearted. He's not really eating and he barely moves. I don't know what to do for him.'

Lawson dropped to his knees and rubbed Buster's neck. 'Give him time. His master only died yesterday. How are *you* doing?'

'I've been better,' she said as she spooned coffee granules into mugs. And *that* was saying something.

He nodded, then stood again and shoved his hands in his pockets.

'How's Ned?' Megan asked, not really wanting to talk about Archie for fear she'd cry in front of Lawson and he'd think she was trying to manipulate his emotions or something.

'He's good.'

When he didn't elaborate, she added, 'And the farm? Have you heard anything more?'

'I've been looking into other possible processors for our milk come July, but I think our best bet is looking at alternative options, like selling off some of our herd or trying to make more of Tabitha's ice-cream business.'

'I'm sorry,' she said because she didn't really know what else to say.

'Thanks.'

She put the coffee mugs down on the table. 'Would you like to sit?'

For a second she thought maybe he'd refuse, but then he dragged back a chair and lowered his large, ridiculously gorgeous body into it. He wrapped his fingers around the mug, lifted it to his mouth and took a sip. 'Good coffee,' he said after a few more moments.

'Thanks. Can I offer you a biscuit?'

She opened the container that was already in the middle of the table, but he waved his hand in dismissal. 'No, thank you. I'm fine.'

Argh. Megan wanted to scream. They were being so damn polite—he felt more like a stranger than on the day they'd first met and it broke her heart. She almost commented on the arrival of his beard, simply for something to fill the silence, but he got in first.

'What was it like being in prison?'

She blinked, surprised by his question, but also grateful that he was no longer dancing around the elephant in the room.

'You don't have to say,' he rushed, sitting forwards slightly. 'It's just I'd like to understand more what you've been through.'

She wanted to ask *why*? Why did he care? Why did he want to know? Would telling him change anything? Instead, she told him straight. 'It was hell. It's not something I find easy to talk about but I want to tell you.'

His gaze dropped to his coffee as she continued.

'People think prisoners have it easy these days with gyms and flatscreen TVs and stuff but, even if that were true, none of that makes up for the showering in full view of strangers. Having to sleep in the same cells as people you don't trust is terrifying. I didn't sleep properly the whole time I was inside. And it was lonely too. I didn't make friends and I got teased and bullied for being a goodie two shoes.'

'What did you do during the day?' he asked.

'For the last couple of years, I worked in the prison kitchen, and I also did any extra learning opportunity that came up—I learned about car repairs, how to build and fix things around the house. I even did a unit on nail art. They were trying to give us skills so we could earn a living when we got out, but I wasn't really thinking that far ahead. I exercised in the yard whenever we had the chance and became obsessed with the gym too; I did anything that helped pass the time and gave me an avenue for my grief that wasn't drugs.'

'And in prison … is that where you finally got help for your addiction and counselling for your grief?'

She nodded, again doing her best not to cry. Most of the time she tried not to remember her time inside and the huge battle she fought to recover. 'Gran had tried to get me counselling just after the fire. Unfortunately I refused to talk to anyone. Talking about things hurt; taking drugs made that stop. It was the shock of seeing someone die that broke the cycle. I didn't shoot the bullet that killed him, but I was there and I associated with the kind of people who could do that kind of stuff.'

'I can't even imagine what it would be like to have gone through everything you've been through, Meg.' He sighed deeply. 'But the fact you couldn't trust me enough to share it? That hurts and I can't help wondering what else you haven't told me.'

'I understand.'

He shook his head. 'I'm sorry. I didn't come here to go over all this; I came because I wanted to check you were okay after Archie. I just wanted—' The ringing of his phone somewhere deep in his pocket interrupted him and he glanced down as he dug it out. He gave her an apologetic look before answering.

'Hello, Lawson speaking.'

A few seconds later, it became clear he was speaking to the school and Megan took a sip of her now-cold coffee, trying not to look like she was eavesdropping. The only thing she could think of to do was clear their mugs from the table but she didn't want to do that because she didn't want him to think she wanted him to go.

He disconnected and shoved back his seat. 'I'm sorry, Meg, but Ned's got himself into some more trouble at school. I'm going to have to go.'

'Of course.' She nodded, also standing. She wanted to ask what kind of trouble because she cared about his son, but she didn't think it was her place any more. 'I hope he's okay.'

'Thanks.' He started out the kitchen and she and Cane followed him down the hallway. Cane as usual took as wide as possible a berth around the stairs and this time Lawson noticed. He frowned and paused a moment. 'He's still scared, I see.'

Then, he rubbed his arms a little and glanced around him. 'Did you find anything else out about Eliza?'

'Yes, as a matter of fact I did,' she said, wondering if it was the right time to offer her thoughts on Penelope Walsh being a murderer. Considering they'd just been talking about her own prison time, it felt somewhat audacious. And he had somewhere else he had to be. 'But it's a long story.'

Lawson sighed. 'Maybe one for another day then? Bye, Meg.'

Where only days ago he would have pulled her into his arms and kissed her till her lips ached, this time he turned and strode off towards his ute as if he couldn't get away fast enough. But even as Megan waved him goodbye, she couldn't help clinging to the little bit of hope she found in his final words.

Another day.

What did that mean? Would she see him again? Did he think maybe they could be friends?

She closed the front door and then leaned back against it, emotionally exhausted from the weirdness of Lawson's visit. While she couldn't deny a certain happiness at seeing him again, in some ways it only made things worse. Him sitting across the table from her was akin to someone waving a chocolate cake under her nose, yet telling her she couldn't taste it.

And what good was a cake you couldn't eat? How could she ever be satisfied with his friendship—if that's what he was offering—when she wanted so much more?

Chapter Forty-two

Lawson gripped the steering wheel hard as he drove away from Meg's house, away from Rose Hill. As worried as he was about Ned, the phone call had been a welcome distraction because he wasn't sure how much longer he'd have been able to withstand Meg's company without losing the plot. Even in old shorts and a shapeless T-shirt, with puffy bags under her eyes, which he guessed were the result of crying and too little sleep, she turned him on like he'd never imagined possible and his body was starting to affect his head.

There was simply something about her that snuck under his skin and made him question everything he'd always thought he stood for. Damn Tabitha for making him go over there. From now on, he'd leave all the do-gooding to her.

He drove all the way to Walsh Primary School with the music up full-bore and ten kilometres over the speed limit—he wanted to get to Ned and he wanted something else in his head besides Meg. As he climbed out the ute, he looked up to see the principal holding the door open for him and realised this was even more serious than she'd conveyed on the phone.

He shoved his keys in his pockets and headed over to greet her. 'Hi Ms Saunders. Where's Ned?'

'He's in my office, and I have to tell you, I'm very disappointed in his behaviour. I was hoping that his week off school would have given you and him some time to discuss acceptable forms of conflict resolution to complement what we've been discussing at school, but once again, Ned has used his fists to finish an argument.'

'I … uh …' Lawson honestly had no idea what to say. He'd never punched anyone in his life and he didn't know where Ned was getting all this violence from.

'Let's go inside,' Carline said, 'and have a proper conversation.'

She led him into her office, where Ned was sitting on one of the seats opposite her desk, his arms crossed tightly over his chest and a scowl on his face. Not a remorseful scowl, but an angry scowl, as if he wanted to punch someone else.

'Ned,' Lawson said, crossing over and dropping into the seat beside him. 'What's going on?'

His son narrowed his eyes at Lawson in response and then looked away, preferring it seemed to face Carline as she sat behind her desk rather than him.

She planted her elbows on the desk and entwined her hands. 'Now, Ned, do you want to tell your father what happened or should I?'

He shrugged, cast one scornful look at Lawson and then turned away again. 'Some kids were spreading lies about Meg, not that you'd care!'

Lawson stiffened. 'What kind of lies?'

He felt Carline's castigating gaze boring into him. Of course she knew the truth about Meg—nothing was secret in a small country town.

'They said Meg killed someone,' Ned said, his tone telling Lawson how ridiculous he thought this, 'and that she just got out of prison.'

'I see.' Lawson could barely speak, his chest squeezing so hard he suddenly found it difficult to breathe.

'It's not true!' Ned shouted. Then in a tinier voice, he added, 'Is it?'

Lawson looked to Ned then to Carline, to Ned again and back to Carline. 'This situation is complicated,' he said. And all his fault. Tab's words about how he needed to explain things properly to Ned reverberated around his head.

Carline raised her eyebrows and nodded slowly. *No kidding*, said her expression. He could only imagine what she must think of him but right now that didn't matter as much as Ned did.

'I know Ned's done something he shouldn't have and we need to deal with that, but I'd like to have a conversation with my son in private first, if you don't mind?'

'Of course.' Carline stood. 'I've got to go do some classroom visits, so I'll leave you in here to talk. Tell Beck when you're finished and she'll buzz me. I'll come back and we can discuss where to from here.'

He'd been envisaging taking Ned home and having a heart-to-heart over some of Tab's ice-cream but maybe it was better to get this conversation over and done with. 'Thank you,' he said as Carline headed for the door.

The moment she closed it behind her, he scooted his chair over closer to Ned's. 'I'm sorry, buddy,' he said, 'but you know those things the kids are saying about Meg … some of them are true.'

Ned's eyes widened and his lip wobbled as he shook his head. 'She wouldn't kill anyone!'

'No, you're right,' Lawson reached out and placed his hand on Ned's shoulder, 'but she was in prison.'

He swallowed, unsure how to go about this conversation. He didn't want to lie to Ned—doing so by omission had got his son into this mess—but he wanted to protect him also. Damn, he wished he'd never met Megan: not only had she wrecked his heart, their association with her had messed Ned up as well.

'What for?' Ned asked, his face crumbling.

'You know how you lost your mum?' Lawson asked. Ned barely nodded. 'Well, Meg was older when her mum died but at the same time, her dad and her brother died as well. She was very sad and to try and handle her pain, she started taking drugs.'

Ned knew all about drugs—well, as much as a kid his age needed to know—because one of the local cops had come in and talked to the school about it.

'As you know taking drugs messes with your head and so Meg made some bad friend choices.' His stomach clenched again—he didn't want to have to tell Ned any of this. As much as Ned pretended to be a big kid, he still radiated such innocence and Lawson didn't want to be the one to strip him of it. But this shitty situation left him no choice. 'One day she went into a shop with someone she thought was a friend and that person tried to rob the shop attendant and things got out of hand. The shop attendant died.'

'But she didn't do it,' Ned exclaimed, shaking his head so hard it made Lawson's own head hurt. 'So why did she go to prison? Why is everyone saying she did?'

Lawson let out a long puff of breath. How could he explain all this in a way that Ned would understand, when he didn't really understand it himself?

Before he could, Ned spoke again. 'If Meg didn't do it, then why are you angry at her, why have you two broken up?'

'It's complicated,' Lawson said. 'Meg never told me most of what I've just told you, I had to find it out for myself—and that hurt a lot.'

'You're such a fake!' Ned yelled, leaping out of his chair and knocking it to the floor with a swipe of his arm. The ferocity of his actions stunned Lawson.

'Excuse me,' he said, standing up and looming tall over his son. 'How dare you speak to me like that! What's got into you? Since when have I ever taught you that violence is the answer to your problems?'

Ned perched his hands on his hips and shouted right back. 'I don't care what you say anymore because you don't practise what you preach. You told me I need to forgive Levi and Tate for being mean to me—you said I needed to understand that when people did bad things it was usually for a reason, that it was because they were hurting, so we needed to forgive them. *And* they keep doing it, but Meg has stopped doing anything wrong at all! And *you* won't forgive *her*!'

Tears burst from Ned's eyes. Lawson wanted to go to him and hug him hard but he couldn't move.

'I don't care what Meg did, Dad. I don't care what anyone else thinks. I love her,' Ned sobbed. 'And I'm so sad without her. But you know what? You are too. *Please*, forgive her. I want her back.'

Ned's heartfelt words shot right to Lawson's heart. Tears formed in his eyes because he felt exactly the same about this woman who had been in their lives little more than a month. Here was an eight-year-old boy—*his* eight-year-old boy—telling him that he was living his life all wrong, throwing his own words back in his face. His son was *way* smarter than he was.

He suddenly heard Meg's apology loud and clear, properly this time. He realised she hadn't told him because she was scared of losing what was becoming the most important thing in her life. She was scared of losing them. And he was refusing to forgive her out of a stupid thing called pride. She *was* going to tell him, in her own time, as was her right. In refusing to forgive her, he wasn't only punishing her, he was also punishing himself. And Ned.

He was robbing all three of them of a future that could make them the happiest they could be.

'You're right,' he told Ned simply. 'I'm sorry. I do love Meg too and I've been an idiot. Will you ever forgive me?'

Ned wiped his nose on his T-shirt sleeve and then cocked his head to one side. 'You love her too?'

Lawson nodded. 'I do.'

'What are you going to do about it then?' Ned asked, his tone sceptical as if he didn't quite believe what he was hearing.

'I'm going to tell her and I'm going to ask her to forgive me.'

Ned's face broke into a smile and he all but leaped across the turned-over chair in his rush to throw his arms around Lawson.

Man, he'd missed this little body these last few days.

Chapter Forty-three

Megan emerged from the shower to hear Cane barking like a lunatic by the front door. She groaned, wrapped a towel around herself and went across to the window to see if there was a reason for his hysterics. When her gaze came to rest on Lawson's ute parked out the front of her building, she grabbed hold of the window sill to steady herself. As the window was ajar, she heard voices wafting upwards.

'Do you think she's home, Dad? Why won't she open the door?'

Ned! Her breath caught in her throat.

'Give her time,' came Lawson's voice and then she heard a knock on the front door.

She called out the window, 'I'll be down in a moment,' then glanced around her bedroom and grabbed hold of the first clothes she laid her eyes on. She yanked on knickers, snapped on a bra, shrugged a yellow T-shirt dress over her head and then ran out of the room and down the stairs, dragging her fingers through her wet hair as she went.

Cane was at the front door, jumping up against it, his claws making nail-down-the-blackboard noises against the dirty glass.

When she turned back the lock and opened the door, he sprang at Ned, almost knocking him over in the process. Lawson reached out to steady him but Ned was all smiles, laughing as he returned the puppy's affection.

Lawson lifted his hand from his son's shoulder and took a step towards Meg. 'I'm so sorry, sweetheart. I'm so sorry.' And then he grabbed her face between his two big hands and dragged her in. Two seconds later, she was tasting him. And man, he tasted better than all the chocolate in the world. Torn between confusion and bliss, between embarrassment at being kissed like that in front of his son and happiness so strong it made her heart hurt, all she could do was wrap her arms around him and throw herself utterly and completely into the kiss.

When he finally tore his mouth from hers, her heart raced and she looked up at him questioningly. *What on earth was that all about?*

He smiled down at her and then he looked to Ned, who was grinning up at both of them.

'That was totally gross,' the kid said. 'Next time you do that make sure I'm not watching.'

Lawson laughed. Megan didn't know whether to laugh or cry. She thought maybe she'd fallen in the shower and knocked herself out and that this was actually a cruel dream. Yes, that had to be the answer, and if so, she never wanted to wake up.

'Ned and I have been talking,' Lawson said, taking hold of her hand. 'It took one of us a little longer to realise, but we've come to the conclusion we're in love with you.'

What? This declaration was so unexpected she could hardly believe it. 'I'm sleeping, aren't I?' she whispered.

'You look pretty awake to me,' Ned exclaimed, reaching out and pinching her on her leg.

'Ouch!' She yelped and frowned at Lawson. 'I think … I must …' She shook her head. 'I must be hearing things. What did you just say?'

Lawson opened his mouth but Ned got in first. 'He said he loves you and so do I. *Please* say you love us too?'

'Ned, give Meg a moment,' Lawson said, putting his free hand on Ned's shoulder again. 'She doesn't have to tell us anything.'

'But I don't understand. I thought you were angry. And why would you want to be with me when nobody else can stand to look at me?'

'For one, it's the situation I was angry with, not really you. For two, not everybody is judging you. You've got a massive champion in Tabitha and even if you didn't, I wouldn't care. I don't care what the town thinks about you or me or us. The only opinions that really matter right now are yours, mine and Ned's.'

He squeezed the hand he was still holding, looked right into her eyes and continued. 'Meg, you came unexpectedly into my life and, without even trying, you snuck into my heart in a way no other woman has been able to do since Leah died. I honestly thought I could never feel this way again but when I'm with you, I feel alive again and that is quite frankly the best feeling ever. I'd be stupid to throw that all away because you messed up in the past. I *was* stupid. I was proud and self-righteous and stupid. But no more secrets. If there's anything else you've forgotten to tell me, you lay it on the table now and if there's anything you want to ask me, go ahead. You were right: I wasn't completely open with you either and for that I'm sorry. So, what do you say? You want to give the future a try with me and Ned?'

'Okay. That sounds good.' Tears prickled in her eyes but this time there were happy ones. She'd already decided that there were to be no more lies in her future, so it was an easy promise to give him. 'No more secrets. Not ever.'

'Good.' Lawson squeezed her hand again, then looked down to Ned and Cane. 'Ned, why don't you take Cane out into the backyard and throw a ball to him or something.'

'I'm hungry,' Ned said.

'There's a full container of chocolate chip bickies on the kitchen table,' Meg told him, smiling knowingly at Lawson.

He laughed as Ned, followed by Cane, shot off into the house. 'You said the magic words,' he said, pulling her up close and personal again.

'I'd say anything to have you to myself a few moments,' she whispered.

'I like your thinking,' he said, and then he dipped his head and kissed her again.

Meg welcomed him into her mouth and into her heart, smiling inside and out as her temperature rose to meet that of the midday sun. Some would think she didn't deserve this wonderful man and his amazing son, but that wasn't going to stop her grabbing onto them with both her hands, never ever letting go and being the very best she could—for herself and for them.

The time had come to finally forgive.

Epilogue

'Move it that way just a little. Yes, that's perfect.'

Meg stood out the front of the old general store with Ned, Cane and Buster, directing Lawson as he positioned the blackboard sign out the front: *Grand Opening—Eliza's Tea Room.*

'You're a slave driver, you know that?' Lawson said, grinning as he came over to stand beside them. He slid his arm around Meg's waist and pulled her into his side. 'But I guess it works for you because look what you've achieved.'

She playfully elbowed him but couldn't help smiling as she gazed at the building they'd lovingly restored to its former glory. The doors and windows were now so clean they sparkled and bright flowers filled the once-barren garden beds. Today, almost a year to the day she'd arrived in Rose Hill, Eliza's Tea Room would be officially opened. Opening a café-gallery almost in the middle of nowhere with her reputation was quite possibly the scariest thing she'd ever done. And that was saying something. It felt like she'd achieved the unachievable but she knew she could never have done it without Lawson, Ned, Tabitha and their friends.

'When's everyone going to start arriving?' Ned asked, absent-mindedly fingering the fur at Buster's neck as he spoke. Over the last year, he and Buster had become almost inseparable, so that eventually Meg had relented and let Buster move to the farm full-time. She and Cane were very frequent visitors.

Lawson glanced down at his watch. 'We officially don't open for another half an hour but I'd say any time soon.'

'That's *if* anyone arrives,' Meg said, trying to ignore the quiver in her belly. Although she was no longer getting so many terrified stares whenever she went into Walsh, she wasn't naïve enough to think she'd been completely accepted by everyone. People had long memories, especially in country towns, and she kept having terrifying dreams that the opening of the tea room would be a complete flop, with not even one person attending.

'They will.' Lawson turned and then put his thumb under her chin, forcing her to look up into his deep brown eyes—depths she'd never tire of falling into. 'Funky and his family will be here soon for starters and he has a *big* family.'

She laughed and rolled her eyes. There was only so long her business could survive on the kindness of the people who had become her friends because they loved Lawson.

'And,' he continued, 'even if nobody comes, who the hell cares? We'll eat ice-cream and cake and have tea with Eliza till we make ourselves sick. We don't need anyone else.'

As usual, his words and the way he looked at her as he said them eased her jitters. He was right—even if this was an utter flop, at least she could say she'd tried. If she'd learned anything over the past year, it was that she needed to follow her heart, do what felt right and not let what other people might or might not think stop her.

'Are you guys going to stand around outside yakking and leave me to do all the hard work inside?' Tabitha said, appearing in the doorway. She wore a CWA anniversary apron and her usual grin on her face. 'The cream for the scones won't whip itself, you know.'

'Coming!' Meg smiled; Tab had become the sister she'd never had.

Lawson shook his head and glanced down at Ned. 'We're surrounded by slavedrivers.'

Ned giggled. 'What are we going to do with the dogs?'

'We better put them out the back now,' Meg replied.

When she'd first dreamed of opening the tea room, she'd envisaged Cane lounging on the verandah like some kind of mascot, but he hadn't really got to the lounging stage of his life yet. Buster would happily act as mascot but Cane would bark and whine out the back if he were left alone.

'I'll take them,' Ned said, grabbing Cane's collar.

'Thanks,' Lawson and Meg said in unison, then smiled at each other as Ned led the dogs along the verandah towards the side gate.

'Come on.' Lawson took Meg's hand again. 'Let's go whip some cream.'

They went inside and set to work doing the last-minute jobs, which stopped Meg from biting her nails as the time ticked down to the official opening hour.

When it was one minute after their ten o'clock opening and not one person had walked through the door, her heart sank, and she went across to the table in the corner where they'd set up a tea pot with a cup and saucer. A sign sat in the middle of the table— *Reserved for Eliza.*

She slunk into one of the two chairs and sighed deeply. 'I'm sorry, Eliza. I tried.'

Then the little bell above the door ding-a-linged and Meg turned so fast she almost gave herself whiplash to see Beth and her husband tottering in through the door.

'My my,' Beth exclaimed, pausing in the doorway and glancing around, 'you're a miracle worker. Look what you've done to this old building.'

Meg, tears sprouting in her eyes—she'd become quite the crier since moving to Rose Hill—leaped off the chair and rushed across to greet her first customers. She threw her arms around the old woman, who'd remained a supporter even after the truth about Megan McCormick had spread around Walsh. 'I'm so glad you could make it.'

Beth chuckled and patted Meg on the back. 'I wouldn't have missed it for the world. I even made sure Howard wore his Sunday best.' She pulled back out of Meg's embrace. 'Howard, meet Meg; she's a very special girl and a dear friend of mine.'

Meg shook Howard's old, papery hand and then linked her arms through both of theirs. 'Where would you like to sit? You get first choice of a table.'

'Oh, no,' Beth said, shaking her head. 'First I need to have a proper look around.'

'Okay, then.' Smiling, Meg led the elderly couple around the tea room so they could admire the old photographs of Rose Hill and Archie's paintings, which hung on the walls. 'There are more in the gallery—those ones are for sale and all proceeds go towards our new charity.'

In addition to renovating the general store and getting ready for the launch of the tea room, Meg had finished her memoir and started doing drug awareness talks at schools in the region. Her book was now under consideration with a publisher and, inspired by the positive feedback she'd received about the talks, she'd recently started a charity to help survivors of drug and alcohol abuse get back on their feet. It was early days but she finally felt as if some good might come out of all the bad that had gone before.

Halfway through showing Beth and Howard around, Meg had to stop to go and greet the next arrivals. As predicted, Funky walked in the door, followed by his whole extended family, which included a number of nieces and nephews who immediately found the kids' corner she'd set up with paper and coloured pencils. She barely had time to greet them all before Ethan arrived pushing an elderly woman in a wheelchair.

'Gran!' she exclaimed, rushing over to greet Lawson and Tabitha's grandmother. She threw her arms around the woman who'd become like a surrogate grandparent to her these past few months. 'I'm so glad you could come.'

Gran chuckled softly. 'I wouldn't miss this for the world.'

Meg pulled back, giving the older woman a chance to look around.

'I'm sure your Eliza would be very happy with what you've done with the place,' she said with a nod. 'Now, when do I get a cup of tea? My throat is parched.'

'Coming right up,' Meg said and went off to fulfil her very first order.

After that, the people just kept coming.

Meg had hoped the opening would be a success, but she'd never dreamed she'd have to feed that many people. She, Lawson and Tabitha were so run off their feet taking and delivering orders they had to put Funky to work washing up in the kitchen and Ethan and Ned in charge of the ice-cream bar.

Every now and then, Meg paused for two moments to survey the dream-like scene in front of her—a café full of people laughing, talking, eating and admiring the locals' arts and craft.

'Are you going to say a few words?' Tabitha said, coming up beside Meg with a tray of used plates as she headed back into the kitchen.

'Oh yes, I'd almost forgotten that part.' Meg's stomach jumped again with nerves, but she wanted to thank all these people for their support.

Tabitha had a way of commanding attention and a few minutes later all eyes were on Meg as she stood just in front of the cake display cabinet and addressed the crowd.

'I …' She'd planned a speech but now, with all these people smiling at her, she couldn't remember a word of it. 'I just wanted to say thank you for coming and I hope you enjoy the food and beverages. I can't express how much you all being here means to me and—' She couldn't say another word, but nobody seemed to care. They all stood up and applauded.

Lawson came to stand beside her and then, just when she thought she truly could not take another hit to her emotions, he tapped a spoon against a glass and everyone went quiet.

'I just want to add to Meg's thanks. It means the world to me as well as her because this is the woman I love and want to spend the rest of my life with.'

Then, he turned to her and she gasped as he got down on one knee and presented a small black box.

'Megan McCormick,' he said, his own voice a little shaky now, 'there are no words for the light you've brought back into my life. I love you with everything I've got and I was wondering if you'd do me the massive honour of becoming my wife?'

Yes! Of course! She wanted to scream her positive answer so that people all over Australia would hear it. But she couldn't seem to speak at all. With tears streaming down her face, she nodded violently instead and dropped down to the floor to join her future husband.

He laughed, his eyes also glistening, as he slipped the most beautiful diamond ring onto her finger. Meg gazed down at it—she would have been happy with a plastic band from the two-dollar-shop if it meant getting to wake up next to Lawson for the rest of her days—but it fit perfectly.

Applause sounded around them again, but Meg barely heard it as Lawson's lips met hers. When they finally came up for air, Ned was standing beside them.

'Onya, Dad,' he said, raising his hand for a high five to Lawson.

Then, he stepped right up to Meg, threw his skinny arms around her neck and hugged her hard. Lawson's arms came down around them both and they stayed there, snuggled together in one tight unit until someone from the crowd called out.

'Can I get a photo for the *Walsh Whisperer*?'

Meg didn't need to look up to know the voice was Adeline's but she did look up and she smiled, knowing how difficult this must be for the other woman. In the last year, they hadn't exactly become friends—she wasn't sure they'd ever get to that—but they'd learnt to be civil. Adeline had accepted that Meg was part of Lawson's life, part of the town, and Meg had realised that she couldn't blame the other woman for her grandmother's sins. However untoward, Adeline had genuinely had Lawson's and Ned's best interests at heart when she'd dug up the dirt on Meg.

'Congrats, you guys,' Adeline said, lifting her camera to aim. 'I'll put this on the front page.'

And for once Meg didn't mind her life making the news. In fact, right at that moment, she was happy to be the talk of the town.

Acknowledgements

Acknowledgements are one of my most favourite things to read in other author's books—I'm fascinated by who has helped an author in their research and who supports them through their writing on a daily basis. As an author, though, acknowledgements are one of the most difficult things to write—I'm always terrified I'll forget a VIP.

This book is my tenth full-length novel with Harlequin Australia and during this time so many people have formed the team that bring my books to you. Each and every one of those amazing people have worked above and beyond and I want to thank them all. It's too hard to name everyone because there are so many, but I want to thank Sue Brockhoff and James Kellow for leading such a fabulous team and for their personal enthusiasm towards my writing.

Talk of the Town was edited by the brilliant Annabel Blay and the equally brilliant Kate O'Donnell—thank you both for helping me strengthen my story and make my words sparkle.

As always I want to thank my incredible agent Helen Briet-weiser—you're there with me from the beginning to the end of every book and your support is priceless.

To all my wonderful writing friends—thank you for your constant support and the emails that help me procrastinate every day. Over the years we've been writing together, you have become some of my best friends. A special mention to Beck Nicholas—YA author extraordinaire and the absolute best critique partner a girl could ask for. Beck has read every one of my published books pre-publication, offering her advice, wisdom and encouragement, and I wouldn't be without her. Thank you, my love!

Each book requires a little bit of research and a few special people helped me with the factual details of this one. As usual any mistakes are mine, not theirs. Thanks to Bec B for giving me insider info into what life is like in an Aussie high security prison; to the Pitter family and Peta Sattler for offering me a hands-on dairy experience and also to Peta for reading my draft to make sure I didn't get anything too wrong; to Carla for answering my questions about the current state of the dairy industry; and lastly to my fabulous ex-boss, the one-armed wonder woman, Lorreen Greeuw—if my character Tabitha comes across half as amazing as you are, I've done my job!

And a special shout out to Julie Hutchins—who read the beginning of this book in the very early stages and told me it wasn't absolutely rubbish, which gave me the confidence to continue.

Finally, I wish to thank my family. It isn't always easy being the husband, son or mother of a writer, but my tribe take it all in their stride. I'm running out of words to describe how much you guys help me to achieve my dreams … but know this, I love you and am grateful for you all every single day.

Other books by
RACHAEL JOHNS

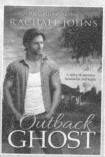

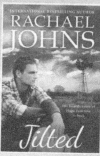

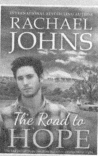

rachaeljohns.com

talk about it

Let's talk about books.

Join the conversation:

 on facebook.com/harlequinaustralia

 on Twitter @harlequinaus

www.harlequinbooks.com.au

If you love reading and want to know about our authors and titles, then let's talk about it.